THE
OTHER
SISTER

THE
OTHER
SISTER

SARAH ZETTEL

GRAND CENTRAL
PUBLISHING

NEW YORK   BOSTON

Copyright © 2018 by Sarah Zettel

Cover design by Brigid Pearson. Cover copyright © 2018 by Hachette Book Group, Inc.

Grand Central Publishing
Hachette Book Group
1290 Avenue of the Americas, New York, NY 10104
grandcentralpublishing.com
twitter.com/grandcentralpub

First edition: August 2018

Grand Central Publishing is a division of Hachette Book Group, Inc. The Grand Central Publishing name and logo is a trademark of Hachette Book Group, Inc.

The publisher is not responsible for websites (or their content) that are not owned by the publisher.

The Hachette Speakers Bureau provides a wide range of authors for speaking events. To find out more, go to www.hachettespeakersbureau.com or call (866) 376-6591.

LCCN: 2018937750

ISBNs: 978-1-5387-6090-1 (hardcover), 978-1-5387-6089-5 (ebook)

Printed in the United States of America

LSC-C

10 9 8 7 6 5 4 3 2 1

To the memory of my great-grandfather,
who bought the fairy tale book to give to my
grandfather, to give to my father, to give to me.

THE
OTHER
SISTER

"Snowy White, and Rosy Red. Will you beat your lover dead?"
—"Snow-White and Rose-Red" from *Kinder und Hausmärchen*
Vol. 2, Jacob and Wilhelm Grimm, 1812

GERALDINE, PRESENT DAY
MICHIGAN, HEADING NORTH

1.

Twenty-five years ago, I killed my mother.

I tried to kill myself immediately afterward. Probably that was from remorse, but I have to admit, I've never been sure. My suicide attempt, though, didn't actually work out. You can tell.

I've been back before for a couple of weddings, a few births, and the big anniversaries. This time, it's my nephew Robbie's high school graduation. I promised my sister, Marie, that I would not miss it.

Marie has never been above playing the Robbie card to get what she needs from me. She knows I love her son without reservation, and that's not a feeling I have about many people. So, if she wants something, she'll say, "Robbie was asking about you." Or "Robbie's hoping you'll be here." Or she'll bring out the big guns, like she did this time, when she called to tell me to keep an eye out for the invitation card and the ticket. "You have to promise, Geraldine. Robbie's counting on you."

A tight smile forms and pulls at my old scar. Robbie. Prince Charming of the Monroe family's fairy tale.

I'm one of the world's experts on the stories of the Brothers Grimm and their influence on pop culture. Therefore, I'm qualified to lecture you about the structure of the basic fairy tale arc. Including the fact that in most stories, somebody comes back during the big transitions: weddings, or christenings, or executions. Sometimes it's that should-be-dead princess returning to claim her castle. Sometimes, it's the witch or the bad fairy appearing to drop the curse.

I wonder which one I am? My smile broadens. It's an old, sharp, nasty smile, and the pull deepens. *Guess we'll find out when I get there.*

Assuming I don't lose my nerve.

It's a tiring drive. Whitestone Harbor, Michigan, is three days away from Alowana, New York, and Lillywell College, where I lecture. You go down through the Allegheny Mountains and across to Buffalo. Over the Peace Bridge. All the way across the flat expanse of Ontario, where you struggle to stay awake and thank God for satellite radio. Over the Ambassador Bridge and through grim, battered Detroit. Then it's point the wheels north, until the world turns green and the hills roll out in front and bunch up behind.

No matter how many times I do this drive, I need all three days to decide if I'm going through with it. Sometimes the shakes come, and memory blots out the road in front of me. Sometimes, I can't stop myself from seeing Mom standing in the ruined driveway—her arms thrown wide, so she's crucified in the headlights. Then, I have to turn around. I have to call Marie and make some lame excuse about a department emergency, or the flu, or the car breaking down.

When this happens, Marie always acts like she believes me. "Are you okay, Geraldine?" she asks. "Do you need help? Do you have enough money?"

"I'm fine," I tell her, every time.

"Okay then, call if you need anything, all right? Don't just text. I need to hear you're okay."

"I promise, Marie," I say, and we hang up and I do call, but it's always to tell her that I went back home and I'm fine, whether it's the truth or not.

Obviously, I haven't been caught, or tried, or punished, for my murder. If I was ever even seriously suspected, those suspicions were quickly tidied away. In Whitestone, the Monroe family name is good for that sort of thing. I got asked a few questions in the hospital, and that was that. It was decided that my mother, Stacey Jean Burnovich Monroe, killed herself. Everybody in Whitestone breathed a great sigh of relief. Especially my father's family.

Perhaps I should say, especially my father.

The two-lane ribbon of blacktop unspools up and down the achingly familiar hills. Every so often there's a gravel drive with a little white shack or flatbed trailer and a hand-painted sign:

STRAWBERRIES
ASPARAGUS
LAST CHANCE

Last chance. The words hover in front of my eyes like a heat mirage. I don't have to do this. I could turn around. I could break down. Let my phone run out of juice.

I could run away for good this time. All the bridges to the world I thought I'd created for myself outside Whitestone Harbor and Rose House are well and truly burnt. I've got my whole life packed up with me. My rusting yellow Subaru is crammed with suitcases of clothes and dishes, and boxes upon boxes of files and academic journals. The parts of my ancient desktop computer ride shotgun on the passenger seat. My sleeping bag and backpack are crammed behind the driver's seat.

I can go anywhere. Marie and I can just keep pretending we don't know what we know, just like we've been doing all our lives.

But then there's Robbie. And there's Dad. If I turn around this time, what will I do about Dad?

"I have gained great wealth through you. I shall take care of you in splendor as long as you live."
—"The Girl without Hands" from *Kinder und Hausmärchen*
Vol. 1, Jacob and Wilhelm Grimm, 1812

MARIE, PRESENT DAY
THE ROSE HOUSE

1.

"Geraldine? Are you sure you're okay?"

"…Marie! It's the battery," Geraldine is saying in my ear. I press my free ear closed with two fingers and lean in to the receiver, like that's going to help me hear over all the family we have in the great room. "Swear to God, Marie, I had the thing checked before I left, but the garage says it'll only be maybe another twenty, thirty minutes. So, I'll be there in an hour, tops. I promise."

"You're already in Whitestone?"

"Petoskey. Almost made it this time."

This is a test, I think. *We are being tested. I knew it would come.*

I take a deep, cleansing breath, so I can answer as cheerfully as I should. "Do you want someone to come get you?"

"No, no. Don't bother. It'll be finished by the time you got here."

"Okay. We'll see you soon then. Robbie's really looking forward to having you here." I glance over my shoulder, reflexively looking for my son. I see my father instead.

He's poised on the threshold between the great room and the terrace, framed by the exquisite stained-glass wall that gives the Rose House its name. Behind him, Monroes cluster around the grills and the buffet table. Dad raises his martini glass and I smile in answer. My father is a handsome man, tall and tan with thick gray hair. His yellow Oxford shirt is crisp despite the unseasonable June heat. He looks like an aging Robert Redford, only with brown eyes. He has an easy smile, an infinite store of patience, and a limitless attention for detail. He might appear relaxed, but I know he is alert to the dynamic of our crowd. Including me. Including this unexpected phone call. It's only natural. This is a family gathering, and family is the focus of my father's whole life.

"Do you have enough money, Geraldine?" I say into the phone.

"Hey, Marie!" someone calls. Carla comes out of the pass-through to the dining room, a knife in one hand and celery stalk in the other. I hold up one finger at her. "Oh, sorry!"

"Yes, Marie, I have enough money. I'm fine!" Geraldine shouts in my other ear, while Carla shouts over the voices. "Didn't see you were on the phone!"

Dad sips his drink. His gaze drifts casually from Carla to the rest of the gathering, before returning to me.

Does he see something's wrong? I squint between my relatives' heads, all tinted gold, green, and red from the stained glass. Grandma Millicent seems all right. She's seated by the hearth, talking with Amber. Amber's mother, my aunt June, is perched on the sofa, ready in case Millicent needs anything. So that's all right.

Out on the terrace, the plates of hors d'oeuvres have been completely disarranged and the buffet table cloths are covered in crumbs. I'll need to fix that, but it's not so urgent. What's important is that people are talking and laughing, circulating smoothly.

Down on the lawn at the bottom of the concrete stairs, boys slap and shove and dance around each other in the teenage male ritual of bluster and negotiation. I pick Robbie out from the crowd. He's shouting and punching shoulders and tearing around with the ball under one arm. They've switched from playing football to playing keep-away.

Just like Geraldine. My sister has been playing keep-away for twenty-five years.

But that's over now. This time, Geraldine is coming home for good. No one knows this yet, of course. I'm not even sure Geraldine knows it. But I do. This time she is staying, and we're going to be real sisters again.

I smile into the phone. "Okay! I'll let everyone know. Drive safe, Geraldine."

"I will. Tell Robbie I'm on my way, all right?"

"I will!" We both hang up before either one has to try to think up more reassurances.

Not that there's anything really wrong, of course. Everything is happening the way it must. It is important to understand that no matter how chaotic things might seem, there is order underneath. This is one of the many important things that life with my father has taught me.

Dad takes another drink of his martini. He slips smoothly through the ripples of the gathering, pausing only to smile in a gentle conspiracy with Grandma Millicent.

"Was that Geraldine?" He comes up beside me, close enough so I can smell how his Ralph Lauren aftershave mixes with the brine and vermouth. Of course he knew I was talking to Geraldine, even from the terrace. No one can read faces like my father. "What's gone wrong this time?"

"Just car trouble." I'm already heading for the kitchen, like I'm not worried, and we can all believe what Geraldine tells us. "Something with the battery. She's at a garage in Petoskey. She says she'll be here in about an hour, maybe an hour and a half."

"She's in Petoskey? I thought she wasn't coming up until next week?"

"No. I told you. The timing worked out better for her to come early."

Dad does not trust this. I can't really blame him. This is Geraldine, after all. Geraldine does not fit. Everyone wonders how someone like her could be Martin Monroe's daughter. A scarred, rumpled woman who spends her life writing for obscure journals that don't even pay money and teaching easy-A courses to slacker kids at a little college no-body ever heard of.

Not that Dad—or anyone else at our family barbecue—would ever say anything like that to Geraldine's face. If they mention her at all, it's to say that really, considering everything Geraldine put us all through, it's amazing how well she's done.

But still, they add and leave the words to dangle and twist. *But still...*

I stride toward the kitchen. I smile at Grandma, and Aunt June, and Amber and Walt, and all the rest as I pass.

A selfish part of me thinks, *Please don't follow me. Just give me a minute.* But I dismiss that. I will not be selfish today.

Carla's standing at the butcher-block island. She's turned her attention from celery to watermelon, neatly sectioning the ring-shaped slices into quarters.

"Is your father on the prowl?" My cousin-in-law is a tall, substantial woman with a big bosom and no intention of engaging in diets or surgeries. All the rest of us Monroe women wear the approved barbecue-night uniform of khakis, open-toed sandals, and striped tank tops or twinsets. Carla wears jeans and a plain T-shirt. Her dark curls are bundled up in a ponytail. She looks more like one of Robbie's friends than one of the family.

I've always liked Walt better because of Carla. She's his first and only wife. All the rest of us have been divorced at least once.

"Dad's just a little antsy," I tell her. "You know how he stresses about these family parties."

Carla glances at me sharply from under her sparse eyelashes. She really should have put on more makeup today. The jeans and the pony-tail are bad enough. People will say she looks tired. Sloppy. I resist the urge to touch my own face. Instead, I stack watermelon pieces on the platter. Pink juice films my fingertips.

"I heard him talking to Millicent," Carla says. "He knows you're planning something."

A melon wedge drops—*splat!*—onto my exposed toes.

"Oh, damn." I grab a towel and wipe frantically at my white sandals.

"That's going to stain." I scoop up the spattered melon bits and toss them quickly into the sink.

Carla leans her ample behind against the counter and picks up her coffee mug. She's the only person over eighteen drinking coffee before dinner. "So, I'm guessing you haven't told him that you and Geraldine want to take over the other house?"

I shake my head, a little impatiently. The "other house" is a small, battered, white building at the bottom of the hill. You can't even see it from here.

What is that quote? Two houses, both alike in dignity…?

But our two houses were never anything alike. Down underneath the trees is where Geraldine and I grew up, and where Mom ran Stacey B's Sandwiches and Stuff while we waited for Dad's assorted businesses to take off. It's also where we waited for the chance to move where we really belonged, the Rose House. This house. But first, Mom's older sister had to die. And so did Mom.

No. Don't think it, Marie.

But it's too late. The skin on the back of my neck prickles and I catch the stale scent of tobacco and beer.

Mom.

My mother has been dead since I was nineteen, but dead does not mean gone. Nothing is ever truly created or destroyed. It only changes form. This house is a perfect example. It's changed forms so many times over the years. Sometimes, I can feel the dank old layers shifting beneath the sheetrock.

"Marie?" says Carla. "Everything okay?"

"Sorry. Woolgathering." I straighten Carla's wedges into a tidier stack. "But you know, Carla, I'm not trying to get Geraldine to take over anything," I say out loud. I wipe my fingers on the dishrag, hard, like I'm trying to get rid of something much more tenacious than watermelon juice. "Mom and Aunt Trish left the houses to me and Geraldine. We are equally responsible for them. Anything that happens, we have to decide on together."

"But your father thinks—"

"What do I think?" asks Dad from the threshold.

Carla and I both freeze. We both see my father's cheerful smile, the one that says, *Gotcha*.

2.

"Oh, great, more watermelon. Thanks, Carla." Dad gestures toward the terrace buffet with his half-empty martini glass. "They're running low out there."

Carla hesitates just long enough to let me reach for the platter if I want to get away. But of course I don't. Dad wants Carla to be the one who leaves.

"Would you mind, Carla?" I ask her. "It's like a swarm of locusts landed out there."

"Sure thing."

I pretend I don't see her sympathetic look as she heads out the door toward the terrace.

Now that Dad's here, I am suddenly aware of how messy I've let the kitchen become. There are Whole Foods bags, empty bakery boxes, an empty plastic container that used to have grape tomatoes in it. Crumbs are scattered all over the counters, along with some lemon halves and a few crisscrossed celery ribs. It's as if the room itself is an indictment of my management skills. I shouldn't feel that way, of course. It's a complete overreaction. I'm always doing that. It's one of the things I need to work on.

"Marie?" Dad asks.

I rip a length of plastic wrap off the roll bolted to the underside of the cabinets and bundle up the leftover celery like I'm afraid it's going to escape.

"What were you and Carla talking about? What do I think?"

"I have no idea. You'll need to ask her."

"Carla's got enough on her plate right now."

I can't turn away fast enough to hide my surprise. "What's the matter?"

Dad arches his eyebrows. "She didn't tell you?" He sips his martini, inviting me to fill the pause. When I don't, he sighs. "Typical Carla. Talks about everybody else when she's the one..."

I will not be led down this road. I can already tell it's nowhere I want to go.

"I don't think Geraldine will be delayed too badly," I say firmly.

This is a clumsy and transparent change of subject. It's also exactly what Dad was hoping for. I can tell by the timbre of his fresh sigh and the tilt of his head.

I have learned so much over the years from my father, but the most important thing is how to really pay attention. You have to remain aware of all the details, no matter how tired you are. That's how I've become such a good hostess and a good manager, and, of course, a good daughter. I really owe him everything. If it wasn't for Dad, I might not even have my son. After all, it was Dad who stepped right in as male parent and role model for Robbie when my husband, David, walked away.

"Marie, I hate to bring this up now, but even if Geraldine doesn't make it, you're still going to have to talk with her about the old house."

There it is. Carla was right. Dad does suspect something.

"She's never going to stay, Marie. You can't keep hanging on to that decrepit old place hoping she'll change her mind."

"There'll be plenty of time to talk houses after Robbie's graduation." I wet a dishrag and start wiping counters. "And Geraldine will be here soon."

"I know you love your sister," Dad says behind me. "It breaks my heart to see how many times she's disappointed you, and Robbie. You have to—what is it they say these days?—you have to try to distance yourself."

"Dad, please," I say softly, and with the pleading little smile that he enjoys seeing so much. "Let's just put it aside, all right? This is Robbie's week. When it's over, we'll talk about the old house and Geraldine and everything else."

Sadness and patience gather behind my father's eyes. He is always so understanding. You can see it in the way he nods, and in the warm, paternal kiss he presses against my forehead.

"All right. We'll do it your way, baby girl," he says, because I will always be his baby girl. I am forty-three. My son is graduating high school. I was married, am divorced, have been troubled, but even when I've been on the edge of disaster, I've remained my father's baby girl. That's how much he loves me.

My hands are shaking.

Slowly, so I can concentrate on each separate motion, I undo the flaps on the bakery boxes and flatten them out. I am fully present. I feel the brush of thin cardboard under my hands. I feel the warmth from the stove at my back. I feel the tackiness of watermelon juice on my fingers and my feet. I will not be distracted by thoughts of the past, or my own absurd ideas about how the universe works, or even my mother's shadow beneath our clean white walls. These things only confuse me and worry Dad.

I do not want my father worried.

Fortunately for us all, he's focused on one of his favorite themes.

"You have to buy Geraldine out, Marie. These constant delays aren't fair to her, or to the property. As long as you let her dither, the place will just sit there empty, and Geraldine won't be able to move on."

"It's a house, Dad, not an ex-boyfriend," I say, lightly, of course. Just teasing.

Dad smiles a little and tips his now-empty glass from side to side. "You can have a bad relationship with a house, too. Look at Patricia Burnovich and this place."

Patricia Burnovich. That's how Dad likes to refer Mom's sister. It helps emphasize the distance that must be kept between us. He never calls her "your aunt," let alone "my sister-in-law." Acknowledgment of those sorts of relationships is reserved for the poised and practiced people he brings into this house. People who know just how much they owe, and to whom.

My aunt June and her daughter Amber are a perfect example. Both wear twinsets (June blue, Amber green) and strappy sandals. Amber's finally given up on her third husband, which puts her just one shy of her mother's total. Each holds a cocktail in one hand, and uses the other to wave and point. Diamonds flash on wrists and skinny fingers.

Aunt June remembers appearances and the importance of keeping up the family reputation. June would never go crazy. She would never starve to death alone in an empty ruin of a house because she was too stubborn to sign it over to people who could manage it properly.

June would never, ever kidnap her vulnerable adolescent nieces in the middle of winter.

But I am not thinking about that. I am in the present. The present is a cutting board to be wiped down, a discarded knife that should be in the dishwasher. A houseful of Monroes to keep fed and lubricated.

"You know that's what your sister is really coming to do," Dad says.

"Please be quiet."

"What did you say?"

I don't even know. Why don't I know? But I am saved from having to answer.

"Hey, Mom! Look what I found!"

Robbie. My tall, beautiful, golden, cheerful son, the star of the day. He strolls into the kitchen and then abruptly steps back.

"Surprise!"

It's my sister. Geraldine's here.

3.

"Geraldine!"

Robbie dodges so my sister and I can hug—Geraldine with one arm and me with both and all my might. My sister is short and soft and scarred, but she's strong. I can hug Geraldine as hard as I want and she will not complain or wince away. She smells like sweat and outdoors. Her hair is snarled, her black skirt is too tight, her top and jacket are too loose. She's wearing a pair of ridiculously high-heeled boots and carries a battered bucket-sized purse slung across her shoulders. But she's here. She made it. Relief rushes up from the bottom of my heart. Everything's going to be all right. This time it all comes true.

"She was sitting in the car." Robbie smirks. "It was like she was trying to sneak a smoke or something."

"Or something," Geraldine agrees sheepishly. Then, she smacks his shoulder. "And you, you can just stop being taller than me."

"Too late!" Robbie rests his chin on the top of Geraldine's head. "Oh, snap! Aunt G, you're getting shorter!"

She shoves him off. "Go away, whippersnapper, or I'll bite your kneecaps."

"I'll get a ladder."

I am so happy to see them together, something is going to burst.

"I'm sorry I'm so late, Marie. Really. I…" She holds up a squashy green cardboard basket. "I brought strawberries."

"Thank you." I take them and I notice her blunt finger ends are all stained red. There is probably a second, and now mostly empty, carton in her car someplace. Geraldine has always adored fresh berries. I look down my nose at her and she puts up one finger, right across the puckered scar that runs from her nose to her chin. *Shhh.*

"Hello, Geraldine." Dad straightens up.

And just like that, the switch is flipped. The cheerful little moment is over, and we all remember we are on display. Aunts and cousins and plus-ones are peering into the kitchen, waiting to see what Geraldine will do now that she's face-to-face with my father.

I mean *our* father, of course.

"Hi, Dad." Geraldine's mouth twists uncomfortably around the scar. She fell hard against the stairs one winter when she was fifteen and it left a permanent mark. I've always suspected she could have done something about it if she wanted to, but that's just not Geraldine's way.

"So glad you finally made it," Dad says. "We were starting to worry."

"I had some car trouble."

"That's what Marie said."

This could become awkward. Fortunately, Robbie is too focused on Geraldine to let that happen.

"So, what'd you bring me?" He bumps his shoulder against hers.

"He's asking for a present?" Geraldine bumps Robbie back. Neither of them notice the tiny wrinkles that appear at the corner of Dad's eyes as he watches this display. "What kind of manners have you taught this kid, Marie?"

Bump. "Not her fault." Bump. "I take after my aunt."

"Explains where you got the good looks."

"So, what'd you bring me?"

"Your graduation's not even 'til next Sunday!"

"Awww...Come on, Aunt G! Please!"

Geraldine sighs and rolls her eyes and digs into that bucket of a purse. "Let's see...nope, nope, what the heck is that? Oh, never mind. Nope..." Robbie is grinning. What's-in-Aunt-G's-Purse is a game they've played since he was little. "Hello, George, you still here?...Nope...Well, I guess this'll have to do."

She pulls out a fat, brown-paper package about the size of my fist.

"It's not a gift card," she says as she hands it over.

Robbie tears off the paper. It's definitely not a gift card. It's a roll of bills. Twenties. My son's jaw drops. So does mine.

"I...but...Aunt G...that's..."

"Pizza, video games, movies, whatever." She waves her hand.

"Thank you, Aunt G!" Robbie throws his arms around her and hauls her right off her feet. "Thank you!"

Geraldine shrieks and laughs, and tears prick the back of my eyes. "Congratulations, Robbie! You earned every bit of it."

Dad picks the roll of bills up off the counter and turns it over. "Wow. This must be, what? A thousand?"

"Two," says Geraldine. "Graduation gift adjusted for inflation. Besides, I didn't know what he'd need."

I'm startled, I admit it. Where did this come from? Geraldine doesn't earn much money.

Dad puts the roll back down. For a moment I think he's going to wipe his fingers on his khakis. "Robbie, you can't accept that. Geraldine can't possibly afford that kind of gift."

"If I couldn't afford it, I wouldn't have done it," she says. "Robbie's only going to graduate high school once, and it's different these days. You need a lot of stuff. Who knows? He might even buy books." She digs both hands into Robbie's fair hair, which contrasts so sharply with her dark waterfall of curls. "Feed this head!"

"All that is taken care of, as Robbie knows perfectly well."

"Come on, Granddad." Surely, I just imagine the hitch in Robbie's voice. "It's up to her, right?"

The white noise of muted conversation has faded. Heads and eyes flick toward us, and away, but no one comes into the kitchen to say hello.

"Yeah, it's up to me, Granddad," Geraldine says through clenched teeth. Her scar is a burning red thread across her pale mouth. "This is my money."

"I understand you want your nephew to know you care, but this is much too much." He says this to Robbie. He says it to me, but most of all, he says it to Geraldine. Patiently, of course, but firmly and finally. "Robbie, give the money back."

"It's my present." Robbie straightens up. "It's my call."

"You're a grown man now, Robbie," Dad reminds him. "I've always taught you that actions have consequences, especially where money is involved. You don't want to hurt your aunt, or your mother, or me."

"Wow. Just jumping right into it, aren't you, Dad?" says Geraldine softly. "Couldn't let me say hi or get a drink…"

"Robbie already knows you care, Geraldine. You don't need to hurt yourself to prove it." Dad's smile is soft and sad.

Say something! Do something! I shout at myself. I should take the money and give it back to Geraldine myself. That will end this trouble before Dad feels he's forced to take action. But I'm paralyzed. He, she, they, he, couldn't give me even five minutes to be happy that my sister is home. To see her and my son laughing together. Not five minutes.

My hand hurts. I look down. My hand is on the cutting board where Carla was slicing watermelon, but the red runnels on the oak board are too bright to be melon juice.

"Oh my God, Marie!"

Geraldine's grabbed my wrist. The paring knife clatters to the floor.

"Mom!" shouts Robbie. "Jesus...!"

Geraldine snatches up the dishrag and shoves it hard against my palm, holding my hand up over my head so the blood runs down my arm.

I wrapped my fingers around the knife blade without even noticing. The blood is hot and it tickles as it drips down my raised arm to the sleeve of my tank top. That's going to stain.

"Robbie, is there a first-aid kit? Bandages? Anything?"

"Yeah, yeah. Hang on." My son thunders up the kitchen stairs.

Now Monroes are crowding around the doorways, come to see the blood and hear what this new shouting is about. Even Grandma Millicent is on her feet. Carla tries to squeeze past Walt, but he's shoving her back.

Now Dad moves.

"It's okay, folks," he says cheerfully. "A little accident. Walt, nobody's got any drinks. Help me out here. June, can you close the terrace doors? It's getting chilly."

He's smiling and shepherding people away. He has to keep the party going and not give anybody a chance to be upset by my clumsy little mistakes.

"Shit." Geraldine's pressing on the cut. "Come on, Marie, let's get out of here. You still in the old guest room?"

Geraldine leads me to the back stairs. I look over my shoulder at my bloody kitchen and ruined family party, and I can't help noticing that the roll of bills isn't on the counter anymore.

It is worth noting that the German title of the Brothers Grimm collection is Kinder und Hausmärchen, *literally "Children and Household Tales." The emphasis here is not on the magic, the fairies, or the exotic monsters in the woods. These are stories experienced by the children, from inside the house.*
—Out of the Woods: Musings on Fairy Tales in the Real World,
Dr. Geraldine Monroe

GERALDINE, PRESENT DAY
THE ROSE HOUSE

1.

Welcome home, Geraldine, I think as I drag my bleeding, stupefied sister into her bedroom.

It's so damn clean, I think. I never get used to that. Even up here, away from public view, there's nothing left of the gloomy, grimy magnificent house where Aunt Trish died.

Marie's in what used to be the biggest guest room. It looks like a picture in a Pottery Barn catalogue. Dad, of course, has the master suite down the blank, white hall.

Dad. I grind my teeth down. Can a whisper ring in your ears? Because I keep hearing his parting shot.

Get her cleaned up before somebody sees.

I bet he doesn't even remember all the other times he said that to me. Only then, of course, he was talking about Mom. So maybe he does remember and just doesn't care.

"It's okay." Marie's whiter than her brushed cotton sheets. Robbie's out in the hall, swearing as he digs through the linen cupboard to find something better than a box of Band-Aids. Downstairs, I just know our father is busy explaining things to the family. It's a minor accident. Marie is so clumsy. Geraldine is overreacting. Some things never change. Walt, that steak looks terrific. Oh, hey, Greg, let me freshen that up for you.

I shove Marie into her bathroom and yank her hand down so it's under the faucet.

"It's not that bad," she whispers. "Really, it's not."

"Shut up."

"Got it!" Robbie tries to jam himself into the little bathroom behind us. He waves an ancient white plastic first-aid kit.

"Disinfectant. Gauze," I tell him. "Shit," I add because I've just peeled back the dish towel and gotten a look at my sister's cut. It's straight and deep and runs right across her palm. Dark blood wells up fast and only turns scarlet once it mixes with the water.

My scar blazes with a kind of sympathetic heat. I am remembering the winter cold and the way my feet shot out from under me on the icy steps as I tried to run away from Dad. The step's edge strikes like an axe. My teeth rattle. Shock numbs mind and nerve. The screams only start when I bring my hand down from my face and stare stupidly at the bright red river pouring between my fingers.

Here with me now, Marie doesn't make a sound.

Robbie dumps disinfectant onto a gauze pad. I pull Marie's hand out from under the water and grab the gauze so I can press it against the cut. Marie sucks in a breath, but clenches her teeth so she won't let out an accidental shout and alarm her son.

"Get back downstairs," I say to Robbie. "Tell Dad everything's fine."

Our eyes meet. Robbie's almost as pale as his mother, but fury blazes behind his dark eyes.

Oh, kid. I'm so sorry.

"Please, Robbie," whispers Marie.

"Yeah, right, sure. 'Cuz what the hell else should I be doing right now?" He tosses the crumpled gauze package onto the floor and stomps out.

This of course sets Marie off. "I've got to get back down there."

"You've got to hold still."

"He can't…Everyone will be upset."

She tries to get up. She's stronger than she looks, but so am I.

"You need stitches." I'm dabbing at the gash. The blood isn't slowing down.

"Just get some more gauze on it, and tape it up," she snaps.

"It's a barbecue, Marie, not a national emergency. What does it matter?"

She looks me right in the eye. Her color's back. In fact, her cheeks are flushed. "It matters," she says, steady as stone. "You know it does."

Get her cleaned up before somebody sees.

"Yes, yes, okay."

Marie winces and spasms as I press down with the layers of gauze and use half the roll of tape to hold them in place.

"Geraldine?" whispers Marie.

"Yeah?"

But Marie's busy reevaluating. The sight of my sister's careful internal calculations triggers a déjà vu so strong I'm instantly motion sick. I once joked my sister couldn't climax until she planned out the duration and intensity of the orgasm.

Not one of my better jokes, or my better days.

The sleek digital clock on Marie's nightstand flicks over another silent minute. Laughter flutters through the floor vent, probably from kids all the way down in the rec room. Nobody else has come up here to make sure everything is okay. Nobody is going to, either, not if I know the Monroes.

"What is it, Marie?"

"There was some trouble down at the old house," she tells me. "I had to change the locks. The new keys are in the top drawer of the dresser."

"Thanks for taking care of that." I pull the neatly labeled ring out of her (dust-free) dresser and I let it lie in my palm, as if testing the weight. There are two brass keys, both with those little colored caps on them so I can tell them apart. Red and green. Front door and back door.

Marie was the one who saved the house. She was the one who realized it would be needed again. I didn't ask her to. I didn't have to. Marie always plans for the long term. Then, she puts the keys in her drawer and waits.

I close my fingers around the keys. My hands are stained with blood and strawberry juice, but I swear to God I smell tobacco and beer. But it's really salt and iron and cold water. Scents of memory, of self-harm and delusion. Mine. My mother's. Her sister's. My sister's. It doesn't matter which. It's all blended together into one great swampy mess.

"Geraldine, you need to make a decision," Marie says slowly and reluctantly. "The development commission is getting ready to condemn the old house." She waves her unbandaged hand, but lets it fall, thump onto the bed.

I stare out the window, over the green hills toward the shimmering silver expanse on the horizon that is Lake Michigan. Right up until this second, it wasn't real. I could still just sneak away. Now, no matter how quietly I leave, Marie will know, and all our plans become just one more secret I'm asking her to carry for me.

"Dad's on the development commission, isn't he?"

"Yes."

"How hard has he been riding you about it?"

"He just thinks it's a waste to have it sitting there unused, especially with property values on the rise like they are."

The shiver that runs through me is far too much like a premonition for anybody's comfort.

"I'll make sure everything's okay downstairs," I tell her. "You are going to lie there for a half hour with your arm up. If I see you a minute sooner, I'll call 911 and tell them you're gushing blood from a suicide attempt."

My sister believes me. She should. I walk out and close the door.

Robbie's standing at the top of the stairs, craning his neck to see past me for a glimpse of his mother.

"Is she gonna be okay?"

"She's fine," I lie, but I do it with conviction. "She's just going to change and take it easy for a bit."

We face each other, this slender, grim boy and I. His full name is Robin James Pendarves. Marie wouldn't let him change his last name after she divorced David, even though I know Dad and Grandma Millicent pushed for it. He's Hollywood handsome with his fair hair and square jaw and those big eyes over fashionably sharp cheekbones. He holds himself carefully, trying not to make any sudden moves with his too-long arms and legs. I see this a lot in my freshman boys. I thank all my stars for those boys right now, because they've taught me how to stay relaxed while looking up into young, hostile faces.

"Aunt G?"

"Yeah?"

"Mom's not going to say anything..."

"Yeah, she never says, does she?"

That cracks his shell just enough to let out a hard, wry smile. He knows that I know, about this house and about Dad. About all of them, really. Or, I should say, about all of us.

"Hell, no, of course not." Robbie shoves his hands into his back pockets. "But she really wants to know if you're going to stay."

I rub at my scar. It's itching. Badly. There's a question I should ask, and now is the perfect time. But I just can't do it. Not yet.

"I'm going downstairs. Gotta say hi to your grandfather and all the family."

"That should be fun," he breathes.

We smile at each other. Tight. Sharp. Angry. I bet his mother has never seen this smile. Robbie's keeping his own secrets. I smell them on his Coca-Cola breath and see them in the black pupils that are too large in his dark Monroe eyes.

Tobacco and beer. Salt and iron and cold fresh water. Sex and danger and blood and friends who will never be invited into this house and plans of his own that don't fit the picture frame he's been shoved into.

I see myself in Robbie's eyes and the terror of it slashes straight through me.

"You didn't answer my question, Aunt G. Are you staying?"

Am I staying?

"I don't know," I tell him. "But I'm going to try."

2.

Once upon a time, the Monroes ruled the town of Whitestone Harbor. Monroes built the first barn, and church, and dormitory from out of the scrub and the forest. We pulled the stumps and planted corn and apple trees. We exploited the local loads of timber, then the limestone and sand. We opened the pits, which brought the workers and opened the roads, which brought the banks and the businessmen to found a fortune that lasted through a better part of the twentieth century.

But the world changed, construction slowed, and it got too expensive to haul sand and stone down from northern Michigan. People moved away, and the Monroe hand on the tiller of Whitestone Harbor shriveled, weakened, and almost gave way.

Then my father came along, with his charm and his savvy, and his rock-hard certainty that Whitestone could be hauled back from the brink. Thanks to him, the Monroes are kings of the castle again. Literally.

I take the long way around through what used to be the children's wing and down the back stairs so I'll come down in the kitchen instead of the great room. The air is filled with the scent of smoke and hot meats, the sizzle of frying food and the clatter of dishes. Carla is stacking empty plates in the dishwasher, a job that, incidentally, allows her to avoid the rest of the family.

"Oh, Geraldine, great! How's Marie?"

"Just a cut," I say, which is true as far as it goes. "But it's messy. I told her to lie down."

Carla smirks. "Yeah, and that's going to work. How are you holding up?"

"Ask me after the third martini. It's still martinis, isn't it?"

She rolls her eyes. "Does anything ever change around here?"

Yes. It does. I shove my hand into my pocket so my fingers press against the keys. We just pretend it doesn't. That way we don't have to admit to all our deals, compromises, and petty thievery.

Carla snaps her fingers. "Oh, I meant to tell you. While you were upstairs your phone rang, like three times."

"Oh. Thanks."

My purse is still where I dropped it on the kitchen island. I don't want to check. I really don't. I'm pretty sure I know who called. He's been calling all three days of my drive from Lillywell to Whitestone. But Carla is watching, so, I dig in among my private flotsam, and find my phone. Yep. I've got three missed calls, all from the same number.

Tyler.

"Something wrong, G?"

Yes. My heart squeezes, a lot harder than it should.

"Just my department." I shove the phone into my back pocket. I'm going to need it later. "Always something."

Carla nods like she believes me, but movement in the other room catches her eye. Dad is out on the terrace, heading over to the grill. Carla's husband, Walt, is forking a piece of steak onto my cousin Amber's plate. Dad whispers something in Walt's ear. Carla stiffens.

And just like that, I know that Marie and I aren't the only ones with secrets here.

"Shit," Carla mutters. "I wish…" She glances toward the stairs and nibbles on her lower lip. "I've got to get the desserts ready."

"Want me to take care of it? I can still slice a mean cheesecake."

"No. You can't hide in here all night." She doesn't look at me when she says this though. Dad puts his hand on Walt's shoulder to give him a little "snap out of it" shake. Carla twists her gold rope chain, and untwists it, and twists it again.

"Well." I take a deep breath and a swallow out of the coffee cup on the counter. It's stone cold, and not mine. I make a face and hand it back to Carla. "Once more into the breach, dear friend."

I shake my jacket back on my shoulders and cross the threshold to the great room.

3.

Our little family gathering has segregated itself by sex. The men cluster on the terrace while the women have taken over the great room. Originally, the kitchen was closed off. Its door opened onto the formal dining room, and that opened onto the great room. But that was too old-fashioned. The walls had to be torn down to make this modern, pillared open plan where everybody can see everybody else at all times.

Grandma Millicent, of course, has pride of place in the square, white Nella Vetrina chair. Aunt June hovers beside her, an uneasy combination of honor guard and lady's maid. The little kids duck between the grown-ups to grab deviled eggs and baby carrots. These are my second and third cousins, the disregarded children of a legion of unsatisfactory marriages.

Danish modern furnishings have been traded for Italian modern since I was last here. This isn't really a surprise. Dad gets bored easily, and Marie is always having to redecorate. Currently, the great room that holds these decorous, gossipy, hard-drinking ladies is pristine black and white, except of course, for the Tiffany glass.

That stained glass is our home's crowning glory. Dark painted evergreens stretch from floor to ceiling in a series of panels that alternate with delicate amber-tinted glass. Glorious scarlet glass roses wind around the French doors. When the light is just right, like it is now, you feel as if you're standing at the edge of a pine forest while the sun streams in from some adjacent meadow.

As I come out of the kitchen, Dad is handing Grandma Millicent a plate of salad and delicate pink salmon. They have identical expressions—their special blend of satisfaction and disdain. Dad straightens and colored light turns the familiar angles of his face into a gaudy, painted mask. But his eyes, as they turn to see through to me, remain clear and bottomless.

He knows. My throat closes. Old, ludicrous adolescent guilt floods me. *He found out what we're doing.*

"Geraldine, there you are!"

I just about jump out of my skin. But it's only Aunt June. She doesn't notice how badly I'm startled. She transfers her dinner plate from one hand to the other so she can throw a bony arm around my shoulders, and give me a pair of loud air kisses. "Is Marie all right?"

"She's fine. Just needed a lie down." I put my back to the enormous fieldstone fireplace so nobody else can sneak up on me. Standing here, I'm draped in the colors of blood, sand, and moss.

Dad smirks and turns his back, dismissing me from his list of immediate concerns.

"Marie works too hard," Aunt June is saying around a mouthful of blackened chicken. "I'll never know where she gets the energy. But look at you! All New York chic!" She steps back so she can properly take in my black jacket, black blouse, pencil skirt, and stiletto boots. I'm a shadow walking through all the pastel and khaki. "Mother, doesn't Geraldine look wonderful?"

Grandma Millicent sets her plate down on the side table and blots her mouth carefully so as not to smudge her coral lipstick.

"I'm so glad you could make it, Geraldine." She gives me her light, cool hand. We will not hug. We have never hugged.

"You look great, Grandma." This is true. My grandmother is as polished, sharp, and strong as ever. "How've you been?"

"I'm old and getting older," she says with crisp modesty. "Will you be with us long?"

So, now's the time for the big announcement. It's appropriate that I tell the Monroe matriarch first. "Well, actually, I'm on sabbatical."

She arches her neatly plucked brows. "Sabbatical?"

"Mmm-hmm. I'm writing my book, and I was planning on working from here."

"A book? *Well.*" Grandma Millicent picks up her plate. "That sounds very exciting. I look forward to hearing all about it."

But not now. Now she has to eat her salad before it gets warm and her salmon before it gets cold. I am dismissed.

"A book!" Aunt June threads her arm through mine and steers me away from Millicent, just in case I didn't get the hint. "That's amazing! I could never write a book. Oh, I should tell you." She snuggles up, all confidential. "The new medical center downtown? They're making a specialty out of cosmetic surgery. Susan Fisk—you remember her? She just had her eyes done and she looks twenty years younger. You wouldn't believe what they can do with lasers these days. If you wanted, I could set you up a consultation for your, you know...?" She lays her finger across her lip, like she's telling me to shush.

I squish my mouth into a smile that makes my "you know" wrinkle and pull tight. "I'll think about it." I slide away from her with a nonchalance I picked up at faculty cocktail parties and come up next to my cousin Amber.

"Well, you made it." Amber rakes me over with gray eyes that have grown colder and harder since I was last here.

"I heard you were out in Seattle," I remark.

"For a while." The weight of her failure makes Amber's words fall flat. "Are you really writing a book?" My cousin has never worked a day in her life. Amber lives off husbands, when she has them, as well as her share of the assorted Monroe family funds that my father doles out.

"I really am writing a book." Amber looks positively panicked at this and I laugh. I can't help it. "Don't worry, it's not a memoir. Strictly pop culture with a little pop psych sprinkled on top. My department wants to shake off the academic dust, get us out in the mainstream, and fairy tales are hyper-trendy right now." *God bless the good ship Disney and all who sail her.*

"So, what's it called?"

"Seven Secrets of Highly Successful Princesses."

Amber stares for a moment longer. "Well, sounds like a bestseller to me, but then what do I know?"

Before I have to answer, Walt steps up to the edge of our little knot. "Hello, Geraldine. You made it." He hands me a paper plate that holds a cheeseburger, rich with grilled onions and cheese on a big brioche bun. "I thought you might be hungry."

"My savior!" Amber, who has been loading up on the salad and chicken, looks away politely as I take a big bite. "Mmmmm!"

Walter's got the beginnings of a serious widow's peak and a blossoming paunch. He blinks at the world from behind round, wire-framed glasses. He beams as I roll my eyes in rapturous enjoyment.

If I've got a direct opposite among the Monroes, it's Walt. I ran away from home. Walt, he ran back. I tore up my father's last bribe. Walter's not only on the family payroll, he's my father's right-hand man, just one rung down from Marie on the ladder of trust. I've never been able to hold a relationship together. Walt has defied the odds and stayed married to Carla for over twenty years.

My mom was killed. Walt's father...well, we never talk about what really happened to Walt's father. In that way, we are both genuine Monroes.

"So," Walt begins.

"Marie's fine, I'm still at Lillywell," I tell him. "But I'm taking a year off to write my book."

Walt not only gets the joke, he actually laughs. "Okay, okay, genius. We are all unoriginal drones and you have broken the mold. I'll find a new question. How about this? You seeing anybody?" Because of Carla, Walt still believes that people like us can fall in love if we just try hard enough. He's a genuine sweetie, and whatever's got Carla on edge does not seem to be bothering him at all. Worry creeps through me and takes some of the enjoyment out of the burger he's made.

"No, not seeing anybody now." I try very hard not to think about the phone I have shoved in my pocket and all the calls I haven't answered.

That's when my shoulder blades twitch. It's Dad. It's got to be. I turn my head, just enough so I can see he's crossed back over the window-forest threshold. Evidently, he feels he's given me enough line. It's time to reel Geraldine in.

As he approaches, Amber and Walt are both suddenly trying to find something to look at that is not my face.

"Amber, you're running on empty," Dad announces jovially. "Walt, you might want to get back and check those steaks. Shame to overcook such good meat. Geraldine, come help me with the refills, will you?"

4.

Dad's study is a haven of traditional masculine competence. The furniture is all rich leather and dark wood. The broad desk is empty except for the blotter and the computer. It's also angled to face the door. Nobody is going to sneak up on Dad.

A curated selection of family photographs hangs on the navy-blue accent wall. Mostly they're of Marie and Robbie. You can track my nephew's growth from a plump toddler to a rangy young man looking stiff and awkward in his sport coat and tie. Dad is there, and Grandma Millicent. There's one carefully composed portrait of Millicent's children: Dad, Aunt June, and poor, dead, deluded Uncle Pete. Grandma's dead brothers are absent. No cousins are in evidence, either, and no spouses, not even Robbie's father. Going just on the photographic evidence, my nephew seems to have been the result of a virgin birth.

I let my gaze drift across our edited family until I find the one representation of me. I haven't moved. I'm still bottom corner, left. I'm eleven years old. Marie in the same portrait is thirteen. We're wearing matching dresses covered in big sunflowers. Marie's got a bow in her hair. I sport a crooked ponytail. That eleven-year-old me hasn't got the scar yet, and her face is freckled and sunburnt. She's been told to smile, but she looks like she's baring her teeth for an attack.

From this angle, eleven-year-old me seems to be looking out past my grown-up shoulder toward Dad at the vintage minibar. There's a whole sideboard full of booze in the great room, but the best stuff stays in here. The imported single malts. The top-shelf vodka. The wine that's been brought up from the (locked) state-of-the-art cooler in the basement. He's slowly mixing up the fresh drinks, giving me time to get all tense and awkward.

It's okay, I assure my young self. *I know this trick.*

"How's Marie doing?" he asks finally.

I ignore him and let my gaze tick backward up the timeline of Marie's and Robbie's lives, to the middle of the wall and the spot I've been avoiding.

And there she is. My mother. Stacey Jean Burnovich Monroe.

She's the only casual shot in the sea of studio portraits. She was caught shoving her hair back from her tanned face. Her hair was always the most remarkable thing about Mom. It's a natural blond so fair it's almost white. Sun streams through the tangles and fine strands, making them glow. It's a close-up so tight, it might be a selfie, if they had had selfies in the late eighties. You can see every line that time, anger, and raucous laughter have carved around her wide mouth and summer-brown eyes.

Since she died, Dad has kept her right in the middle of the office wall. That way, everybody can see how important she still is to him and how much he misses her. It also means you're less likely to notice how this picture is the only trace of the late Mrs. Stacey Monroe left in the whole house.

"Geraldine?" says Dad behind me. "I asked you a question."

"Yes," I agree. I also turn around. Dad is still pouring and mixing, his competent hands running on autopilot. Those hands are gnarled and spotted with veins like tree roots running down the back. They give him away. He's hiding it well, but my father is an old man. I take a little vicious comfort in this.

"Like I told everybody, Dad, Marie is fine. It's just a messy cut. You must have heard me. I only repeated it about six times."

"Is it the truth?"

And they're off!

"If you're worried, why don't you go up and check? I'm sure she'd love to know how much you care." I bare my teeth. Me and eleven-year-old Geraldine.

"Marie knows I love her," says Dad softly. "And what worries me..." He pauses for a sigh, like he needs to collect himself for what's coming. "Is what you've been telling her. Yes, I heard you say her hand is fine. I also heard you say you're on sabbatical."

"That's right."

"Now, I know it's been a while since I was in college, but I seem to recall it's professors who get sabbaticals. The last I heard, you were just a lecturer."

"*Sabbatical*'s a blanket term. When you're in the humanities, you're pretty much expected to write a book. If you've been a good little worker bee, you get time off to do it."

"I see."

Dad folds his arms and leans against the minibar. Casual, in command. I feel short and squat, the dark and lumpish invader in this lean and golden family. I used to pretend I was a changeling. I used to climb trees, up so high the branches would barely hold me. I'd hide there, waiting for my real family to come get me. My real family were gnomes and trolls and crows. Dark and dangerous monsters who rode black horses, and trailed ghosts and secrets. Unlike the daylight family I'd been stuck with, my real family could command their ghosts, and they would share those secrets with me.

"You're lying, Geraldine," says Dad. "Like you lied about your car breaking down. You're not on sabbatical. Something's happened to you."

He waits for me to deny it, or blanch. Or maybe start crying. I'm sure any or all of those would do.

I shrug. "Gold star for you, Dad."

"Are you going to tell Marie and Robbie? Or do I have to?"

"Are you going to tell Marie you stole Robbie's graduation present?" I say back. "Or do I have to?"

Dad, of course, receives this bitter repartee with all his usual patience and understanding.

"I am not playing your games, Geraldine. Do you think for one minute I will let you come in here and ruin my family?"

"Your family?"

"My family. You abandoned us years ago."

"After you told me it would be better if I wasn't around anymore."

Dad's gaze doesn't flicker, not even a little. "Since you were bent on suicide, I thought you should at least kill yourself someplace your sister didn't have to watch."

Memory digs its teeth in—the hospital room, the terrible lethargy that was the aftermath of blood loss and hypothermia. Marie's face was stark white then, just like it was when she saw the cut on her hand.

Mom was dead, but I didn't know that yet. Dad was busy with the people who mattered, covering up his wife's undignified departure from this world, as well as my unsuccessful attempt to follow along.

But I didn't know that yet, either. I just lay there hating Marie with all the strength left in me. I hated her because there she was sitting beside my hospital bed, and because my last, desperate, and unsuccessful attempt to spark even a tiny desire to live involved getting drunk and screwing a guy I barely knew. Who just happened to be her then boyfriend. How the hell could she still love me after that?

Away in the real world, I smell beer and tobacco, and I jerk my head around.

"My God," whispers Dad. "After all these years, you still twitch like you're the one who got bit. How do you live with yourself?"

He moves forward. With each step, the years slide away. I shrink down until I'm just a fifteen-year-old girl, bloated with fear and anger. This isn't the suicide time, or the murder time, we're regressing to. Oh, no. We're headed straight back to Disappearance Week. I'm shut in our bedroom again, and there's no way out. There's never going to be

31

any way out. There's just my father's patient, searching eyes and his cold, steady voice telling me what's going to happen next. And the pain. The pain of my stitched-up lip fills my face and my skull so full, I'm sure it's never going away.

If you want to hide from everybody who loves you, then you get to hide, he says. *You're going to bed for three days. You're not coming out, no matter how hungry you get or how bad you have to pee. If you do, you'll be staying in bed for four days. Then five.*

What about Marie? I hear my shaking, stammering self ask.

Don't you dare try to blame Marie, he whispers. *Marie is a good girl.* She *loves her father and understands what is expected of her. She never would have done this except for you.*

My father's words are like handcuffs and deadbolts. They're actually worse than blows. Because while I'm shut in our bedroom, Dad's going to tell our teachers that Marie won't talk about what happened at Aunt Trish's house. He'll tell them we were only gone a couple of days, not a week. He's going to tell them I won't leave my room. No matter how much he begs or shouts, I won't even get out of bed. No one would believe the truth, not when the lies sound so much more reasonable.

I'm so worried about my girl, he's going to whisper to them all. *What should I do? Please, what should I do?*

"I won't let you put Marie and Robbie through this, Geraldine," says my father. "You're going to leave, right after graduation next Sunday. I'll let Marie down easy. She doesn't have to know you've lost your job, or that you're trying to buy Robbie's affection with money that isn't yours." He pauses because despite my best efforts, he sees something in my eyes that isn't simple anger or old fear.

He knows. He sees I'm planning something, we're planning something. In that moment, I'm so sure of this, it's all I can do to keep it together.

"Whatever's going on can stay your private disaster," he tells me.

He's sure this'll work. Why wouldn't he be? It's worked every other time I've tried to come back. Usually, he doesn't even have to say anything. At most, I can stand four or five days of his sad, loving commentary on my every move. Then I lose my patience and my nerve and take off all on my own.

Because there has always been something about Dad, about being here, that makes it impossible to think straight.

Anger presses down against me. This is nothing like the bright, impulsive fury that makes you yell at your boyfriend or throw rocks at your ex's car. This is old, thick, and slow. It's sick and sweet, built up across the long years of our lives. I inhale it deeply and hold it in my lungs for as long as I can, because I know that as long as I feel this way I can do anything, and I will not give a shit what happens next.

"You stole two thousand dollars, Dad. It was sitting right there on the counter. Robbie didn't take it. Marie couldn't. There was nobody else in the kitchen. You stole from me, and your grandson."

We're toe to toe, almost nose to nose. I smell the martini and aftershave. Inside I'm crawling and I'm screaming and trying to get away. But I can't. I'm sneaking out the window to save myself, but always creeping right back. I'm falling hard, slamming face-first onto the steps. My teeth and skull are rattling, my skin is splitting wide open to let out the blood and the pain. I'm swimming out into the frigid lake, trailing yet more blood into the black water.

But this once, I am not backing down.

"I'm staying, Dad. I know what you're really doing, and so do you."

Right on cue, my phone buzzes in my pocket. I yank it out.

"You're going to take that, now?" Dad asks, scornful and surprised.

I glance at the screen and my hand shakes, just for a second. *Tyler. Tyler. Thank you, damn you. Go away, Tyler.*

"If it's so important you'd better go ahead." Dad's permission comes mixed with equal parts contempt and resignation.

"It's just a faculty friend," I lie. "From the business school."

"Lillywell has a business school?"

"Well, it's pretty small, but it does have one specialty that gets it into the top ten lists."

It's news to Dad that my college is considered good at anything, and it puts a particular gleam in his eye. The one that says, *Maybe there's something useful here after all.*

"What's the specialty?"

Don't, G. You're going to screw everything up.

"Forensic accounting," I say.

I watch that gleam of pride and condescension fade. Will I regret this later? Oh, yes. I know I will.

But for now, I smile and I smile, and I keep right on smiling.

Where do stories really begin?

True beginnings are easy to miss. The story of Snow White and the Seven Dwarves is a good example. The story does not begin with Snow White herself. It begins with another queen who sits sewing by her tower window. We're never told if she has a name. But she does have power. When she pricks her finger and blood falls on the snow covering the ebony windowsill, she says, "I wish I had a daughter with skin as white as snow, hair as black as ebony, and lips as red as blood."

And it happens, just as she asked.

Fairy tales are filled with women whose wishes come true. Usually, they are the "real" mothers of the heroes and heroines. They have no names and, with few exceptions, are never mentioned once the heroine's journey gets under way. But it is their unnamed presence and their disregarded power that shapes the story.

—Out of the Woods: Musings on Fairy Tales in the Real World,
Dr. Geraldine Monroe

STACEY BURNOVICH, SEVENTEEN YEARS OLD THE ROSE HOUSE

1.

Later, Stacey would remember how happy Martin looked the first time he walked into the Rose House. His coffee-brown eyes swept the foyer, taking in the slate floor accented by art tiles, the broad staircase that turned at precise angles as it traveled to the second story, and the heavy ceiling beams with their iron bands. Only then did those glittering eyes settle on her.

"Beautiful," he said.

"It's a crypt." Stacey shrugged, pretending she didn't realize he was talking about her. She'd dressed to impress in her white tube top and frayed cutoffs with the sunflowers on the back pockets. She'd spent an hour teasing out her stupid, freaky, white hair so it floated around her bare shoulders.

And it was all paying off. Martin was looking at her, slow and careful. He had dressed for the occasion, too. He wore a crisp white dress shirt and dark slacks pressed so they had a crease in them.

Like he's going to church.

"Show me around?" Martin asked.

"Okay." *Oh, yeah. Come into my parlor, you pretty boy.* Stacey's skin heated up. Pete was going to flip out, and it would serve him right. So would Trish, and it would serve her right, too.

"The first thing that greets the visitor to Rose House is the grand foy-ay." Stacey began in her snottiest fake English accent. "The overhead beams and graceful staircase are carved from local red oak. The accent tiles were custom designed by the Potawatomi Pottery Company to match the magnificent art glass window created by the studio of Louis Comfort Tiffany, which we will see later."

"No way."

"Yes, way. They did a layout of the place in some magazine back in like the twenties. My mom could recite it from memory." Stacey did the game show hostess walk. "If we look to the left, we see the beautifully proportioned pocket door, leading to…" She grabbed the iron handle and heaved the door open. "The front parlor!"

Martin stepped across the threshold like he was stepping onto the stage.

"What makes this room remarkable are the walls, hand-painted by Addison Walters, the oldest son of Hamish Walters, who built the Rose House." Stacey fell back, one hand on her cocked hip, the other gesturing to the room. "A noted local artist, Addison drew his inspiration from Whitestone Harbor's magnificent landscape. This room, as you can see, allows the viewer to feel they are standing on the peaceful shores of Lake Michigan."

Martin turned, looking at the painted walls, with their fake pebbles and the beach grass and rippling sand. He lingered on the gray storm clouds and delicate sunset colors up above the three picture windows. Stacey was glad he was taking his time. It let her get a full look at him. Hmm. Not much in the butt department. Or in the shoulders. Of the brothers, Pete definitely had the better build. Martin's glory was all in that perfect face and sunrise-gold hair. Those deep, dreamboat eyes.

Stacey couldn't even remember the first time she'd seen Martin Monroe. Growing up, he'd always been just another boy in the halls of the Lincoln Monroe Comprehensive School. But suddenly, he was everywhere: in the cafeteria, in study hall, at Janice Wilkinson's party, and Judy Mayor's and Beau Shamanski's. It was like she couldn't turn around without seeing him behind her, staring.

At first, she thought it was because he didn't like his brother going out with her. If she was being honest with herself, she'd have to admit she'd only started dating Pete Monroe because she knew it would absolutely kill his stuck-up old bitch of a mother, Millicent.

But after a couple months of Pete's fumbling and complaining, Stacey found herself wondering if she'd picked the right brother. So when Martin looked, she started looking back. When he started saying hi in the halls, and at the parties, and the stupid school dances that people only went to because there was nothing else to do, she said hi back. And when Pete took off for a smoke with his buddies, she danced a couple of dances with Martin.

And finally, there was today.

"It's even more amazing than I imagined," Martin breathed.

"You imagined it?" Jesus H. Christ. He could not possibly like this place.

"Mmm-hmm. Full of crap, aren't I? But you don't know how many times I've looked up here and thought, it must be great, having a place like this, where nothing can touch you."

"You wouldn't say that if you had to live in it." Stacey folded her arms, trying not to see the shadow of her mother sitting on that sofa, quiet, calm and absolutely at home. "I told Trish we should sell the place. It's not like we need fifteen rooms and a three-car garage." It wasn't like they'd be throwing crazy parties here, or having to get away from any more screaming fights, or...or...or...anything.

"You need it because it's yours," Martin said. "Once you start giving away what's yours, you never stop."

"Oooo, so serious."

"It is serious. If you want to have a real family, you've got to have a place for them. This"—he gestured at the room—"holds people together."

"Like a prison."

"Like a castle."

"You sound like my sister. Maybe I should be jealous. Maybe you actually wanted to be up here with her, so you guys could cream over this place together. Have its fucking baby, why don't you?"

"How can you hate it? It's your home."

"It's not my home!" Stacey snapped. "It's a museum! Everything here belonged to somebody else. You can't touch it. You can't move it. If I had my way, I'd rip it all out. Every hand-painted, hand-carved, hand-forged, custom-ordered piece. I'd put a disco ball in the foyer and a hot tub in the great room and let all those dead Walters and Scropes and Burnoviches rear up out of their graves so I could laugh in their stupid rotting faces!"

She wiped at her cheeks. Oh, she was not crying. She'd spent forever on her mascara and now she was going to look like a raccoon. Martin must think she was nuts. Now he'd hate her, like all the rest of the kids did. Like his snotty mother Millicent did.

But Martin just smiled, moved closer, and pulled something out of his pocket.

"A handkerchief?" She laughed. "Who carries a handkerchief?"

"The oldest son of Martin Monroe Senior. Because even if the whole world is headed into hell in a handbasket, his children will remember who they are and where they come from. Go on. Take it."

Stacey did, and she blotted the corners of her eyes, carefully. Martin watched for a few seconds. Then, he extracted the cotton square from her fingers, and dabbed it across her upper lip and across her forehead.

"You talk about not being able to move. About everything belonging to somebody else? That's my whole life. Every second of every day belongs to my dad."

He drew the cloth down her cheek, to her neck, and the hollow of her throat, right where her heart was pounding.

"How old were you when he died?"

Martin watched his own hands as he folded the cloth and slid it back into his pocket. "You mean when he killed himself."

The words played back in Stacey's head, stretched and distorted, like a warped cassette tape. He said them so casually. Like he didn't care.

"I didn't know," she whispered.

"Nobody does." Martin moved over to the wall and leaned in close, like he really wanted to check out the faded piping plover that peeked through the dune grass. "But it's the truth. He couldn't hack it anymore and climbed up onto the roof and jumped. Pete found him. I was ten," he added. "Pete was eight."

"Jesus. That's awful." Somehow, in the four months they'd been going out, Pete had never thought to mention this particular little pile of facts.

Martin shrugged. "It's not as bad as having to spend the rest of my life with his ghost looking over my shoulder. But I guess you know about that."

"I'm learning." *I will not close my eyes. I will not cry. There's nothing to be upset about. Mom and Dad are dead, and it's not like they're going to get any deader.*

Stacey looked at Martin through the dusty sunbeams and saw how clear and sharp and distant he looked. He *glistened*, like all the brittle disdain he felt for the whole rotten life he'd been stuck with—they'd been stuck with—shone right through his perfect skin.

Stacey suddenly wanted to kiss him.

She'd planned to get at least that much from the get-go, but until this moment, she hadn't felt any physical desire for the boy in front of her. Now that she saw him in that bright uncaring light, she wanted to kiss him so deep she'd peel back all the layers behind those drowning eyes. They could share the truth of their hideous lives. She could learn what he knew—how to not to care. Not just fake it every day, but to really, truly, honestly, finally not care.

"You've got goosebumps," Martin whispered. "Are you cold?"

Stacey shook her head, intensely aware of how her hair brushed her bare shoulders. She should have braided it. Put on a nice dress. Done something better with her face. For the first time, she wished she was a better match for the house.

No. Stacey stiffened against the idea. That was Trish's deal, not hers, and Martin…he was here strictly because she wanted to see how he stacked up against his brother. She dug her hand into her back pocket until her fingers brushed the foil.

I'm the one in charge.

"So, you want a drink? There's some bourbon in…the den." She didn't say "Dad's den."

Martin didn't answer. Not right away. First, he let his gaze wander all around the room, from the dark window frame, across the straight lines of the Greene and Greene furniture, to the open door.

"Where's your sister?"

"Work. She doesn't get home 'til seven."

There'd been some insurance and stuff, but Trish had forked it all over to Mom and Dad's lawyer for the mortgage and taxes and shit. That meant the only money they had to live on was from Trish's job doing billing at the hospital, and what Stacey could pick up after school.

"She doesn't mind you inviting me here, all alone?"

"What if she does?" Stacey sauntered up to him, her hips swaying. He wasn't fazed at all. The fact she couldn't get to him once she turned on the juice should have made her mad, but instead she felt a sizzle right under her skin.

"You know, Martin, you're not what I expected."

Martin lifted one of his thick, pale eyebrows. She liked them. They made his eyes look even more intense by contrast. "What did you expect?"

"If I was lucky?" *Let's see how thick that ice really is, pretty boy.* "A semi-decent fuck."

The corner of his mouth curled up. She'd expected his eyes to dip, to take a gander at what was on offer. But that dark gaze stayed fixed on her face. "Now, see, that's what you do."

"What do I do?"

"You try to shock people. You know what you look like. Delicate. Shimmering. And then you go and shoot your mouth off like that, just to scare the hell out of them."

Tou-CHAY. And even that didn't piss her off. What was so different about the way he talked?

Stacey took another step forward. "Do I scare the hell out of you?"

"Nope."

Another step. Right up into his face. Hands in her sunflower pockets, so her fingers touched the condom wrapper. So her elbows pointed behind her and pushed her breasts toward him. "I'll have to try harder."

He was looking now, right down her cleavage. Phew. He was a normal guy after all.

Martin met her eyes again, and Stacey had to stop herself from licking her lips.

"You think this is your scene, Stacey." He leaned so close his cheek brushed hers, lightly, prickling the delicate hairs. "You don't know who I am. I'm the big bad wolf. You let me in, and now it's too late for you."

"Are you going to eat me up?" she whispered back.

"Every bit of you." His breath swirled against her ear and carried his words down to her throat, her lungs, her heart. "Every drop of blood, every perfect little bone. I'm going to swallow you whole and you're going to enjoy it."

"Promises, promises." She smiled, to deny his power and his eyes and the screaming need they woke inside her. But she failed, and he knew it.

"I would like that drink," he said, and he stepped back.

The world came back in an ice-cold rush. Unnerved, Stacey headed for the door in the corner, the one she hadn't walked through since the accident.

Just do it. Do it quick. She jerked open the door and ducked inside. *There's nothing in here. It's been six months. It doesn't really still smell like him. Just open the cabinet. Grab the bottle and the glasses. Mom and Dad can't see what I'm doing. They don't care. They're gone.*

They're gone and they left me here alone and they can't even care.

Stacey slipped back out into the parlor. She stuffed the bottle and glasses into Martin's hands so she could drag the door shut and get her face under control.

Too late.

"You okay?"

"Yeah, sure. Pour the drinks, will you?"

"Sure."

The heavy-bottomed tumblers clicked against the cabinet table as he set them down. She heard how smoothly he pulled the wrapper off the bourbon's cap and poured. Her mouth watered. Oh, she needed this.

By the time she turned around, Martin was holding out a glass with three fingers of Wild Turkey in it.

Stacey held her hand out to take the glass. Martin looked at her fingers as she reached. She'd put a fresh coat of coral pink on her nails. He let his gaze travel up her arm, to her bare shoulder, to her face, to her eyes.

He set the glass down and grabbed her hand. He was bigger than she was, his hand was broad and warm and soft, but not mushy, unlike some. Martin held her hard, like he knew she could take it. He turned her palm up and ran his thumb along the lines etched there. Warmth trickled outward, down her fingertips and up her wrist.

"Pete knows I'm here."

"Oh yeah?" she said, even though her tongue felt thick and clumsy. "How?"

"I told him."

Sudden anger short-circuited all the feeling from the slow circles he rubbed against her palm. "What the hell for?"

"Because I don't lie, ever, about anything." Martin put the bourbon glass into her hand. The cold glass was a shock to her skin. "That means if you're with me, you can't lie, either."

"Not even one teensy-weensy white lie?" She made her words into a purr, but he ignored it.

"Not even. Because I'll know. And then all bets are off. Understand?" He didn't smile, or even blink.

So she smiled for both of them. "I understand, Martin." Then, she leaned forward and kissed him on his hot, hard mouth.

He didn't respond. At all. She grabbed his face with both hands, stabbing her tongue at his mouth. But he didn't open. He didn't even move.

Humiliation flooded her. She jumped back, breaking the kiss with a loud smacking sound.

"What is the matter with you?" she demanded. "I thought you wanted it! You a secret homo or something?"

He should have got mad at that. Every guy did. But not Martin. He just shook his head.

"I just want you to know," he said.

"Know what?"

Now he did move. He curled his hand around the back of her head, knotting his blunt fingertips into her hair. Her heart banged out of control. Fear, excitement, and need flooded her, and something else besides.

"If we do this, we really do it," he said. "It's not just a one-off. It's for real. Forever."

"Forever?" She tried to make a joke, but her heartbeat reverberated through her whole body, robbing her of calm. "Jesus, Martin Monroe. Who do you think you are?"

This time, he was the one who kissed her. His hard hands traveled down her back. He was just on the edge of rough as he squeezed her ass and shoved his fingers between her thighs.

Her body responded instantly. She pressed closer, matched and mimicked his caresses, rough and rowdy.

Let's see how you like it.

And he did like it. He was hard as hell between them, and Stacey would have grinned if she hadn't been so wide open to his kisses. Desire obliterated strength and thought. Her knees started to buckle. He dug his fingers into her ass to hold her upright against him. Stacey kicked off her flip-flops, wrapped one leg around his nonexistent butt, and rubbed her breasts hard against his chest. God, it felt good.

"This," he whispered against her jaw, and her throat, his teeth and his breath grazing roughly against her skin. "This is who I am."

"Then you'd better come here," she gasped. "Show me the rest of what you got."

"Forever?" he asked.

Her eyes found his and Stacey felt like everything slotted into place. Her skin, her dreams, had whispered to her about this heat, this guy who could come up here and make it feel like nothing about her nightmare life mattered. Only right here mattered, only right now.

"Forever," she said back. And she did not lie.

2.

He dragged her down to the carpet, just like she wanted. It was fast and it was unforgiving. She knew she'd never erase the sensation of his hands on her skin and she knew she'd never want to. She was going to memorize him with her whole body. The rasp of the wool carpet against bare skin just added to the thrill. So did the whiskey they poured down each other's throats and sucked off each other and out of each other. They wrestled and rolled together until they slammed into the wall under the window. They laughed out loud and rode the hilarity and the ragged, messy, gorgeous heat all the way down.

She was alive. She was total. She was insane and she didn't care.

Eventually they fell off each other and faded into a bleary, warm doze. At least, Stacey dozed. Martin pretty much passed out. He snored, too, which cracked Stacey up, without her really understanding why.

He looked so perfect and pale and still, Addison Walters could have painted him.

Martin fit here, Stacey realized. Really fit. When he walked into the room, it was like the whole place rearranged itself, just to make him comfortable.

Stacey tugged her strapless bra back into place and went over to the cabinet table. She opened the drawer, and the old checkers box, to pull out the pack of cigarettes and lighter she had stashed there. She blew a cloud of smoke at the ceiling and watched it disperse into the slanting, dusty sunbeams.

"You shouldn't smoke. It'll ruin your complexion."

He hadn't moved, just opened his eyes. She had no idea how long he'd been watching her. But that was okay. That intense, confident look felt as good as anything he'd done while they were busy fucking each other's brains out.

"Who'd even notice?" She blew out another billow.

"I would." He pushed himself upright and plucked the cigarette from her mouth. He looked at it skeptically and took a huge, long drag. And promptly fell over coughing and gagging. Stacey fell over on top of him, laughing.

"Ah-ack! You're tougher than you look. Here. Keep it." He shoved the thing back into her mouth, too hard, so it squashed against her teeth.

"Watch it!" She grabbed it from him and took another drag. They both sat there against the painted wall, knees up, heads against the windowsill. Stacey smoked blissfully. Martin found one of the tipped over glasses and ran his finger around the inside and held it out to her.

She lapped at it, thoroughly and with good humor, but not a lot of energy. But when she lifted her head, he was giving her that look again.

"You've got a dirty mind for such a pretty girl." He dug his fingers into her hair, dragging them down to watch the baby-fine strands flutter. "I mean look at you, all sunshine and satin."

There was reverence in his voice, but she couldn't keep her thoughts from flashing straight back to those same fingers touching the sofa arm, and the piping plover on the wall.

"I bet you say that to all the girls." She stubbed the cigarette out in the bottom of her empty glass.

"You are all the girls. You're perfect."

"Not even close." She picked up his glass, too. Reality was leaching out of the walls around her. She was hungry. She needed to pee. Now that they'd finished, she was disappointed to find nothing felt new, except she was raw and itching inside, and had dust smears down her arms. Her hair probably looked like a rat's nest.

Shit.

Nothing changed. Nothing ever changed. A minute ago she'd been floating on a river of post-come mellowness and good sweat. Now it was all collapsing under the weight of the house and its shadows.

It was six thirty. Trish would be getting home soon. She'd better get Martin out of here, because when it came down to it, Stacey knew she didn't have the nerve to let her sister see.

Because deep, deep down, she didn't want her sister to see.

"Do you ever hate yourself?" Stacey's words bubbled from nowhere. "Do you?"

"Every day." She poured what little bourbon was left into Martin's glass. The remainder was drying across the floor, making it tacky under her bare feet. She'd have to clean it up, or Trish would smell it, even under the tobacco.

Martin came up to her and turned her around. He took the glass, set it on the windowsill and brushed her hair back from her bare shoulders.

"Now?" he asked, drawing his hand slowly around her breast. "Do you hate yourself right now?"

46

This time his touch didn't get down inside her. It was just there, like the sticky bourbon underfoot. She looked up at him bleakly, so that he saw, so that he understood.

And when he smiled, she felt the shadow deepen.

"You want to hate yourself?" he breathed. "Try knowing you are a loser from a line of losers, and that your dad's the biggest fucking loser of them all. Try knowing your family used to own this whole town, and that the entire point of your existence is to get it all back. And even if you do, that's not going to be enough." He kneaded her, his fingers digging in, until she hissed. But he didn't stop.

"Shit."

"Yeah, shit."

Now he did stop. Now he turned away. Stacey's breast felt cold. She wanted his hand back.

Stacey, you are truly twisted.

"So, what are you gonna do?"

"I'm gonna do it. I'm gonna buy the entire fucking town and wrap it all up in a bow. Then, I am going to shove it down my family's fucking throats."

Fear trickled into Stacey's blood, a slow, cold warning. *Get him out,* it told her. *You've proved your point. Pete knows where he was, he'll know what you did. That's enough.*

"Why?" she asked. "Why not just leave?"

"You can't leave home."

"Screw that. The second I turn eighteen, I am outta here."

Martin shook his head slowly. "There is no out. Home never lets you go. So you have to be the one who owns it." He tucked his hand into her hair again and wound one long lock tight around his finger. "Besides, you don't really want to leave. I can tell. No matter what you're saying."

"You're nuts."

He laughed. "You want control, Stacey. You want your sister to do what you say. You want this house to be yours, not hers."

She tried to muster the strength to argue. The problem was, she was ready for him again. Her body screamed that he did know all about her. More than that. He understood her.

"Trust me, Stacey." Martin slipped his hands around her bare waist. His voice was soft and controlled, even though she could see his erection and feel the sweat on his palms.

"Why should I?" she whispered back, in one last attempt to keep from being dragged away by her own needs.

"Because I know everything."

"Everything?" she asked.

"Everything," he agreed. "You better remember that, too."

3.

Later, Stacey would say what happened was Trish's own fault. If her sister hadn't been such a raging bitch when she came home and found them together. If she hadn't tried to treat Stacey like she was a baby. If she hadn't tried to totally take over Stacey's life and threaten to kick her out unless she stopped seeing Martin. If Trish had let Stacey make one single decision about her own life, she never would have run away with Martin Monroe. At least, not like she did, not without even finishing high school or anything. There would have been another way out. She and her sister could have at least stayed friends, and none of the rest of it ever would have had to happen.

For a long time, Stacey was able to believe that. But not quite long enough.

"Next Sunday you must come out to me. I have already invited guests. I will make a trail of ashes, so that you can find your way through the woods."

—"The Robber Bridegroom" from *Kinder und Hausmärchen*
Vol. 2, Jacob and Wilhelm Grimm, 1812

MARIE, PRESENT DAY
THE ROSE HOUSE

1.

My hand hurts.

That's my first thought when the dark, dreaming fog lifts away and I have to wake up. My bedroom is full of dawn's dull light. I don't need to see the clock to know it's about five a.m. Time to be up and moving. I have work to do.

I sleep on my side, I always have. It's a holdover from when I was a little girl and I had the top bunk bed. I was always afraid I'd fall off, even though there was a railing. So, I propped myself up against the wall where I felt sure I was safe.

What's the matter, Marie? David asked the first time we woke up together. It was in this room. This bed, in fact. Even though we were married, there'd never been any real question about living anywhere but the Rose House. At least, not for me. Well, not for Dad. *You think I'm going to sneak up on you? And grab you…like this?* He wrapped me tight in his arms and rolled us over and I shrieked and beat on him with both fists, and eventually remembered that he must be joking, and let him kiss me and make love to me. I was even able to laugh for him.

He always let me sleep next to the wall after that, starting right when we left on our honeymoon the next day. He thought it was cute, until he stopped thinking anything about me was cute. Until he went the way of all Monroe spouses.

My hand really hurts. The stain on my bandage is black. I feel the skin on my palm pull and the unseen scab breaks. The stain spreads, fresh darkness under the neutral beige of the bandage. That's probably symbolic of something. Maybe I'll ask Geraldine about it when I see her.

Yesterday's barbecue ended without additional incidents. I was able to wait out Geraldine's thirty-minute exile and come downstairs, smiling. *Just a cut*, I was able to say. *Nothing to worry about.*

I spent the rest of the evening helping Carla keep the plates of side dishes and desserts filled. I took Grandma Millicent her tea. I smiled at Robbie whenever he barged through the kitchen, trying to pretend he wasn't checking up on me.

Dad, of course, didn't bother to pretend.

"You're sure you're all right, Marie?"

"Yes, I'm fine. Really."

"I just want to be sure Geraldine didn't upset you."

"How could she? Where is she, by the way?"

"She left before you came down." He says it slowly, concerned, I'm sure, that the news might worry me. "I'm afraid she didn't say where she went."

No. She wouldn't. Not to Dad.

I wonder where she spent the night. I hope that she didn't do anything foolish. I should not think that way. I have to trust her. It is too late to do anything else.

I climb out of the bed, tug the covers back into place, plump the pillow, and turn down the hems so there's a tidy collar of sheet over duvet. Geraldine left the box of gauze pads and more bandages on the sink. I wince at the mess, although I am glad I don't have to do any extra rummaging around. It's awkward to work one-handed, but I strip away the old gauze, press a fresh pad onto the cut, and tape it down.

It hurts, but I work quickly. I wonder if I'll have a scar and if it will stay red, like Geraldine's. That idea hurts worse than the actual cut. Scars make you vulnerable. They show the world that you can be broken.

Just in time, I remind myself that Geraldine is home now. We are together. My sister can teach me how to live with scars, and I will let myself learn.

I wash, I dress, I dry my hair and brush it out. I take a deep breath and I lift my gaze to the mirror.

And there she is.

Marie Monroe smiles back at me. She is not pretty. She is not ugly. She is middle-aged and middle-sized. She has fair hair cut in a practical bob. Her face is still smooth, except for a few crinkles around her eyes, and the tiniest bit of crepeing under her chin. Her brows are perfectly plucked, and her mouth is refined by a hint of gloss and liner. She wears no perfume. Her deodorant has no scent. She shopped around for years to find a soap that's got no odor. It's a brand made especially for people with allergies.

Marie Monroe's shoes are soft flats. Her sleeveless navy-blue top and beige pants skim her figure, which is still quite good, for a woman her age. Otherwise, she's no one you'd look at twice.

I fully committed myself to perfecting this reflection when I was still seventeen, just after Geraldine's first major escapade, the one where she hauled us up to Aunt Trish's for a week, forcing Dad to come to drag us both home.

Bring, I mean. Rescue, maybe. Find, of course. Not drag. He didn't drag me home.

Us. I mean us.

But that is all the distant past. Aunt Trish died in this house and was removed, and then Mom died and it was all left to Marie to manage. And here she is, rested and ready. It's time to begin her day. Routine is important. She cannot let little upsets like a cut throw everything else out of kilter.

Household comfort and efficiency is found entirely in the little details. My bedroom door, for instance. I've oiled it and polished and planed it so it opens noiselessly. The carpet in the hall is soft pile. It cost a mint, but it doesn't crunch underfoot.

I feel the hallway strain and shift around me as I walk, but I keep a straight line down the exact center, and I make no sound.

Dad took over the master suite as soon as we moved into the house. Even David didn't think of asking him to move during the time we all lived here together. I've treated his door exactly like I've treated my own. The knob turns, the door opens, but unless you felt the ghost of the draft against your skin, you'd never know.

Dad sleeps on his chest, arms and legs all sprawled out under the white sheets. Always white. The walls are a very pale blue. It's colder in here. This room has a separate thermostat so Dad can adjust the temperature to his personal specifications. His life needs to be seamless. That way, there's no reason for him to stop and look around, and maybe decide things have to change.

David shouldn't have tried to insist we move out. It didn't matter if we could afford it. Dad needed me to stay here. He depends on me. I'm his baby girl. If David hadn't kicked up a fuss, Dad wouldn't have decided David needed to leave. We could have stayed married.

The white bedroom carpet is the same make as in the hall. Dad doesn't shift as I come to stand at the bedside. I lean across, carefully, so my shadow doesn't fall across his eyelids.

Dad sleeps with three down pillows spaced evenly against the headboard. That way, no matter which way he rolls over, he doesn't have to adjust anything. He will always be comfortable.

I smell tobacco and beer. I know my mother's shadow waits just beneath the cool, blue walls, watching to see what I will do.

I lift up the nearest pillow. I hold it over my father's head. His eyes twitch underneath their lids. There's a catch in his breathing. I make myself count to ten. I grip the pillow. My scab cracks. My heart bangs against my ribs.

Dad's breathing evens. I lower the pillow, smoothing it carefully back into its place. There's no stain on the white case. I back away, I close the silent door. Dad does not wake up.

Even with the bandage and the bloody hand, I can manage whatever needs to happen. Just as soon as Geraldine and I are ready.

But, goodness, there's so much left to do.

2.

By the time Robbie comes thudding down the stairs, I've finished breakfast and I've spent an hour in the front room on my laptop, checking, ordering, organizing. There's all the usual lists for the houses I'm staging. Our family business involves managing properties for the elite families who consider Whitestone Harbor their second home. My job is to furnish the houses. That means I spend a lot of time scouring the internet for exactly the right accessories.

Still, I do find a moment for a little online me time. There's a new Tiffany vase up on eBay, and the Potawatomi art tiles I've been searching for have finally surfaced. The bids are already ridiculously high, but I put in a new one anyway. There are last-minute emails to be sent about Sunday's graduation party, and bills to be paid. Other things— other accounts and lists and little details of interest to no one but myself.

When I close the final window of my web browser, I pause and sit very still, just breathing. Stillness allows me to savor this rare moment where no one is watching me. Robbie is in the kitchen, whistling and beat-boxing to the rhythm of clinking china and glass. I hear the rattle of the cereal box and the squeak of sneakers against tile. The muffled pop as he opens the refrigerator door and then the healthy glug of milk.

He's being himself, relaxed and undisturbed. I do not need to intrude. I do not have to play a role. I can just listen and feel my love for him, without hesitation or correction.

Of course it can't last. I need to speak with Robbie. I close the laptop and take a moment to make sure I'm wearing the right expression.

One that is concerned but not judgmental. Only then do I start for the kitchen.

Robbie's in the fridge a second time. He's got one earbud in his ear and the other dangling loose. He's puffing out his cheeks and bobbing and boxing to whatever he hears. The bowl's in the sink, because he's considerate like that, but he's bringing out the milk again.

He doesn't hear me.

"Robbie?"

It takes him a minute to realize I'm not just more noise in his head, but he does turn.

"Yeah, Mom?"

"I need to ask you something."

He pulls the other bud out of his ear and tucks it into his pocket with his smartphone "What?"

I look up at my tall, perfect son. No, not perfect anymore. Adolescence came down hard, and left scars on his skin. The sight of them makes me feel better about my aching hand. It is not right that my son is scarred when I am not. His are small, thankfully. Not enough to ruin his dramatic good looks or keep the girls at a distance. It's the wariness in his eyes that hurts me. It runs deeper than it should, and nothing I do now can smooth it away.

"I'm not going to be mad, I promise."

Robbie shakes his head and pours milk into a tall glass. The cover's off the plated coffee cake I set out last night, and two pieces are already gone. "Mom, I'm not twelve. Whatever this is, just say it, all right?"

So, I do. "Did you take the money? Aunt Geraldine's money?"

"That's what this is about? Shit."

"Robin."

"Sorry," he mutters mulishly. "Why shouldn't I take it? She gave it to me."

"I know. But your grandfather..."

"Is a control-freak bastard."

"Robin!" The shock is real this time and I can't help the way my eyes dart toward the stairs. Dad could be up there, listening.

Robbie sees. Robbie knows. He grew up in this house with his grandfather. Of course he knows. I watch him make his decision and my heart twists beneath my ribs.

"I'm…it's true! You gotta stand up to him, Mom! You gotta get out of here." He leans across the counter. "Come with me."

Oh, no. Oh, no, Robbie. You're not supposed to say that.

All at once, it's Geraldine I'm staring at, not Robbie. She's stick thin and pale and her eyes and arms are bruised. I'm about to get married, and she's half-dead but she's still talking to me like I'm the prisoner.

Come with me, Marie! Fuck Dad. Fuck all the Monroes and every last horse they rode in on. You need to get out of here. Fuck David too if he can't see that!

I cannot breathe for the love and guilt and fear. I cannot tell whether I'm proud or terrified at Robbie's poorly timed attempt to make me agree to the kind independence he can recognize.

"I know you care, honey." *Smile, Marie. The bright, self-deprecating smile. You can do it.* "But you don't want your old mother hanging around you at college, trying to make sure you eat right and dress warmly enough."

Robbie must see something in my eyes, because he snaps his jaw shut and looks away, the picture of a young man's stubbornness. "It's not fair. You're just staying because Granddad likes having someone to order around."

"Robbie, you know things are complicated with your grandfather…"

"No, I don't! Because they're not. He's a bully and a bastard and he just keeps you here because he can!"

Fear closes over me. It oozes out of the walls, sliding thick and cold from the deep shadows. It's heavy and resists being shaped into words.

"Robbie, your grandfather has been looking after his family for a long time. He can be overprotective, and that's hard for a young man. Just remember you've only got another couple of months, and then you start your new life."

Oh, when did my son learn to hoard so much anger? I tried to protect him. I've tried so hard. What did I miss?

He opens his mouth to tell me the truth. I don't want to hear it, whatever it is.

Please, I try to tell him. *I need time. Please, Robbie. Please...whoever can hear me. Just a little more time, and it will all be better. I promise. I do.*

Does he understand my silence? I don't know. But the moment breaks anyway.

"I gotta go," Robbie tells me. "Chuck's band is playing this graduation thing in Petoskey. I promised I'd help set up the equipment and stuff."

"Will you be back for dinner?"

"Chuck's having his thing the day after, so I was just gonna stay over, be back Wednesday night." He stops again. "You know I don't care about the stupid graduation party Granddad's making you put together for Sunday, right? As far as I'm concerned, you can tell him to stuff it."

"Yes, I know."

"But we're doing it anyway."

"Yes, we are. And you're putting on a clean shirt with a collar, and you're going to smile at everyone and talk about how excited you are to be going to the University of Michigan."

A thousand expressions flicker across my son's face, too fast for me to read, but not too fast to understand.

Robbie gulps his milk, shoves a third piece of coffee cake into his mouth, mumbles an apology for cramming, and grabs his car keys off the hook on the cabinet.

"I didn't take the money," he says over his shoulder.

"I know," I say, but only because he's already left.

The garage door slams and I listen to the familiar noises of the car engine starting and the slight rattle of the automatic door opener. My son is gone.

I close my eyes, and I breathe, deeply, steadily. When I've finally stopped shaking, I get to my feet.

I have to get out of this house.

I'm supposed to be here when Dad wakes up, smiling and ready to demonstrate that nothing's wrong. I'm supposed to hear his gentle reminders and loving criticisms, and all those special little last-minute requests he makes in his most offhand manner. Dale Watts and his wife are coming to dinner tonight. And tomorrow we're going out with Jack and Margot Spitzer.

But some days, it is better to take a little time out until one is completely calm again. This is slightly self-indulgent, but I can't risk any careless mistakes. I'll tick some items off the to-do list: some party shopping, some visits, a few necessary conversations. I can check up on Geraldine.

Yes. That will work. I take my own keys off their hook and curl my good hand around them so they don't rattle. No one will even notice I'm gone.

3.

"Marie!"

Aunt June waves with her free hand. Her other arm is wrapped around Grandma's, supporting and guiding her, but with dignity. Grandma Millicent always commands respect.

I'm coming out of Trey's bakery, where I'd stopped to pick up some of Dad's favorite almond macaroons, while Grandma and Aunt June are coming out of Haabs Restaurant.

"Oh, hello!" Cheeks are kissed. Both of them are wearing sun hats. June's is pale pink straw with a dark pink ribbon and pink rhinestones for trim. Grandma Millicent's is navy blue, like her skirt, and very plain, like her sleeveless white blouse.

"What are you…" I begin, but I interrupt myself. "Oh, of course, it's Monday." On Monday, Grandma Millicent has breakfast with her club ladies. There's some formal name for their association, but I don't think they even remember what it is anymore.

"What a treat to see Geraldine last night." Aunt June leans in. She smells of Chanel and Bloody Marys. She's not an official member of Grandma's club, but she gets to sit in and drink. "I thought she looked really good, all things considered. And writing a book!"

"Yes, it's all very exciting."

"How are you holding up? So much to do and, you poor thing, nothing to look forward to but that empty nest time."

"Oh, I'll manage. I think I'll enjoy having some time to myself."

"As if the lord of the manor will permit that!" June laughs brightly so I'll know she's joking. "I know you, Marie. You'd never be happy without someone to take care of."

"Well, now there'll be Geraldine," says Grandma Millicent.

"Assuming she stays," adds June. "Do you think she'll stay?"

"I think so," I say, although it's not entirely clear which of us she's asking. "I hope so."

"Time will tell," says Grandma Millicent.

"We should invite her to dinner!" cries Aunt June. "Wouldn't that be nice, Mother? I can't remember the last time we had Geraldine for a family supper."

Geraldine would certainly have a great deal to say about that. Now, however, is not the time to bring this up.

"I'm sure that would be lovely." Grandma smiles. "Oh, by the way, June, didn't you say you wanted to pick up that new Anne Tyler novel while we were out?"

"Yes, I did, didn't I? Where is my head? You know my weakness for weepy books, Marie."

"Well, why don't you go ahead? I'll just wait in the car. Marie can keep me company."

Of course June agrees and heads off down Main Street without questioning. June knows her mother as well as anyone and has learned it is best to comply with her little ways.

I open the door on the blue Town Car and help Grandma inside. I climb in after her and shut the door on us both. The car windows are all tinted, so it's dim in here, but it's quickly heating up. It's going to be in the high eighties today, even though we're barely halfway through June. Even Grandma has a little sheen of perspiration on her lip.

"I'm so glad we ran into you, Marie. I wanted to talk to you at the barbecue last night, but there simply wasn't any opportunity."

Grandma's hard gaze digs beneath my skin, rooting around among the veins and nerves to find the one that's the teeniest bit frayed. If I'm being honest, we've never had an entirely easy relationship. Grandma Millicent never quite forgave Dad for marrying our mother. At least, not until he laid the title for the Rose House on her table. Until he began making real money buying and leasing the other properties around town. That his first acquisition once housed his own now-deceased brother is something we never mention.

"And where on earth did Geraldine vanish to?" my grandmother asks. "I didn't have a chance to say good-bye."

"She left early. I guess she was tired from the drive."

"She left? I assumed she was staying with you."

"We hoped she would, but…she decided she'd rather stay down at the old house."

"Ridiculous. That house is not safe."

"I know. I told her that."

"And she didn't listen." Grandma presses her lips together in a thin, pale line. "You would think just once she might try to go a day without raising a ruckus."

I drop my gaze. My left hand is on top of my right, hiding my bandage, but exposing that vulnerable place where my wedding ring used to be. I fold my fingers together. There. Better.

Grandma, of course, sees. "Something's the matter, Marie. I can tell. What is it? You know you can say anything to me."

I do know it. Without question. And knowing, I take a minute to gather my nerve. It's my turn. "I'm worried about Dad." I get the words out in a rush.

"Why?"

"I think…" I rearrange my hands again. I tuck my purse closer to my side. I am too nervous. I am too ashamed and awkward. I want to disappear.

My concerned grandmother watches closely.

"I'm sorry," I say. "I'm jumping the gun. I'm sure it's nothing." I make myself smile at her, stiff and unconvincing.

"Well. Now you have to tell me, Marie, or I'll be losing sleep over it." She is trying to joke. It almost works.

I have to tell her. There is no getting out of it. "There was some money … it's gone missing."

This stings her. Grandma was getting all set to explain to me that I am overreacting, again, but I've mentioned money.

"What money? Missing from where?"

I tell her about Geraldine's graduation present to Robbie and how it vanished. I am ashamed. Every bit of me displays it. Nervous hands, downcast eyes, tremulous voice. Poor little Marie. Daddy's baby girl. Marie doesn't know what to do.

Disapproval hardens like a mask over Grandma's features.

"Marie. Why on earth would you think your father had taken it? Simply because he pointed out to Geraldine she shouldn't have made such an extravagant gesture?"

"No, it's not that." I stop again. Breathe again. Her gaze chisels into me. Whatever I say next, she will believe. Grandma Millicent knows I am incapable of lying to her. I have worked hard to make sure of that.

"Dad's been talking with Jeff Seward more lately, and Walt. I think there might be trouble with the business."

Trouble with the business. The words hang between us, vibrating in the building heat. *Trouble with the business.* It's the one thing all Monroes fear. Trouble with the business means being left without money. Trouble with the business means shame and all our dirtiest laundry exposed for the entire world to see. Grandma's mind is already racing ahead, fitting pieces together, drawing conclusions. I wish I could see inside her. I want to watch the pictures take shape.

"I'm sure it's nothing." She takes my nervous hands, and holds on, forcing my fidgeting fingers to be still. "You've just been too stressed with Robbie's graduation party."

"I know. I know. I just...Dad won't talk to me."

Her hands are all sharp angles. The softer flesh wore away years ago and what's left is granite and iron. "Don't worry, Marie. I'll speak with him."

"But you won't tell him I told you?"

"I said don't worry." Grandma pauses and her fingers dig deeper into mine. "It's not just your father who depends on you, Marie. We all do, but that means you must depend on us."

"I do, Grandma." I lean forward and so very impulsively kiss her cheek.

Her smile is small, doling out the expected level of approval, but nothing more. "Well, now. That's settled. Would you go find June for me? I think it's time to go home."

Of course I will. I climb out with my box of almond macaroons and hurry down the street toward Lakeshore Books. I don't look back. She doesn't need to see my face. Not that she'd bother looking toward me. I've been managed and am therefore no longer a matter of concern.

But thanks to our confidential conversation, she does know something's gone wrong with Dad. That is a matter for concern. It will worry at her until she discovers all the details and devises some means to make the problem go away.

Good.

One under-examined aspect of the Household Tales is the princes. The ones who come to the rescue and who always seem to think choosing a wife from a family filled with witches, murderers, and cannibals is a good idea.

It's unsurprising that those princes get behind the idea that the family branches need a little pruning, starting with the bad sisters and wicked stepmothers. These men are, after all, royalty. They represent the power of high and low justice. Why shouldn't they use it to secure happiness and peace of mind for their new bride? Of course, it also secures them a castle, and a kingdom.

Somehow, this calculation never renders them less charming.
—Out of the Woods: Musings on Fairy Tales in the Real World,
Dr. Geraldine Monroe

GERALDINE, PRESENT DAY
STACEY B'S SANDWICHES AND STUFF

1.

The phone's ringing.

I wake up with a start. I'm in my driver's seat. Sun streams through the windshield. The car smells of stale coffee and overripe strawberries from the wilting container on the passenger seat. My toes are cramping inside my damp socks.

My phone's still ringing.

I spent the night in my car. This was strictly my choice. Even though the tourist season is well under way, there are still plenty of vacancies in the motels by the highway, and no matter what my father believes, I'm not that broke yet.

But I wanted to watch the old house and see if anything happened. I didn't seriously believe that any of my relations would come and burn the place down or call the cops to report suspicious activity. Not yet anyway.

I also did it to see if I still could. If something else went wrong and I had to leave in a hurry, did I remember what I needed to keep close? How to sleep with one ear open in case somebody came around looking for a dollar or a grope? Even before I left Lillywell, I put a couple changes of clothes and other useful stuff in my backpack, where I could get to them easily. Shimmying out of my party clothes in the dark was a little awkward, but nothing I hadn't done before.

Once I was in my old jeans, white men's T-shirt, and plaid flannel, I found my flashlight and pepper spray, and hunkered down to wait for morning. The sound of the wind in the trees mixed with the rush of the occasional car was as familiar as my name. So was the smell of cool summer night. I was home, whether I wanted this to be home or not. My body and my brain recognized it and relaxed. I fell asleep. No dreams found me. Thank God.

The ringing stops, just long enough for me to roll my shoulders, flex my toes inside my worn boots, and crick my neck.

And it starts again. I swear and root around in my purse, until I drag the annoying little device up from the bottom to check the screen.

Tyler.

Shut it off, I tell myself. *Wait it out. He'll get the message.*

But I can't. It is physically beyond me to turn him away again. I touch the *Accept* button and hold the phone to my ear.

"Geraldine?"

I close my eyes and swallow like I'm drinking his voice.

"Geraldine, come on. I just want to know you're okay. That's it. I promise."

How can I be okay? Tyler's voice is in my ear and I can see every lean, clean inch of him, with his chestnut hair flopping over his forehead and his beard cut so close around his jaw it's almost a five o'clock shadow. His café au lait eyes under their heavy black brows. The way he smiles with only one side of his mouth. Cheekbones to die for. Shoulders, arms, chest, waist. I'm remembering him with mind and hands and mouth.

So, I know exactly how he looks when he gives out that sigh that slips into my ear. "All right. We're not talking. Just…just tell me you're okay," Tyler whispers. "Please, Geraldine."

I swallow, and swallow again. Finally, my throat unsticks enough to let a trickle of breath thread its way through.

"I'm okay."

"Where are you?" The question is eager, and a little desperate. "Nobody back at Lillywell would give me anything."

I open my mouth to tell him, but catch myself just in time.

"This is a bad idea, Tyler."

"Do you want to know where I am?"

Yes. I do. I want to climb through the phone and be there, too. I want to wrap myself around you. I want you to hold me and say that everything will be all right even though it's never going to be all right again.

"Ty…"

"Chicago," he says before I can get any further. "I'm finishing up my paperwork at Northwestern. I got a graduate lecturer job."

"You didn't tell me you'd applied to Northwestern."

"I was saving it for a surprise."

Chicago. That's only ten hours away, nine if the traffic cooperates. Tyler is less than a day away from me. Way less if he flies into Traverse City and rents a car.

Tyler's in Chicago with a job and a chance to start a new life. Not still a student at Lillywell with scandals and old crimes sniffing around both our heels. The fact of it goes straight down to my stupid, starving vagina, and all at once I'm dripping and straining with raw need.

"Pay's for shit right now, but it'll look really good on the CV," he says. "I told you it'd work out."

"You did." I can admit that much.

"I love you, Gerie."

"Don't call me Gerie." The words are automatic.

"I love you anyway."

It's our very own call and response. We've repeated it in bed, at the table, in the woods, in the shadows of my office after we've almost broken the desk and the chair. After I've made myself drunk again on his scent and his hard, eager, delighted sex.

That, of course, was all before the department found out I was living the biggest cliché imaginable and sleeping with a student. Before Jeannine got scared and fired me and I had to make sure she didn't do worse.

My fingers curl around the steering wheel, because if I pound it, he'll hear me. "We can't. I can't."

"Sorry. You were breaking up there for a second."

"Don't joke about this, Ty!"

"I'm not joking. Where are you? Are you coming here, or should I come get you?"

"We agreed to separate."

"You said you were going away. I couldn't stop you, because of that little thing where you left in the middle of the night without saying good-bye. That is not an agreement to separate."

I should scream at him. Pour out all the hateful, insane things I thought in the dark as I packed up this car back in Alowana. Then, I should hang up and let him sit in Chicago with all that ringing in his ears (only ten hours away, nine if the traffic cooperates, even less if he flies into Traverse City). Let the anger and the pride and the pain make it easy for him to stay away. It would be for his own good.

That's not what I do. "I'm sorry. I shouldn't...I should have found another way."

"Then make it up to me. Let me come see you," he says. "Please, Geraldine. I just want to talk. Or you come here. I've converted to the way of the deep-dish pizza. You were right. I can't ever go back now." He purrs the last words, a tone of faux seduction that never fails to make me laugh.

It doesn't fail either of us now. I'm throwing my head back against the seat and I'm laughing. It hurts. Oh, God, it hurts so bad.

"I do not want to give us up, Geraldine. But, if you tell me that's not what you want, I'll hang up. I'll drown myself in the lake, or in pizza sauce. Whatever. But you won't hear from me again."

"Don't drown yourself," I say. "It hurts way more than they tell you."

"Okay. I won't. But I have to see you, Gerie."

He's twenty-four, and he calls me Gerie and I call him Ty. He's handsome and I'm eighteen years older than he is and I spent every minute until we got caught not caring. Because I was finally alive, really, physically alive in my own battered body. I had a pulse and hope and a reason to make a life that I could share with another human being. With Tyler I believed in Once Upon a Time and Happily Ever After. I wanted to clear everything between the two away.

And God help me, for a minute there, I believed that I could.

"I'm home," I say. "At my old house."

"Nice?"

I stare through the driver's side window at the dirty white aluminum siding. I think about the other house on the hill, looking down. "No."

"How about your sister? Is she there?"

I'd told him a little about Marie, once. After the regular phone calls started last year.

I've got some stuff that I have to work on, Ty. We'd been in bed, of course. It was sunset. Which I suppose was appropriate, symbolically speaking.

Everybody's got something.

Not like this.

What is it?

I can't tell you. Not yet. But... Marie, my sister, called. We've been talking. I might need to go home for a while and... You're just going to have to trust me for a bit. I'm doing this so we can be together.

Then I'm all for it.

That was before he and I got caught. Before I had to work my little bit of blackmail on Jeannine.

"Geraldine?" Ty prompts. "Can you hear me?"

"Yes," I croak. "Yes. I…Marie's son, my nephew, Robbie, he's graduating this weekend. That's why I'm here. I promised him."

"Gonna be a big party and everything?" We're talking about nothing, but we're talking, and I am not sending him away.

"Massive party. My father has a thing about entertaining. Probably half the town's going to be there."

"And that's not nice, either?"

"No. It isn't." Because it'll be the half that knows me, or used to.

"So, tell me what you're doing there again? I mean aside from avoiding me in an epic fashion?"

I am not hanging up or erasing his number or the hundred or so photos I've got of him on my phone. I am not letting him go for his own good or mine.

"I'm trying, Ty. I swear to God, I'm trying."

"I know. I just…I want to help. Why don't you come down here? Just for a couple of days."

He needs me. He wants me. I can trust this. Trust him. I always could. That's the part that gets inside and twists. "I can't."

"Then I'm coming to you."

"Stop saying that!"

Silence, heavy and stunned, leaches through the phone and into my mind.

"I'm sorry," I croak. "I just…it's complicated. I don't…I can't deal with us right now."

Please understand. Please go away. I love you. You have to stay away. I can't let my father know I've found someone. He'll pick us apart to find our weak spots and pour the poison in. Just like he did to Marie and David. And I don't know if I'll be able to stop him.

"I love you, Gerie," Ty says.

I shut the phone off. I drop it into my purse and grip the steering wheel so tight the plastic is pressing against bone.

"Don't call me Gerie."

2.

I met Tyler while we were both attending the same conference in Las Vegas. Even experts in anthropology and European folklore get a conference in Vegas at some point in their careers. We didn't actually meet at the conference. We met at a magic show in the next hotel over. We'd both forgotten to take off our name badges. We laughed about it and sat together. Afterward, we went disco dancing and ate too many mini eclairs at the buffet and drank Asti Spumante like freshmen at a Sweetest Day sorority party. We watched the rows of women playing the slots and made up fairy tales about them, and then numbered them all according to the Aarne-Thompson folktale classification system. Then we admitted we both hated the Aarne-Thompson system. We laughed until I was regretting the eclairs, but not the fact that I was falling fast and hard for the first time in a very long time.

He wasn't my student then. That didn't happen until September rolled around. He walked into my lecture, and we stared at each other, both utterly blank-faced.

He should have walked out, but he didn't. He slid into his chair in the auditorium, flipped up the desk, and pulled out his laptop.

I should have walked out. I should have written him a tidy note explaining that my having crazy-hot sex with a Lillywell student—any Lillywell student—while employed as a lecturer would be considered entirely inappropriate by the department. I was not a professor. I didn't have tenure. I could be fired at any time, with or without cause. With or without the fact that the dean and I went *waaaaaay* back.

But I just dimmed the lights, made sure the connection between the screen and my laptop was working, and launched into my introduction about how the popular culture influences of the Brothers Grimm had expanded beyond the Household Tales into ideas and pop myths about Jacob and Wilhelm themselves.

Tyler came to my office hours. I locked the door. We talked. I cried.

"How the hell did I pick now to finally fall in love?" I demanded, in a whisper, because the walls and the door were both really thin.

He wrapped his arms around me before I found the nerve or the strength to get away. "You need to stop talking like you're in this alone, Gerie. I'm here with you."

That was that. End of discussion. We thought.

I eat the rest of the strawberries for breakfast and drink the coffee left in the Starbucks cup in the dash holder. It is truly terrible, but we do what we have to.

I stare at the long, low prefab building across the yard that used to be Stacey B's Sandwiches and Stuff. Like the house, the old store has gone gray and green from dirt and mildew. Random memories waft in through the open window. Summer days when the tourists came for Pringles, Coke, beer, sandwiches, and slices of pie in polystyrene clamshells. The clusters of tourists. Mom and sometimes Dad. Me, and everything I turned into.

The house keys sit in the coin tray down by the stick shift. I squirm in my seat. I'm going to have to either go inside or use the woods, real soon. But I know what's waiting for me among the trees even better than I know what's waiting for me in the house.

So, which do I go and face first? Woods or house? Life or death?

The petty urgency of biology makes the choice for me. I grab the house keys, shove them in my coat pocket, and climb out of the car.

3.

Last night I dreamt I went to Manderley again...

The line from *Rebecca* drifts through my brain as I round the house's corner. My old boots crunch down dandelions, lamb's tongue, and ambitious raspberry shoots that have pushed their way up between the gray gravel that used to mark the parking lot. Not that the little white house I've been staring at all night is our Manderley. That title belongs to the Rose House up on its hill. This...this is just the place I grew up. Bequeathed with the Rose House to me and Marie by my mother and my aunt, partly so we'd always have a someplace of our own. Partly to stick it to my father in the only way they had left.

A maple sapling sprouts out of the sagging gutter. Half the roof is covered with moss, dead leaves, and maple seeds. The rest is wrapped in a blue plastic tarp to try to keep out the weather.

One white metal lawn chair lies on its side, a leftover corpse from when we used to sit out here in the shade. I set it carefully upright, then wipe my rust-smeared palms on the seat of my jeans.

That's when I realize the big maple is gone, and everything freezes.

Somebody cut down our tree.

Some *goddamn bastard* cut down our tree!

I walk over, slow and tentative, like if I give it enough time I might realize I made a mistake. No such luck. All that's left of the broad sugar maple is a gray stump. Black, spongy rot has hollowed out its center. The tree's heartwood had gone bad. I can see it needed to be taken out before it broke and fell. That doesn't stop my surge of anger at whoever gave the order.

It might even have been Marie. I turn away toward the house. I'm sick and sore and I haven't even gotten inside yet.

Shit.

The aluminum screen door has no screen left, and no spring. It flaps open, exhausted. The front door is steel. Its paint is flaking and it's rusted around the edges. The new key fits, but the lock sticks. I rattle the key, kick the door, and swear a few times. One of those does the trick, and I'm in.

I make a beeline for the bathroom. Marie has kept the water and the electricity turned on. I'm not surprised. My sister would never make me come back to a dead house. I use the toilet (I keep a roll of paper in my backpack, because you never know). I wash my face with my bare hands and rinse my mouth out in the sink. The water still tastes like iron and sulfur. I wipe my face on my hands and my hands on my jeans.

Out in the main house, the morning scents of earth and leaves are warmed and concentrated by the sun streaming through the windows. The mice have been, well, everywhere.

Marie has kept me updated. I know this place has changed hands three or four times since I left. There was a family who wanted a summer cottage, and at least one experiment with a manager to rent it out during the summer, like Dad does with his starter mansions for the one-percenters. I don't feel any of those other people. This is our house. We—my sister, me, my mother, our father, the living and the dead— we all haunt it together.

There is where I discovered that if you throw spaghetti at the wall, it really does stick.

There's where Mom always hung the calendar. This is where Marie and I spent two weeks putting together the thousand-piece candy jar jigsaw puzzle.

This is the place Marie once swore she'd never go back to, after I'd pulled her out of the snow, frozen close enough to death that I thought we'd never get warm again.

I turn one more corner. I walk down the dim hallway. My damp boots squeak on the scuffed floorboards.

The door to our old bedroom is closed. All the other doors have been hanging wide open, but not that one. I need to go in there. There's something I've left behind. For Marie. She never told me if she found it, not even during our recent flurry of phone calls. I have to know if she found it. It's going to make a difference about what happens next. All the difference, actually.

I wrap my palm around the smooth, familiar knob and push.

I come up into our old room like I'm coming up for air. I have to wait for my heart to slow down and for the ripples of memory to finish sloshing against my skin and my mind. Eventually, though, I can see I'm just standing in another empty room of my empty house. The metal blinds are down over the windows, and it's as stuffy as the rest of the place. The damp smells are just as strong. There's a dead moth on the windowsill and a cobweb in the corner where our bunk beds used to be.

Our room has one heating vent. The cover's got thin, vertical bars and is painted over with the same dull white paint as the walls. Like kids do, Marie and I figured out that if you scrape the paint away, you can loosen the screws and take that barred cover off. It became our hiding place. Packs of Twinkies and Ho Hos we stole from the store went in here. Allowance money. Marie's notebooks. My stash, for a little while anyway.

And one other thing.

A week after Mom died, we moved into the Rose House. A week after we moved into the Rose House, I left home with a pocket full of cash and a prepaid credit card that did not belong to me. I did it in the middle of the night so Marie wouldn't try to stop me. I was afraid if she did, I might end up telling her about my last conversation with Dad.

Not the one at the bottom of the gully behind the house. The one after that.

But before I met up with the kid who would drive me out to Buffalo in exchange for gas money, I came back here. My home was already empty, already cold. Left for dead, just like Mom.

I used a quarter to unscrew the vent, and I put a note inside. It was my confession to Marie. All of five words long.

I did it. I'm sorry.

When I decided to kill myself, I didn't leave a note. But when I decided to stay alive, I also realized Marie deserved to know I was the one who killed our mother.

I have never known whether this was because I loved my sister, or because I hated her, or because I wanted her to be able to hate me like I deserved. Maybe it doesn't matter.

Like the door, the vent takes some work, but I'm ready for it. I carry a Swiss Army knife in my glove compartment for the same reasons I carry toilet paper and a flashlight. Because you never know. I use the screwdriver blade to scrape away the four or five layers of cheap white paint that have been slapped over the vent and its screws since we left.

If the space is empty, Marie found the note: *I did it. I'm sorry.* She read it. She knows what I did, and she wanted me back anyway. She trusted me. She kept this house, our real home, so there'd be someplace for me to come back to.

There are only three screws. One vanished down a crack in the floorboards when we were still kids and was never replaced.

If the note's still there, she didn't look. She didn't trust me and she still doesn't know what I did. She kept the house alive just because she's Marie, and Marie keeps up appearances.

I line the screws up by the baseboard. My hands have gone cold. I hear the songbirds and crows and the wind outside. No cars, though.

I curl my fingers through the grating and lift the vent cover away.

Inside the hole, there's more dust, more old mouse droppings and desiccated insects. There's a gray stone too, the size of my fist. It sits on top of a slip of paper that's gone as brown as the dead leaves littering the sagging roof.

It's still there. Right where I left it. She never found it. She never even looked.

I'd been so sure. I just knew that after I disappeared, my sister would go to the old hiding place. I was positive she must have read the note and forgiven me, or at least understood on some level what I'd really done. Almost positive. At least, I wanted it to be true. Badly.

That's why I listened when she called last summer. That's the real reason why I came back.

I snatch up the pointless, childish confession that my asinine, shallow, selfish bitch of a sister couldn't be bothered to look for. The rock rolls aside, clanking into the little dark tomb, and there's something else. It rustles and it flutters.

Another paper.

It's old and dirty and stained and speckled and nibbled around the edges. It's been here a long, long time. Almost as long as the note I left, but not quite.

I unfold it. I see my sister's handwriting, and I read her message to me. Mine was five words long. So is hers.

I did it, Marie writes. *I'm sorry.*

4.

Gradually, I am able to move. Eventually, I can put my note back into its place. I lay my sister's on top of it.

Then, I take the stack of two thousand dollars out of my pocket. I use the stone to weigh all that precious paper down so it can't escape.

Lastly, I set the vent back in its place so no one will see what I've done.

Fathers in fairy tales do not receive a lot of critical attention, which is surprising. These are, after all, the men who marry the wicked stepmothers. Then they passively agree to abandon their biological children, or fail to protest when those children are turned into swans, ravens, or scullery maids. Sometimes they die before the story arc truly begins, which gives the stepmothers free rein for their evildoing. Other times, however, the father is right there when children return, having successfully avoided being eaten by the witch or burned at the stake for murder or witchcraft. At this point, King/Father typically demonstrates righteous remorse. He helps punish his new wife, and then it's happily ever after.

I can't help believing this all must lead to some awkward family dinners. Because the father did *abandon his children. He did* not *curb the elaborate murder attempts. He didn't even go looking when his children vanished.*

Children tend to notice these things.

—Out of the Woods: Musings on Fairy Tales in the Real World,
Dr. Geraldine Monroe

MARIE, EIGHT YEARS OLD
GERALDINE, SEVEN YEARS OLD
STACEY B'S SANDWICHES AND STUFF

1.

Marie Monroe knew every hiding place within a half mile of her home.

The very best was the maple tree right on the edge of their full-acre yard. This was no skinny forest tree. It was a fat field tree, with three trunks and a sprawling crown of tangled limbs. It was as easy to climb as a ladder, even with Mom's old purse slung over her shoulder to hold important items, like her notebook and pencils and a can of Faygo Redpop.

No matter how hot it was in the summer, up here it was green and cool and shady. It even smelled different—a sweet blend of warm leaves, bark, and maple sap. Marie could sit with her back against the trunk, as secure as if she was curled up on the living room sofa. Only here was better, because nobody could see her except the squirrels and the robins.

And her sister, of course. There was no hiding from Geraldine.

Marie had just gotten settled. She flipped back the cover to expose the page she'd been working on, and pulled out her pencil with her favorite pink pinwheel topper over the eraser. She opened the Redpop, sucked up the fizz as it fountained out, and then clamped the can between her knees so she could hold the notebook more easily. That, of course, was when the branches shook, and the pop almost spilled, and the little twerp practically hopscotched up the branches.

"Whatcha doin'?"

"Go away." Marie hunched further over her book.

Geraldine stuck out her tongue. She also climbed up to the next branch, so she could look down. Marie snapped the book shut before Geraldine could see her sketch, splashing Redpop as she did.

"I said go away!" She blotted the cover with her bare arm.

But Geraldine just pulled down a handful of the tan, winged seeds everybody called helicopters and sent one whirling down onto Marie's head.

"Quit it!" Marie swatted at the seed pod. Geraldine giggled and let another one drop. This one, by sheer dumb luck, slithered into the pop can.

"You little jerk!"

"Two points to Mighty G! Marie's a loser!"

Marie dropped the can, sending up a shower of sticky red sugar water as it bounced to the ground, stuffed her notebook into the old purse, and yanked herself up after her sister, but Geraldine was already long gone.

Marie gritted her teeth and stretched her longer legs to climb after Geraldine, even though she knew this was exactly what Geraldine wanted all along. The next branch wobbled under her weight. Marie faltered and clutched the trunk. Geraldine grabbed her wrist. Her hand was warm and stronger than it should have been for such a little kid. Marie eased her hold on the trunk. Geraldine was a baby and a twerp, and had made her waste a whole can of pop, but Geraldine would never let her fall.

When Geraldine felt Marie find her balance, she let go and stretched out on the neighboring branch like a cat, her legs wrapped tight around the slender, bobbling end.

"One day, I'm going to build a bridge," said Geraldine as Marie settled down in the fork between trunk and the new branch, letting her feet dangle. "A great big long rope bridge through the trees. And I'll cross that, and sling another one, and another. It'll be a whole rope highway."

This was a make-believe they'd played forever. Lately, though, Marie had started to feel like she was too old for the Going To game. Geraldine was still only seven, but Marie would turn nine in three and a half weeks. Like her growing body, reality was getting heavier. It was harder to climb out from under it to think about rope bridge highways or castles made from sand or shells, or any of the other things they came up with.

But Geraldine was looking at her hopefully, so Marie sighed and dug deep in her brain.

"I'm going to build a tree mansion, off an exit ramp of your rope highway. I'll live there all the time and never invite anybody."

"Except me."

"Except you," Marie agreed. "You don't count as anybody."

While Geraldine was still trying to figure out if this was an insult, the sound of tires crunching on gravel rose up from the parking area. Geraldine twisted herself until she was sitting upright on the branch, one finger pressed against her mouth. Marie nodded. Together, they scooted closer to the trunk and craned their necks to see who was coming.

Both girls recognized the rusted-out, red pickup that rolled into view. It belonged to Uncle Pete, Dad's brother. His jeans had patches on the knees and he wore a blue work shirt with the elbows so thin you could see his arms underneath. Everything about Uncle Pete was like that—worn down, beaten up, and awkward, like he wasn't used to it, or to himself.

No pride, Dad always said. *No sense of where he's from.*

"Stacey!" Uncle Pete shouted, like he couldn't just walk into the store. Or maybe the CLOSED sign was already up. "Stacey!"

Out beyond the green curtain of maple leaves, a screen door creaked and then slammed.

"Jesus H. Christ, Pete! What is your problem?"

"Uh-oh," whispered Geraldine, and Marie clutched the branch tightly.

Down below, Mom stormed into view, a cloud of cigarette smoke swirling behind her. She wore her work clothes—jeans and blue tennis shoes and a white apron over her T-shirt with the faded sunflower right across the front.

"This is my problem, Stacey!" Uncle Pete flapped the piece of paper in front of her. "This is from your goddamn husband!"

"Are you going to tell me what it is, or are you just going to keep waving it in my face?" She swatted at the paper like it was a moth.

"It's from a lawyer. Your husband is kicking me out of my house!"

"What the fuck!" Mom snatched the cigarette from her mouth and tossed it to the ground. It bounced off the pop can. *Ting.*

Geraldine held her breath. Marie did, too. Picking up the litter in the yard was their job. If Mom shouted for them now to come and get this G-D can, she'd see them climb down. They'd be busted. Worse. Their best-ever hiding place would be ruined.

"He bought the property. He's evicting me!" Pete shoved the paper at her, and this time Mom grabbed it and stared at it. Geraldine inched closer to Marie, slowly, so she wouldn't shake the branch.

"He wouldn't. You're his brother."

"You think he cares? After what he made you do to Trish, you really think…?"

"Shut up, Pete. This is not about Trish."

There was a long, grim pause between the two adults. Geraldine nudged Marie's shoulder, and Marie knew they were both wondering the same thing.

Who's Trish?

"He knows," Uncle Pete said. "He figured it out."

"Of course he didn't!"

"You sure?" Pete flapped the paper at her again.

A jay screamed in the woods. A crow cawed back. Marie bit her lip. Geraldine leaned against her. Marie wanted to wrap her arm around her sister, but she wasn't sure of her balance anymore. She didn't dare let go with even one hand.

Underneath them, Uncle Pete turned his back and marched away, stuffing the paper back in his shirt pocket as he did. Mom hesitated for a split second, and then ran after him.

"Pete, wait." Squinting through the leaves, Marie could just make out how they stood so close together. Mom had her hand on Uncle Pete's sleeve.

"Wait for what?" he asked.

"Take me with you," Mom said. "Let's do it. Let's just go."

Go where? Cold crept into the pit of Marie's stomach. Understanding threatened, but she forced it away. Geraldine nudged her.

"I can't," said Pete.

"Do you want me to say I was wrong? I made a mistake and picked the wrong brother? Okay. I did. I'm sorry." She walked toward him, hands in her pockets, elbows pointed backward, until she was so close, she had to tilt her chin up to look into his eyes. "Please, Pete. I was a kid. I was confused, about my parents, and Martin said…he said a lot of things."

"Yeah, you were a kid," said Pete slowly. "And now we've both got kids."

"We'll grab them. We'll leave, right now. Stop at Kmart and get what we need on the way out. He's in the house messing around with that computer. He won't even notice we're gone."

"Marie…" breathed Geraldine.

Marie squeezed her eyes shut.

"He'd destroy Florence. And he'd find us. You know he would."

"He's not God, Pete."

"Don't tell him that. Anyway, what about Trish?"

"What about her?"

Pete shook his head. "That's some kind of answer about your own sister."

Sister?

"Please, Pete."

"Mom has a sister?" whispered Geraldine. "Did you know Mom has a sister?"

She can't have a sister. She never said. Dad never said.

"If you want to leave, Stacey, why don't you just go? There's gas in the car. Go on."

For a second, Marie was sure Mom was going to say something back, but she didn't.

"See?" said Uncle Pete. "We're all trapped."

Uncle Pete climbed back into his truck. The engine started on the third try and he pulled out. Mom stood there for maybe one second longer. Then she reached down and grabbed the pop can and threw it hard after the truck. The girls heard the can hit the blacktop and rattle away. Mom stalked out of sight. The door creaked. The door slammed.

"Okay. Now," whispered Geraldine. She eased herself down so she could balance her feet on the next branch.

"No, wait," said Marie.

Creee-ahh-k went the shop door. *Slam!*

Geraldine froze, stomach braced against the branch, elbows bent into an M.

Below, Mom reappeared. She plopped down into the rusting, white chair with its seashell back and dropped a whole blue and white case of beer beside her.

Oh, no.

Mom yanked out a can of beer, popped the top and put it on the grass so it was ready for her. She dug her pill bottle out of her apron, shook two out onto her palm, paused, and added a third.

Oh, no.

She tossed all three pills into her mouth all at once and tilted her head back for the beer.

Marie edged right up next to Geraldine. Below them, Mom tossed the beer can away and reached for the next.

"Stop her," breathed Marie right in her sister's ear.

"I can't…"

"Stop her! She'll listen to you. Please, Geraldine. I just make her mad."

Geraldine swallowed, and nodded. Bending and twisting and shimmying, she worked her way down, keeping to the back of the tree. Marie watched and tried not to feel like a coward.

Mom threw away the second can and reached for a third.

Marie clung to her branch. Down below, Geraldine walked out from behind their tree, easy and natural, like she'd been there the whole time.

"Where'd you come from?" Mom's voice was already thickening from the pills and the beer.

Geraldine didn't answer. She just stood there, letting Mom's foggy attention focus all the way on her.

Marie slid one branch lower.

"Cat got your tongue?" asked Mom.

Geraldine shifted from foot to foot. Marie reached down with one toe to find the fork in the trunks.

"Well, we'll have to see what we can do about that. How about a story?"

Geraldine nodded. Marie bit her lip and wriggled her sneaker into the fork.

Mom drained the beer and tossed the can away. "Come on, climb up." She slapped both thighs. "I'll tell you a good one."

Geraldine settled down as easily in her mother's lap as she did in the tree's crooked branches. Mom must stink from sweat and beer mixed with cigarettes. But the smell was never as bad as the blotchy, greasy anger that seemed to ooze out of her skin.

"Once upon a time," Mom began slowly. "There was a queen, and she lived in a castle called the Rose House. Its walls were made out of trees and the windows had roses growing on them, and there were fairies living right inside who took care of her and did whatever she said."

Marie reached the ground. Mom reached for another beer.

"Why did they?" asked Geraldine.

"Why did who what?" snapped Mom.

"The fairies? Why did they do what the queen said?"

"Well, she made them." Mom paused and took a long drink of beer. "The queen was not a nice lady. She threw all kinds of parties, and that made some people think she was nice. But really, she was mean and selfish and she wouldn't share what she had, not even with her two daughters. So people hated her, and that included the fairies. And since she went around telling all kinds of lies about people, they hated her even worse."

"Was there a king?"

Mom sighed, a long, gusty rush of breath that ended in a belch. "Yeah, there was. And he tried, you know? Argued with the queen all the time, but, he just couldn't get her to be nice. Nobody could. She was too strong. So, they all just had to sit there and hate her and wait for her to make some kind of mistake."

"Did she?"

"You bet she did. See, she had two daughters."

Marie slipped down the tree. Her sneaker touched the ground. Geraldine's eyes flicked left. Marie froze.

"The oldest daughter was just like her mother, only worse," said Mom. "She was mean and selfish, and wanted everything her own way. The youngest one...she was so beautiful that all the princes wanted to marry her. But that daughter, she had her eye on one prince in partic-ular. He was from a rich kingdom, but they'd lost all their money and they were poor now."

Marie pressed herself against the tree. She needed to get past without being seen. She could do it. It was all about picking the right minute.

"Then one day, the queen and the king got into an accident and died."

"What kind of accident?" asked Geraldine.

"Car accident."

"Kings and queens don't have cars. They have carriages."

"Well these had a car. Now shut up, I'm telling the story."

"Sorry, Mommy."

"'S okay, G. Anyway. They died, and the old queen left the castle to the older, selfish daughter, the one she really loved. But!" Mom waved the beer can. "The younger daughter, the pretty one, she finally got together with her prince, see? And they made a deal. The prince promised the pr-pretty princess that if they got married they'd find a way to rule both kingdoms. And the pretty…pretty princess promised the pretty, pretty prince they could live in the big castle with the roses and the fairies on account of he loved it soooo much."

"What about the bad sister?"

"Well, see, the prince, the prince, the prince and the pretty, pretty princess…" Mom's words slurred, growing distant and mushy. "They had a plan. After they got married…" Mom belched. "After they got married, what they did was they got a bunch of…of guards together to go after the oldest sister. They were going to prove to the guards that she wasn't just mean, she was crazy. So they would take her away and lock her in the asylum."

Mom set the beer can down carefully by the chair. She fumbled her apron pocket and pulled out a pack of Virginia Slims and a blue Bic lighter.

"When the bad sister was gone, did the prince and princess live happily ever after?" asked Geraldine.

Mom blew the stinking white cloud up to the sky. "Well, now see,

83

that was the problem. The bad sister, she was smart. Bad people can be. She wrote down a whole set of spells and used them on the guards and the fairies. Then, she barricaded herself into the castle."

"So what happened to her?"

"Nothing happened to her. She's still up there." Mom pointed up the highway with the cigarette held in the V of her fingers. "She just sits there, getting uglier and angrier by the minute. She won't even talk to the good sister."

At last, Marie moved, quick and light, smooth and sure. She didn't break stride, she didn't look back.

"She's not even a princess anymore." Mom's voice drifted across the summer air.

"What is she?" asked Geraldine.

"Can't you guess, G? She's a witch." There was a pause. Marie slipped into the house. But as the door closed behind her, she heard, "And maybe, baby, what we need is a goddamn witch."

2.

"Dad?"

Dad's study was a plain room. The dull white walls had metal-bracketed shelves full of paper and books and binders. There was an electric typewriter on the desk, along with the fat, stacked boxes of the new computer.

"Dad?"

Dad was staring at the glowing green print on the new computer screen and making notes on a legal pad. He didn't turn around.

"What have I told you, Marie?"

Oh, no. She didn't think. She messed up. Marie knew exactly what she was supposed to say, but the words had all lumped together in her throat. "Only good girls can come in here."

Dad clicked a few more keys and made another note on the pad. "And do good girls disturb their fathers when they're working?"

"No, sir."

Another few clicks, more shifting and stirring of green numbers on the black screen. A period jabbed into the yellow page.

"Are good girls messy, with dirty hands and tangled hair?"

He knew. He didn't even have to turn around. Mom said she had eyes in the back of her head, but Dad really did. "I'm sorry, Dad. I'm a bad girl."

"And I forgive you." He laid his pencil down and swiveled the chair around. "Because I love you, Marie."

Marie waited for the warm and fuzzy feeling that usually filled her when he said that. But this time, her stomach stayed cold. "Dad, I'm sorry, I really am. I'll clean up right away, but…"

"But what, Marie? You look scared. Don't tell me I scared you?"

"No." Good girls were never scared of their fathers. She knew that. "It's Mom. She's drinking. She's got a whole case of beer and she took three of her pills."

"Well, at least the store is closed, so no one will see."

No one will see. Marie's stomach turned over. He didn't understand. Dad had to come out and stop her. If he didn't, Mom was going to keep drinking. She was going to shout and laugh and throw things, and pass out, maybe right in the yard.

"Geraldine's out there too," Marie tried. "She'll see."

"Well, then, Geraldine will let us know if anything's really wrong. You just worry about getting yourself cleaned up, okay?"

Marie was shaking. She shouldn't be bothering Dad. He was right. It was a mistake to come in here. But she needed…she needed…she didn't even know what. She wanted to explain how Geraldine was only seven. Not that much more than a baby. How could she tell if something was really wrong?

The venetian blinds rattled and a fresh breeze brushed Marie's sweating forehead.

The window was open.

She heard the rumble of a car tearing down the hill, and another laboring its way up. If she could hear the traffic, Dad must have heard the shouting. He must have heard the whole argument between Uncle Pete and Mom.

Except he couldn't have, or he would have come out. He wouldn't just sit in here, listening.

"Oh, now you look sad, Marie. How about I tell you a secret? Will that cheer you up?"

But before Marie could decide, Dad leaned forward. "I've gotten hold of a very valuable piece of land, and I'm going to sell it, and when I do, we'll have lots of money." Dad chuckled. "All kinds of other people wanted it first, including my sister, June."

"*Your* sister? N-not..." Not Mom's? Marie swallowed the question just in time. "Uncle Pete?"

"Don't stammer, Marie. You're too pretty for that. And I've told you, Uncle Pete's a failure and a lousy manager. He could never afford anything like this."

Marie had never met Aunt June or Grandma Millicent or any of Dad's family, except Uncle Pete. There had been some kind of big fight before she and Geraldine were even born. But Dad told stories about Grandma Millicent, like he told them about his father, who was also named Martin and had died a long time ago.

He died, Dad said, because he was a failure. Failure was like a disease, Dad said. If you got infected with it, it would kill you. Boom. Like that.

"When I sell the property, we'll be able to buy all kinds of things. But that's not the important part." Dad held up one finger. "The important part is my family will have to talk to me about the deal. They'll have to start being nice to us. You and Geraldine are finally going to be part of a real family with a grandmother and aunts and uncles and cousins."

Dad beamed and it was like all the sunlight in the world poured into the room. The warmth swept straight through Marie and she threw her arms around his neck to hug him. It was only then she realized what land he must mean, and who it must have belonged to.

She felt the weight of her heavy body pull her backward.

"You're talking about Uncle Pete's house."

"It's not his house," Dad corrected her gently. "He only rented it. I bought the land it's built on, and so I own the house, and the lease, and if he can't pay the rent, he has to leave."

But…that wasn't right. Aunt Florence lived there, and Walter was in fourth grade and Ruby had just turned two. Marie had given her a box of crayons. She tried to eat them.

"Smile, baby girl." Dad made a V with his two fingers and pressed them against Marie's mouth to push the corners up. "Things are finally going to come together for us."

This was all wrong. Mom and Uncle Pete. The open window. The way Dad was talking now.

"Why does it have to be that house?" Marie asked slowly. "What about the other house?"

"What other house?"

"The castle. The Rose House. What about that one? Couldn't you take it from the witch and sell it instead?" Witches were bad. It'd be okay to take her house. At least, it'd be better than taking Uncle Pete and Aunt Florence's.

Dad sighed. "So, your mom finally told you about that, did she?"

He hadn't heard after all. Marie felt a rush of relief, but she didn't know why.

Dad settled back in his chair. "Unfortunately, baby girl, this is one of those complicated grown-up things. The Rose House belongs to your mother's older sister."

"How come you never told us Mom has a sister?" *You talk about family all the time. Why not her?*

Dad sighed again. "How can I explain this, Marie? It's a bad thing to fight with your family. But, once the fight starts, you have to make sure you win. You see, when we found out you were going to be born, your mother promised you would grow up in the Rose House, like she did. But because your mother wouldn't fight hard enough, she couldn't keep that promise. She just walked away and never wanted to talk about it."

"She failed?" Marie whispered.

Dad nodded. "Yes, Marie. She failed and now we're all stuck with it."

Dad pushed both hands down on the chair arms and levered himself all the long way up. Marie tried to scoot backward, but she wasn't fast enough. Dad's hand dropped onto her shoulder.

"Now, since it's so important to you, Marie, let's go find out what's really happening."

3.

Geraldine was still curled up on Mom's lap. Mom had stopped talking. She just smoked and stared at the empty highway. A fresh beer can sat on the ground beside her. Sun and shadow played across her pale skin and made her brown eyes flicker. Strands of white hair floated around her head. She looked strangely beautiful. She looked simply dangerous.

Dad walked Marie across the lawn to stand in front of Mom and Geraldine. He kept his hand on her shoulder. Geraldine scrunched her face up at Marie, and Marie felt her cheeks heat up with shame. But she didn't know what for.

"Weeell, well, well," drawled Mom. "Martin. Where have you been?"

"I've been working, Stacey."

She snorted. "I can tell. Did you see the notice from the phone company?"

"I took care of it."

Geraldine slipped off Mom's lap, but she stayed by the chair, with both hands holding Mom's arm down.

"Pete came by." Mom reached down for her beer with the arm Geraldine wasn't holding. "Seems he's losing the house, and guess who he said was taking it?"

"It is not my fault he can't pay, Stacey." Dad's hand tightened on Marie's shoulder. Not hard or anything. It was just a reminder that she should be a good girl and hold still. "I don't know why you're getting angry at me. You were the one who said the financial game wasn't going to work out. Not long term." He smiled. "I should have listened to you and remembered how my family built Whitestone in the first place. The money, and our future is in real estate."

Mom moved to pop the top on her beer can, but Geraldine was still holding her one arm down. Confused, Mom handed Geraldine the beer. Geraldine set it on the ground.

"You're always going on and on and on about how we need the money," said Dad. "And that is a valuable piece of property going to waste. Now, it's going to be a revenue generator for us and our daughters."

"We've got the store!" In a sudden burst of energy, Mom heaved herself to her feet. Geraldine stumbled backward.

Now she'll run away, thought Marie. *No one's holding her. Nobody expects her to be good.*

"I'm in there ten hours a day, every single day while you're sitting on your ass…!" Mom lurched forward, flinging out one arm.

"And always telling me how it's not enough," Dad reminded Mom, gently. "You're right, Stacey. This will be a new start for us. We need one, since you weren't able to get the Rose House back like you promised."

"Oh, here it comes!" Mom threw up her hands. "The house, the house, the goddamn house!" She stopped, she lurched left, then right. Geraldine gasped and started forward. "You're scaring the girls, Stacey," said Dad.

But Mom wasn't listening. "Where did you even get the money to buy Pete's place?" she demanded out of thin air. "If we're so broke…" She stopped. "Oh, no. Oh, Jesus fuck, Martin!"

"What?" he said back, the word flat and heavy. "Why all the surprise, Stacey? You were there. You signed the papers."

"I never signed anything!"

"You did. I sat down with you and we went over them and…oh…oh no." Dad squeezed Marie's shoulder again. *Pay attention,* that squeeze, said.

"What?" said Mom.

Squeeze. Pay attention, Marie. This shouting is because of you. You wanted me out here.

"Never mind." Dad's voice was soft, but his eyes were bright and hard, like glass, like ice.

"What?" shouted Mom.

Squeeze. This. This was about failure, and being dead, and the bad princess who became a witch and the real house on the hill.

"I think, maybe, when we went over the papers, you were drunk," said Dad.

This fight was because she'd bothered Dad when she knew she shouldn't. Things were bad, and she'd made them worse.

"When was I so drunk I don't remember signing over our house?"

Marie was a bad girl. She made stupid mistakes.

Dad waved with his free hand. "It's not your fault. Those pills for your back, they don't mix well with the beer."

"How did you…this place isn't yours! What did you do?"

"We needed the money, Stacey. For the girls." *Squeeze.* "But don't worry. We'll be fine. You know I love you and I'll always take care of you and our daughters, no matter what."

She should have found another way. One that didn't bother Dad.

"You never loved me!" Mom shouted. "You hate me! You love that stupid fucking house and you hate me!"

"Why do you care so much about what happens to Pete, Stacey?"

Silence dropped down. A car roared by. Another. A crow cawed. Its brother answered.

Mom staggered forward, and sideways, and forward again. Dad didn't even flinch. Marie shrank back against him. He was solid and warm, and all the skin on her back shriveled up where it touched him.

"I love you, Stacey. It doesn't matter to me what you've done. I will never leave you alone."

"Stop it," whispered Geraldine.

"I can't," breathed Marie.

But Geraldine wasn't talking to her. "Stop it!" She balled up her fists and her face turned beet red. *"Stop it, now!"*

Mom spun, but too fast. She screamed and toppled over, yanking on Geraldine so they went down together. Marie shrieked and lunged forward. Dad's fingers dragged hard against her shoulder the entire way. Mom was laughing and sobbing and couldn't find her feet. Geraldine struggled to get out from under her.

Dad didn't move.

Marie dodged Mom's flailing arms and pulled Geraldine out of reach. Mom crawled around in a tight circle, looking for something she lost. She didn't find it and collapsed in a heap.

"Go," breathed Marie into Geraldine's ear. Geraldine was trembling, stiff as a board, glaring at their father. "Go on." Go into the house. The tree. The woods. Anywhere.

Mom blinked helplessly. Then, in one abrupt movement, she rolled over on her side, and vomited, a thin, brown stinking stream. Marie whimpered and hid her face.

Dad still didn't move.

"Just look at how ugly you've gotten," he muttered. "How you teach our daughters to behave."

Geraldine pulled out of Marie's grip, but she still didn't run. She took two giant steps forward and plopped down next to Mom on a clean patch of grass, arms folded, faceup.

"Geraldine," said Dad. "Get up and go stand with your sister."

Geraldine pushed her lower lip out and shook her head hard.

"This is how bad girls behave, Geraldine. You need to be good, like your sister. Marie obeys her father."

Marie felt like she would split in two. She wanted to shout at Geraldine to run, to get away. She wanted to tell her to come here, like Dad said. Before things got worse. Before he really decided she was bad. Before...before...

Mom groped sideways and her arm snaked around Geraldine's shoulder. She struggled to get up onto her knees. Geraldine flinched, but she staggered to her feet, a tiny, dark little thing helping her pale mother stand. She glowered at Dad, and Marie wished the ground would open up and swallow her whole.

She just wasn't sure which "her" should get swallowed. Maybe all of them.

"All right then," said Dad quietly. "You pick her over me, Geraldine? Fine. She's your responsibility now. Go get her cleaned up before somebody sees."

Dad walked away and left them all there.

All of a sudden, Marie hated her mother. Hated them. The stink and the falling down and the beer and the pills. She hated the way Geraldine could decide to stand next to their sick, dirty mother and leave Marie over here, all on her own.

But she couldn't hate. She had to be a good girl. Good girls didn't hate anybody. Not their sisters or their mothers.

And most especially not their fathers.

Once upon another time, there was this other princess. You've never heard of her. The Brothers Grimm didn't even record her name. When it came time for this princess to get married, this nameless girl's mother pricked her finger and let the blood drop onto a handkerchief, which she gave to her daughter as a token of protection.

Along the journey, an evil servant caused that handkerchief to fall into a stream. After that, the princess is robbed. Her horse is killed. The prince marries the wrong girl, for a while, anyway.

What's interesting here is that it's not the wish that causes the trouble. It's when mother and daughter lose control of the wish that all hell breaks loose.
—Out of the Woods: Musings on Fairy Tales in the Real World,
Dr. Geraldine Monroe

MARIE, PRESENT DAY
THE ROSE HOUSE

1.

Dinner with Dale and Deborah Watts goes off perfectly. I'm intensely grateful to be able to slip into my hostess role. This is absurd and I know it. But when I'm a hostess, I understand precisely what is expected of me. If Deborah remarks that I seem a little tired, I am able to laugh about how busy we all are with Sunday's graduation party. I do not pull away when Dale takes my wrist to look at my injured hand, tut-tut, and run a manicured finger along the edges of the bandage. He suggests to my father that he should be taking better care of me.

We all smile, and as I pull my hand away, Deborah and I exchange a little eye roll. *Men.*

Dad changes the subject smoothly and hopes the Wattses will accept his invitation to the party on Sunday. This is a polite nothing, just a demonstration of how much he values them as friends and clients. They know this, and demur. So all the boxes are checked, and everybody leaves content.

"Well." Dad sighs as the front door closes behind them. "I'm sure we could both use a drink."

He doesn't wait for my answer and heads to his study.

I do not refuse, although I really would rather be left to myself. The air is shifting uneasily around me. I thought Geraldine would have called by now, to let me know she's settled in. But she hasn't. She's out there in the dark, and I don't know what she's doing or thinking.

I hope nothing's gone wrong. I hope there hasn't been any new trouble.

But of course, I will not let Dad know any of this. There's absolutely no reason for him to worry as well. So, I make myself focus on the details of my surroundings. The foyer is broad and white. The old beams have been replaced by modern white bracket supports. The whole space was to be pure white to contrast with the dark slate floor, and—although this did not need to be said out loud—to cover over all traces of Aunt Trish's final vandalism.

Once that was done, of course the accent tiles clashed with the clean, modern décor and had to be replaced with plain stone. The color here and in the front room comes strictly from the abstract art my father selected for the walls.

I am not hesitating, of course. I am centering myself so I can be fully present for my father. I must pay attention to everything—the change from slate to carpet under my stocking feet, the change of temperature against my skin as I pass through sunbeams and shadows. There may be signs in any or all of these, laid down by the house and my mother and all the other lives this place cradles. I do not want to miss them.

I must be ready for whatever is coming.

2.

By the time I reach the study's threshold, Dad is already busy at the minibar, pouring two Scotches, neat. I have never liked Scotch. It tastes like acrid mud. I can't remember if I've ever tried to tell him that.

I take the glass Dad holds out to me.

"So." He sighs. "Did you hear anything from Geraldine? Debbie was beginning to joke about you leaving to check your phone so often." He smiles and raises his glass to me. I take a little sip of my drink in answer. "I said you were waiting to hear from Robbie."

"I'm sorry, Dad." I really am. Dad abhors lies, even little social ones. My forcing him to fib will have soured the entire evening.

"I should have been paying more attention, but I had asked her to call when she got settled...at her motel," I add, but slowly.

"Marie. When are you going to learn we can't rely on Geraldine for anything?"

"Never, I suppose."

I smile sadly. People say you can judge the sincerity of a smile by how it reaches the eyes. But eyes have no expression. They are damp marbles that take in light and block off the skull. Expression is created by the complex interplay of tiny muscles around your eyes. These can be controlled. Any actor knows this.

"So, are you going to tell me why you asked her back?"

Dad's question does not startle me or challenge me. I know we have to talk about Geraldine. Despite everything, she remains family, and it is important I know what he is thinking about her.

"You know why I asked her. Robbie wanted her here for his graduation." I press hard against the rising guilt that comes with bringing my son's name into this.

"And so you decided to give him what he wanted, even though you knew she'd start making trouble the second she got here?"

I don't answer. Instead, I study my father—how his gray hair slants across his forehead, and the way his shadow falls on the carpet.

I am relaxed. We are just talking, the two of us, like we always do. We are so close. He loves me. I know he does. He demonstrates it in a thousand little ways. Some of them can be hard for those who don't really know him to understand. But I do understand. I always have to.

"I was hoping this time...She loves Robbie so much..."

"And just how many more times are you going to let her do this to you, Marie?" He sounds so tired and so disappointed. "I keep trying to warn you, but it's as if you don't even listen."

But I do listen. I hear every single word you say, Dad. I always have.

"You have to be strong, Marie," my father tells me. "I know it's hard, baby girl, but it's the way things are."

Yes. Yes, I know. I close my eyes to try to center myself. But it's too late. It's starting. The room is moving.

Around us, the walls bulge and shift uneasily, like ragged breathing. Like all the living and the dead in this house are breathing together. Rising to the surface. Listening. Watching.

Dad will pretend that nothing is happening. He is much better at this than I am. I have never been able to completely ignore the changes of pressure against my skin and my skull.

"So now, the question is, what are we going to do about the mess with that money?"

Breathe, breathe. Focus. It will be okay.

"You can't be worried that Robbie will say anything in front of people?"

"Oh, no." Dad waves this away. "We've raised him better than that. He won't make a fuss. But Geraldine is another story."

Beside us, the walls split, slowly unzipping themselves. They exhale cold and mildew.

It's Mom.

I know it is. I never see her, but I always know when she's behind me. I can feel her presence drape across my skin. She's heard Geraldine's name. She worries about Geraldine. She never worried about me, or trusted me. I should have tried harder when she was alive.

I set my glass down and clasp my hands. That's appropriate. Outside, the roar of the wind in the trees dies away. Inside, I feel my mother press closer. I can stand it. I will stand it.

"I'll talk with her," I say, and for a bad moment I can't remember whether I'm promising about Geraldine or Mom.

"You're going to have to do more than that, Marie. She can't come to the graduation party. Dozens of our best people will be there. What are you going to do if she makes a scene?"

Who? Which?

"And I don't suppose you thought to ask her what really happened to the money while you were busy handing over the keys to the old house."

My head snaps up.

Dad smiles wearily. "Oh, baby girl," he breathes. "You think you're so good with secrets. Did you really think I never noticed you kept the spare keys when we changed the locks?"

Of course he noticed. He sees too much. He sees what is happening with the walls and the floors. But he keeps it all to himself.

"Geraldine's not actually at a motel, is she?" Dad asks. "She's down at the old house."

This time, he wants an answer. But he won't wait forever. I have to give it to him before…well, before he decides he needs to try another tactic.

I can clench my hands a little. That's appropriate. I can press my ankles together, too. I study the fiber patterns in the carpet. They spell out words, sometimes. All the house's oldest secrets. I can read them sometimes, but I never remember what they say.

Mom is right behind me.

"I'm sorry, Dad. I didn't know. Really. I didn't."

"But you gave her the keys."

"And that was wrong. I know, but she asked for them, and I didn't have the heart to turn her down."

I blink up at him, my eyes are bright with tears. Mom is still now. The whole room is still. Waiting for my father to decide what he believes.

And, it seems, he believes I am incompetent.

"You should have gotten her to stay here, Marie." Dad sighs and swallows the last of his drink. "I don't know how you couldn't figure that out. We have to be able to keep an eye on her while she's home. For her own sake, Marie. If the gossip mill gets going again, it'll chew her up and spit her out."

"I know. And I did try, but she said she wanted to see the house. What could I do? It is her property."

Dad crouches down in front of me. He takes the glass from my hand, and then takes both my wrists. He holds me firmly. Not hard. Not so I will be hurt. Just so I will pay attention to him, and not the room. Not the patterns. Not the cold on my shoulders and the splits in the walls.

"It's *your* property, baby girl." He frowns at my wounded hand. The tape holding down my bandage itches. I hate it. It's ugly. I want to rip it off and miraculously reveal a perfect palm underneath. "You've been taking care of it since your mother died. She's done nothing to earn it."

Which she? I struggle to remember how many conversations we've had about the undeserving "shes"—the ones who didn't earn, didn't pay attention, needed to be taught a lesson.

You have to focus, Marie. He wants to talk about Geraldine. Say something.

But Dad speaks first. "I know it was my fault Geraldine ran away after your mother left us." He releases one of my wrists to cover my bandaged hand instead. His palm is warm and moist. It is costing him to make these admissions. "I couldn't...I couldn't understand how badly she was hurting, too. All I could think was how dare she do that to me, to us, when we all needed to be there for each other...I wanted to kill her, Marie. I really did. And she knew it and she's never forgiven me. I can't blame her for that. Or you, either."

His eyes are hollow as he looks at me, and the rings under them stand out, even though his cheeks are flushed. I try to remain detached. I try to be open to the details of setting and atmosphere. The arrangement of the bottles on the sideboard. The crows cawing in the woods. The tilt of the pillows. They are all full of meaning, but I can't make myself understand them. I can't understand anything.

There's only one thing I can do that will ease my father's mind.

"It was my fault," I tell him. "I wasn't there for Geraldine, or Mom. I was all wrapped up in my own little world and I stopped paying attention to what was happening with my own family."

With that, Dad smiles, sadly, patiently. "Oh, baby girl, you can't blame yourself. There were so many people to take care of," he whispers to our joined hands. "I leaned hard on you after, well, after your mother became so incapacitated. She never recovered from what her sister did, trying to abduct you both. But I needed you, Marie. And it wasn't that I didn't understand what it's like to be saddled with so much responsibility. It was just the same for me after my father died."

The walls shift uneasily, but Mom at least is drifting away. We are not talking about Geraldine anymore. We are talking about him and his life. She's heard it all before.

"My father failed us all, Marie, just like your mother failed you. He left us with nothing. That should have taught me better...but I loved your mother, Marie. I couldn't help myself. Sometimes...I hated myself for how much I loved her. Maybe it was a mistake, not divorcing her. I just...all I wanted was to keep the family together."

And just like that, we are back on familiar ground. He's said this so many times, I have memorized every break and ragged inflection of his voice.

"You did everything you could, Dad. For all of us. Geraldine has always had a cruel streak," I try to bring us back around to a more comfortable direction. "I guess I thought, maybe this time, now that Robbie's leaving, we could try again, but, now I just don't know..."

Dad squeezes my bandaged palm. The scab breaks beneath the loving pressure of my father's hand.

"I was too harsh. I didn't always let you know how much I loved you, how much I've always depended on you."

"But you did, Dad." I give my hand a little shake to assure him. He loosens his fingers so I can draw away, before he realizes I'm bleeding again. "I couldn't have ever asked for a better father." *Smile, Marie. Smile and be brisk.* "I'll go down and talk with Geraldine tomorrow, right after I see Carla about Windward Hill."

"All right." Dad straightens himself up so he's looking down at me. "I guess that will have to do. If you're really too busy to take care of this first thing…"

"Well, you know that anything with Geraldine takes ten times longer than it should. I don't want to delay things for the Dickinsons' house if she decides to be…difficult."

Dad nods in sour agreement, and our eyes meet. He sees right through me, sees how calm I am remaining, how well I can pretend everything is normal.

"All right, Marie. We'll do it your way."

Dad smiles, and I smile. I let him see my relief. Why shouldn't I? It's real. We are back on the right path. The symbols and shadows sink into the carpet. They are no longer needed.

"Do you want another drink, Dad?" I get to my feet, carefully, in case the floor shifts.

"Nah, I think I'll hit the hay." He stretches his shoulders. "Where's Robbie got himself to?"

"He's in Petoskey, playing roadie for his friend's band and staying over for a graduation party. He'll be back Wednesday." *I think. I hope.* "Why don't you head up? I'll clean up here."

"Thank you, Marie." He kisses my forehead. "Goodnight, baby girl."

"Goodnight, Dad."

He leaves me there to pick up the glasses, find the cloth to carefully wipe the damp ring off the table, and take care of all the other small business to restore perfect order.

Because that, after all, is what his baby girl is for.

When we talk about the Household Tales, we eventually have to turn our attention to that other sister—the ugly one, the wicked one, the natural child of that evil stepmother. Whatever her mother says—go out into the cold, commit murder, cut your own foot—that ugly daughter does, no questions asked.

The natural conclusion is she must love and trust her mother.

But there could be something else driving her.

After all, the wicked sister knows she's not pretty, and that people don't like her. She gets to watch that other girl—the pretty one, the good, beloved one—be sent to her death.

How could the other sister keep from wondering if it might be her turn next?

—Out of the Woods: Musings on Fairy Tales in the Real World,
Dr. Geraldine Monroe

GERALDINE, PRESENT DAY
STACEY B'S SANDWICHES AND STUFF

1.

About a quarter mile back into the trees behind our house, there's a gully, a long, V-shaped gouge carved out by years of spring runoff and passing deer from the hills. On its slopes, the maples and oaks are slowly taking over from the pines. One birch waits like a ghost. Sprawling clusters of Boston fern unfurl wherever there's enough sunlight.

I've been avoiding this place. All day yesterday, I kept to the house—unloading the car, fixing up what comforts I can with the stuff I brought along. Compared to some places I've been, it's not too bad. Like the night on the edge of the Gobi when Shin Liu and Daniella and I had to shut ourselves in the car to keep from being smothered by the sandstorm. The old house is positively paradise compared to that. Then there was that night in the truck stop parking lot outside of Pittsburgh, with that skeezy long-haul guy who was not going to take no for an answer. That was really bad. I wonder if his knee ever healed.

But this, this is bad, too. Because down there at the bottom of the gully, that's where they found my mother.

I stare down the slope. It's steep. Almost a cliff. A seasonal stream trickles over the rocks.

They found Mom down there, sprawled on her back in the mud, an aging Snow White, thrown out of her coffin to make room for a better princess.

Overhead, the crows shout at each other.

She's here! She's here! Here! Here! Here!

She is here. I feel her. Her presence coils under the leaves. It snakes up through the soles of my shoes, into my ankles and my shins. It burns through every scar—all that need and greed and hot, bitter resentment. I feel her cold skin under my hands, the slouching weight as I heave her into bed, yet again. The sour, sick smell of her all the mornings when I cleaned her up.

I imagine her staring up at the trees, mouth open. *Hey, somebody get me a drink! Jesus, G, get the lead out. Do you expect me to wait here all day?* Every detail, including the smells of blood and mud and fresh water is a part of me, despite the fact that I never actually saw her dead.

The last time I really saw my mother was in the driveway of the Rose House. She flung her arms out and tipped her white face up to meet the rain while she waited for me to gun the engine and put us both out of our misery.

When Mom was lying on her back at the bottom of this gully, I was in the hospital with tubes in my arm and up my nose. Because despite my very best efforts, I had survived the glass shards and the lake and the hospital room to be released to my father's care.

He brought me straight here.

Shaky as a kitten, I followed him down the hillside, using roots as steps and sapling trunks as handholds. My skin strained against my scabs and stitches. The rain had freshened the stream, and it was running cheerfully down the hillside, adding its chatter to the birdsong and the wind. The deep, cloven impression of a deer track made a little puddle at the edge.

I thought you should see, Dad said. *I thought you would want to know.*

And he proceeded to tell me all about it—how Mom was found, where she was found, what the sheriff and the EMTs and everybody else had to say about it. How quickly they assured him it was an accident. Sheriff Boyd had already told him they'd probably find out she'd been drinking too much, again.

I stood there in the mud, listened to every detail, and waited for my grief to come.

Instead, intense, insane euphoria boiled up from the bottom of my broken heart. With every word he spoke, I wanted to laugh and spin around and fling my arms out.

Look at me! I ran down my drunk of a mother and she stood there in the middle of the goddamned driveway and let me do it! Ding-dong the witch is dead! Whee!

I wanted to ask, *How did she even get here? I killed her up at the Rose House. That's, what? A mile away as the crow flies?*

But all I did was shove my freezing hands into my jeans pockets and look up into my father's eyes.

Oh, Geraldine, he breathed.

With those two words, I understood. He knew what I'd done. But he was never going to tell. So, I couldn't tell, either. He folded his arms around me. He was always physically strong, and he crushed us together. He smelled of fresh air and sweat, and he held me tightly against him until my ribs burned.

I didn't pull away. I can still feel the press of his polo shirt against my cheek as I hugged him back as hard as I could.

I thought he was glad I'd done it. My becoming a murderer was a sacrifice for the good of the family, like he always talked about. I thought it would bind us together. Now, he would finally love me, like he loved Marie.

In that moment, for the first time since I woke up in the hospital, I was glad I hadn't died.

Maybe for the last time, too.

But that was twenty-five years ago. Now, I stand up here on the edge and feel like I should pray, maybe. Apologize. Maybe then I won't have to do the rest of it.

I wonder, weirdly, what Marie is doing now. I wonder if she ever comes back here.

But this is all just delaying the inevitable. I made my choices. There is only one way out for me.

My heart skips a beat, and I lean into my anger. I'm flying. I'm falling. The pain, when it comes, is bright, and I welcome it.

The Household Tales have changed over time, sometimes out of all recognition. Let's take Cinderella as an example.

In the original, when Cinderella's mother dies, she plants a sapling on the grave. Then, when she's told she can't go to the ball, Cinderella runs to that tree and calls, "Shiver and quiver, my little tree, silver and gold throw down over me."

A beautiful dress and shoes drop down from the branches. Cinderella goes to the ball on her own to steal the prince from her stepsisters.

Then comes the self-mutilation, and later, the maiming at the wedding by Cinderella's friends, the birds of the forest.

It's worth noting how many times it turns out that the good sister is not as helpless as she looks.

Or as good.

—*Out of the Woods: Musings on Fairy Tales in the Real World,*
Dr. Geraldine Monroe

GERALDINE, NINE YEARS OLD
HEADED UP THE HILL ABOVE M-131

1.

POSTED:
PRIVATE PROPERTY
NO HUN ING
NO TR SPA IN

The metal sign had been peppered by so much buckshot that the bottom line was pretty much chewed off. Geraldine didn't even slow down. She waded past through the hip-high Queen Anne's lace and blaze-orange Indian paintbrush, dodging the clusters of poison ivy. She had to hurry. There was a storm rolling in. Clouds scudded overhead, propelled by a wind that smelled of lake water. The sky to the west had already turned an ominous charcoal gray.

Marie, though, stopped at the shot-up sign. "You're gonna get in trouble!"

"So will you! You better go home!"

Two whole summers had passed since Mom told Geraldine the story of the Rose House and its bad-princess-turned-wicked-witch. Since then, Aunt Florence had packed Ruby and Walt into the pickup truck and left Uncle Pete behind. They were in Detroit for a while, and then Indianapolis. Then, nowhere.

When Marie found out their aunt and cousins were gone, she'd started crying. But Dad sat her down and told her she didn't need to worry. They weren't losing a family, they were gaining one. Now, they would have whole bunches of Monroes to be friends with.

Geraldine didn't cry; she was too angry. Mom didn't cry, either.

Dad was right about the family anyway. Walt and Ruby were replaced by a fresh flock of cousins, as well as aunts and uncles, some of whom kind of came and went. Every Friday now they had to go to dinner with them all at Grandma Millicent's. Geraldine and Marie had to put on dresses and get their hair braided, which was a pain. Sometimes, Geraldine eyed Mom's big sewing scissors and thought how nobody could braid her hair if it was, like, really short.

"What are you even doing up here?" Marie had finally caught up with her. "There nothing up this way except…"

Geraldine broke into a trot. Black-eyed Susans and meadow grass rasped against her bare legs.

"It's not safe, Geraldine!" Marie clutched at her elbow, but Geraldine shook her off. "You can't go up there!"

But "there" was already in sight. "There" was a wide, low house, so battered by the weather it was almost as gray as the gathering clouds that seemed to crawl out of the hillside. But it crawled blind, because it had no windows, just sheets of plywood covered in graffiti.

Whitestone was full of abandoned houses, but this one was special. It was big and it had been famous once. Everybody told stories about it at sleepovers and Halloween parties. They said it was home for rats and bats and ghosts and bloody killers with hooks for hands.

It had taken Geraldine forever to realize that this haunted ruin must also be the witch's castle Mom told her about.

And if this was the castle, then the witch might still be inside.

"It's condemned," Marie was saying.

"It's ours!"

"What are you *talking* about?"

Geraldine didn't have the breath to explain the whole long idea chain, so she just said, "Mom's sister lives up there."

A flash jerked Geraldine's gaze to the horizon. Clouds sagged low and lumpy over the lake. Lightning flickered down.

One, two, three, four . . .

Every four seconds between lightning and thunder was a mile. Geraldine made it to twelve before the low rumble rolled lazily up the hill.

"We gotta get home." Marie labored through the weeds behind her. "Besides, Mom doesn't have a sister."

"She does. She told us. Don't you remember?"

Marie shook her head, and Geraldine felt her eyes bulge with disbelief.

"How could you forget? You're the one that's so in love with fam-i-ly." She drawled the last word.

The very first dinner with Grandma Millicent and the new family, Marie started kissing up. She trailed around after the new cousins and lost every single cutthroat game of Hearts or Monopoly they played. That should have made them like her better, but never did.

Geraldine hated the way these cousins treated Marie, almost as much as she hated the way Grandma Millicent and the new aunts treated Mom. Almost as much as the way everybody pretended like Aunt Florence and their real cousins were dead. No, it was like they never existed in the first place.

She knew she was supposed to behave, but she just couldn't. Instead, she shouted at them all. She hid from the cousins and wouldn't kiss Grandma.

Not that Mom seemed to mind. She'd just laugh and say, "You tell 'em, G! Let 'em have it." Which should have made Geraldine laugh, too, but somehow it just made her confused, and that made her angrier.

Dad, though, Dad got upset. Afterward, he gave Geraldine talking-tos that lasted for hours. He grounded her for days at a time, so she could only come out of her room to take care of Mom. He threatened to lock her in on Friday nights, unless she started acting like a real part of their family.

Geraldine found herself eyeing that threat like she eyed the scissors and her too-tight braids. Except, some part of her got frightened, too. Dad stopped talking about their cousins and their cousins disappeared. If she was locked up in her room, he might stop talking about her, too, and then she'd be the one who disappeared.

Which was way stupid and she knew it, but the idea wouldn't go away. Not even up here, in broad daylight with Marie bouncing along beside her, looking confused.

They reached the end of the meadow. Somebody'd been up here with a riding mower or something and cut the weeds and wildflowers down almost to the sandy ground.

"Wait. Geraldine," Marie panted as she kicked her way out of the flowers and sweet grass. "Did Mom really say she had a sister?"

"I can't believe you don't remember."

Somebody had built a stairway into the hillside—broad, cracked concrete steps with brick walls and posts on either side. There were dead leaves and moss and bird poop everywhere. Shiny green poison ivy crept over one of the walls.

Geraldine started climbing on the non-poison side. Marie was still following. That was a surprise.

"If Mom's got a sister, why don't we ever see her?"

"Why didn't we ever see Dad's family 'til just now?" shot back Geraldine.

"He said they got mad at him, and they were too proud to ask for help. Like Uncle Pete is." Uncle Pete stopped coming around once Aunt Florence, Walt, and Ruby vanished. He'd started living in the crappy apartment over the garage where he worked.

"But we always knew all about them," Marie reminded her. "Mom never even mentioned a sister."

She was right, in a way. Dad had always talked about his mother and siblings, and so it felt like they had always existed. That was the way it went. When Dad talked, things were real. When he didn't, they weren't.

The wind blew cold against Geraldine's bare arms. She rubbed the goosebumps smooth. The light around them was fading from clear gold to watery gray.

Boy, would Dad be furious if he found out all that stupid stuff with his on-again, off-again family was what gave Geraldine the idea to come out here. If bits of families could be swapped around, why shouldn't she go find Mom's sister? Draw her out of the card deck and add her to the shuffled pile of relatives. Then Mom would have somebody else who could help take care of her.

And maybe Geraldine would, too.

"Geraldine," said Marie in her most serious I'm-the-big-sister-here voice. "You know you can't always believe what Mom says. She makes stuff up."

"Not as much as Dad."

"What are you talking about? Dad hates stories."

Oh, good grief. "Dad hates other people's stories. He's always telling his own, though."

Marie stopped in her tracks. "You're wrong. He never lies!"

"He does and you know it!"

Keep your mouth shut, G. But she couldn't. She couldn't stand the idea that Dad had Marie fooled that badly. It felt like he'd stolen her. Geraldine could stand losing cousins and uncles, and she wished the whole stupid flock of Monroes were at the bottom of Lake Michigan. And sometimes in the depths of her heart, she wished Mom was with them.

But he did *not* get to take Marie.

"Dad lies. All. The. Time."

"Shut up!"

"He lies about me and Mom, and you. About his family, about houses and Uncle Pete and the cousins!"

"You're the liar! The big fat baby liar!"

"I am not! He is! He lies about everything!"

Marie hit her.

Geraldine never even saw it coming. She just staggered against the far wall, and the poison ivy. The leaves smashed against her hands and her bare legs. She jerked away so hard, she teetered on the edge of the stair.

Marie grabbed her and they stood like that, Geraldine open-mouthed and Marie looming over her, breathing so hard, it made her whole body shudder.

"Take it back," Marie demanded. Her face was dead white. "You have to take it back!"

"No!" Geraldine yanked her wrists out of Marie's grip and put both fists up between them. "You want to start something? Come on! You big, fat, dumb scaredy-cat!"

"What in the holy hell are you two doing down there?"

Both sisters jumped, and turned, and somehow crowded close together in the same move.

A woman stood at the top of the stairs. She wore jeans and a plain gray sweatshirt. She had a big, saggy bosom and planted both fists on her round hips.

But it was the hair that was the giveaway. The woman's short hair was a blond so pale it was almost white. And when the wind gusted, it made a crooked halo all around her head.

It was all true. Mom had a sister. This was her. This was the witch.

2.

Marie grabbed Geraldine's hand. "We're really sorry. I was just…she's my sister and I was coming to get her. We didn't mean to trespass."

Geraldine decided now was the time to ignore Marie. "Are you Patricia Burnovich?"

"Who's asking?"

Marie was trying to drag Geraldine backward. "We're leaving. Come on, Geraldine."

"Geraldine?" snapped the witch. "Geraldine Monroe? Don't tell me you two are Stacey's kids?"

"And you're our Aunt Trish." Geraldine twisted her hand, but Marie was not letting go.

The witch trotted down the stairs to stand on the landing just above them. Marie shrank back, but Geraldine stayed where she was. It wasn't easy. Trish Burnovich was a big woman, and when she bent close, she smelled like dirt, sour milk, and mint. Her blue eyes were strangely cloudy, and they flickered restlessly back and forth.

Then, she chuckled, a low, hoarse, bitter sound. "Well, well. Isn't this a terribly interesting development? Did you tell your mom you were coming up here?"

"No." Geraldine finally wrestled her hand out of Marie's death grip. "She doesn't know. Nobody does."

The witch, Aunt Trish, chuckled again and bent even closer. "Now was that smart, Geraldine? Hmm? You've got to be careful. What happens if the two of you just…disappear?"

"We're sorry," repeated Marie. "We're going home. Now!"

"Are you?" The woman sneered. Her teeth were gray and crooked, and for the first time real fear trickled into Geraldine's belly. "Let's see. If she"—she pointed, and Geraldine resisted the urge to duck—"is Geraldine, then you must be Marie."

That was when the first hard raindrop smacked against the top of Geraldine's head. Another splashed on her arm.

All three of them looked up, because that's what you do when the rain starts. Another drop landed on Geraldine's nose.

"Well, now you're going to have to stay. Can't show yourselves to the mighty Martin Monroe looking like a pair of drowned rats. Come on, let's get inside."

"We're not allowed to go into strangers' houses," said Marie, even though she was ducking her head and wrapping her arms around herself.

"But I'm family." The woman touched her nose. That was crooked, too, like Bobby Warshawski's after he broke it. "Think about that for a second."

Trish Burnovich began trudging up the stairs. Geraldine stared at the near panic on Marie's face, but then turned and ran after their newest aunt.

3.

"Why's it called the Rose House?" asked Geraldine. It wasn't like the place had any flowers anywhere, unless you counted the weeds growing between the terrace's stones. It wasn't even pink, and somebody'd bolted a padlock onto the front door.

"Because of the rose windows." Aunt Trish rapped on the plywood sheet as they passed. Geraldine recognized maybe four of the names spray painted across it. "They're by Tiffany. Do you know about Tiffany?"

Probably she didn't mean Tiffany Hausmann in the fifth grade, so Geraldine shook her head.

"Well, maybe I'll show you sometime."

The terrace turned the corner of the house. Marie crowded close to Geraldine, ducking her head as the rain started to come down harder. The grassy space had been turned into a vegetable garden, with tidy rows of bush beans, carrots, beets, and tomatoes and a big sprawl of zucchini vines, their leaves drooping and quivering under the rain.

"No rampion," said Aunt Trish when she saw Geraldine looking.

"What?"

"Never mind. Hang on. I need to put these away."

A rusted wheelbarrow full of rakes and hoes and stuff waited by the terrace wall. Aunt Trish trotted down the side steps to push it all into a brick shed that looked as old and battered as the house.

Marie yanked Geraldine under the eaves. Rain dribbled off the ends of her braids and ran down her neck.

"We are going home. Right now."

"You want to go, go. And quit grabbing me." Geraldine shook herself loose again.

Marie ignored this. "What about Mom?"

That just wasn't fair, and Marie knew it. Geraldine bit her lip.

It'll be okay, she told herself. Mom was asleep on the couch, which was allowed. Geraldine had counted the beer cans and checked the pill bottle and so she knew how much Mom had taken. She wouldn't wake up for hours yet. But just in case, Geraldine had tucked her up under the afghan and put a cup of coffee and a glass of water on the table by her head. There was a wastepaper basket next to her too, in case.

It's fine, she told herself. *She's fine.*

Aunt Trish pulled a ring of keys out of her pocket and unlocked the door to the house. "Come on, if you're coming."

"What's even in there?" Marie asked.

"The kitchen. How else am I going to bake you into meat pies?" Aunt Trish walked through, leaving the door open behind her.

"She's kidding," said Geraldine.

"How do you know?"

Out past the eaves, the rain started falling in a steady sheet now.

Thunder growled and grumbled. Marie shivered, and looked at the sky.

"I'm going home."

Lightning flashed. *One, two, three…*

Thunder.

"Fine. Run away and leave me alone with the cannibal."

Geraldine scooted through the door before she had a chance to think about it again.

4.

It was dim inside, but Aunt Trish didn't turn on the lights. The wind whistled under the eaves, and Marie jumped as she crossed the threshold. Geraldine didn't know whether to shout or just roll her eyes. There was nothing to be scared of. It was just a big, old kitchen. Sure, some of it looked weird. The counters were wood, and there was a monster cast-iron stove like the ones on *Little House on the Prairie* looming over the smaller white one with normal knobs and stuff. The double sink looked deep enough to bathe in, but the fat, rounded fridge was barely taller than Marie. There was plenty of normal stuff, though. Like the Corelleware bowl upside down on the counter, and the coats on the hooks by the door, and the phone on the wall.

The whole place smelled like damp and dirt and…

Gingerbread? Geraldine wrinkled her nose.

Aunt Trish picked up the phone, dialed a number, and waited while it rang, and then waited again. Geraldine heard the beep of an answering machine.

"Mrs. Monroe?" said Aunt Trish. "In case you're wondering, your daughters are waiting out the storm with me." She hung up.

"Hungry?" she asked. Even though neither of them answered, she lifted up the bowl to reveal an unfrosted brown cake. "Get a couple plates, will you?" Aunt Trish picked up a knife and cut a huge wedge.

Marie wasn't moving. Geraldine wasn't sure she could. But the white cabinets had glass doors, so she could see the stacks of gold-rimmed plates. As she reached three down, more details started sinking in. Like how that huge sink was full of dirty dishes, and the wooden counters were heaped with mail and newspapers, and how grease and dried catsup splattered the top layers of letters. A folding cot with an olive-green sleeping bag stood in front of the Little House stove, and a Coleman lantern waited on the floor.

But that wasn't what bothered Geraldine. Something important had just happened. Besides the phone call, and the fact that Aunt Trish had called Mom "Mrs. Monroe." There was something else, but she couldn't put her finger on it.

Aunt Trish finished cutting gingerbread slices and shoved a plate toward each of them.

Geraldine picked her piece up.

"Don't!" Marie smacked her hand. She stared at Aunt Trish, waiting for punishment, or, maybe something worse.

Aunt Trish just rolled her eyes, and took a big bite out of her wedge.

"Okay?" she asked, spewing crumbs. "No poison, no drugs. Flour. Molasses. Eat. Jesus."

The rain rattled the window panes. Geraldine ate. Marie didn't. Geraldine looked at her aunt, and her aunt looked at her. Now, they both rolled their eyes. Geraldine giggled. Marie flushed red.

"Okay, okay, that's enough." Aunt Trish dusted the crumbs off her hands. "So. Tell me. Why'd Stacey send you two up here? It was Stacey, wasn't it?" she added sharply.

"I told you. Nobody sent us," said Geraldine. "We just came. Well, I did. Marie followed me."

Aunt Trish waited for Marie to contradict that. She didn't. "Okay. Why'd you just come?"

"We wanted to…" What? There were so many answers, and not all of them were things Geraldine could say out loud.

"Meet you," said Marie, at the same time Geraldine said, "Find out if you were real."

That made Aunt Trish look away. She licked her lips slowly, catching all the crumbs left around her mouth. "All right. You've met me and I'm real. Now what?"

"I just want to go home," whispered Marie. "Please."

Don't joke. Don't joke, Geraldine thought toward Aunt Trish. *She's really upset and you'll make it worse, and I don't want to have to yell at you.*

But Aunt Trish didn't joke. "Yeah. Okay. And believe it or not, I understand. At least let me loan you a raincoat?" She didn't wait for an answer this time, either. She just headed toward the staircase at the far end of the kitchen.

"Can I come?" asked Geraldine.

"Nobody's stopping you." But Aunt Trish was looking at Marie as she said it. When Marie didn't answer, she muttered something under her breath, and stomped up the grimy white staircase. Overhead, a door creaked open.

"I'm going," Geraldine said. Marie shrugged both shoulders, and Geraldine felt a twinge. She probably shouldn't leave her sister alone when she was so freaked out. But she might never get a chance to see inside this place again. Especially if Dad got home and checked the messages before Mom woke up.

That thought froze Geraldine where she stood. That would be really, really bad. She wouldn't even be allowed to get out of bed for days. Last time, she'd had to pee the sheets because he was watching her and she couldn't climb out the window to go like she usually did when he grounded her. Her whole body flushed with shame just remembering.

"I'll be right back. Swear." Before Marie could say anything, Geraldine ran up the stairs.

Which meant she ran into the dark. The only light was what filtered up from the kitchen and leaked around the shutters. Slowly Geraldine's eyes adjusted and she saw...

The wild woods.

The walls were covered by a painted pine forest complete with meadow flowers, and birds: plovers and hawks and crows and jays and finches. But there was more than that. Little winged girls and boys peered out from the flowers and swung from the tree branches. They even rode tiny ponies between the blades of grass.

Geraldine's jaw dropped. "The fairies." Just like Mom said. "Did you paint these?"

"Nah. It was a guy named Addison Walters. He was a relative, about eighty years ago. Now, he really was crazy."

"A crazy guy did all this?"

"Yeah, well, they kept him shut up in the house, so he had to do something." Aunt Trish turned her head this way and that like she was getting her bearings. "Right." She jerked open a door in the middle of the left-hand wall.

It was a closet, but in the twilight, all Geraldine could see inside was a bunch of blobs. It was hot up here, and it smelled like mildew and dust. Something she couldn't see skittered away.

Geraldine shivered. *Stay put, Marie.*

"I'd give you a ride home, but I think Marie really would pass out." Aunt Trish shoved her arms up to the elbows into the closet's junk and started rummaging around. "Martin's done one hell of a job on her, hasn't he?"

Geraldine's tongue stuck to the roof of her mouth. Nobody talked about Dad like that.

"You...I mean...he..." But she couldn't figure out what she wanted to say.

"I know, Geraldine," said Aunt Trish. "We all know, even if we won't say it out loud."

"Mom calls me just G," she said, although she didn't know why.

"Okay. G. Ah-ha. I knew I still had something. Here." She handed Geraldine a bundle of thin plastic. Geraldine struggled for a moment to untangle it. It wasn't a raincoat, but it was two opaque plastic ponchos. "Don't worry about bringing them back."

"Thanks." Geraldine bundled the ponchos up again and crushed them against her stomach. The mildew smell got stronger.

"Now, you'd better get your sister home before she pees her pants, or tries to call the cops on me for kidnapping."

"Can I come back?"

Aunt Trish looked around into the dark, like she was afraid somebody was waiting there. Geraldine hugged the poncho bundle closer and heard a clock somewhere, ticking.

Aunt Trish leaned forward. Shadows filled the lines and hollows of her face, but her eyes shone like they were lit from inside.

This was her. This was the wicked witch, the ghost, the bloody murderer.

"If you tell Martin Monroe you came up here, I will not only cut your head off and turn you into meat pies, I'll bury your bones under the juniper tree where nobody can find you."

She's just trying to scare me, to see if I'm like Marie after all. "I wouldn't tell him anything, ever."

Aunt Trish nodded, and she pulled up, shrinking back into the shape of a (kinda) normal woman in blue jeans who happened to have Mom's pale hair. "Go get your sister out of here, G."

Geraldine did.

They slipped and splashed all the way down the hill and back into the house. Mom was still asleep. Marie changed clothes; Geraldine erased the message on the answering machine.

When Dad came home, Marie didn't say anything. She just made dinner and pretended like nothing had happened. When Dad asked how they got the poison ivy, she acted all confused.

In fact, Marie acted so well, it was weird. Geraldine decided not to worry about it. Marie was just like that, especially around Dad. And she couldn't exactly blame her sister. Keeping Dad happy made everything else easier.

5.

It was bedtime before Geraldine finally realized what was strange about Aunt Trish's phone call. She didn't look up their number. Not in the phone book, or even off a list like Mom kept taped up next to the phone in the store.

Patricia Burnovich, Aunt Trish, Mom's wicked witch sister who nobody ever, ever talked about, knew their phone number by heart. That must mean she and Mom called each other. A lot.

And Mom never said anything about that, either.

You gotta wonder some days how evil picked 'em. How did these women know? Did they wish too? Were they just bad at it?
                                        —Dr. Geraldine Monroe (margin notes)

MARIE, PRESENT DAY
THE ROSE HOUSE

1.

Windward Hill is a timber A-frame house overlooking the winding "Color Mile" stretch of M-131. It has five acres of hardwoods, manicured lawns, and a drive with gated entry and remote control. It's light and bright and modern and a perfect fit for Mrs. Ashley Dickinson.

I get in first and go into the kitchen. I set my briefcase on the black granite counter and pull out my planner and my phone. I see a text from Carla saying she's running a few minutes late, which gives me time to check if there's anything new from Robbie.

There isn't, not since this morning. Thankfully, my son did text to confirm he was in Petoskey, sleeping on his buddy's couch and planning on being back tomorrow night. So, my little lie to Dad wasn't a lie at all. Of course, the message came through at three in the morning, which means there will have to be a little Mom talk. But only a little one. A young man needs some freedom.

I hear the front door open. A moment later, Carla walks in carrying a cardboard box.

"Good morning! Are those the finials?" I ask.

"They came while I was at the office." She sets the box on the polished counter beside my open planner.

"Thank you." I slit the packing tape with my key and shake the packing list open.

"How's Martin today?"

I pull a tea towel out of the drawer to lay on the counter, as much to protect the granite as to cover my surprise at the question. Carla is not usually concerned in my father's feelings, or his health. Not even casually.

"Dad's fine," I tell her. "Busy. Apparently Jamie Kellerman's got some new friends coming up for him to meet."

Dad had told me this when we shared our coffee this morning. I suspected he was being a little frugal with his facts. Probably he was also going to talk with Grandma Millicent, and probably about money. I'd happened to see her number flash on his phone. Which was fortunate. Forewarned is forearmed, after all, and I was able to spend last night reviewing records, accounts, and emails to make sure everything really is as it needs to be. And the truth was, I was glad to do it. It gave me something to focus on while I was waiting to hear from Robbie.

"Is something wrong?" I ask her.

Carla shrugs with one shoulder, but she is also suddenly very interested in her own hands as she sets her briefcase on the other end of the counter and tucks her sunglasses into the side pocket.

"So. Staffing," she says. "Are we going to need to find a personal chef?"

"Yes. Mrs. Dickinson wants the whole package."

Actually, she wanted Dad to know how much she relies on him, so she made a great show of letting him talk her into it. But this is a purely academic distinction.

"Okay, I'll get a call in to Parris Catering." Carla brings out her phone and stylus. "Marie?"

"Mmm-hmm?" I lay out all six wrought-iron finials in a neat line on the tea towel. I have to be sure there're no flaws or scratches.

Carla sighs and sets down her phone. She is clearly trying to come to a decision. Cold sweeps through me, but I rise above it. Carla is, after all my friend, as well as my cousin, and Geraldine's.

"Marie. We need to talk."

No. We do not. We need to finish here so I can go see Geraldine and make sure she's all right. I need to take care of my own business and all its details.

Stop it, Marie. That doesn't matter. Carla has something important to say and you must hear her.

"About what?" This is bad. I sound too testy. I need to calm down, to be open and present. But between the last night's conversation with my father and the fact that he wasn't entirely forthcoming about where he'd be today, I cannot entirely dismiss my own concerns.

"What's the matter?"

"I had a fight with Walt this morning."

"Oh, Carla, I'm sorry." I am not relieved. Of course not.

Carla shakes her head, brushing this away. "He's been staying out late, and last night he didn't come home at all. I...God, this sounds so *Real Housewives*...I thought he might be cheating on me."

Relief beckons. That's why she was watching him at the party, just in case she caught him flirting with someone. I remember Dad and Walt together at barbecue night, and how Carla twisted her necklace so nervously when she saw them together. This is what was behind that. It makes perfect sense.

But then where is this cold on the back of my neck coming from?

"It turns out I was wrong," she says.

"Well, of course!" I say. "Walt loves you!"

She ignores this and plunges straight ahead. "It turns out all those nights when I thought he was seeing another woman, he was staying late at the office, going over the books."

Oh my lord. I have literally gone weak in the knees. It's happened. It *worked*.

This is so much sooner than I expected. I thought I would have to drop more hints, and more breadcrumbs in the accounts. Walt is so very loyal to my father, and so very weak. His own father—poor, lost Uncle Pete—was such a disappointment. I didn't think Walt would have the vision to see what was happening until there was no possible choice.

Clearly, I've underestimated him.

Carla mistakes the reason for my hesitation. "Marie? Walt says Geraldine threatened your dad with some kind of audit. Did you know about this?"

There's no satisfaction in deceiving Carla, but this once it's necessary. "Oh, you know Geraldine. She'll say anything to provoke a reaction, especially from Dad. And the situation with the house is so complicated..."

"Marie, cut it out, okay? We're friends, and I'm trying...I'm trying to warn you. Walt says there's something wrong with the accounts. He's been going through the receipts. He said the charges for services weren't matching up. At first he thought...well, never mind."

"No, tell me." I need to know how far he's gotten. I have to know how much more I need to do.

"You know, when the AbsuHomes deal fell through, and money got tight and Martin came back with that private loan..."

"Which Walt never liked." I sat with Walt for over an hour that day, doing my best to reassure him that everything would turn out fine. But the whole time, I had to gloss over just how little I knew, or wanted to know, about where that money Dad insisted was "just to tide us over" came from.

It was in that moment, listening to all Walt's fears, that the future opened up. I remember going breathless with wonder, because finally I knew what I could really do, for my father and my family.

I knew how to bring Geraldine back to us.

"Walt's always thought that 'loan'"—Carla pauses to make the air quotes—"might have been sneaked out of the family trust. Now he thinks Martin is having trouble getting the money back."

Yes.

"He says that the charges to clients for services are higher than they should be. The invoices don't match up."

Yes.

I make myself stare at the finial I'm holding in both hands. I have to take my time. What I say next has to be absolutely right.

"So, Walt thinks, what? That Dad's been padding the accounts to try to get the money to pay back...whoever that loan came from?"

Carla hesitates. She's trying to see inside me, but thanks to all Dad's training, there's nothing there for her.

"Yes," she says and her eyes glitter. "Walt thinks Martin has been cheating the clients, probably for tens of thousands of dollars, maybe hundreds."

I'm sorry this hurts you, Carla. I'll find a way to make it up to you. I would not be doing it if wasn't important. I need Walt to tell the story. It can't just be my word.

"But it's you, isn't it, Marie?"

2.

"Wh-what?" The world spins and the finial squirms abruptly in my fingers.

Carla does not apologize or clarify. She just looks at me, and I can tell she feels the cold rising around us. She sees the finial coiling, ready to strike. I set it down and rest both hands on the counter instead.

"You do all the billing, Marie. Martin barely looks at the accounts. He just hands it over to Walt. If something's being snuck through, you're the one doing it."

The cold fills my mouth. If I try to speak now, I will choke on it. I swallow, and I swallow again, but I cannot clear my throat.

"Marie...we trust each other, don't we? You know I see how much Martin puts you through. I want to help. I do. That's why I'm telling you this. So you can stop before things get any worse."

I cannot believe this. I was certain I could count on Carla to see things correctly. Carla and Walt have always known Dad is the one who makes all the decisions. I am the good girl. I just carry them out.

"Walt says he's going to have to tell Martin."

Oh. No.

But of course that's what Walt will do. Walt is good and honest, and so very weak. Walt is the only one of Pete's children to ever come back. His mother and sister won't even talk to him anymore, so we— so Dad—is all he has left. Dad decided to give him a welcome and a job and a real place when even Grandma Millicent was uncertain how to greet his return. This has meant that Walt's loyalty is not to the Monroes as a whole, but just to Dad.

And Carla, of course.

"You told him he couldn't do it," I say. "You told him he made a mistake."

"No, Marie, I didn't."

The counter bunches abruptly under my palms. I am going to tear the polished surface in two.

Carla leans across and grips my hand. Does she see? Is she trying to get my attention or trying to stop me from ruining the beautiful, restless countertop with a careless gesture? I can't tell. Clearly, Carla is better at pretending than I realized.

"I know what a bastard Martin is. If you want to get out, I'll help, I swear it. But you've got to trust me, Marie."

I did! I trusted you to see what Dad is doing! Not me. Never me! I just do what I'm told!

And I know what I need to do now.

"Carla. Walt needs to let this go." I cover her hand with mine. I wince, just a little as I wrap my fingers around hers.

"Marie, listen. We do all kinds of things when we're desperate. But if you need money, I'll loan you..."

"What I need, Carla, is for you to listen very carefully to what I am saying. Walt does not want to go any further with this."

There is no way to count or track the calculations going on inside Carla. I let her go and rescue my planner before it can be shrugged off onto the floor.

"It's not forever," I say as I return the planner into my briefcase. I do not want its words spilling out. I do not have time to pick them all back up. "Just for another week or so, while I take care of a few last things."

"Marie, what are you doing?"

"Carla, I asked you to please *listen*. The audit Geraldine wants to start? As things stand, it's not going to turn up anything about Dad, or about me. But it will turn up a great deal about Walt."

Carla's mouth shapes a few words. I decide not to hear.

"You're right, I do the billing. I know exactly what is in the books and how it all got there." I take a moment, adjust my expression and for once, I let her see how difficult that is to do. "I'm going to see Geraldine just as soon as we're done here. I'm going to try to convince her that she can't just go charging into a situation she doesn't fully understand."

Carla stares at me, comprehension and horror dawning together.

"No one is going to get the idea that Walt did anything wrong, not if I can help it. You have to trust that I am working to make sure every loose end is cleared up, so there are no misunderstandings if Geraldine does decide to be…difficult." I let her see how very sorry I am to have to say these things. That much is easy. Perhaps later I will be able to explain. Or perhaps I will let her stew, until she can feel something of what her jumping to conclusions has almost cost.

No. I will not be that petty. Just as soon as things with Dad are finished and Geraldine has decided to stay, Carla and Walt will be as free as the rest of us. Then, I'll be able to begin making up for all our bad decisions and these hard choices.

But right now I have to get to Geraldine.

Fathers in the Household Tales routinely make questionable parenting decisions, but the one in "The Armless Maiden" really stands out.

In this story, the father meets the devil and volunteers to exchange "what's standing in the yard" for endless wealth. When he finds out he bartered away his daughter, the father tells her she has to get ready to go to hell, or the devil will take him, and his new wealth, instead.

The daughter agrees to do what she's told. That's the surprising part. Or is it? After all, what choice does she really have?

—*Out of the Woods: Musings on Fairy Tales in the Real World,*
Dr. Geraldine Monroe

GERALDINE, PRESENT DAY
STACEY B'S SANDWICHES AND STUFF

1.

I've just made it back to the old house and closed the door behind me when I hear the tires on the old gravel. Overhead, the crows scream.

I put my hand up to my face. I thought I'd have time to clean up a little. The pain has faded to a persistent throb, but the blood drying on my cheek and chin has started to itch like a son of a gun. I stumble into the room that used to be Dad's study and peer out from behind the blinds. An enormous black Escalade pulls up into the remains of our parking lot. Fear squeezes my lungs.

But the door opens and my sister climbs down from the driver's side. I let out a long breath and head to the front room.

I've rehearsed the story I have to tell.

My sister stands stunned on the disintegrating welcome mat when I open the door. I'm braced for her shock, but not for the way she goes dead white. And definitely not for her scream.

"Oh my God, Geraldine! Your face! Your face!"

Oh my God, Marie! Are you scared of a little blood? Is that what this is?

But I don't say it, because Marie's shaking, and her color fades from white to gray.

"Jesus." I wrap an arm around her shoulders, half-frightened, half-annoyed. She was always supposed to play her part as the concerned sister here, but this is something more that her usual expert playacting. She's really about to fall apart. "Come on, Marie, you need to sit down."

I push her into a sitting position on the living room floor and kneel next to her. She mouths a few soundless words, and stops. And starts again.

"What happened, Geraldine? How…who…Geraldine?"

"I don't know who it was."

"You have to tell me!" She shouts and grabs me by the wrists, yanking hard. Her thick bandage presses against my skin. "Who was it? I have to hear it. Who…!"

"I don't know! Marie!" I swat her hands away. "Marie! I don't know!"

My shout finally gets through. Marie gasps and slaps both hands—the good one and the bandaged one—over her face.

"Oh, God. Oh, Geraldine, I'm so sorry. I don't…I didn't…"

"It's all right. And I'm okay. Really."

But if she even hears me, she doesn't listen. "I can't do this. I know what we said. I know…I thought I could. I thought as soon as I saw you, as soon as I knew you were home, I could do anything, but I can't, I can't…"

Exasperation bites down anyway. *You've got no business falling apart when I only waded into this because you asked! I was happy before you started calling! For once in my goddamn life I was happy!*

But I remember the two notes I found. I press my fingers hard against my bruised cheek. Pain shoots through flesh and bone, and snaps me back into focus.

"You don't have to do anything, Marie. Just sit here. I'll go get cleaned up."

I had enough time before she got here to pull my first-aid kit out of my backpack, so I've got antiseptic and bandages ready in the bathroom. I lean in close to the mirror.

I might owe Marie an apology. I look way worse than I thought. I knew my right eye was pretty much swollen shut, but not that bruises around it were already starting to turn blue. By tomorrow they'll be black. And I didn't realize my old scar had opened up quite that much, or that there was a new messy split up by my hairline.

Yuck. I did know it was bad. How could I not? I must have spent twenty minutes just sitting on the gravel out front, trying to find the strength to make it the last ten feet into the house.

The pipes gurgle and splutter. The water's cold. I've got no towels, so I do the best I can with my hands. I swallow a couple of Tylenol, too, and wash them down with water from my cupped palm.

Back in the living room, Marie is still sitting against the wall.

"Hey, look at us." I gesture at my padded head and her wrapped hand. "Bandage twins."

"I…" Marie clears her throat, but doesn't get any further.

Come on, Marie, stay with me. I sit down cross-legged next to her. *Yeah, okay, we're both hurt, but we've got to deal with it. This is only the beginning.*

"You have to tell me what happened, Geraldine," she says finally. "You can't expect me to believe this was some kind of accident."

There we are. That's the Marie I know.

"It wasn't." I take a deep breath. "I was unloading my car, and this pickup pulled in. These two guys say they're looking for Plover Beach." *Come on, sell it, Geraldine. Make it real.* "I go to show them on the map and one of them grabs my arms, and the other…" I gesture at my face. "I got one good kick to the nuts in, though."

"Did you call the police?"

"No."

"What? We have to…" She reaches for her purse.

"You do, and I'll tell them I tripped and fell down Mom's gully and hit my face on a rock."

"They won't believe you," she says.

"And there's jack shit they can do if I won't swear out a complaint."

"Why are you doing this, Geraldine?"

I look her right in the eye. At least, I think I do. My vision's pretty blurry. "Because it's my choice, and there's jack shit anybody can do about that, either."

Silence falls, and I feel the old telepathy surge between us. We are telling each other that the forms are completed and the boxes checked. I have said what I had to, and so has she. We can move on.

I settle back against the wall and dangle my hands over my knees.

"That is some car you've got."

She blinks, and frowns at me. "It was my birthday present from Dad when I turned forty. He wanted me to be safe."

"So he bought you a tank."

"You know he has his own way of showing he cares."

"That's for sure."

Her fingers tap at the edges of her own bandage. She hates that thing, too, and wants to rip it off. Her wound was accidental, a sign that she's not entirely in control. That kind of thing gnaws at her.

"Where are you...Geraldine, you're not sleeping in your car again, are you?"

"With a perfectly good house here for me?" I answer back, because whole truths are not what the situation calls for. "I'm not that crazy. Come on and see base camp."

I climb to my feet and hold out my hand. Marie stares at it for a minute. Then, she lays her palm against mine so I can help pull her up, like I used to when we were girls climbing trees.

Let's not do this, Marie, I think before I can stop myself. *Let's just get out of here. We'll load all the gear into your car. We'll take the money. We'll take everything and we'll run. I know how to now. I'll get us some fake IDs. We can leave the country if that's what you want. I've been around the world. I know how to live through a night in a Walmart parking lot or a sandstorm in rural China. I can get along in four languages. We can do it this time. It won't be like before.*

I wish I could say all that, and more. I wish I could make her believe it. But when has that ever worked? So, instead I lead her into our old bedroom so she can see what else I've been doing with my morning.

I lined the file boxes up under the window. I turned over a couple of milk crates to make a platform for my desktop computer, and a third to use as a table for the gooseneck lamp. My backpack leans next to the closet, and my few changes of clothes and my spike heel boots are arranged on the shelves. I stretched my pad and sleeping bag out where our bunk beds used to be. Right beside our hiding place of a vent.

But Marie's not really seeing any of this. Her attention is captured by the photographs I taped to the wall.

They're all snapshots of me and Marie. We're little girls throwing autumn leaves at each other. We're young women at a birthday party for mutual friends. There, Marie is all dolled up in pink with her hair blown out Farrah Fawcett style, ready for the prom. There, I'm in full goth mode for Halloween.

She doesn't look at the vent. Not once.

I found the note, Marie.

There, we are holding hands over each other's heads in a triumph that was so long ago and so fleeting I don't even remember it.

I found your note. You found mine. Marie. Marie... what did you do?

Marie's eyes slip from one moment to the other in this crooked display of our messy, ordinary lives. I see the doubt in her. Was this really me? Did any of it really happen?

Yes, Marie. This was all real, too. Including your wedding day.

Because Marie's wedding is here, too. There's the whole lineup of us girls. I was maid of honor in a Laura Ashley dress. Up until now, it was my longest return performance in Whitestone. I'm practically skeletal and I look like hell in all that pink and green, but I'm smiling for the camera and my sister. There's no photo of me trying to convince her to leave her fiancé at the altar.

I'm going to say it. I am. I am going to break the silence.

Here are David and Marie together, holding each other's hands. We spent that entire week maneuvering around each other to try to avoid being alone together in the same room.

In the photo, Marie smiles at him with that look I know so well— the deep, desperate hope that she will be allowed to keep just this one thing.

I'm going to do it now. It's just five words, after all. Five. Marie, what did you do?

"I'm glad you kept these," Marie says. "I wasn't sure you would. Dad didn't like having them around, especially after the divorce. They didn't..."

That's as far as she gets. It's okay. I know what she means. These photos didn't fit in the home Dad crafted, so Marie had sent them to me.

Because there's shots of Mom, too. Here, she's holding our hands with our toddler selves. There, we're all in the lake, splashing each other. And there, Marie and I are out front of the store with the banner we painted declaring HAPPY SEVENTH ANNIVERSARY STACEY B's! Aunt Florence, Walt's mom, shades her eyes with her hand and waves. Mom wears red oven mitts and hoists a pie over her head.

Here, she's hoisting a beer to the camera.

There, it's a glass of vodka and a cigarette.

In the present, Marie is whispering, almost like she's trying to explain things to this cluster of long-gone moments. Then, she spots the lone black-and-white photo. I salvaged this all on my own, and when I ran away, I took it with me.

It shows two girls in peg pants and tight sweaters with their arms around each other. They both have the same pale hair and they stand on the terrace in front of the stained-glass forest, framed by the roses. The shorter girl leans her head on her sister's shoulder.

It's Mom and Aunt Trish. It's the only evidence we have that, once upon a time, they really were sisters. And in a kingdom far, far away, those two princesses really did live in a castle on a hill.

Until the king and queen died.

Until the prince came and charmed the younger sister.

Marie touches that old picture gently. The pressure of unspoken words squeezes my eardrums and my bruises. We are both wondering the same thing: Is she going to say *it* out loud? Will she risk it? Will I?

But then the pressure bursts and Marie turns her back on the photos and their faded memories.

"Geraldine, you can't stay here. Not after this." She gestures toward my damaged face and just like that we are back on script.

"I'll lock the doors," I promise.

"At least let me call David. He's working for the security company we use."

I suck in a deep breath. I keep my voice steady as I answer, but it's hard, especially with the long-past image of David in that ridiculous tux staring up at me from the wedding photo.

Especially when I'm remembering that other night. The one where I sat on the hood of my car with my knees pulled up to my chest and stared out at the lake, drinking David's beer and feeling the reality of what I'd done settle in. I tried to send David away from my—our—disaster then. But leaving was never David's way. Every single other ex–Monroe spouse has, by pure coincidence I'm sure, decided to leave Whitestone Harbor. Most have left Michigan altogether. But not David. Never David.

Treacherous memory flits from David to Tyler. I hang my head, because suddenly my assorted aches are clamping down hard, despite the Tylenol. Old, sick cravings stir in the pit of my brain.

I press my bruise again.

"Okay, Marie. If you insist, I'll talk with David."

"I insist. I…there's something else you need to know."

"Why doesn't that surprise me?"

"It's Carla."

"*Carla?* Jesus! I thought…" I stop myself just in time. "What's happened with Carla?"

Marie takes a deep breath and chooses her words with exquisite care.

"Today she told me that Walt thinks he might have found some discrepancies in the billing around the summer houses."

Might have. Walt thinks. She told me. There are all kinds of demurrals and ways to backtrack in that sentence. Good job, Marie.

"She said she thinks I'm responsible for them."

The words drop between us, sinking fast into cold silence. But she's not done.

"Walt knows you've threatened Dad with some kind of audit."

Keep it together, Geraldine. I press my bruise. Pain clears the shock. I suck air. "Yeah, well, I figured Dad would tell him right away. I mean, Walt's handled the books for how long now?"

Marie refuses to be distracted. "He told Carla because he was worried about…things…he's found. I told her I'd talk to you. That I would get you to back off for a week or so, so I could get things cleaned up." She pauses for a very long time. "I said that I needed time to make sure no one would blame Walt for…whatever comes to light."

Oh, good job, Marie. Really. Because if there's anybody I give a shit about besides you, it's Carla. And poor, stupid, goddamned cousin Walt.

But before I can work out how to answer, the sound of tires on gravel rattles through the room. Marie's head jerks around.

"Who's that?" Marie is shaking again. Jesus. I'm the ex-junkie, ex-cutter, ex–suicide attempter, but she's the one who looks like she's going cold turkey.

"Who do you think?" But even as I say it, fear lances up the familiar straight line from my ankles to my scarred mouth.

"I'm sorry, Geraldine," Marie whispers. "I'm sorry. I thought I'd be all right. I thought I could do this, but I'm not. I can't."

I want to slap her. I want to scream. I want to throw everything into the car and drive away. Change my name. Forget her, forget myself. Swim away into the dark and this time never to come back.

Instead, I face my sister, who is standing in front of the fading evidence of our other lives, and I make myself speak with absolute calm.

"You'll be fine, Marie. Just as soon as I open the door, you'll know exactly what you have to do."

I walk across the threshold and down the hall. I do not look back. Marie has to decide for herself whether she's going through with this.

Lights. I cross the empty living room to stand at the front door.

Camera. I pull back the door.

Action.

"Hi, Dad. What brings you out this way?"

2.

"I wanted to make sure you were all right," my father breathes.

I try not to notice how much he looks like Marie right now, down to the way the color drains out of his healthy, tanned cheeks.

"I'm fine. What's this? Groceries? Aw. You shouldn't have." I lift the paper bags out of his arms. I can see a couple of little supermarket deli trays of cheese and sausages, another of cut vegetables. Some boxes of crackers. And a big bottle of rum, and another of Diet Coke.

"Gee. Thanks, Dad."

I carry both bags into the kitchen to set on the one section of counter that is the only thing still standing. The appliances have all been ripped out, and I do mean all. There's a hole where the stove used to be, and the cheap green linoleum curls around it.

Another man, seeing his daughter hurt, would insist on taking her to the doctor. He would at least come touch her, make her sit down, try to get the full story. Not my father. He stays right where he is, drinking in every last raggedly little detail of me and my injuries.

Despite all my plans and resolve and bravado, I finding that hard, distant gaze surprisingly hard to take. "Can I get you a…Oh, no, I guess not." I pull out the two-liter bottle of pop and the massive bottle of white rum. "Wait. I've got some glasses in the boxes. Just give me a sec…"

"What are you doing, Geraldine?" snaps Dad. Oh, I've managed to rattle him good.

"Just trying to remember my manners." My palms are sweating. Jesus. I wipe my hands on my jeans. "You're my guest."

"Dad?" Marie's voice startles me. I didn't hear her come out of the bedroom. "I didn't expect you to be here."

Marie ghosts past me to our father's side, close enough that I feel the brush of her warmth against my hand. As a piece of choreography, it's exactly what the moment calls for. Also, it puts her just out of Dad's line of sight. This is no accident.

"What happened here?" Dad asks her.

"It's nothing, Dad," she answers, too quickly. "An accident."

"She told you that?"

"Leave Marie alone," I snap. "If you've got questions, ask me."

"I've tried that. It never goes very well, does it?" Oh, all that sick, sad, eternal patience in his eyes. People call them bottomless. That's just another word for empty.

Empty, and yet his gaze still penetrates all the way to the bone.

Over my dad's shoulder, Marie's mouth moves. She shapes one word. I see it, her, from the very corner of my vision.

Now, says my sister. *Now.*

Action.

"Not that you should have a whole lot of real questions anyway. You already know how this happened." I tap my bruised temple.

Anger burns deep behind my father's smug, perfect eyes, and I enjoy it. Oh, this is bad. I cannot let emotion wash me away. Not now. But I've been waiting so long to break open this man's armor of money, pride, and family. I want to pry him out and leave him naked on the ground in the cold, in the snow, in the dark.

I smell tobacco. I smell beer. The reek of memory and home and the mother I could not save. I smile and it hurts.

"Was there something you wanted, Dad?" I ask. "Because I was planning on heading out for the graveyard. I want to take Aunt Trish some flowers. Maybe toss a few over the cliff for Uncle Pete on the way."

"Geraldine," Marie prompts. It sounds like a warning. But she already gave me the go-ahead, and I am going to follow through.

Now.

"So that's what this is about." Our father gathers himself fully back into his Martin Monroe armor. "You came back to accuse me of murder. Again."

3.

Murder. Again.

The words ring through the room, bringing the past down over me like a bell jar, sealing me off from sense and reason.

I am thirteen, with clenched fists and obscenity dripping from my angry tongue. Mom is huddled on the sofa, her head in both hands, sobbing. It's the first time I've seen her cry for nothing but sheer sorrow. I'm responsible for her. I have to make sure she doesn't get hurt or go off drinking again. And there's Dad, making everything worse, telling her everything she's done wrong, every way she's screwed up and disappointed everybody. But this time it's different. This is the time I realize that he's doing it on purpose. That it is always on purpose.

In the present, he says, "You know how Pete died, Geraldine. And so did your aunt, and so did your mother."

"Oh, yes," I tell him. "They knew. Isn't it funny how I'm the only one who left town and the only one who survived?"

"Pete came to me for money to leave town," says Dad calmly. "I gave it to him, but in the end, he couldn't stand the shame."

"Yes. I remember what you told us." I make sure he's looking me full in my wounded face as I speak. I want to make sure he picks up on all the little nuances here. "I also remember you had your hands bandaged pretty good for a week there, afterward. Like you'd cut up your knuckles."

I am fifteen, spitting blood and swinging out so he cannot grab me and take me away with him. It doesn't matter how hard I snarl, or bite, or claw. I can't get away. He ignores my blood and my screams and bears me down to the icy bricks.

Why? I scream. *What do you even care? You don't want me! You never wanted me!*

Because you're mine, Geraldine, and you always will be, he whispers in my ear. *I do not give up on what is mine.*

"I know why you did it, too."

Marie doesn't move. Marie doesn't matter. This is between me and him. Dad steps forward until his shadow slides across me. He's still a tall man. Still a powerful man. I'm already shrunken and hurting.

"You thought Mom was having an affair with Uncle Pete. You were sure she betrayed you by screwing your loser of a brother. But that wasn't what they were doing," I go on, forcing my voice to carry beyond the depths of memory. "At least not by then. You got it wrong, Dad."

I am seventeen. My stitched and stapled ankles throb beneath their bandages. I'm staring, stupefied while my father describes in loving detail how my mother's body was found. How she was bruised and broken, and dead. I'm euphoric because I'm free of her. I'm horrified, because of what I've done. I'm lost, and this time I know I'm never going to be found. Because with every glance, and every sad word, my father is telling me he knows what I did, and that he is going to forgive me. And I want him to. I want it so bad I can taste it.

She's your responsibility now.

There, at the bottom of the gully, I feel my father's understanding wrap around me like his arms do. He wanted me to kill her, to free her, and the rest of us, from her suffering and addiction. I pull back from our embrace, so I can look into those eyes that have no limit. I want to see love in them. After everything that he has done and I have done. With the ghost of my mother already dissolving into the earth, I still want him to love me.

This is the thing I can never explain, not even to myself. This is why I couldn't trust myself with Tyler. Because what kind of sick fuck could stand in such a place and need the love of such a man?

That's not even the worst part. The worst part is knowing that if he'd given me even a hint of affection just then, I would have stayed. I would have become like Marie. And for exactly the same reason.

In the present, in the old house, I am saying, "You got everything *wrong*, Dad. And you didn't even know it."

"Geraldine." Marie's voice is light as silk. "You need to stop this."

Dad and I both turn. My sister has drawn herself up and holds her purse neatly in front of her. Her expression is perfectly composed, patient, and just a little sad.

This is the Marie our father crafted. The one who will quietly bundle her whole life into a box and send it away because it does not suit his purposes. The one who could stand on the steps in the dark and lie about the woman who saved her life.

The sight of her hurts worse than any bruise.

"Geraldine, I came down here to ask you to see reason and come back to the Rose House," Marie tells me. "I was going to tell you how worried Dad and Robbie are. I thought that if you didn't care about my feelings, you might just care about theirs."

I try to let this slide off me. She has to do this. It's what the script calls for.

Now. It's my turn.

"You always were on his side," I sneer, and wipe my palms on my jeans again. "But let's talk about the elephant in the room, shall we? Neither one of you has any idea how much Mom told me before she died, or how much I'm going to be able to prove. That's why you really came down here, isn't it, Marie? To try to keep crazy, junkie loser Geraldine from derailing the Monroe family gravy train."

Our eyes lock. The silent waves of understanding surge between us—sister to sister, heart to heart, fear to fear.

"You're scared that I've found out just how long Dad's been playing with other people's money. Starting with how he got that first mortgage on this place when his name wasn't even on the title."

Dad decides this has gone on long enough. "Your sister does not deserve this treatment, Geraldine."

"No," I admit. "But you do."

Two white spots appear on his taut, tanned cheeks.

"You made me responsible for Mom," I remind him, sliding the knife in as easy and slick as I can. "I was seven years old. *Seven.* And when she drank, when she passed out, I either got her hidden away or I got punished. I missed school. I *ran* that goddamned store so we could have enough to live on while you were busy swindling the entire fucking town." I lean in. My father doesn't move. He's as still as a statue of himself, except for those eyes. Those eyes gleam and flicker back and forth, but they do not blink. Not once.

"You wanted to make me hate her." My voice rasps against my throat. "Well, it worked. Congratulations. I'm one big ball of hate. But that doesn't mean me and Mom didn't talk. Maybe she even told me something the night she died. We were alone together for hours that day. Maybe that's why I'm back. Maybe I can finally prove what you've done."

"That's it, Geraldine." Marie's words slice cleanly through the pause I've left. "I am not going to listen to this. The only reason you came home was to stir up trouble. You can…" She swallows. "You can just go right back to your college and leave us alone."

She has to say this. She has to make sure Dad believes she's on his side. But her words still press hard against me and the bones of my cruelty crumble.

I am thirteen and there is nothing inside me but a child's burning hatred.

I am fifteen. I am blundering through the snow, dragging my sister with me, praying I am strong enough to get us to shelter, even if shelter is the witch's house.

I am seventeen. I am at the family gravesites, in the lake, in the freshly abandoned house, leaving my confession behind. I finally know all that I am, and all I am not.

I am forty-two. I am here, now, in my empty home. I lift my gaze to my father, to show him a glimpse of the labyrinth he has helped to build inside his daughter's soul.

But Dad doesn't feel the need to look at me anymore. He walks to Marie and laces his fingers through hers.

"We should go, Marie."

She presses the side of her free hand under her nose so she won't sniffle. Oh, wicked Geraldine. You're making your good sister cry.

"I'm sorry," I say. "Really, Marie. I am."

Marie shifts her feet, just a little, like she's going to step toward me, but, of course, Dad doesn't let her go.

"Robbie's graduation is Sunday," she reminds me.

"Do you want me to stay away?"

She is careful to glance at Dad before she speaks. "I want...I'm sorry, Geraldine. I...Robbie is looking forward to you being there, but you can't keep acting like this."

"I'm sorry," I say again.

"I wish I could believe that."

Dad puts his arm around Marie's shoulders and steers her toward the door. How disappointing this is for him. He hates to have to choose between his daughters, but I've forced this on us all.

The screenless door slams behind them. As soon as it does, I move. Ludicrously afraid of being heard, I run on my tiptoes into the room that used to be Dad's office. The window is open in here, just a little, not enough so anyone would notice.

I press my ear to the frame, hold my breath and listen to the voices drift in from the old parking lot.

"Marie, what just happened in there?"

"Nothing, Dad, really. It was just Geraldine..."

"Don't tell me that was just Geraldine being Geraldine. She's been talking to you, hasn't she? You've been listening to her lies."

"I'm just trying to do what you asked, Dad. I came down to talk to her. To tell her she can't make trouble at Robbie's party."

"But you never got around to disinviting her until I was there to see you do it."

"Dad, we all love Geraldine despite everything. You didn't have to come down, but you did. And you brought groceries."

My sister is trying some gentle teasing, to remind Dad that we are all family. Of course he cares about me, and so does she. Blood's thicker, isn't it? Even when it's spilled on the stairs and on the snow.

"Marie, what did Geraldine really say to you?"

"About what?"

"Those accusations of hers. Did she tell you anything? Did she try to convince you...? Oh, my poor baby girl. She did, didn't she? What did she say?"

"Nothing, Dad. Really. We barely had time to exchange two words before you got there."

"Marie, don't you trust me? Please. You can't tell me Geraldine's finally going to get between us."

Marie doesn't answer him. Marie doesn't answer for a long time.

Dad says something I can't hear. So does Marie.

It'll be all right, I tell myself. *Marie's got it handled. I mean, she told me to go ahead.*

In my mind's eye, I see her mouth moving again, shaping that one word. Fear stops my heart cold.

Now I can hear him. I can hear the shock, and the horror.

"You believe all this crap Geraldine has been spilling," Dad says. "You believe I actually had my own daughter beaten up, that I killed... that I *killed*..."

Your brother. Your wife. Her sister.

But he's not angry. Oh, no. He's disappointed, and that's so much worse.

"No, Dad," says Marie. "I tried to get her to talk to me about what happened to her face. But she just said she fell in the woods and promised that she'd stick with that story no matter who else asked."

"That's what she said? Those words? That she'd stick with that story?"

My heart starts again, pounding so my face throbs in time.

"Yes, Dad. That's exactly what she said."

Maybe there's more between them, but their voices are lost under the rush of the wind. Eventually, I hear the sound of one car door opening, and an engine, and tires on gravel. My strength drains away and

I slump down until I'm kneeling on the floor underneath the window, listening to my sister, and then my father, drive away, back up to the Rose House, where I don't know what he'll say or what she'll do.

Because I might have moved too fast, I might have said too much.

But Marie told me *now*. I was so sure she said *now*.

Unless she said *no*.

As has been noted, if you're a heroine in a fairy tale, your life is going to be defined by some truly terrible parenting decisions. But it makes a difference whether those decisions are made by your mother figure or your father.

If you do what your father says, you end up with a happily ever after.

Even if he wants you to go live with the monster he robbed.

Even if he wants you to stand in the yard and wait for the devil to come take you away.

Even if he wants you to hold still while he cuts off your hands, because the devil told him to.

But you do what your mother wants—

Go with the huntsman, dear.

Go gather the strawberries, dear.

Cut off a piece of your foot so the shoe fits, dear.

—You just end up dead.

—Out of the Woods: Musings on Fairy Tales in the Real World, Dr. Geraldine Monroe

GERALDINE, THIRTEEN YEARS OLD
STACEY B'S SANDWICHES AND STUFF

1.

Geraldine had a system.

She laid out the white bread in a double line down the counter. Groups of five. Egg salads first. Then salami and cheese. Then roast beef and mayonnaise. Then PB&J. Smear, slap, slice, wrap, done.

Geraldine Monroe, super sandwich spreader. She tried to make a joke out of it, but she never really could. She looked at the clock. The school bus was coming in ten minutes. Marie, of course, had driven with Dad. Marie was getting her learner's permit and now she drove Dad every morning. Geraldine asked once to ride along, but Dad said he was afraid she'd be a distraction. Marie, he said, needed to concentrate. Now, if Geraldine missed the bus, she'd have to ride her bike, and then she'd miss first hour, which would be better than missing the whole day, again, and having to sit and listen to Stick-up-the-Butt Stucholtz go on about responsibility, but...

The screen door creaked. Geraldine jerked around so hard she almost fell off the footstool.

It was Mom. Her hair was damp and her T-shirt stuck to her. It was like she'd tried to take a shower but hadn't been able to dry off all the way. She walked carefully, softly. Geraldine swallowed and turned back to the sandwiches. Ten done. Ten to go. Ten minutes for the bus. She could do this.

Mom came behind the counter, a whole cloud of tobacco and lavender soap coming with her.

"The store looks good, G," she said.

"Thanks." Geraldine dug the knife into the mayonnaise jar, smearing the bread, white on white.

"I mean it," Mom said, a little more loudly, in case she hadn't heard. "You've been doing a great job. I...don't expect you've been getting a lot of help."

Geraldine clenched her teeth. If she answered that, she was going to cry or scream, and she didn't want to do either. She peeled slices of roast beef off the mound and laid them on the mayonnaised side of the bread and started slapping the lids on.

"You shouldn't have to do that."

"It's okay."

"Let me help you."

"I said it's okay."

"I said I'm helping." Mom started gathering up the bread slices and the jar of peanut butter.

"Leave it alone!"

Mom stared at her. Geraldine braced herself, her heart pounding, but she wasn't sure what for.

Mom lifted up her hands, and everything fell. The bread bounced onto the counter and the giant industrial-sized jar of peanut butter hit the floor.

Geraldine stared at it all and then, without thinking, without wishing or wanting or even anger, she jumped off the stool and sprinted for the door, grabbing up her backpack as she ran past. She crossed the parking lot and made it to the shoulder of the road, but it was too late. The bus was already on the top of the hill, and then it was gone.

Just go, she told herself. *Just get your bike and go.*

But the sandwiches weren't done and the register wasn't open and Mom was in rough shape, and…and…and a thousand other ands. And she hated them all, and she was still turning around and slouching back into the store and flopping the sign from CLOSED to OPEN.

Mom was sitting on a stack of Coke cases with her head buried in her hands. She looked up as Geraldine came back around the counter. Tears streamed down her face and strands of white hair stuck to her cheeks.

"I'm sorry, G. I'm so sorry."

"It's okay, Mom," said Geraldine. The words were automatic. Meaningless. She tried to tell herself she didn't want to go to school anyway. What was one more day? Everybody there was lame. School was lame.

She picked up the peanut butter jar and found a towel to wipe off the lip. No hurry now.

Mom watched her, but didn't try to help anymore. "What's happened to me? I wanted…I thought once I got out of that house, it'd all get better. I didn't even make it out of town…" She ground the heel of her hand into her eyes. "I've screwed up so bad."

Geraldine knew she wanted reassurance. *It'll be okay. I love you. It's not your fault.*

Geraldine couldn't sound out any of those words. Not now. Instead, she turned away and started picking up the scattered bread slices and tossing them back into the wrapper. She'd put them out for the birds, or just hide them in their room, because you never knew.

"I wanted to do better," Mom said. "I've been trying."

Geraldine couldn't even look at her.

"Can you keep a secret?"

Geraldine's hand stopped halfway to the last slice. "What do you mean?"

"I mean can you keep a secret, G?"

Don't listen, Geraldine tried to tell herself. *Finish up. Just let her talk.*

But she wasn't that strong. She turned and saw how Mom leaned forward, her elbows on her knees. Geraldine looked into her eyes for a long time. They were red-rimmed but clear. The real Mom had surfaced above the pills and the beer, at least for now.

"We've got a plan to get out of here."

Geraldine had to play that over in her head a few times. It wasn't easy. Her thoughts seemed to have gone sludgy. Which was stupid. After all, Geraldine had thought about running away, sometimes.

But that was in her own head. Mom saying it out loud somehow made it sound more nuts and less nuts at the same time.

"We've got a plan?" Geraldine said finally.

"Me," Mom croaked, her hands rubbed together faster. "And Pete. And Trish."

Geraldine's heart was hammering. She had to turn away, and fumble with the stupid plastic tab that held the bread wrapper shut. So she could breathe, so she could calm down. She was not going to cry. This was stupid.

"Where are you going?"

"Indianapolis. Pete's working on patching things up with Florence. They've got a house. As soon as she says okay, we can stay with them while we sort things out."

"Oh."

There was noise behind her. Rustling. The squeak of damp sneakers on the tile. The smell—Ivory soap and tobacco and beer. Mom's cool hands on her shoulders. "You're coming with us, G."

I can't handle this. I can't. I have to…I need to…

What? She didn't even know. Her ideas broke to bits before she could even think them. Geraldine turned and looked up into her mother's exhausted eyes.

Mom nodded. She meant it.

"What about Marie?" Geraldine asked.

"She'll be fine. She's got her dad."

"What do you mean *her dad*?"

Mom started itching the back of her right hand, hard. "Well, he hasn't exactly been a real dad to you, has he? It's you and me, G. And we are getting out of here. I promise." Her head drooped. "Jesus. I'm sorry. I gotta…I gotta go lie down."

She stumbled as she turned, and slapped one hand against the counter to steady herself. Geraldine watched her, uncertain what to do, or what to feel.

Don't do this, she begged silently. *Don't tell me we're running away and then fall down. Please, please don't.*

Mom levered herself upright but did not turn around. "You can trust them, okay?"

"I don't get it."

"Trish, and Pete, G! Trish and Pete." She bit her lip and her voice wobbled as she tried to get it under control. "If anything…bad happens. If I can't…If I don't…you can trust them, okay?"

"Yeah, okay." But it wasn't.

"Come find me when you're finished, okay?" said Mom. "I'll drive you to school."

"Sure."

Geraldine turned back to the counter and the unfinished sandwiches.

Don't think about it, she told herself. *It's not real. It can't be real. Mom just says stuff she wants to be true. That's all.*

But Mom's words wouldn't leave her.

Her Dad. Geraldine's hands shook as she dug the knife into peanut butter.

She'd always looked different from the rest of the family. They were all skinny and blond, bright-eyed and bushy-tailed. At thirteen years old, Geraldine was round enough that the kids at school called her the Pillsbury Dough Girl, and the Monroe cousins liked to show off their fake concern by giving her magazines with the diet plans bookmarked.

Geraldine's dark bangs dropped into her eyes and shook. *Her Dad.*

It couldn't be. It was stupid. It couldn't be true that somebody else was her father.

Like, say, Uncle Pete.

She couldn't belong to Uncle Pete. He was the failure, the loser, the black sheep. He could not possibly have stayed in town after Aunt Florence left because he was in love with Mom, and because she was really *his* daughter.

A family came in and wanted chips and sandwiches and Cokes, so Geraldine had to get the cash drawer out of the safe and set the register up. And another came in and wanted directions and the bathroom and a bag of Chips Ahoy cookies to keep the kids quiet, and Mr. Kushner and Mr. Shamanski came in and wanted beer and the last of the pie. Which meant she had to cut more and get it into the clear plastic clamshells.

Her dad.

She tried to forget her stupid ideas. Tried so hard not to believe it. Because if she started hoping, it'd all fall down. Because it always fell down.

He hasn't exactly been a real dad to you... It's you and me, G.

Geraldine swallowed, and turned the sign on the door to CLOSED. Heart in her mouth, she walked to the house. Mom wasn't in the living room like she expected. She was in the bedroom, lying on her back on the white crocheted bedspread, with her arm angled over her eyes.

Geraldine stopped in the doorway.

"Mom?"

There was no answer.

"Mom?"

Mom rolled over and her arm flopped sideways.

Geraldine bit her lip. She took the bottle of pills off the nightstand and put it back in the cupboard and took the vodka bottle into the kitchen.

She stood there for a long minute, gripping the edge of the counter. She should go back and take care of the store. She should do a hundred things.

She grabbed her keys off the hook by the door and ran out to the shed to get her stupid rusty bike before she got the chance to be sorry.

2.

He was heaving a tire up onto a stack beside the garage door. The long shadow from the ED's AUTO sign slanted across him. One of the men inside the garage shouted something. Pete shouldered the tire stack straighter, and shouted back.

Geraldine stopped next to the air pump, one foot on her bike pedal, one foot on the ground, trying to decide what to say. Before she could figure it out, though, Pete turned, rubbing his forehead with his sleeve.

They stared at each other. Pete Monroe, her uncle, her father's younger brother, was kind of a wreck. He kind of always had been, but now it was worse. His hair was shaggy and greasy, his jeans were streaked with dirt and oil.

He pulled a grimy shop towel out of his back pocket and wiped both hard hands on it. "What are you doing here? Is everything okay?" His forehead wrinkled. "Is it your mom?"

Geraldine shook her head and Pete's shoulders slumped in relief. "Then what's going on? I mean, I'm working here."

Yes. He was working and she was an idiot.

"I'm sorry. I was, it was stupid." She got ready to push off.

"Geraldine, wait." Uncle Pete held out his hand, but didn't actually touch her. He glanced back at the guys in the garage, who all seemed to have stopped what they were doing to watch the show. "Come upstairs."

He trotted up the rickety stairs bolted to the side of the garage and waited at the top while Geraldine locked up her bike.

Turned out Dad was right about something. Pete's apartment really was crappy.

There was only one room and everything in it was crooked and sagging and chipped at the edges. It smelled like the garage, exhaust and gas and oil. No beer though, which kind of surprised her.

Uncle Pete stopped in the middle of the room and looked around him, like he'd forgotten something important. Geraldine found herself staring at him, looking for traces of herself in this skinny, greasy, sunburnt man.

Did she have his chin? His nose? Was it there, around his eyes, or in the way he grimaced just a little before he turned to face her?

"What's going on, G?" he asked.

Anger surged. She was being stupid, and he didn't get to call her G. And the two things didn't make any sense and that just dug further under her skin.

"Is it true you and Mom are leaving?"

"What?"

"Mom says you're leaving. She says you made up with Aunt Florence and you and her and Aunt Trish are all going to live in Indianapolis and I can come too but not Marie and if you said that, you're some kind of goddamn shithead to talk Mom into leaving Marie behind!"

If she'd been talking to Mom, Mom would have popped open a beer right now. Dad would get all soft and patient and start telling his endless stories, like he thought if he just kept talking long enough she'd have to believe him.

Uncle Pete pulled his torn flannel shirt off from around his shoulders. He was wearing a sleeveless undershirt, and his arms were tanned, twisted, and ropy. He balled the flannel up and threw it at the wall. It flopped down on top of the ancient TV set.

"Shit," he said, but not angry. Just, flat. "How'd you find out?"

Hope reached out from nowhere at all and twisted Geraldine's heart.

"I won't tell. I won't tell anyone ever. I promise. But you've got to take Marie, too. I'll figure out what to tell her. I promise I will, but—"

"No, Geraldine. That's not it. It's not." He took a deep breath. "Look, your Mom and me…it's complicated, all right?"

"UnclePeteareyoumyrealfather?"

Geraldine had to watch for eight strained seconds while Uncle Pete sorted the lump of sound into words.

"I'd ask where you got that idea from, but I don't guess it matters."

Geraldine swallowed and shook her head. She wasn't sure whether she was agreeing with him or just trying to keep from crying.

"And no, honey, I'm not. I'm sorry."

"Do you know who is? Because it's not him. I know it's not him. He hates me. He can't be my father. I swear to God I'll never tell as long as I live. I just want to know."

But Uncle Pete just sighed.

"Look, you hungry? It's lunchtime. How about we go get a pizza?"

She did not want pizza. She wanted an answer. She wanted him to say he was taking her and Mom and Aunt Trish *and* Marie all to Geraldine's real family. But some part of her felt sure saying the words would end everything. As long as she kept quiet, there was still a chance it'd work out.

"Sure. Okay."

"Okay. Let me go get a fresh shirt. Hang on."

3.

There was exactly one place to get pizza in Whitestone Harbor. Unless you counted Charlie's out on M-131, but that was a bar and Geraldine was pretty sure Uncle Pete wasn't taking her to a bar. That left the Flat and Round.

Geraldine and Pete didn't talk much on the way, they just walked side by side, Geraldine pushing her bike, and Pete digging his hands in his pockets.

The Flat and Round was built like an old barn. Inside, it was one big room with a cement floor and a bunch of picnic tables. She'd lost track of time. It was lunch hour at the high school and the place was almost full of juniors and seniors, clustered around pizzas on pedestal trays and pitchers of Coke and root beer.

Stupid. Never should have said yes.

A few kids looked up when Uncle Pete and Geraldine walked in, the beam of sunlight cutting through the gloom. Most of them went right back to scarfing pizza and shouting at each other.

But some of them stared, like the two who were sitting toward the back, right at the very end of one of the long tables, with an untouched pie between them.

It was Marie. And David Pendarves. Marie's wide eyes flickered from Geraldine to Uncle Pete and she went dead white.

Geraldine grabbed Uncle Pete's arm. She figured he'd take the hint and they'd leave. But Pete ignored her. He walked up to the window, so she had to either let go or be dragged along.

"Whaddaya want, G?" he asked. "Pepperoni?"

"Yeah, sure. Okay."

"Coke?"

"Yeah."

Pete gave Mr. MacInnerny the order.

"Get us a seat," he told her. "I'm gonna go wash up."

Pete headed for the men's room. Marie wouldn't stop staring, even though David was talking to her. Everybody else was done paying them any attention. They were busy eating, talking, laughing about stuff that was way more interesting.

Anger reared up slowly inside Geraldine, defiant and familiar. She waved twinkle-fingers at her sister, and sat down on the nearest bench, elbows on the table.

Marie said something to David without looking at him. She pressed both hands against her table and stood. It must have taken her two whole minutes to slow walk across the room. When she finally got to Geraldine's table, she was breathing like she'd had to run a whole marathon.

153

"What are you doing here?" Marie demanded, in a whisper-shout, like they used at home so Dad wouldn't hear. "You're supposed to be home with Mom. I'll get your homework. What if somebody sees…"

Geraldine let her gaze wander around the busy room. "Too late."

"Dad's going to find out!" hissed Marie.

"Dad doesn't care about me."

"That's not true."

Except it was and they both knew it, and Marie's refusal to admit the stupid truth of their stupid lives made Geraldine nasty. "He will care a whole lot if he finds out you're going out with David Pendarves and you didn't tell him."

"I am not going out with anybody. He just asked me if I wanted to get a pizza. For lunch."

"And Uncle Pete asked me if I wanted to get a pizza. For lunch."

"We're not supposed to talk to him! You're going to get in trouble!"

"Go back to your boyfriend."

"He's not my boyfriend. I don't have a boyfriend!"

"Wonder why that is?" piped up Luke Lindowski at the next table, and for a second, Geraldine thought her sister was going to faint.

Somebody snorted. Somebody snickered. David got to his feet and strolled over to Luke and his buddies.

"You're a dick," he said.

"Better than being a pussy-whipped cunt face."

David swung. Luke ducked, and struggled to get out from under the picnic table. David was leaning forward, ready to get in a couple good punches before Luke got his legs free. But Uncle Pete strode up from behind, wrapping his ropy arms around David and hauled him backward.

"Cut it out, Pendarves!" he shouted, just as Mr. MacInnerny came charging past the counter.

"Take it outside, you little shits!" MacInnerny roared.

Pete let David go. David wiped his mouth and looked at Marie, and at Geraldine. He looked at Luke, too. Then, he curled one fist tight, turned around, and walked out. Marie stared after him, after David.

Geraldine saw something strange in her sister's face. It was like hunger, but worse. Her anger dissolved like it had never existed.

Of course, Luke started to follow David, but Pete clamped one hand down hard on the boy's shoulder.

"Don't be an idiot. He'll beat the snot out of you."

"Let me go, you old ass-wipe." Luke shook free and took off.

"Come on, Marie." Geraldine tugged at her sister's elbow. "Sit with us."

But Marie just swatted weakly at her hand. She didn't even turn around. "I h…I have to go." And just like that, she left. In fact, she ran.

Geraldine plopped back down on the picnic bench. The rest of the place went back to what it was doing. Mrs. MacInnerny brought the tray of pizza and a pitcher of Coke. Uncle Pete sat down on the other side of the table and waited. Geraldine just kept staring out the door.

"Pizza's gonna get cold, G."

"Yeah. I just…I think I better go make sure Marie's okay."

Pete sighed. "Margie!" he called to Mrs. MacInnerny. "Can we get a box?"

Geraldine didn't wait.

It took a minute, but Geraldine spotted Marie and David by the Dumpster. She was staring up into his face and he was touching her cheek. Geraldine didn't know whether to gag or cheer.

Then, behind her, Uncle Pete swore, the most tired sound Geraldine had ever heard anyone make. She whipped around and saw why. A brand-new silver Taurus was pulling into the dirt and gravel parking lot.

It was Dad.

4.

Geraldine didn't stop to think. She grabbed Uncle Pete's hand and pulled him close to block the view of Marie and David.

Instead, Dad only saw her and Pete. Side by side, with Pete holding her with one hand and a pizza box with the other.

"Pete."

"Martin."

Dad had this way of looking at her when he was angry. It was slow and steady and unblinking, and somehow it always made Geraldine feel like she'd been rolling in the mud. "Little young for you, isn't she?"

Pete muttered something under his breath, at the same time, he gave Geraldine's hand a squeeze. "What do you want?"

"Well, I could ask what your intentions are toward my daughter."

Get out, get out, get out, thought Geraldine toward Marie, but she didn't dare look back. Right now, Dad's attention was busy being taken up by Uncle Pete, and her. She couldn't blow it. She just had to hope Marie was fast enough.

"Just getting my niece some pizza." Pete held up the box as proof.

"Because she's so clearly wasting away." Dad looked Geraldine up and down an extra time. She felt like she was inflating while he watched. "Where's your mother, Geraldine?"

"She's home. Asleep."

"Well, we'd better go check on her." Dad leaned over and opened the car door.

"I need to get my bike," said Geraldine, pointing to where she'd locked it to the crooked apple tree.

"Leave it," snapped Dad.

Geraldine swallowed, and climbed into the passenger seat. *I won't cry,* she promised herself. *I won't look. I won't do anything. I won't give him anything.*

"Martin…" said Pete.

Too late. Dad gunned the engine. Gravel spat out from under the tires as the car jounced over potholes and out onto the road.

He drove in silence, but not for long enough.

"What did Pete want?"

"Pizza. He told you."

"Geraldine. You should know better than to try to smart talk me."

Yes, she should, but she wasn't going to be scared. She wasn't going to show him how bad she wanted to crawl away. "It's true. I missed the bus this morning, so I rode my bike to school. But I had a flat and at lunch, I went out to use the air pump, and Uncle Pete asked if I wanted to get a pizza."

"So what did you two talk about over pizza? Or were you going back to his place so you could be alone together?"

Geraldine's stomach cramped up. "He asked about school and...stuff."

"What kind of stuff? Like your mother?"

Geraldine looked out the window at the green blur of trees. "I guess. Maybe. Why's it matter?"

"It matters because Pete is a liar and a cheat. He wants what we have, and he won't stop at anything to get it. That includes using you and your mother to get to me."

"Well maybe if you hadn't stolen his house and busted up his family, he wouldn't have to!"

Dad didn't say anything. Dad acted like he hadn't even heard. Dad just drove.

But not home. He turned off M-131 onto Barstow, where the ground leveled out into cornfields and barns and falling-down houses.

"Where are we going?" asked Geraldine.

Dad glanced at her, just long enough for her to see his lifted eyebrow, and his tiny little smile. "Too cool to take a drive with your old man?"

"No, I, I just...I'm going to be late for class."

"Now that's really strange that you should be worried about that now. Because Mrs. Stucholtz called me earlier. She said you weren't in school at all today."

Busted. Geraldine felt herself shrinking down in the seat. She was going to be locked in her room again, sneaking out the window to raid the store and pee in the woods again.

It wasn't *fair*.

"Patience, Geraldine," said Dad. "It'll all be over soon."

The cornfields and the apple orchards rolled past them. The sky was flat and blue and the sun beat down on the car. Dad didn't have the air-conditioning on and Geraldine didn't dare roll down the window.

At last, up ahead, Geraldine saw a building. It stood on its own in the middle of a lawn that was burnt brown by the sun. It was tall and square and made of orange brick with neat rows of little windows. But what really stood out was how it was surrounded by a chain-link fence, topped by big curls of barbed wire.

Dad pulled up onto the far shoulder and shut the engine off. She could hear the crackle of road dust settling around them.

Dad was waiting for her to say something. She could tell. She swallowed and tasted more dust.

"What's that?" She pointed to the building.

"That's the loony bin, Geraldine," answered Dad. He sounded cheerful, like this was a real treat for him. "The insane asylum. That's where they lock up crazy people. Like Patricia Burnovich. Or people who drink too much, like your mother."

"You're going to lock Mom up?"

"No. You."

He turned to her. He was smiling his saddest, most patient smile.

There was no air. She was going to be sick all over the seat. She couldn't move. All these things were true at the same time, and she didn't know which was worst.

"You don't go to school, Geraldine." How could anyone sound so sad and so happy at the same time? "You're always getting into trouble. You're failing everything."

Because I have to take care of Mom! Because I have to watch the store! Geraldine balled up her fists, ready to shout. But then she looked again at her father's face. It was flat, dead. The sunlight streamed through the windshield, but none of it touched his eyes. They weren't even dark. They were blank. She couldn't tell what he was going to do. They were all alone. They hadn't even seen another car for…ever. She could scream and scream and scream and no one would hear.

"Your teachers are calling me, Geraldine," he said. His voice had changed again. All that strange, cold cheerfulness was gone. Now, his voice was trembling, like he was on the edge of tears. She looked at his eyes again. Still empty. Still cold. The contrast with his tearful voice made everything inside her lurch hard. "I tell them I don't know what the matter is. I tell them how worried I am." He paused, like he was trying to pull himself together. "They say maybe you've got a problem. They say maybe it's drugs."

He leaned forward. Uncle Pete smelled like work. Mom smelled like cigarettes. Dad smelled like aftershave, which smelled like nothing real at all.

"This is where they put girls who take drugs, Geraldine, because drugs make you crazy. They have to keep them here so they can't hurt themselves and their families anymore."

This was bullshit. Geraldine knew it. She knew plenty of kids who spent half their lives stoned out of their minds, and nobody put them anywhere.

But none of those other kids belonged to Martin Monroe.

She couldn't look at him anymore. She couldn't stand it. She faced forward. She stared at the rectangular orange building on the other side of the fence. She stared at the slanting lines of the barbed wire.

It's bullshit. It is. It IS.

A house finch landed on the barbed wire, looked confused, and took off back the way it came.

"Are you going to hurt us anymore, Geraldine?" Dad asked.

"No," said Geraldine.

"Are you going to see Pete anymore? Because he's a dangerous man, Geraldine. He gets little girls into trouble. I'd hate to have to tell the school, or the police, that he was getting you into trouble. But I have to protect my daughters, don't I? Even if it's from my own brother."

Geraldine swallowed her spit. It tasted metallic and burned in the back of her throat. "No. I won't see him anymore."

"Well, then, I guess we don't have a problem after all." He cocked his ear toward her. "I'm sorry, I didn't hear you?"

"No. There's no problem."

"Good girl!" He clapped a hand on her shoulder and shook it. "Now!" He started the engine again, gunning it hard before he shifted into gear. "Let's go find your sister."

Cinderella is the most famous good sister. But the original Cinderella is the one with the biggest contradiction in her narrative.

At the end of the story, Cinderella invites her wicked stepsisters to her wedding. But as they're coming out of the church, Cinderella's birds land on their shoulders and peck their eyes out.

Those birds were Cinderella's special friends. They obeyed her. Cinderella could have stopped them.

But she didn't.

—Out of the Woods: Musings on Fairy Tales in the Real World,
Dr. Geraldine Monroe

MARIE, PRESENT DAY
WHITESTONE HARBOR

1.

Even though it's barely eight o'clock by the time I pull into the public parking lot on Main, the sidewalks are crowded with families and young people. Summer is at its height. Our visitors are breakfasting at Mama's Pancake Diner or buying supplies for day trips on the trails or the lake. The marina is full of boats of all sizes and makes. Sailboats tack across the blue and silver surface of Lake Michigan.

It's the lake that brings in the tourist trade that supports the lifestylers. The lifestylers brew the craft beers and raise the heritage breed pigs and create the other local luxuries that help lure in our more gracious elite, the men who sail up on their yachts or fly in on private planes to enjoy summer on the lakeshore.

Of course, it takes more than craft beer to support a gracious life. There are also Mexicans to work the orchards and the cornfields, and

Jamaicans to work the hotels. But these people live under the power radar and are generally only the concern of those who hire them. They don't vote and don't buy houses, and everyone tells themselves they prefer it that way.

In general, the town works as a tidy unit and looks like picture-postcard perfection. So different from when I was a child. People don't run away from us anymore. We are where they run to.

Of course I can't take any real credit for Whitestone's successes. All the kudos must go to my father. He is the one who has watched so carefully for every opportunity, so we could benefit when those chances came. But I have done my part, and I'm sure I can be forgiven if I take a little quiet pride in the way things have turned out. I have made certain I understand how everything works. Even a small town is a complicated piece of machinery, with dozens of moving parts. And naturally, we have our problems. Old-timers and young wrecks who live in rusted-out trailers behind the blind ruins of the farmhouses. They work odd jobs, or they repurpose abandoned houses to make meth or bath salts, or to package the marijuana they grow in the woods.

But nobody talks about them when they talk about Whitestone, and this morning, at least, that's not what I have to worry about. My worry right now is much closer to home. I have to talk with Walt. I have to make sure he understands what is really at stake.

I cannot let all my hard work unravel. Not again.

Monroe Real Estate and Property Management takes up the second floor of a grand, gothic sandstone building on the corner of Main and Washington.

"Good morning, Bethany," I say as I push open the doors to our reception area. Bethany jerks her head up and shoves her phone into the desk drawer at the same time. She means well, but the truth is, she's not the brightest intern we've had. I'm afraid her appearance—corn-fed, Midwestern, blue-eyed, blond—reinforces the impression that she can't be taken seriously. And I'll have to talk with her soon about dressing for success, among other things.

"Good morning, Ms. Monroe. I um, was just trying to get hold of you." She rubs the drawer nervously, revealing the lie in her words. I do not remark on this, yet.

"Is there a problem?"

Before she can answer, Geraldine's disgusted exclamation echoes down the oak-paneled corridor.

"Jesus, Walt, are you ever gonna grow a pair?"

I freeze. *Oh, no. Not yet. She was supposed to see David next. I haven't even talked to Walt. I haven't got him ready…*

"You *know* he's a lying rat bastard!" my sister continues.

It's extremely difficult, but I make myself smile. "Well. That definitely does sound like a problem."

"Is she really…? I mean…"

"Yes, Bethany, she really is my sister." My smile is perhaps a little sharper than her skepticism warrants, and I stride past.

The office is an extension of my father's study at home—solid and timeless. Here he let me preserve the original oak paneling and several of Addison's oil paintings of the harbor and the quarry. People like a sense of continuity and solidity when they come to an office like ours.

Inside the front conference room, Walt finally manages to speak up. "All I'm saying, Geraldine, is that I need to talk to your father first."

"Why? It's not his house. It's mine."

I take a second to fix the appropriately sunny expression on my face, and then throw open the door.

"Geraldine! This is a surprise. Good morning, Walt."

But Walt does not look like he's having a good morning at all. His button-down shirt is wrinkled. He hasn't shaved, and his wiry hair is sticking up on end. There's a suit bag hanging off the back of the door, so he's been home at some point, but he looks like he hasn't been to bed.

Of course facing down Geraldine when she's on the warpath would be disconcerting to a stronger man than Walt, especially this morning. She has not bothered to dress for coming into the office. She's in a pair of old cargo shorts and a flannel shirt and her hair is bundled into a messy ponytail. Her hands are already dirty and her face…I can barely make myself look at her face. Her bruises have darkened, and the fresh scab has turned her scar into something from a bad horror movie.

"Marie," Geraldine shoots back. "I should have known it'd be you next."

"What's the matter?" I ask with as much surprise as I can muster.

Walt answers first, plainly pleading for help. "I was just telling Geraldine that when it comes to your old house, she should talk with your…"

"He was just telling me that he is not going to hand over the deed and paperwork to my house. But he won't explain why, since it *is* my house."

I find myself more than a little frustrated with Geraldine's choice of tactics. She knows Walt has always been dependent on others—Dad, or Carla, or Grandma Millicent, or me. She really should not be picking on him now.

"I'm not even sure we're keeping the title here." Walt is looking at me. "We moved all those files to storage last year."

"Did you move the house files to storage, Marie?" Geraldine asks me.

"Well, even if we did, it won't take that long to get them out again. Bethany can do it, and of course you can have a copy of whatever you want."

Except Walt clearly thinks it is a problem. He tries to muster some courage. "Geraldine, you can't just come storming back in after twenty-five years and demand we drop everything to cater to your whims."

"That house is mine, and I want the paperwork, including"—she leans forward and stabs at the conference table—"any outstanding mortgages, or liens, or anything else that might be encumbering the property."

Now it is time for me to intervene in earnest. If only to stop poor Walt's lip from quivering.

"Geraldine. You know very well the house is in both our names. I couldn't do anything without your permission. If there was a loan, you would have had to have known and approved."

"Yeah, right." My sister snorts. "I know all that. Just like I know Dad's never ever played fast and loose to keep what he wants."

She says this slowly, like she's enjoying the taste of each word. I try to see through the cold reflection in her eyes. How much of this is for show? I should be able to tell, but for the moment, at least, Geraldine has closed herself off from me.

Considering what happened yesterday at the old house with Dad, this is understandable. I remind myself I am not angry. I knew this was going to be difficult from the beginning.

"Walt," I say. "Why don't you see if Bethany can get copies of the paperwork, or at least links to the files, so Geraldine can print whatever she needs."

Walt, however, does not seem to be interested in making things easy on himself. "Marie, can I talk to you for a minute?"

"Why, Walt, I didn't think anything was the matter," sneers Geraldine.

"Marie, please," says Walt again.

"Geraldine?" I ask, and triumph glitters in her bruised eyes.

"Don't bother. I've gotten what I really need. But you might want to know, I'm also getting a lawyer."

The word rings much louder than it should. Walt blanches, which is, of course, the reaction Geraldine was hoping for.

"That's not going to be necessary," I tell her. "If you come back this afternoon, I'm sure we'll have copies of everything attached to the house. I know for a fact there isn't that much. Have you gotten hold of David yet?"

Geraldine, however, is not going along with my attempt to change the subject. "I'm sure there'll be copies of everything you and Dad think it's okay for me to know about. But that's just not going to be enough."

Geraldine pushes past us. Her hiking boots clomp hard on the floor and leave crumbs of black dirt behind. I try not to wince, or to let the shame crawl over me.

"I'll go talk to her," I tell Walt.

"Marie." His voice stops me before I reach the door. "Do you think she'll really hire a lawyer?"

I wish Walt would stop fidgeting. Really. A grown man should have more control over himself, especially in a professional setting.

"Probably. You know how she is. Always trying to stir things up."

"Yes, Marie, I know how she is. But do you?" Walt steps closer. He smells musty. I wonder briefly if he's been drinking. But no, it's just the lack of a shower. There's something different about him, though—a silent warning, a hardening of his features—that wasn't there before.

"Walt, Carla told me you've got…concerns." I think for a moment about taking his hand. That's the sort of gesture Dad would make. But I just grip my purse strap. "Did she tell you we talked?"

He ignores my question. "Marie, you have to stop her. I don't want to make waves and I don't want to hurt Uncle Martin, but Geraldine does not care. She'll blow the lid off and she won't care who gets hurt."

"I know, Walt. You've always looked after Dad's best interests and…"

"And nothing," he says, and his voice is so taut you'd think something was about to snap. "Marie, you are on the edge of serious trouble. I'm only going to be able to cover up so much, especially if Geraldine is serious about audits and lawyers."

"She can't really call an audit."

"Actually, she can. She's still got an interest in the family trust."

How should I respond to this? I thought we'd have another day at least, perhaps even as much as a week.

"And you need to think about this," Walt continues. "Martin's done a lot of good for Whitestone, but not everybody appreciates what he had to do to accomplish it. There are people who remember that Geraldine is a Monroe, and that she might just know where some of the bodies are buried. If anything happens, you're going to have a tough time weathering that storm."

He's threatening me. For Dad's sake. With his hangdog face and ragged mustache and a suit that was tailored for him but still sags and bags because he doesn't stand up straight. He actually thinks he can frighten me.

I cover my mouth and look away. Because it is not funny. Not at all.

"Marie, you're family. You've...you've been through a lot. I don't want to hurt you, I don't, but Geraldine's...she could really do some damage." He pauses and tugs at his mustache like he's trying to pull out fresh words. "Did she tell you how her face got so cut up?"

My heartbeat speeds up, just a little. "She told me she fell."

"Do you believe her?"

I'm about to say that of course I do, but my phone plays a staccato drumbeat. It's my special ring tone for Dad. I cannot ignore this. I glance at Walt and he nods, as if he could withhold permission.

It's a text. I read:

Can't make brunch you take it sry short notice

I slide my phone back into its pocket. "I...I'm sorry. I have to go. I have to take a brunch meeting for Dad."

Walt folds his arms and looks at the suit bag, and the gym bag underneath it. For some reason, my thoughts have flickered to Bethany and her cell phone, and then to Carla and her fears. The combination is laughable, of course. It is impossible a girl like her would look at a man like Walt. If she was going to take on an older man, he would need an air of glamour, or escape, things Walt most decidedly does not have.

And yet, I think, Walt is not the only one who can raise silly concerns.

"Walt, is everything all right between you and Carla?"

This startles him. He tears his eyes away from the bags. I was right. He didn't get to bed last night. He might not even have gone home. "Of course! Is...has she said something?"

"No, no," I assure him. "Well, maybe a little something. She was just worried Dad might have, well, maybe been teasing you a little. You know he and Carla don't always get along, and he can be a little careless with his words."

"Oh." Walt is visibly relieved. "No, nothing's wrong. Or, at least, well, you know how much overtime I've been putting in."

"Well, you need to talk with Carla. Set her mind at rest."

"You're right. And I will. But Marie…"

"I'm so sorry, Walt, I can't right now."

Walt falls back, defeated. "Sure. Right. Fine."

"Walt, I have heard everything you said," I tell him firmly. "I want to explain. Just give me a little time and then we can have a sit down and decide what to do together." I swallow and I lay my hand on his arm. "All I'm asking for is a couple more days."

"Okay, Marie. But that's all I can give you."

"Thank you." I flash my most grateful smile. "And go home, tonight. Please. Carla is worried about you."

"Yeah, right. Of course. Please. I…Marie…"

But I've already turned away. I have to. I can't be late. And I can't let him see the worry on my face.

2.

The Cherry Tree is only half full when I get there. Miranda is at the hostess station. We exchange a few trivialities and she shows me to the reserved table by the windows overlooking the lake.

This is my favorite of the new restaurants in Whitestone, and not just because Teri and John took my suggestions on the décor. Although, privately, I have to admit it turned out beautifully. I love the clean lines and natural wood of the Arts and Crafts era, and the murals of the lakeshore are beautifully done.

I notice that Sally Wyatt is here, brunching with Marsha Jankowski. Rebecca Cliffords sits at another table, alone, and drinking a mimosa. We do our best to ignore each other. Lawrence Kappernick is here, too, hunched over a small table so covered in papers there's barely room for his plate of smoked whitefish and bagels.

An idea forms. A possibility. Just for a little insurance.

I tell Miranda to leave the menus on our table and excuse myself. Lawrence looks up as I approach and his face splits into a wide grin.

"Marie! Looking lovely as always! Out doing the old man's work for him?" His laugh at his own joke is hearty and rich. I smile.

"Shh! That's our little secret, Larry." Lawrence is one of Dad's oldest clients and knows a lot of people. He's on the boards of any number of corporations and trusts and so forth. With everything that is happening, it wouldn't hurt to have a few extra resources in place, in case they're needed. "I just wanted to ask, are you free later in the week? There's something I need to talk with you about." It's best to remain a little vague, because I'm not yet sure exactly what our conversation would need to be about.

He squeezes my hand in both of his.

"I'm always free for you, Marie! Nothing serious, I hope?" He lays his hand on my forearm and looks attentively into my eyes.

"Oh, no, nothing. There are just some questions with a new client."

"Well, then, call whenever you need to. My time is yours." He gives my arm another of his little squeezes.

I politely extricate myself and move to settle down at my own table. I hope to have a few minutes to settle down and fix myself properly. There's so much happening, I feel like my head is about to start spinning. But no. Miranda is already leading a beaming Ashley Dickinson toward my table.

"Marie!" We air kiss, both cheeks. She sounds cheerful, but her light has dimmed perceptibly now that she sees I'm the only one at the table. "Martin didn't tell me you'd be here, too."

Her tone reminds me I should have texted her as soon as I'd heard from Dad. "I'm sorry, Ashley, but my father was detained."

The light switches off. Ashley doesn't even bother with a façade of courtesy. She just grabs the menu card and stares at it. Our server comes by to pour the ice water and take our drinks order.

"Bloody Mary," Ashley snaps, like the server is already late.

"Just coffee for me, thank you."

Ashley Dickinson is blond, of course, and gliding through her mid-forties. She has a long face but a snub nose. Her sleeveless pink sheath dress displays a body that's the kind of fit-thin achieved with a certain amount of help from surgeons, dietitians, and personal trainers. Her jewelry is, well, *bold*, I suppose is a good word. Gold cuffs shackle her tan wrists. That broad gold collar must hurt when it bumps against her exposed collarbones. I wonder idly what she's hiding under there.

"Have you been here before?" I ask cheerfully. "The Mediterranean eggs are delicious."

"Mmm." Ashley pulls out her phone and checks something on the screen. I respond by bringing out my planner.

"You'll be glad to know your house is almost ready. Oh, and those finials you liked so much are in. I'd love to schedule some time so you can see what we've done, and let us know if there are any last-minute changes."

"Oh, yeah. Anytime." She taps her screen a few more times. "No, wait. I've got a massage scheduled tomorrow...you're sure Martin said he couldn't meet us?"

"He asked me to tell you how sorry he is. It was unavoidable. I'm afraid this is our busy season."

Our drinks arrive and Ashley takes a long swallow of Bloody Mary, tilting her head back as if she was trying to down a handful of pills along with tomato juice and vodka. My skin curdles and I look away just in time to see Miranda threading her way through the dining room again, this time with my father following closely behind.

Ashley catches me staring, turns her head and sees. The switch is thrown again. Mrs. Ashley Dickinson sets down her Bloody Mary and lights up like a Christmas tree.

"Ladies." Dad pauses to put a hand on the back of Ashley's chair. He gives her his best smile, the one that can make the rest of the world fade away. "I'm so sorry I'm late."

"Marie said you weren't coming." Ashley holds out her slim hand.

Dad takes her hand. He doesn't shake, just holds it for a minute. Under her tan and the precise layers of concealer and powder, Ashley turns a shade of pink that a woman her age should have left behind years ago.

"I didn't think I was going to be able to get away," Dad tells her. "But…in the end, I just couldn't help myself. I had to be here."

Dad is playing up to Mrs. Dickinson, part of what he calls keeping the client sweet. I've seen it many times. He has a knack for creating an air of comfort and friendship, and it truly shines when he's around these women.

Dad sits between us and picks up the menu card. "What are we having?"

"Well, I was thinking about the Mediterranean eggs," Ashley says.

"Oh, no, no. You've got to try the blueberry pancakes."

"Oh, I can't possibly. I have to watch my figure."

Dad smiles and leans forward for a stage whisper. "You've got nothing to worry about. And they're delicious. My favorites."

"Well…Maybe I can indulge just this once." She hands him the menu card and preens in the glow of his approval.

"You'll love them." He turns to the server as she arrives. "Krista, blueberry pancakes for two, and Marie? The eggs?"

"Yes, please."

Dad is entirely focused on Ashley. In response she smiles up into his deep eyes and leans forward, her perfectly manicured fingers toying with her necklace. *Eating out of the palm of his hand.* Dad's gaze flickers toward me. We share the cold joke of her hopeless flirtation, and she doesn't see a thing.

"Now, have you seen the house?" Dad asks.

"Not yet. But I'm sure it's perfect."

"It is. Marie has done her usual magnificent job." Neither of them look toward me, but her air grows smug. She imagines I am here to act as secretary.

"Will Todd be coming up this week?" The words slip out of me, and I have to work to keep my face casual. It is the wrong time for that question, and I know it. I am off my stride this morning.

"*Ppppbbbtt.*" Ashley takes another gulp of Bloody Mary. "Somehow this has managed to be his busy season, too. Funny how that happens, isn't it?"

Dad *tsks* softly. "I hope he's not going to make a habit of staying away. I'd hate to think of you in your lovely new house, all alone. The princess in her tower." He smiles at the metaphor, and so does Ashley.

"Oh, don't worry about me. After all, I'm up here to relax, aren't I?" She flutters again.

Dad leans in, leading her on. Not that it's hard. Like so many others, she wants him to save her from her particular gilded cage.

She's going to be trouble.

Women like Ashley do not understand. They are useful because they convince their husbands and boyfriends to spend extra for the services that come with the houses—the housekeeping staff, the personal chef, the driver and car. Not one of them can see past the surface of his eyes to his abiding indifference. The only woman in his life was my mother. No one else has ever been able to give him anything he truly wanted. But so many of them want to try, I've learned to size them up in advance. Unfortunately, experience tells me Ashley is going to be one of the ones who calls every day for the first few months, trying to get past me to talk with Dad. It's always painful to hear their manufactured excuses and their petulance.

That, of course, is part of the reason Dad likes me to be at these meetings. By showing me how ridiculous these women make themselves over a few smiles and a little carefully choreographed attention, he is teaching me how to behave. Still. Always. Forever. Until death do us part.

The pancakes come, each stack sizzling in a little cast-iron skillet. Dad slices into his, but watches Ashley. She takes up a forkful, tilting her head back as she swallows, just like she did with the Bloody Mary.

"There now," he says. "Didn't I tell you? Aren't they perfect?"

"Oh, you were so right."

My skillet holds eggs in tomato sauce and two slices of grilled ciabatta. I occasionally turn a page in my planner as I eat. I am not required for this part of the conversation.

I should also call Geraldine. After our last encounter, I have to at least leave her a message. It would look strange if I didn't. Maybe I should stop by the house again.

"Well, don't worry. That's why we have Marie. Marie?"

I have kept a careful half an ear on the discussion, so I am able to answer without hesitation, despite my personal maunderings. "We should have the last details settled by next Tuesday."

"It must be lovely to have a daughter who's so devoted," remarks Ashley. "I can't even get Portia to come home on the weekends."

"Well, between us, Marie's the one who runs the show. I couldn't find my socks without her."

I find myself staring at my father's hands. The twisted patterns of veins beneath his spotted skin. My father does not monitor his blood pressure the way he should. He works too hard. The risk of stroke is very serious. "Even the bills?" Ashley folds her arms on the table, in an attitude that incidentally pushes up her cleavage. "Wow. I've got absolutely no head for numbers. I'm just a little beach bunny."

"Oh, Marie knows where all the bodies are buried. She dug the graves herself."

My father is looking right at me. I will not clench my pencil. I will only raise my eyes and smile with perfect comfort to show how well I share the joke.

At the same time, I picture him on the sidewalk outside, facedown. People gather around to gawp at the sprawling old man with his spotted, veiny hands spread out to catch the sun. Someone snaps a picture to post on Facebook later. Someone remembers to call the ambulance. But they are all too late.

And where am I in this little scene? Up at Windward Hill, because Ashley Dickinson decided she wants her draperies all changed to forest green, something my father suggested at the last minute.

How terrible that would be.

3.

I walk out of the Cherry Tree a little too quickly. After Dad's remark about how much I know, I was unable to settle back into my role as audience and enabler. Dad will have something to say about that later, I'm sure.

I climb into my Escalade and make sure the tinted windows are rolled up. The parking lot faces the groomed beach and the lake. Gulls hover on the brisk wind. The silhouettes of children and families stroll, or trudge, against the bright background of blue sky and blue lake.

Why can't I calm down?

It must be overwork. It's been a busy few days, and there's the party on Sunday, and, of course, Geraldine, and, unexpectedly, Walt. They're all pushing too many plans along too quickly. Who wouldn't get a little stressed?

Maybe I'll give myself an afternoon off. Take a little drive down to Petoskey, maybe. Do some window shopping for Geraldine. We're going to need to redecorate when everything's over with Dad and she's moved back into the Rose House. She hates to shop, so I'll have to know exactly where to go to find what she likes. She'll probably want Aunt Trish's old room. I'll have to show her how much I've already done, but she's sure to have a few ideas of her own...

This is when I see Robbie.

I recognize him even in the middle of the crowd of other teenagers. They're striding up the beach, all in a bunch, dodging the kids and aiming kicks at the gulls. Robbie has his hands shoved in his jacket pocket and he's shouting something.

I recognize Shelly Bronski, Lauren's Bronski's oldest, and that's Max Koepler. There are two others I don't know. They've all got torn jeans and wrinkled T-shirts and their hair is bleached and dyed all sorts of rainbow colors.

I don't like them. My son shouldn't be with them. He shouldn't be here at all, not when he was supposed to be in Petoskey.

But I can't criticize. I can't yell, not when he's with his friends. But I am still his mother. I can't just *leave* him here.

I glance at Marie in the mirror and make sure her face is sunny, and I climb back out of the car.

"Robbie!" I wave. I will apologize for embarrassing him later. "Hello!"

I ignore the expression on his face and the way the others snicker. He mouths something like "back in a sec," trots up the sand, and edges between the parked cars.

"Mom. What's going on?" He hasn't shaved, and I can smell tobacco and beer on his breath. Anger rises in a bubble, filling my throat, and I have to press down hard.

"Nothing." I smile and rub his arm. "I just missed you. Are those your band friends?"

They're clustered together on the sand, not coming any closer, but not looking away. I know their kind. I went to school with them. Nothing changes but the clothes and the hair.

"A couple of them. We were gonna go out for pizza. I was gonna text you."

It's a harmless enough lie. Something Geraldine might have said when she was his age. But there's that smell on his breath. Not even the constant wind off the lake can take it away.

"I'd like to spend a little time with you, Robbie." I do not let my smile waver. "You can tell your friends you'll go out with them another time."

"No, Mom. I'll be home for dinner. Promise."

"I want you home now." *No, Marie. Stop, Marie. There is no need for this.* But in the back of my awareness, Mom is laughing at me. She knows I cannot control my son, not even now when it's so important that all the pieces stay where I put them. "There're things we need to discuss."

I need time. Just another couple of days. Just until after the party. That's all.

"Like what?" he demands.

"We are not going to be talking about personal business in the middle of a parking lot," I snap. "I'll give you a ride."

175

"I've got my car, Mom."

"And you smell like a brewery!"

Robbie glances behind, to see if my shout carried. The others are clustered together, looking at the lake and each other. It's impossible to know if they heard.

"Jesus, Mom! Why are you so…"

I adjust my look, ever so slightly, and Robbie's mouth closes. He looks away, and looks back.

"Okay. Okay. Just gimme a sec."

I watch him trudge back to the others. I am very glad I can't hear what's being said between them. I know I should just let him go. I'm overreacting. I need to get hold of myself. What does it matter what his friends look like? He'll be away from here soon. Once he's settled in Ann Arbor, he'll be free to come and go as he chooses, and decide life for himself.

Unlike Geraldine. Unlike me.

Robbie slogs back across the sand and climbs into the passenger seat. I shut us both into the SUV my father gave me and drive away in silence.

All the way, I can feel Mom in the backseat, enjoying the show.

The Household Tales came out of a country ravaged by decades of war. So, perhaps it's not surprising they are boundlessly bloody and full of impossible dangers. What is a little surprising is how they also emphasize the absolute importance of being kind to strangers.
—Out of the Woods: Musings on Fairy Tales in the Real World,
Dr. Geraldine Monroe

GERALDINE, PRESENT DAY
LAKE MICHIGAN SHORELINE

1.

"Why here?"

That's the first thing David says to me as I sit down next to him. We're on a curved stretch of sand and stones, using a driftwood log as a bench. Lake Michigan spreads out in front of us. It's evening and the sky above the lake is burning orange and fuchsia pink. The wind's kicking up. White-capped waves curl up and crash down, filling the rapidly cooling air with the scent of fresh water. All at once I'm dried out and thirsty and I want nothing more than to strip down and dive in.

"I wanted to see if you'd come," I tell him. "And if I would."

He's wearing a cap with the Whitestone Security logo. There's a matching logo on his police-blue polo shirt. His fat gold wedding band still flashes on his left hand. The flesh bulges around its edges and I wonder if it's ever going to come off. Every time I see him, his hairline is a little farther back and his belly is a little more prominent. What really hurts, though, is watching his strong shoulders slump under the weight of a life he has no way to get out from under.

I wanted to meet earlier today, but David had to wait until he was off-shift. He takes long sips of coffee from a Starbucks cup and is not looking at me. I've already had so much caffeine today, I feel like I'm going to shake apart.

The last time David and I came here together was the night Mom died. Back then, you could drive right onto the sand, if you didn't mind bottoming out a couple of times on the way down. David sprawled beside me on the hood of my car, the murder weapon. We smoked cigarettes and drank beer and stared at the lake. He kept passing me bottles of Budweiser and I kept downing them, hoping the rip current of alcohol and nicotine would drag me past what I had just done.

I don't know why I decided to screw him. I don't know why he decided to go along with it.

"Why'd you stay, David?" I ask him now.

He makes a face like the coffee's turned to ditch water. He also changes the subject.

"That's a hell of a mess you've made of your face there, G."

"You should see the other guy."

"Are you serious?"

I don't answer.

He sighs and lets the Starbucks cup dangle between his knees. "Everybody says you're staying down at the old house."

"Everybody's right."

"The place is pretty much a wreck."

"Not pretty much. It is a wreck."

"And there's been some trouble."

"Drugs. Yeah. I heard. In Whitestone Harbor. What is the world coming to?"

David tugs his hat brim down, shading his tired eyes from the glare on the stones and the waves.

"I was hoping you might know who can help me fix the place up," I say. "I can do some stuff on my own, but not the roof, and I'm going to need a new stove hooked up."

"You have any money?"

"Some."

His eyes travel across me. He's remembering, just like I am, and comparing those memories to what he sees now.

"Like two thousand dollars?" he asks me.

I bite back my first reply. "So, I take it you heard Robbie's graduation present went missing?"

"Yeah, I heard."

"Did Robbie tell you?"

He drinks more coffee, which is pretty much all the answer either of us needs.

"Okay. Yes, I have some money that is all mine, and no, none of it is the two thousand I brought up to give to my nephew. Dad's got that stashed somewhere."

I give him time to digest this.

When I was teaching, there was always some student who asked why in the stories the townspeople never went up to the mysterious castle to chuck the monster out. Why'd they always wait around for the hero? They only ask that because they're young, and they don't understand that when you've got a job and a family to think of, you're a lot less willing to make trouble.

People in Whitestone like the fact that there are jobs and houses and Walmarts and Meijers. Dad has made sure he gets the credit for all that. The way this town sees it, as long as Dad isn't disturbed, he'll just stay in his castle, and their lives can go forward mostly how they're used to. This gives him power.

So, to take that power away, I've got to convince the town that they don't know their particular devil at all. That takes a new story. A better, more interesting story. Or, at least, a more awful, unstable one.

I've spent a lot of today in town. I've been seeing and being seen. It's important people have a chance to exclaim over the fact that I'm back and, of course, the black and blue ruin of my face.

I fell, I tell them. *No big deal.*

Not one of them believes me. They know something's wrong. That means they'll listen a little more closely when they hear the next story.

I feel guilty about using David to move the plan forward, but I'm not going to stop.

As usual, David's first instinct is to be decent. He's more willing to talk home repair than theft. "If you need roofers, I know some guys. I can make a call, if you want."

"Thanks. And since it looks like I'm not going to be smart and leave, have you got any ideas about what should I do about security?"

We both stare down the beach while he considers his answer. There's the remains of a bonfire a few feet down the stony slope, with some dead bottles clustered around it. A twinge of resentment tightens my shoulders. Is that because somebody else was using this place I consider mine, or because they didn't invite me?

"Well, if you were a client of mine, I'd recommend an alarm system. But what'll really help is lights, and fixing the place so it looks lived in as fast as you can. If it's just shenanigans, whoever's doing it will find someplace less risky to hang out."

"It's not just shenanigans." I rub my forehead and wince because I get too close to my healing scabs.

"If you think it's some drug dealers wanting their squat back, you should call the police."

"It's not dealers, David. It's Dad."

His rounded jaw works back and forth. There's something in this silence I can't read.

"Not really Martin's style." David gestures vaguely toward my eyes.

"You sure about that?" I do not mention my uncle, but then, with David, I don't have to. "It's kind of weird how this happened right after I hinted that some accounting friends of mine might get all up in his business."

"You 'hinted'?" He makes the air quotes with his free hand. "That was not smart, G."

"I got mad. I am notoriously not smart when I'm mad."

David mutters something under his breath. I pretend not to hear.

"I'm going to find out what he's up to, David. Will you help?"

That raises an actual laugh. "Help blow up the mighty Martin Monroe, who just happens to be my boss? Not real fucking likely."

"What if I said this isn't just me stirring the shit pot? What if I told you Marie thinks something's wrong, too?"

The decent guy evaporates. David's eyes go hard and sharp. This is the security guard beside me now, who's used to being on watch for trouble.

"Marie's been calling me for months, trying to talk me into coming up to help her." This is the thing I need him to hear, whether either of us likes it or not. "She thinks Dad's really in hot water this time. Some deals haven't worked out the way they were supposed to, and it's messed up the cash flow and it's starting to come back on him."

"And you think this..." David sketches a circle around my face. "This is because you've decided to take full possession of one ratty old house?" I face him fully, and he answers his own question. "You own it, and he wants to sell it."

"Maybe. Or maybe there's something a little...easier to hide. I went to talk to Walt this morning about getting a copy of the title and any other papers, and he really, really did not want to give them up." I rub my hands on my worn jeans. "I think Dad maybe had Marie do something with the house. Use it as collateral on a loan or something, you know, without bothering to tell me." There's all kinds of things you can do behind a house and its mortgages. A lot of them come under the heading of money laundering. But David knows this, too.

Our silence, the waves, and the wind swirl around for a while. David takes another swallow of coffee. It must be stone cold by now.

"Dad's done some hinky shit with his houses before," I remind him.

"Which everybody knows."

"Including Marie, and you, David." I let that sink in. "And before you say we're overreacting, you should know Marie also says Dad was leaning on the development commission to try to get the house condemned, which would get me kicked out, if I don't decide to leave on my own."

But David doesn't say a thing about overreacting.

"Look at me, Geraldine."

I do. I'm ready for him to ask for details about the guys who did such a number on my face. But I'm wrong again.

"Did Marie really ask you to come back?"

This is when it hits me. David still loves Marie. After all I did, and she did, he still loves her.

I don't know whether to cry, or laugh in his face. I settle for telling him the truth. "We've been talking about it for maybe six months, maybe a little longer."

"Jesus."

The waves in front of us rush forward and the traffic behind us rushes away. The wind catches up all the noise and adds its own.

"Geraldine," says David finally. "You know Marie's not okay, don't you?"

I shrug. "Marie's never been okay."

"I mean really not okay. Like, clinically not okay."

I sit still for a second, waiting for his words to start making some kind of sense. "What are you talking about?"

"She sees things, Geraldine. Secret signs, in the carpet and in the trees. And she talks to ghosts." He pauses and he looks at the confusion in my eyes. "You didn't know?"

No. I did not know. I never knew.

"But, she, I ... are you sure?"

"I slept next to her for ten years. Yes. I'm sure."

And I slept next to her for seventeen. And I didn't see anything.

Did I? No. He's wrong. Marie is my sister. Not even David knows all the shit we've been through. I know her like I know myself. Even when she's closed herself off from every single other person. I can still see through.

"If ... if that's what's going on, why didn't you do anything?" I mean it as a challenge, but it sounds like a plea. "Why didn't you call me?"

"Are you fucking kidding?"

And just like that, I realize David knows what I did. He knows how I gunned the engine and aimed the car straight at my mother, and how she stood there and let me to do it. He knows that's why I got drunk and screwed him, and why I sliced my ankles with a shard from a broken bottle and walked into the water after I sent him on a beer run. He's known for years. Maybe since he threw himself into the water after me.

Does he know the thing I missed? That if I'd really hit Mom, there should have been a dent in the bumper. The rain would have washed the blood away, but there should have been a dent. Like when you hit a deer.

But there wasn't.

But we're not talking about me, about then. We're talking about him, and now, and our words are bitter.

"You really can't figure out why I stay?" he says. "You think I don't know your dad's got my balls on an anvil? I feel that hammer come down every fucking day. I stay because it's the only way I can even get a look at my son, or be close when he needs somebody. And I stay because I'm a complete fucking idiot, Geraldine. Because some part of me keeps hoping that someday I'm going to wake up and find out Marie's come to her senses just enough to pack her bag and we can all drive off into the sunset together and maybe I can finally get her some kind of help."

If it had been anybody else in front of me, I might have grabbed that cold coffee and thrown it right in their face. But this is my sister's ex-husband, and Robbie's father. There's a chance, just a chance, that he's telling the truth.

A truth I missed.

David is unfolding himself, getting ready to leave. I look up at him, mute and pleading. For what, I have no idea. He can't help me. He has no idea what his words really mean, or how many foundations he's just kicked out from under how many plans. I knew I could only trust Marie so far, but I did trust her. It took me years, but I finally understood that Marie was playing a part to keep herself safe. To keep her son safe. And me.

That was why I came back. That's what I'm seeking forgiveness for. For all those years when I didn't understand.

But what if I'm wrong again? What if she's not playing? What if living with Dad has just taken away her mind?

My tongue is thick with thirst and confusion. "Does Robbie know?"

"No."

"Does Dad?"

"You think she'd still be walking around loose if he did?"

No. Of course not. Dad does not allow for flaws in the fabric of his life. If things around him aren't perfect, something will be done to bring them into line. The old county asylum he threatened me with was closed down years ago. But I'll bet there's a whole string of doctors at the new medical center willing to sign off on the form saying Marie is a danger to herself and others so Dad can commit her. He's probably already wined them and dined them and whispered his concerns about his poor daughter. Setting up the story of his tragic, beloved family in case he needs it.

Just like he did when it was his poor sister-in-law.

And his poor wife.

I don't want to see the expression on David's face as he looks down at me. "You want to kick over the anthill, Geraldine, I can't stop you, but I sure as hell am not going to help."

He leaves me there, but I do not watch him walk away.

Marie. I missed it. Jesus H. Christ. Robbie. I missed it.

What else have I missed?

2.

The lake is still here, and it still doesn't ask any questions. I strip down and step into the water up to my ankles.

GOD! That is COLD!

It shocks every nerve to life, and despite everything, I laugh. This is real. The water laps at the tops of the straight, white scars on the inside of my pale calves. I'm up to my knees, then my waist and my breasts. I duck my head under and toss my hair back. I throw myself forward and I start swimming. Cold washes like a blessing over the cuts and bruises on my face.

I am crazy. Marie is crazy. I am frightened. Marie is terrifying. I am bad. I am lonely. I am doing awful, terrible selfish things to people who have never hurt me. I am breaking open my fragile sister because she has asked me to, and because inside, I hope to find my forgiveness.

The water doesn't care.

At last, when my lungs are gasping, I roll over onto my back and float and spread my arms and legs out starfish style. My body is my own. Nothing can touch me here. I am clean and cold, and I am strong.

I roll over onto my belly and start swimming toward shore. The sand seems farther away than I remembered, and the cold is starting to hurt, but I wash up eventually, clumsy and heavy, struggling through the breakers.

There's somebody there. My eyes are full of lake and I can't see clearly. It's a dark, blurred human shape. A man, I think.

The silhouette takes a cigarette from its mouth and tosses it into the sand. I shove my hair back and knuckle the water out of my eyes.

It's not David. It's a ghost. Or a dream.

Because it cannot really be Tyler standing here.

3.

No. Impossible. Tyler Prescott is in Chicago. He is not here, grinning at me, handing me a towel from the trunk of my Outback. I never did remember to make him give me back his spare key.

I'm going to kill him.

"What the hell?" I say.

"I wanted to see you," he answers.

"How'd you even find me?"

"It's a small town. I asked at the gas station." He's from a small town, too, so he knows how it works. You find the oldest place. That's where the locals are sure to be. You talk about the weather and the roads to establish you're an okay guy. Then you get around to asking the real question.

"Then, I got lost," he said. "But I saw your car on the shoulder. You told me about how you guys used to go swimming." Tyler steps toward me. His fingertips trace my cold cheek, outlining my bruises. "This looks bad."

I am going to fucking kill him and ship his lifeless corpse back to Northwestern with a note attached saying they shouldn't let their little boy lecturers out after dark.

I'm going to break down crying.

I'm going to do something, anything, other than what it is I am doing, which is standing here, dripping wet in my bra and bicycle shorts letting him touch me.

"I told you to stay away."

"Yep. I am a bad, bad, stalker-style boyfriend. And there's nothing cute or appropriate about any of this."

His fingers gently brush my stringy wet hair back from my forehead so he can see the cut there.

No one was ever gentle with me. Not my other lovers, not my family. Only this man. This is what undoes me, every time. I know how to fight back against so many kinds of cruelty. Gentleness is beyond me.

The goose pimples come out so fast they hurt. Memories come just as fast. Laughing and dancing and walking together with Tyler under the glare of the lights on the Vegas strip. Hiking through the woods and laughing about wolves and Red Riding Hood and finding a meadow carpeted with wild strawberries.

Waking up in a tangle of sheets and pillows. The ache that comes from wishing this didn't have to end. The surprise in finding that maybe it doesn't.

"You should dry off." Tyler touches the corner of my mouth. "You're turning kind of blue."

"You are not the boss of me."

He grins, that stupid, gorgeous grin that makes him look about seventeen. "Want me to wait by the car?"

"Yes."

"Okay."

And as suddenly and as simply as he arrived, he leaves me alone on the beach with my heap of clothes and the towel he brought me.

Goddamn you for not giving me anything to fight against. Goddamn you for always being where I need you, not where I want you.

I towel myself off, trying to rub away goosebumps and need and failing. I pull my clothes on over my still-damp underwear. There is no way he's watching, because Tyler wouldn't do that, but I am not ready to be naked for him even at a distance.

Sure enough, when I climb over the guardrail, Tyler is leaning on the back of his antique blue station wagon, watching the pines, the crows, and the clouds. Not the beach. Not me.

He straightens up as I march past him to the Outback. "So, where are we going?"

"My house." It hits me that this is the first time I've said it like that out loud since I got back. My house.

"Great. You lead."

I will. And as soon as we're there, I'll remember what really brought me up here. I'll find the right words. Not the truth, just the right words.

Standing in the old house, I'll be able to send him away again.

4.

We pull into the parking area. I've got some flat-pack furniture from Walmart—a couple chairs and a table in the back of my car. Tyler carries boxes so my hands are free to wrestle with the door. We don't even talk about it. It just happens.

He leans the boxes against the living room wall and surveys my empty domain.

"Needs work," he says.

"It's got potential."

"Definite potential," he agrees. "Got anything to drink?"

I nod toward the kitchen. He finds the Diet Coke and the plastic bag with the cups and plates I pulled out of their box earlier today. He does not comment on the rum, or the snack trays.

It's getting warm in here. I wrestle the windows open. I'm going to have to get new screens.

Tyler pulls out his Swiss Army knife and starts slitting furniture boxes open.

I don't even bother telling him to stop.

We don't talk much. We don't need to. I don't want to. We wrestle with Allen wrenches and stupid directions, and by the time we're done, there are a couple of uncomfortable chairs and a lopsided table in the rapidly dimming living room. He pulls out a pack of cigarettes and a lighter. I glare at him and he shrugs and heads outside to blow smoke at the crows. While he's gone, I stand on one of the new chairs to screw a lightbulb into the overhead fixture.

Tyler comes back in with a handful of daisies. He fills one of the plastic cups with water and sets the flowers on the table.

"You're secretly gay," I say when he comes back in.

"Caught me. All that crazy-hot sex is an act." He sets the jelly jar on the table, sliding it back and forth a couple of times to find the least sloping spot. "What's in the other building out there?"

"That's the old store. We used to sell sandwiches and pie and stuff to the tourists."

Suddenly I'm remembering the dough under my hands, the smell of sugar and my hands sticky with juice. Fear comes with it. Fear that I will get it wrong. That I won't be able to get everything done in time to do my homework, in time to open up, because Mom is out cold in the bedroom.

"What's in there now?" Tyler's voice cuts through the memories.

"No idea. I haven't looked yet."

Tyler plucks a baby carrot out of the nearest snack tray and pops it into his mouth. As he chews, he leans his butt against the counter and stares thoughtfully out the kitchen window.

"Did you always do this to me?" I ask, and he just grins.

"How soon they forget."

"I'm not ready." For him or the store? Both. Neither. I don't know.

He points another baby carrot at me. "But what if it's Bluebeard?" he asks.

It takes me a minute to get the reference, but when I do, I stare at him. "You think there's a room full of dead women in there?"

He shrugs and crunches down on the carrot. "We're a long way out. Anything could happen. You should check."

I plan to tell him that I know what he's doing and I won't be goaded. The store is as empty as the house was. I don't need to look. But right then, my phone rings.

Saved by the bell.

"Hello?"

"Geraldine? Hello! It's me!"

I didn't recognize the number, but I certainly know the voice. "Aunt June! Hi."

Tyler has wandered over to the front door, chewing on yet another carrot. He squats down to get eye-to-eye with its recalcitrant lock. I can all but see thoughts of adjusted screws and WD-40 flitting through his head.

"I hope you don't mind," Aunt June is saying. "But I got your number from Marie. You are coming to dinner next week, Geraldine, and I'm not taking no for an answer."

Surprise yanks honesty from me. "Oh, Aunt June, not yet, okay? But soon. I promise."

"Oh, no. You are not leaving us dangling. How about Tuesday? Give us all time to recover from Martin's graduation party." Aunt June seems to have forgotten we're supposed to pretend it's Robbie's day.

"Okay, okay. Fine. I'll be there."

"Wonderful. I'll tell Mother. So looking forward to a catch up!"

Oh, I'll bet. Aunt June thrives on gossip. If our family drama was the French Revolution, she'd be in the front row with her knitting. We say good-bye and I stuff the phone back in my purse.

Tyler's opened the screwdriver blade on his knife and is scraping a layer of paint off something.

"Important?" Tyler blows away some paint fragments.

"My aunt. I've got a command performance at dinner with my grandmother."

Tyler straightens up. He folds the blades back down and clips the knife back onto his belt. "Am I invited?"

No. No you are not. You are leaving long before then. You are not getting anywhere near that house, those women, this family, and...

I can't possibly say that.

"Ty...you don't want to do this. It's going to be an emeritus faculty wives' lunch on steroids. All the good china and lace-edged napkins and mini quiches on a silver tray and a maid in uniform."

"Should I wear a sport coat?"

"Did you bring one?"

He shrugs. "I didn't know what I was going to run into. Be prepared." He raises three fingers in the Boy Scout salute.

I take a deep breath, inhaling sweat and the evening breeze. My skin is prickling, my nerves are all singing. I have only felt this way once before, the moment David dragged me out of the lake and I realized that I was going to live, whether I wanted to or not. "Tyler?"

"Hmm?"

"I'm sorry," I tell him.

He closes his hand around mine, wraps his warmth around my chill. And that's all it takes.

His mouth is hot against mine. His beard rasps against my cuts. He drags me to him, digging his hands under my shirt and up my sides, kissing every part of me he can reach.

I missed you.

That's what I tell him with every touch. My hands are hard and heavy against his skin. I am clumsy. Starvation has made me that way.

We're up against the wall, I'm not entirely sure how. Now, we're forcing each other toward the bedroom.

The new roll-away is impossible, so we drag my sleeping bag down onto the floor. His jeans slide off just as easily. He is magnificent. I yank my shirt off over my head and we wrestle with my sports bra and my breasts slap down a split second before he takes them both in his hands. And I throw back my head and groan in welcome for his touch, his mouth, his raw sound of delight.

He is laughing. Vindicated. Delighted. He rolls me over, kissing me deep and hot, ready to give me everything I want. For him it is celebration. For me…I don't know, and I don't care. I want him. I want this—heat and scent and friction. This filling of my straining, empty body.

I want him to absorb the understanding of me through his skin, slick with our sweat. He needs to know all I have done and all I am about to do. I want this act to serve as my confession.

I want to never leave him.

I swear someone is watching us—some ghost, some fear—just out of sight. And I do. Not. Care. I'm screaming—*I love you!*—and I hear all the crows cawing in outrage outside the window. It makes me laugh and press him harder against me, and he's laughing too and shouting because he's never been able to keep quiet and that only makes it better.

We are together. Nothing else is needed.

If only for now.

There are not many stories in the Grimm canon featuring sisters who love each other. In fact, there are just two. The lesser known is "Snow-White and Rose-Red." Snow White and Rose Red are full siblings. They have a stable home and a loving relationship not only with each other but with their mother, and they watch each other's backs. They also invite a bear into their home and it all comes out okay. No mutilations, no death, and the only transformation is of the bear into a charming prince.

That is the power of sisterhood.
—Out of the Woods: Musings on Fairy Tales in the Real World,
Dr. Geraldine Monroe

GERALDINE, FIFTEEN YEARS OLD
A QUARTER MILE FROM STACEY B'S

1.

This is stupid.

The wind blew hard, driving the snow into Geraldine's watering eyes as she trudged along the side of the road. These weren't any fluffy feathery flakes drifting on the gentle breeze. These were tiny, stinging needles that felt like they were tearing her cheeks where the skin was exposed above her scarf.

I'm stupid.

But she'd promised Becca Mayor she could bring some primo shit to the party. The fact that Ken had offered to buy some off her didn't hurt, either. But it didn't make wading through a blizzard at twenty-fucking-below any easier.

It wasn't as dark as it could have been. The gray clouds and the white snow gave the night an ice-cold sheen. The pale shadows stretched across the silver ground.

Geraldine hit the drainpipe where M-131 crossed the gully and she stepped off the shoulder into the woods. She stumbled through the drifts, slipping on the hidden leaves. She shouldn't have promised. She shouldn't have bragged. What the hell did she need to go sharing her stash with Becca Mayor for? It wasn't like Becca didn't have her own fucking weed. She'd moved her stash to the old root cellar about a month ago. Keeping it in the house was starting to feel dangerous. Her sister had been acting weird lately. Marie said everything was fine, but Marie always said that. Maybe there was just a problem with David. Probably they wouldn't last much longer. Marie couldn't bring herself to tell Dad she had a boyfriend, and if Dad found out on his own, he'd totally and completely lose his shit and then they'd all pay for it.

Geraldine shuddered and kept moving.

The root cellar wasn't really a cellar. It was a hut kind of thing built from fieldstone, a leftover from when somebody'd tried to farm up here. There was a real cellar hole, and Geraldine hoped like hell she didn't miss her footing in the dark and fall into it.

Shit. Geraldine wiped her mittened hand across her stinging eyes, gritted her teeth, and slogged forward.

The cold was sinking deeper in, despite her parka and scarf and two layers of socks.

Just grab the stuff and go.

She could see the cellar now, a solid lump of black in the middle of the gray and silver world. But as Geraldine pulled herself from tree to tree, she saw a deeper black inside. An extra shadow.

It moved.

Her heart blocked her throat shut.

Cool it, G. Don't be such a freakin' baby.

Because it was just a stray dog, or maybe a coyote, or some big-ass raccoon. Could be a bear.

Shit, I hope it's not a bear.

"Shoo!" she shouted. "Go on! Get away from my shit!"

The thing shifted again. Whatever it was, it wasn't moving like an animal. What if it was somebody who was lost?

"Hey? Hello?" Geraldine stumped up to the doorway, shivering and squinting, and peered inside.

The shadow moaned and huddled closer to the filthy stones.

Oh my God.

Oh, no, no, NO!

It was Marie.

The poor child was now all alone in the great forest, and she was so afraid that she just looked at all the leaves on the trees and did not know what to do. Then she began to run.
—"Little Snow-White" from *Kinder und Hausmärchen* Vol. 1, Jacob and Wilhelm Grimm, 1812

MARIE, PRESENT DAY
M-131

1.

It is dark on the road. I have been driving for a very long time.

I must calm down. I must think. It's a test. A test. When doing something as momentous as remaking family, one must expect to be tested to the absolute limit.

I have done so many things wrong today. I handled Walt entirely the wrong way. I did the same with Robbie.

Then I went to see Geraldine. I should have gone back to talk to Walt. I know that. But I was weak. I didn't think I could be who I needed to with Walt. Instead, I wanted to try to take comfort in the fact that I had done one thing right so far. I had brought my sister home.

And I saw...and I heard...

I love you!

I cannot be angry. If I am angry, Geraldine will leave again. She might not even stay long enough to finish what we've begun.

I love you!

I am sick. I am filthy. I am a stranger in my own skin driving through the dark, heading back to the Rose House.

A blur crosses the dark road. I swerve and slam on the brakes and I'm in the ditch. The car stalls and I'm staring at the dark slope of the tree-covered hill, hearing the deer crash away through the underbrush.

I bow my head and slam my bandaged hand on the steering wheel, and slowly, for the first time in years, I start to cry.

Shame crawls through every inch of me. The mask that is my best self is shattered. This is what it hides. This scarred, filthy, useless, creature wailing alone in the dark. I thought she was gone. I thought I burned her up and scattered the ashes.

But, there is one thing left in that useless, discarded soul.

Hate.

That hatred burns inside me now—hotter than anger, stronger than fear. Hate is the last resort, but it did not fail me years ago, and it does not fail me now. Love would be better. I love so much. But love hurts and it's slow. I do not have time to wait for love to do its work.

But then, I lift my head. Because I realize what this is. It's obvious. This is Geraldine's rebellion. She's picked up a man somewhere—at Charlie's Roadhouse, at the marina, in a parking lot.

This is her way of taking control. And really, it's a good sign.

It means Geraldine feels home—me, us—pulling on her. That frightens her, so she's lashing out. Doing something naughty. Saying (screaming) to some stranger the one thing she has never said to me.

I love you! Tears threaten again, but this time I am able to push them easily away. I smooth my hair back with both hands. I am above the chaos and thinking clearly.

I have to do better for her. I will soothe her fears, ease her worries, draw her in. I will hold her here until she can hold herself.

I start the car and work the gears to rock it back and forth until I'm level on the shoulder, and then on the road. I am myself again. My storm is passed. The test is passed. All is right again.

At least for now.

2.

I've had a bad morning.

It's nothing to worry about. We all wake up on the wrong side of the bed on occasion, and that's what's happened to me. Just a little distracted. After that little bit of bad timing with Geraldine yesterday, it would be surprising if I wasn't a bit rattled.

After the little incident last night, I have done my best to maintain my routine. I came home and changed and lay down in my bed. I dressed with all my usual care. My makeup is as flawless as my clumsy, bandaged hand can manage. As I take care of the rest of my routine, I feel no movement beneath the chill. I sense no shift in the air or the walls.

I make a big breakfast. This is for Robbie. I feel a need to make up a little for dragging him away from his friends yesterday. I know he feels the house is on edge and it's getting to him. Robbie has always been very sensitive, and events are moving very quickly. I need to find a way to slow them down again. To keep the hardest of the truths from revealing themselves until after he has left for college.

By the time my son clumps down the stairs, I have a stack of French toast on the kitchen island beside a platter of bacon. There's milk and orange juice as well, along with coffee for me, of course, and for Dad when he comes down.

"What's this?" Robbie blinks at the platters of food.

"Breakfast. I'm not going to have many more opportunities to spoil you, so I didn't want to miss the chance."

I expect at least a show of gratitude. What I get is a flicker of suspicion. But, he does plop himself down on the high stool and fork over three slices of toast in one swift motion. I do not chastise. I pour myself a cup of coffee.

"I'm finalizing party plans today. I'm probably going to need you to run some errands, so I want you to stick close to home."

My son pauses in mid-chew. "I was gonna…"

"This is your party, Robbie. You need to take some responsibility."

As soon as the words are out of my mouth, I realize I have made a mistake. Robbie swallows his mouthful in a single lump.

"How is this my party? It wasn't even my *idea*." He is shouting in a whisper. Robbie is an expert in this. He learned, as we all learned, that whatever the crisis, we cannot disturb my father. Geraldine and I used to do the same thing. "I told you I don't want this, like, a hundred times. Did you even listen?"

"And I understand it's hard for you to see why you have to make room for your grandfather's business associates on your big day…"

"It is not *my* big day! Can't you stop pretending for even one second?"

He's saying something else. I sense it under the words. He's desperate for me to hear and understand. But I can't. I want to. I mean to.

I can't.

Before I can summon some kind of appropriate answer, we are interrupted by the sound of footfalls on the main stairs.

"Good morning, everybody!" Dad cruises into the kitchen. He's in his jacket and tie. There are several important meetings today. It's giving him extra energy. "Have you got my coffee, Marie?"

"Yes, of course." I reach for the pot, but Robbie beats me to it.

"Hey, Grandad, let me get that for you," he says and pours out a fresh cup.

Dad stares at him. His eyes slide to me.

Robbie pushes the cup across the counter, right up to the edge.

"Anything else you need, Granddad? You should try some of Mom's French toast. It's terrific!"

Dad presses the lid onto his travel mug. He is watching me the whole time. "That's very thoughtful of you, Rob. But I'm already running late."

"Gee. Can't have that. I'm not blocking you in or anything am I?"

"No, I don't think so."

"Well then, you'd better get going. See you tonight, Granddad!"

Robbie stands there, beaming. I can see all his teeth. Dad nods at us both and takes himself, his cup, and his briefcase out through the door to the garage.

As soon as the door closes, I round on my son.

"Robin James Pendarves, I don't know what you think you're doing…"

But Robin just blinks and the scold dries up inside me. "Just making sure Granddad's got everything his way. Isn't that what we're all here for?"

"It's not like that, Robbie, I promise…"

But I cannot finish. Because he's facing me fully, and for the very first time, I see how much my son looks like his grandfather.

The floor heaves violently beneath my feet. I clutch the counter so I don't fall.

"Please," I whisper. "Just be home tonight. That's all I'm asking."

He does not hear my panic. Instead, he scowls at his plate. I am relieved, because at least he looks like himself again.

"Please," I say again. I am begging my child. I should not. I am his mother. I am the one who shields him. It is what I have always done. It is what every sacrifice has been for. Just like I sacrificed for Geraldine.

Please hear me. I just need a little more time. That's all. It will all be over soon.

Robbie pushes back from the counter and our eyes meet once more. There it is. His grandfather inside him.

Robbie turns and walks away. I stay where I am until I hear the garage door, and the car engine. Then—slowly, deliberately—I turn and walk to the sink, lean over, and vomit.

3.

"Oh, Ms. Monroe!" Bethany looks up startled and shoves her phone into her drawer as soon as I walk in. "I wasn't sure you'd be in today!"

I suppress my impatience. I'm going to have to talk to her, as soon as there's time. Once I have calmed down.

"Mr. Pendarves called." Bethany peels a sticky note off the side of her monitor and hands it to me.

The message is brief:

Please Call. Important.

And just like that I've forgotten my plans to talk with Walt, and Carla, and all the other things I meant to do in my father's office before he gets here. I hurry into my own office and let the door swing shut behind me.

I have David's number on speed dial.

"It's me," I say as soon as he answers. "Is something wrong?" *Is it Robbie?*

"No, no, everything's fine. It's just, I wanted...I was hoping we could talk."

I'm glad I'm sitting down. Relief has robbed me of all my strength, and the better part of my diplomacy. "It's not a good time, David."

"Yeah, I guess not, but, look, can we just...please?"

No. No we can't just "please." I have too much to do.

But I cannot turn David away. I need him. I have never stopped needing him. The dream of being together again with David has driven my plans, almost as much as Geraldine. When this is done, we will all three come together as a true family. We will share a real home where nothing is painted or plastered over, and no one has to pretend not to see what is really happening.

But there is so much work to do before that happens, and I am so tired.

"I'm sorry, David," I tell him. "It's just been one of those mornings. What did you want to talk about?"

"Marie...this would really be better in person, but...I've been talking to Geraldine."

I suck in a deep breath. I am ready for this, of course I am. After all, I'm the one who sent Geraldine to David. That was always part of the plan. I cannot refuse to hear the result.

"Well, David, now you have to tell me what's happening, or I'll just spend the entire morning worrying."

"Geraldine said something might be up with Martin."

"Yes." I manage a regretful sigh. "She...well, some money went missing and Geraldine has worked up an entire conspiracy theory about it." An idea occurs to me. "Did Walt tell you about their argument?"

This is a shot in the dark, but given how quickly things are moving, I should try to cover all possible bases.

"No. Haven't heard from Walt recently."

Good. Then I can manage that part, at least.

"But yeah," David's saying. "Geraldine told me about the money and what she suspects. I got worried, so I made a couple of phone calls."

"Who did you call?"

David's silence reaches out from the phone. I can feel its fingers sliding through my hair and digging into my scalp.

"David, please. Whatever it is—"

"Did Geraldine tell you she got fired?"

4.

Calm descends. It is complete and perfect. I can admire it from this place I seem to have been put, in the back of my own mind. The reflection of Marie, the Marie I put on every morning, is speaking now.

"I'm sorry, David," that Marie says. "You've made a mistake. Geraldine's on sabbatical."

She told me she could get the time. She told me it wouldn't be a problem.

"Yeah, I'd heard, but I know some guys who know some guys who work at Lillywell. Campus security and stuff. They put me onto somebody in the administration staff and..."

"That's quite the chain of somebodies." Marie gives a little laugh.

"It wasn't just a downsizing or like that." David's words have taken on an edge. This is bad. I try to open up, to be present and focused. But Marie from the mirror is blocking me. "People were hedging when they talked about it. So, I haven't found out exactly what happened yet, but I probably could if you wanted me to."

Marie from the mirror is making me smile. I have to get past her. I do not want her here. She is only supposed to be my mask. Why is she here now?

"She's using you, Marie," David says and for a moment I wonder if he's read my mind. He might have learned that trick from Dad when we lived together. "I didn't…I'm sorry. This isn't what I wanted to find out."

"Yes. I know. Thank you."

"I was trying to make sure things were okay. But I didn't…I don't want to see her hurt you again."

"Yes. Thank you."

There is another pause. "Marie? Are you even listening?"

Do you even listen? The memory of Robbie's accusation stabs through that other Marie.

"Yes, David. I'm listening." At last, I am wide open. I am in past and present all at once. I am aware of all the details, as if they were lake stones I cupped in my hands.

Geraldine and I swore from the beginning that we would speak only the truth to each other. We would not say anything that could be misunderstood or misinterpreted. Even when we were alone, we would speak our lines and wear our masks. Because we might have to detail our conversations to the police and the lawyers when everything was over and done with.

But if what David says is true, then Geraldine—my sister, whom I loved and missed and worked for and saved all this time—she has lied to me not one time, but two, and maybe more.

She said she would help me. She said she understood the plan and agreed it was the only way.

Did she lie about that, too?

"Do you want me to find out what happened?" David is asking.

"Let me do it," I tell him, and the words feel hollow. "But I promise I'll call you and tell you anything I learn."

David's silence tells me he does not think much of this answer. In response, I do the only thing I can. I change the subject. "David, have you seen Robbie today?"

"Not yet. Is something wrong?"

"No. I was just wondering."

"If I do see him, I'll make sure he calls."

"Thank you."

I hang up the phone. For a long time, I sit where I am, stock still.

You played the hero for her. You saved her life. You could have drowned, and you didn't care.

That was why I married you. Neither of you ever understood that. I didn't want you in spite of the fact you fucked my sister when she needed it. But because you did.

You saved Geraldine. You were supposed to save me, too.

Of course, that's just what he thinks he is doing. From his point of view, he's protecting me from Geraldine's predations. Because like everyone else, he knows I am helpless. They can all tell by the way I live—so careful and sheltered and fragile, always at someone else's command. I am obedient and therefore must be weak. Everybody knows that. I have spent years making sure of it.

That was why my plan was going to work. It uses what everybody knows.

Just like everybody knows I am helpless, everybody knows Geraldine is a troublemaker who hates her family. Everybody knows that if Geraldine got a whiff of wrongdoing in my father's business, she would immediately make it public.

Everybody knows my father has danced on the edge of legality before. Everybody fears that he might decide to do it again, especially those Monroes who are dependent on him. Because Dad's actions affect the businesses, the jobs, and the Monroe family trust.

So, all that needed to happen was to create a mismatch between the paper trail and the online accounts. Once that was ready, Geraldine could come back and make the right kind of noise. There would be visible attempts to make her go away, or discredit her, or both, but being Geraldine, she would just keep on making her noise.

I would watch, of course, and be horrified. I would try to smooth things over and, reluctantly, try to help discredit my sister's rumor-mongering. But instead of answers, I would find questions, and more worries.

Alarmed by this confluence of events, Walt—sturdy, reliable Walt—would eventually find the discrepancies. And the missing money. And my father would have no way to explain any of it.

And with that, the protected life that I have lived, the shelter I have known under my father's loving, patient gaze, would be stripped away under the landslide of a sordid small-town scandal. There would be nothing left for me to do but try to pick up the pieces and begin again. With my sister. With my husband. With my son.

Geraldine swore she would help. Geraldine agreed the time was right.

Geraldine owes me.

I have to find out if David is right.

5.

"Marie!" Lawrence Kappernick greets me at the door himself. Mrs. Lopez, his housekeeper, must be busy elsewhere. He takes my hands as I step across the threshold, and kisses me on both cheeks. Not air kisses, real kisses. It's something he's always done and I am used to it. "Lovely to see you, as always. Come in. Can I get you anything?"

"No, thank you. I'm fine." I telephoned Lawrence from my office. Even when I met him at the Cherry Tree, I had hoped I would not have to make use of him, but David's revelations left me with no choice. Lawrence has information I need, or, at the very least, he'll know how to get it.

Lawrence leads me to the lovely, open-pattern living area. I decorated this house, a favor to an old friend of my father's. I am perfectly comfortable in this place and with Lawrence's old-fashioned courtesies, like how he holds my hand as I sit in the chair he offers.

"Now." He scoots the vintage wing-backed chair I found for him on a buying trip down in Grand Rapids. "What can I do for you?"

I cross my ankles and fold my hands, letting him see how I am taking the time to collect myself.

"I'm afraid it's...it's a little delicate."

"I see."

"I wouldn't be here except, well, my father..."

"Marie." Lawrence lays his hand across both of mine and gives them a little shake. "I hope you know you can tell me anything."

I pat his hand so he knows I am grateful before I remove my hands to brush back my hair. "I'm going about this all the wrong way, I'm afraid. You see, it's not really about my father. It's about my sister."

"Oh, yes. I'd heard Geraldine was in town. On leave from her college, or something?"

"Yes. And I think I remember that you're on the board of trustees for the University of Michigan...?"

"That's right." His eyes narrow shrewdly. "I hope you're not going to ask me to find your sister a job?"

"Oh, no, no, it's nothing like that. I was just wondering if you might know...anyone at Lillywell."

The gentle paternity of Lawrence's manner shifts. "Marie, what's this really about?"

I have to phrase this correctly, but it's surprisingly hard for me to find the words. "Geraldine has been telling us that she was on sabbatical. But, well, there's a possibility, that wasn't quite true. My father...I...we're afraid there might be some serious trouble of some kind."

"I see."

"She's my sister," I whisper. "Despite everything. We want...we want to help, but we can't if we don't know what's going on." This is almost honesty, and it frightens me. What if I am showing him too much?

Lawrence smiles, beneficent and benign. "Now, now, Marie. I'm sure it's nothing. If she has been laid off, she probably just didn't want the bad news to get in the way of Robbie's graduation. Lecturer is hardly a secure job. It's not like being a tenured professor. Generally speaking, it's one of the first positions cut if a department has budget problems. But!" He reaches out to give my hand another quick pat. "If it'll make you and Martin feel better, I'll make some phone calls. See what I can find out."

"Thank you, Lawrence." I smile in slightly misty gratitude.

He pats my hand once more. This time he lets his fingers linger, just a little, before drawing them off slowly. It's a meaningless caress, the kind old men take when they think they've earned it.

"I really wish you'd call me Larry, Marie. We've known each other long enough, don't you think?"

"Larry," I agree, and I get to my feet.

"Already?" He struggles a little to rise with me. "I was hoping we could have a drink."

Now he's just being silly. It isn't even ten o'clock. "I'm sorry, my father's expecting me."

"Well, I guess I'll have to let you go then." He moves just a little closer. "Although it is with great reluctance."

Lawrence brushes my hair back from my collar, and leaves his hand on my shoulder.

"You've always been very special to me, Marie. I hope you know that."

I suppress my impatience. Men of my father's generation enjoy a little detour over the line now and again. There are tried and true methods for dealing with it. Usually, the best thing to do is make a joke of it. Gently, of course.

"Oh, dear, Larry." I sigh, as I take his hand and give it a squeeze before I let it go. "Don't you think I'm a bit old for you?"

He touches my cheek. "You've never looked a day over eighteen."

"Flatterer." I dip down to collect my purse and briefcase. "Thank you so much for being willing to look into things at Lillywell for me. I'm sure you're right and that it's all nothing."

He sighs as he steps back. "You know, Marie. I had hoped when you said you were coming here, because you needed me, it might be for…a little more."

It is time to end this. "Larry, you shouldn't tease a poor old lady like this. Now, I really do have a thousand things to take care of. It's our busy season, as I'm sure you know. We'll see you at my son's graduation party, won't we? Do tell Dottie I won't take no for an answer. And I do appreciate everything you're doing for me."

He takes my hand. "Well, I can see we'll just have to talk about that later, won't we?" He kisses my knuckles and smiles into my eyes.

I should be able to find an answer to this, but I cannot. I draw away and he lets me find my own way to the door. Behind me, I can feel his delight at the fact that he has disconcerted me. He thinks I am flustered, and flattered.

I cannot correct him.

Because of course this is my own fault. During all the years that I have been made to sit at the table with the women like Ashley Dickinson, I have also been made to sit in the rooms with their husbands and boyfriends. While they chatted with my father about their money and their possessions and how he can help them, I have come under their curious eyes and fleeting touches.

Men appreciate a gracious woman, my father has always told me. *It's not politically correct to say so, but it's true. I can count on you, right, Marie? You'll be my finishing touch, to put the deal over.*

I came here intending to use this fact for my own ends. And I have to accept the consequences.

I cannot be angry like this. This red-black anger like blood on the snow cannot be mine. I have to smile instead. I have to love and be patient and perfect and understanding of everybody. It's the only way.

I cannot be angry.

I cannot be.

If we're attempting a real critique of the Household Tales, we have to save at least some attention for the good sister. She knows at least as much as the wicked sister about their family circumstances. After all, she has suffered for them. One would hope, in those stories where she's not confined to a coffin and so on, she takes a moment to explain to the prince what he's getting himself into.

Unfortunately, that seldom proves to be the case. Being good, in the world of the household story, does not necessarily include being honest.
—Out of the Woods: Musings on Fairy Tales in the Real World,
Dr. Geraldine Monroe

GERALDINE, PRESENT DAY
STACEY B'S SANDWICHES AND STUFF

1.

The third time I wake up, it's nearly evening. Long, amber sunbeams slant across the floorboards and the open sleeping bag where we're lying. Tyler's sprawled out, half on the sleeping bag, half on the floor. His face, and the rest of him, is slack with sleep. He snores.

What am I going to do with you? My handsome prince. My would-be hero. My lover who has no place in this tortured story of mine.

I got my first book of fairy tales from Aunt Trish. Or, to be completely accurate, I stole it from her. It was one of the times I snuck up to the Rose House to see her, back when she was still alive and we were both pretending she could keep the place from falling down around her ears. Or rather, I should say, all three of us were, because Uncle Pete was there too, sometimes. Doing what he could.

The great room was a library then. Old Addison had painted

looming pine trees and black crows between the built-in bookshelves.

"In the pines, in the pines, where the sun never shines," Aunt Trish would whisper in my ear. "And I shiver as the wind blows cold."

And I did shiver, but I loved it, too. It was one of our secrets.

The books themselves were rotting, like the house and Aunt Trish. Some of the shelves had given way, making their contents slide down to one end. But I'd go in there anyway, and trace the outlines on the boarded-up rose window with my fingers. Sometimes I'd try to organize the books, but half the time they just fell apart in my hands, so, eventually, I stopped trying.

I don't even know why I took the fairy tales. I think I was afraid Aunt Trish was going to fall apart, too, and wanted something to hold on to. If she ever even noticed, she never said a word.

But I did take it, and I read it until the pages broke away from the spine. These were the unexpurgated tales, the ones where murdered boys get fed to their fathers, and Cinderella lets her birds peck her sisters' eyes out, and Snow White is saved because the prince's servant drops her coffin and jolts the apple slice out of her throat.

All those strange, convoluted stories of death and magic and blood and guts made instant, perfect, sense to me. I knew, if I could just dig down far enough, I'd find myself there.

When I finally worked, cajoled, and cheated my way into the folklore program at Lillywell, I met earnest, intellectual kids who had grown up with Disney and all the other sanitized versions of the Grimm canon. They talked about feminist interpretations and patriarchal iconography. They didn't understand what the stories *said*.

Tyler understands. And that's the problem. He understands about monsters and castles, and what it's like to have to search for some way to explain the insides of your mind to yourself.

But Tyler is still from the outside world. I can't let Outside into this house. Outside asks stupid questions, like, why doesn't she just *leave*? I cannot, no matter how hard I've tried, make Outside understand what it is to be us.

I climb stiffly to my feet and fish my panties and flannel shirt out of our pile of clothing. Minimally dressed, I tiptoe into the decimated kitchen.

So far, Tyler and I have devoured two of the party trays Dad brought, and even cracked open the rum. I ignore the sweating remains of unrefrigerated snack food. Instead, I lean my back against the wall and fold my arms.

What am I going to do?

Because it is becoming increasingly clear I am not going to do the smart thing and send Tyler away.

It's not a big deal. He's got a job. He can't stay here for that long. I'll just tell him . . . I'll just tell him . . .

The lie won't form. Not even in the privacy of my own mind. But there is no way I can keep my promises to Marie and keep Tyler in my life at the same time.

Maybe if I hadn't lost my job, it would be different. I could play my part and I could leave.

That was the original plan. My original plan anyway, no matter what I told Marie. But now . . . but now . . .

Now, what?

From here, I can see the old store. Its back porch is listing visibly. Cornflowers, lamb's tongue, and one determined sumac sapling poke green fingers up between the slats. A goldfinch lands on the rusted gutter, dips its beak for a quick drink, and flies off again. My fingers rake against the counter and come up against the house keys. I tuck my finger into the ring and twirl them restlessly.

And stop. And stare.

I'm still staring when I hear footsteps pad against the floorboards. Tyler rounds the corner. He's dressed, mostly. He's also carrying my jeans.

"I brought you pants."

"That's a switch."

"I like to keep you on your toes."

I put the keys down and pull my jeans on. He watches, lovingly, hungrily. It's exasperating. It's exhilarating.

He waits until I'm all zipped and buttoned to talk again. "You look like you got some bad news."

"No. Well, yes. No. I don't know."

"What don't you know?"

Where do I even start? "My sister, Marie, she's been looking after the house. She said there was some trouble, kids and drugs or something, and she had the locks changed." I rattle the key ring at him. "She gave me the keys for the house, but not for the store."

"Maybe she just forgot."

"That is not the kind of thing Marie forgets. She didn't want me in there."

"Why?"

"That's what I want to know." I stare at the store again. "I mean, there shouldn't be anything left in there."

Curiosity itches hard. Curiosity, and that old craving, not the one that screams for the junk and the pills. The one that screams for me to break something, just to show that I can.

Maybe they're the same thing.

This is me just wasting time. It's not like it's important. Except it is. Because it's a detail, and Marie does not forget details.

It's important because of what David told me down by the beach. I do not want to believe it, but it won't go away.

Tyler wraps his arms around me from behind and rests his chin on my shoulder. His beard scrapes my cheek. "Tell you what. We can either go try to get inside, or we can drink rum and Diet Coke, and finally have that meaningful conversation about how you and I move forward from here."

There is only one answer to that.

"Get your shoes on."

2.

"You got a jimmy in the car?"

"What, you don't?"

Ty is back in less time than it takes me to drag the rusted chair over to the store window. I choose a back one, so we can't be seen from the road. This really isn't breaking and entering because the store is my property, but old habits die hard.

This window still has a screen, but that's easy to take down from this side, if you know the trick. The glass is so filthy it's impossible to see inside. Ty passes me the jimmy. It's nothing but a thin strip of metal with a hooked end. He steadies the chair and I slide it between the window halves and wriggle until I feel the latch snap back.

I hand Tyler the jimmy. We grin at each other. Tyler puts his finger to his lips. I cannot believe I am doing this. I cannot believe I am enjoying this.

No, actually, I can.

I heave the window open, scramble through, and drop onto the other side. Tyler is right behind me.

"Well," he says as he surveys the dim space. "Something of an anticlimax."

It takes me a long time to answer. I knew it'd be hard standing inside the store, just like it was walking into the house. But the blow catches me dead center anyway.

Like the house, the store has been stripped down to its bones. Empty shelves—too heavy or awkward to move, I guess—line the walls and stretch down the center of the single long room. A couple of rusted wire racks stand sentry by the counter where the register used to be.

God, I used to love this place. Before I learned to hate it. Before I learned how to use it.

When I loved it, I'd stand on cases of beer or Coke to help smear peanut butter and grape jelly onto slices of white bread. Me and Mom would sing along to the classic rock radio station. Sometimes, she'd grab me around the waist and we'd dance up and down the aisles.

When I hated it, I sliced pieces of apple pie and thought about slicing my father's throat with the same knife. That was when every day started with checking to see if Mom was too hung over to open up. Which meant being late to school again, or skipping altogether. The people would come in for their sandwiches and whatever and they'd say, "Shouldn't you be in school?"

"We've got a day off," I'd say back, and they'd move on to asking about what grade I was in and did we have any of those hand-warmer things and could I get down another pack of cigarettes?

Not that all that time on my own wasn't educational. For instance, I learned to fake the inventory so no one would notice how much stuff was going missing, especially the beer. By the time high school hit, I supplied pretty much every party in Whitestone, even before I started a sideline in low-grade weed.

I also learned how to shortchange people and pocket the extra cash, along with anything else I could get my sticky little fingers on. More than a few driver's licenses and credit cards went missing from tourists when I was behind the counter. The same kids I supplied with beer were willing to pay some pretty decent money for those.

That was why when Dad tried to hand me that wad of cash to leave town for good, I was able to tear it up and scatter the little green pieces all over his study floor, and leave anyway.

Tyler prowls the edges of the long room, rattling windows and going up on his toes to try to adjust the cover over one of the fluorescent lights. "So, what was the big deal in here again?"

"No idea." I drift behind the prep counter to the register counter and slide the drawer open. It's empty: of cash, of pill bottles, of everything except my jumble of memories. "Maybe she thought I'd give into an uncontrollable fit of sandwich making."

"Sounds good. I'm hungry."

"There's a surprise." I roll my eyes.

I close the drawer. There's nothing here. Nothing at all. Time to move along. But I don't. I can't get past the fact of the missing key. I should wait and ask Marie. That'd be a perfectly normal thing for normal sisters to do.

Instead, I head for the door to the basement. That's locked, too. I rattle the knob a few times, and of course Tyler notices.

"Need the jimmy?"

"Nah. Credit card should do it."

Tyler extracts his wallet and hands one over.

"This is why you love me," he reminds me as I wriggle the card back and forth between the tongue and the threshold.

You have no idea. The tongue snaps back and the knob turns under my hand.

The stairwell is dark. I try the switch and the light snaps on down below.

I feel Tyler come up behind me. I expect him to start humming the *Twilight Zone* or *Jaws* theme or something, but thankfully he doesn't.

The cellar is much older than the building above. The floor is dirt, packed hard as cement. The walls are undressed fieldstone. The place smells of dirt and damp, mildew and skunk.

And it is full to its dark, dank gills.

Cardboard boxes and Rubbermaid tubs stand on wire shelves. Furniture has been wrapped in plastic sheeting and duct taped to the point of unrecognizability. Tiles are stacked beside plastic portfolios, and three-ring binders are shelved like library books.

"Smugglers' cave?" Tyler suggests. "Illegal PB and J?"

I don't bother to answer. I just reach down to one of the binders and flip it open.

It's a scrapbook. Carefully clipped articles and Polaroid photos have been pasted onto (I'm sure) acid-free paper.

I recognize them all. The grass and the clouds and the birds. The twining roses, the tall dark pines (*where the sun never shines,* whispers Aunt Trish from memory). And the bright-eyed crows perched above and around the chimney piece.

"It's the murals," I breathe.

"What murals?"

"All the rooms in Rose House used to be painted, by one of our ancestors. Addison Walters. He…my aunt said he was crazy and the family had him shut up in there."

"Was he? Crazy?"

"I don't know." I turn the pages. The photos make a kind of time-line. Marie must have taken some of these before Dad's first big re-model, because they're showing the ruin from when Aunt Trish lived alone there—the gouged-out patches, red and black obscenities painted with great slashing motions, the water stains and the clumsy attempts to "fix" the fairies and the songbirds.

I remember Aunt Trish, creeping around with her bucket of brushes. She talked to the fairies and the birds and the clouds. She begged them to be patient with her.

This time it will be okay, she told them. *This time for sure.*

Tyler whistles. "These are amazing. Where they aren't, like…" He draws his fingertips down a photo showing a beach scene made leprous where patches of paint have fallen away.

"Dad painted over them."

"What? You're kidding."

I shake my head. "He made Marie do it. I remember when I came home the first time and saw all those blank, white walls." I touch a close-up of a pair of piping plovers from the front room. "I felt like my skin had been scraped off."

Tyler pulls down a magazine sheathed in a plastic cover. *Michigan Country Home.* There's a picture of the Rose House on the cover. I put the binder back and pull down another magazine. *Home and Garden,* 1939. And another. *Gracious Living,* 1932.

All of them featuring the Rose House. And that's when I realize what my sister has done.

Dad made Marie dismantle the old house. I'm sure he watched while she dutifully stripped it of everything that would remind everybody of Patricia and any other Burnovich, including his wife. He gave good lit-tle Marie precise instructions on how to rework the past according to his exacting specifications. No detail would be left to chance.

And Marie obeyed, because she is the good daughter. But the good daughter gathered up all those bits and pieces. Just like she gathered up all her old photos that didn't fit in the life he envisioned. But this time, instead of sending things to me, she hid them down here. Because that is what Marie does. She puts the keys in a drawer, and she waits.

I'm standing on the brink of something in my own mind. My breath is harsh and heavy against my throat. Something is coming out of the dark to get me, but I can't tell what it is.

That's when I see the shoebox. It's different from the rest of the tidy, secure packaging on the rest of the shelves. It's battered, for one thing, and it looks old. Like the one full of photographs Marie sent to me. The seams at the corners of the lid are torn and mended with yellowing Scotch tape.

Don't.

Whatever's inside the box shifts as I pick it up. It smells like dust. The lid is held on with a rotting pink rubber band.

Stop. Don't. You don't want to know.

I carefully work the band off and I lift the lid.

Inside are two squat, heavy-bottomed tumblers, the kind used for basic, hard drinks—whiskey and soda, vodka on the rocks. They both have brown stains in the bottom, the ancient remains of whatever the last drink was.

And there's a bottle of pills. A big one. It's about half full of white tablets.

No.

I lift the bottle. The plastic is warm against my skin.

She didn't. Tell me she didn't.

I turn it over so I can read the label.

Stacey Jean Burnovich Diazepam 20 mg capsules. 1 capsule by mouth...

I go cold. Pain ripples through my bruises. Slowly, I put the pills back, close the box and return it to its shelf. I back away, like I think it's going to reach out and pull me back.

"Geraldine?" says Tyler.

I'm not listening. I'm running up the stairs. I'm slamming against the door, cursing and kicking until I can make my shaking hands work the lock and I can fall out into the fresh air.

Because those are Mom's pills. From her nightstand. Marie saved them. She tucked them away in a shoebox and hid them. Now I know what her note meant.

And I know who was supposed to be the one to die.

3.

"Geraldine?"

I make it as far as the stump of our old tree before I stop myself. I stand there, staring at the woods—where we went to live, where we went to hide, where Mom and Marie went to die. The wind feels like winter brushing across my skin. I can't stop shaking.

"Come on, Gerie. Talk to me."

I can't turn my head. I can't look at him.

"Don't…don't…"

Tyler sighs. There's a rustling and I hear his voice coming from somewhere around my knees.

"When I was a kid, every night after dinner, my dad would make us all line up in the living room. We were a quiver family, you know? There were seventeen of us, born to serve God and spread the Word. So, of course we had to be raised with strict discipline. He'd go down the row, oldest to youngest, and each one of us would have to confess all the sins we committed that day."

I don't answer.

"The one who he decided sinned the worst would get the beating. Right in front of the others."

I don't answer.

"My oldest sister, Angela, she started making things up. Just whatever popped into her head, as long as it was bad. I'm pretty sure she confessed to screwing the Pope by the end of it. So, she was the one who got it the worst. But she was doing it to try to save the little ones."

My throat loosens. "Did it work?"

"For a while. Then Pop figured it out and started beating the little kids anyway, to teach her a lesson."

"Shit."

"Yeah," he agrees.

"Is that supposed to make me feel better?"

"It's supposed to let you know you're not the only one with a massively fucked-up family."

Finally I am able to turn. He's sitting cross-legged on the grass. I kneel down beside him to wrap my arms around his shoulders, and press my face into the crook of his neck.

I don't know how long we sit like that, with my arms around his neck and his arms around my shoulders, but eventually, my knees start to ache and I have to let go.

"So," he says as I knuckle my dry eyes.

"So," I agree. "You hungry?"

His mouth twitches, and I hold my breath waiting to see if he's going to let me get away with changing the subject so drastically.

"Starved," he says at last.

"Have you ever had whitefish?"

"Isn't that grandpa food?"

"Shut your mouth, young man, and get in the car." I swat him on the shoulder as I heave myself to my feet.

I'm just buying time, and we both know it. Tyler's going along, because he knows every minute I let him stay will make it that much harder for me to break things off again. We have both, after all, been down this road before.

I tell myself it will be different this time. I do not let myself remember all the times and all the ways I have said that about other things, or how I have always, without exception, been wrong.

I just get us into the car, and drive up the hill.

4.

There's a line.

Bob's Fish Fry is a relic from my past. It's nothing but a white shack perched on top of a long, sandy slope. Inside, there're a couple of fryers and a flat top behind the counter. The only seating is the picnic tables on the dune. Bob's been burnt brown by a combination of sun and fry grease, and he works the whole show with the flourish of a stage magician.

This is not nouvelle cuisine. But that beer-battered fish was alive at eight this morning, and it's meaty and flaky and tastes like fresh water. The fries are hot enough that they burn your mouth. You can get a milkshake, or homemade root beer, or something God-awful from a can, like Pabst or Budweiser.

Tyler and I sit side by side so we can watch the sunset spreading melted gold over the lake. He puts catsup on everything, the Philistine. He also steals my fries, which is okay because I steal his. Around us, the other tables fill with locals and a few lifestylers who have ventured out from the brewpubs.

There are even people here who know me. Not family, but people I grew up around, some of whom I even liked. We chat, about our jobs, about friends, about Whitestone. Old jokes get revived, pictures of kids get brought up on phones, or even pulled out of wallets. I introduce Tyler. Everybody shakes hands. Nobody thinks it's weird I'm with a man half my age. Or if they do, they keep it hidden behind an impenetrable wall of small-town Midwest polite.

And for a moment, everything is normal. For a moment.

Then, I hear a familiar voice.

"Geraldine!"

Amber, one of my cousins via Aunt June, threads her way between the picnic tables and comes up next to me and Tyler. The wind whips her Monroe blond hair across her face. She keeps pushing it down, but it doesn't do any good.

"I thought I...oh, hello," she says as it sinks in that Tyler is not just near me, he's with me.

And here we go. "Ty, this is my cousin, Amber Hearst. Amber, this is Tyler Prescott."

Amber's eyes narrow suspiciously. Tyler ignores this and they shake hands.

"I didn't think this was your kind of place," I say to her.

"I saw your car."

I have got to get a new car. "So, what do you want?"

Amber eyes the picnic bench, and Tyler, and me. She finally decides we're probably not that contagious, and sits.

"I just...I wanted to let you know you can count on me."

"For what?"

She shrugs, trying to look casual, but she can't stop shifting her gaze toward Tyler. I'm about ten seconds from saying he's with me and she better keep her hands to herself, although this probably wouldn't do any of us any good.

"If you need help with your book. Or whatever. I just wanted to let you know, I'm here."

Whatever it is she wants to say, she really does not want to talk in front of my boyfriend. I am not in the mood to humor her. "Seriously? You came all the way up here and that's it?"

She turns fully toward me. Our eyes meet and I can see it. Amber has never managed to break free on her own. She thinks I'm going to blow things up, and she wants to be there when I light the fuse.

The realization twists my guts. I want to sneer at her, full of righteous contempt, but I don't. I also can't let her get any closer, because I know her too well. She cannot wait. She cannot plan. Amber just reacts to whatever comes her way.

She is not like Marie.

"Thanks for the offer," I tell her. "Maybe we can talk on Tuesday. Did your mom tell you she and Grandma have invited us to dinner? Should be a hoot, don't you think?"

Amber does not like this answer. Her eyes crinkle, even though her thoroughly Botoxed brow stays flat and smooth. "You know, Geraldine, you might want to consider treating the rest of us like something besides deaf, dumb, and blind assholes."

"Why?" I ask, and try not to notice Tyler wince.

"Because then I might be motivated to tell you that I was at the Marina Club this morning, and Uncle Martin was there with a bunch of his buddies, schmoozing it up. I heard your name get mentioned. And Lillywell."

I keep my face neutral, but it's not easy. I do not have chemical assistance. "What did they say?"

"Gosh, you know, I just plain couldn't tell, 'cause I'm a deaf, dumb, and blind asshole." She swings her legs back over the bench and stands. "Have a nice life. You, too, whoever you are."

"Shit." I struggle to my feet and run after her. "Amber. Wait."

For a moment, I think she's going to keep ignoring me, but, thankfully, she's too angry for that. We only make it to the edge of the parking area before she rounds on me.

"You know something? You're just as bad as your sister. Neither one of you can see past the ends of your own noses."

"Has Marie said something to you?"

"If she had, do you think I'd be here trying to beat it out of you over the whitefish?" Amber snaps. "By the *way*, who's your friend really?"

I almost say "no one," but I catch myself just in time. Not soon enough to keep my skin from crawling that I even thought it.

Amber shakes her head. "You see, this is the problem. The two of you think you're different. Better. Well, in case you hadn't noticed, *cousin*, you're right back where you started from, just like I am. And pretty soon, you'll be crawling to Daddy with your tail between your legs asking for your handout. Just. Like. Me."

She's wrong, but I can't tell her that. I can't even really get angry at her for being so wrong, no matter how much I want to. Because we are different, me and Marie. We're the ones who lived in that house. The others don't know, and what they do find out, they don't believe. Dad spent years making sure of that.

That little reminder stings me into action.

"Look, Amber, I'm sorry." I mean it, too, even if I'm having to force it out through gritted teeth. "You're right. There is something going on, and it's big. But I haven't got the proof yet."

She leans in. There's booze on her breath, which shouldn't be a surprise, but it is predictable enough to be disappointing. "What are we talking about?"

"Has anybody checked the trust's books lately?" I ask.

"You think Uncle Martin's been messing with the *trust*?"

I hesitate. "That's what I'm trying to find out."

Amber's eyes flicker toward Tyler's table, and away again.

"Do you want me to ask around?" she says. "Walt might talk to me."

Never in a million years. But I smile anyway. "Would you?"

She nods. "Count on it."

It's almost too easy. Poor Amber. It's not her fault she's like this. We're all victims, of the money and the family and our own endless, human flaws. It's left her broken, just like the rest of us.

I wish I were better than this, but I'm not.

"Listen, Geraldine, you should know, there's a council of war happening up at the Rose House right now." She lowers her voice to a stage whisper. "Uncle Martin, Grandma, Marie. I think Mom's there, too, but probably she's just getting sloshed while everybody else huddles about the Geraldine problem."

Already? Electric excitement slides through my veins. *I thought it would take at least another week before they got that worried.*

I suddenly become acutely aware of Tyler sitting patiently back at the table, and that excitement turns to ice. "Thanks, Amber," I whisper.

She touches my shoulder sympathetically. "Good luck," she says. "See you at the graduation party."

She leaves, and I slowly return to my spot next to Tyler.

He pushes my milkshake cup toward me. "So, that's your family?"

"In a nutshell." I twirl the straw, and suck some vanilla shake off the end.

"Explains a lot." Tyler bites into another dripping french fry.

"Yeah, it really does."

"So. Are you going to tell any of them about...what happened? With Lillywell?"

No. I'm not. Because that's when you'll have to leave. And I'm going to hang on to you until the very last second, and then I'm going to make good on my promises to Marie. And never see you again. Never leave here again. Finally pay all my debts, take all my punishments.

Except even as I think that, I feel the rebellion rise. Or maybe it's desperation. Maybe that's all it ever was. The drugs and the cutting and the petty crime, it was all just a way to try to stay alive in the face of everything that I thought was trying to kill me. And Marie.

Marie, who only tried to run once. Who spent the rest of her life hiding. Hiding herself. Hiding our past in a hole in the ground. Hiding those pills inside a box inside a heart, inside an egg, inside a duck, inside a well, inside a forest, inside a story that someone else made up about us all three, four, five hundred years ago.

All the time planning. All the time waiting. All the time slowly stewing in her own hate.

Just like the rest of us.

I face Tyler. "Ty...Wanna meet my family?"

He drags the end of his last french fry thoughtfully through a catsup blob. "You are talking about the family in the big house on the hill?"

"Yes. Them."

"The ones we previously planned to meet at the formal dinner, once I'd had a chance to comb my hair and put on my good jacket?"

"Yes."

The sunset catches in Tyler's brown eyes, and I'm reminded that for all his good-natured Mr. Fix-It vibe, I'm not the only one here who likes to break things.

"Let's go."

5.

We gather up the wrappers and pop the last of the fries into our mouths. Tyler dumps everything in the dented trash can while I start the car.

"Do we have a plan?" he asks as I ease us onto the highway.

"No," I tell him.

"Well, yee-haw!" He mimes settling a cowboy hat back on his head.

I laugh because I can't help it. Because being reckless and angry still comes more easily to me than anything else.

Because I'm saving myself and betraying Marie, again. And if I stop to think about it, I'll lose my nerve.

We're rounding the bend when I catch the red gleam of a taillight. I swear and swerve, and as I do, I see somebody's put their car into the ditch.

"Stop, Gerie!" says Tyler. "Somebody's hurt back there."

I brake hard and yank the wheel so we bump onto the shoulder. Ty's got his seat belt off and the door open before the car is fully stopped. I jump out as quickly as I can behind him, cell phone in hand, cursing myself for having left the first-aid kit back at the old house.

Ty sprints along the shoulder and kneels beside the figure on the slope. I'm trying to dial 911 on my phone and run at the same time, so it takes me a minute to see clearly.

But when I do, I forget the phone and just run like my life depended on it.

Because that skinny young man on the edge of the ditch is Robbie.

The girls never get to take back their own castle. Don't know why I thought my story would be any different.
—Dr. Geraldine Monroe (margin notes)

GERALDINE, FIFTEEN YEARS OLD
THE ROSE HOUSE

1.

"Goddamn! Goddamn!"

Aunt Trish reeled backward and Geraldine all but fell into the ancient kitchen, dragging Marie with her. Their aunt put out her withered arms to catch them but failed, and the sisters crashed to the floor. The freezing wind blew in sparkling snow like pixie dust to settle around them.

"Help," Geraldine gasped as she struggled to get out from under her sister. She hurt. Oh, God, she hurt. She was soaked and shivering and the snow was caked up around her knees. There was nothing left to feel but cold and pain.

But Marie was worse. Marie had no coat, no hat, nothing. Geraldine had given her her hat and her scarf, but it didn't make any difference. Geraldine wasn't even sure she was alive. Somehow, for some reason, by someone, Marie had been left out in the snow to die.

Geraldine hadn't been at the Rose House in months, but it was the only place she could think to go.

Aunt Trish blinked. Slowly, heavily, she got down on the floor with them, one knee at a time, hissing through her teeth. She dug her twisted hands under Marie's body and heaved. Marie flopped onto her back. Geraldine tried to pull herself upright, but she couldn't. She was frozen. A fallen statue. All she could do was watch and shake.

Aunt Trish set her jaw, raised one hand, and slammed it down across Marie's face.

Marie screamed and Geraldine shouted and tried to scramble to her knees.

"All right, all right! Get up!" shouted her aunt. "Goddamn! You gotta help me. Move it! You didn't bring her all this way to freeze her here!"

Somehow, Geraldine managed to get to her feet. Trish grabbed Marie's left arm, Geraldine got her right. Marie moaned and tried to roll up into a ball.

"None of that," said Trish ruthlessly. "Come on. In here."

Between them, they half-carried, half-dragged Marie into the great room, kicking aside the corpses of rotting books. Heat touched Geraldine's skin, a bright brush of pain. There was a fire in the fireplace and the complex smell of burning wood and paper.

Trish dumped Marie on the flagstone hearth and started tossing wood scraps into the fire. There was a hatchet, a broken chair, and a heap of books.

Geraldine felt sick.

"Get those clothes off her."

Geraldine stared, open mouthed and dull from cold and exhaustion. "She's freezing!"

"Do as you're told!"

Trembling, Geraldine did. The touch of her sister's ice-cold skin sickened her, but she yanked and struggled and got her socks and jeans and sweater off, until Marie was in her underwear. With every touch, Marie whimpered from the pain. She screwed her eyes up tight. Geraldine was furious—and terrified.

"Put your arms around her," Aunt Trish ordered as she stumped toward the door. "You got to get her warm!"

Aunt Trish disappeared into the house's darkness, leaving them alone. Geraldine didn't know what else to do. She lay down on the stones in front of the fire, grabbed Marie tight and pulled her close. Marie screamed and she coughed.

"It's okay," said Geraldine. The fire beat at her back, Marie's cold froze her front. She was caught shaking in the middle. "It's okay, it's okay. We're here. We made it. It's okay."

But it wasn't. Marie was going to die from cold and pain and fear, and she'd never know why.

Geraldine screwed her eyes shut and tried to will what little warmth she had into her sister's body. She heard rustling and thumping and swearing. All at once a blanket that felt like it weighed a hundred pounds dropped over top of them. It scratched like it was full of pricker weeds. It stank of mildew and mothballs. Geraldine huddled under it like it was the only shelter left to her.

But Aunt Trish yanked the covering off Marie.

"Come on, honey," muttered Trish. "Come on, girly, bumblebee, little fairy girl, bumblebee. Gotta see if you're frostbit. Come on, bumblybee. Let me see if it got you anyplace."

Her twiglike fingers poked and prodded ("Toes first, fingers next," she muttered). The fire's warmth was turning Marie's white skin red ("no gray, no gray, no gray," whispered Trish with each poke. "There? No gray").

By the time she finished, tears were streaming down Marie's face, but she wasn't shaking anywhere near as bad. Geraldine turned her sister to face her and pulled the filthy blanket over them both.

Aunt Trish crawled backward to the very edge of the hearthstones. She just hunched there and watched the two of them for a long time.

2.

Geraldine didn't remember falling asleep. But when she woke up, the gray morning light trickled through the rose forest windows. At some point, a section of plywood had either fallen or been taken down. Frost tinged the red roses with white.

Marie was asleep on the blanket, her skin warm to the touch. When Geraldine put her hand on Marie's cheek, she just rolled over, taking most of the blanket with her. There was nothing but a heap of glowing coals in the hearth, but Geraldine could feel the waves of warmth pounding against her skin.

Someone chuckled. Geraldine, startled, sat up.

Aunt Trish was still perched on her corner of the hearth. There were two mugs on the hearthstones, along with a heap of rubbish—sticks and trash and weirdly shaped chunks of wood. It slowly occurred to Geraldine that Trish must have been there all night feeding that fire, making sure it stayed alive so the two of them stayed warm.

Geraldine was starving. She was going to die of thirst.

"Here." Aunt Trish nudged a mug at her. "Go slow."

Carefully, Geraldine eased her way out from behind Marie. Her sister trembled a little, but didn't wake.

The mug held cocoa. It probably had been hot, but it was lukewarm now. It hit her stomach like lead. At the same time, it felt like she'd never get enough.

"So, you gonna tell me what happened?" asked Aunt Trish as Geraldine slurped.

"I don't know," she said. "I just…found her. Out in the old root cellar. I wanted to take her home…"

Geraldine didn't get any further. Marie shifted, and slowly she sat up. Her skin was a healthier pink now, but her eyes had sunk deep into her skull. Her fair hair hung lank and filthy around her ears.

"I'm not going back," whispered Marie. "Ever. I'm not."

Aunt Trish slurped in a long breath. "Did he finally get at you? Your mother thought he might."

"No," said Marie, but her voice shook. "No, no, no, no, no!" She curled up, hugging her knees to her chest.

"Hey, hey, it's all right. Here." Geraldine pushed the second cocoa mug into Marie's hands. "Come on." She moved Marie's hands to her mouth and made her drink. Marie swallowed, and swallowed some more.

Geraldine glowered at their aunt. "You say anything like that again, I'll knock your teeth out of your stupid head!"

Aunt Trish chuckled and mumbled. "Good luck with that."

"No," Marie pulled away. "She didn't mean it. She didn't. Please don't be mad. Please don't..."

"Don't worry, Marie." Aunt Trish patted the hearth around and behind her, and dragged out a third mug. "I'm not mad. And I'm not sending you back to him." She glanced around the room. "What did happen? Huh? What'd he finally do?"

But Marie just curled in tighter on herself. I shook my head.

Aunt Trish shrugged. "M'kay. Keep it to yourself. Your choice, kid."

"Thank you," said Marie.

Trish's withered grin split her face. Which was when Geraldine saw she had no teeth left at all. "Don't thank me. We're all going to be in the shit for this. Just you wait and see."

You have to believe they saw it coming. You have to. Otherwise…
—Dr. Geraldine Monroe (margin notes)

MARIE, PRESENT DAY
THE ROSE HOUSE

1.

When I finally lock up the office, the sun is setting over the lake in a blaze of melting gold. It is absolutely glorious, but does nothing at all to lift my mood.

Robbie has not texted me, let alone called. I do not know where he is, or if he kept his promise to be home tonight. I am trying to remember if he even did promise when I pleaded with him this morning, and I cannot. Too much has happened since then, and very little of it good.

Walt had already left by the time I got back to the office from seeing Lawrence Kappernick. Bethany was vague about where he had gone. I couldn't tell whether she genuinely didn't know or whether she'd been told not to tell me. I considered calling Carla, but decided against it. That would only make things worse.

I spent the rest of the day in my office. The whole afternoon wore away underneath a tide of party details, and there was still no word from Robbie. Dad did get in touch, though, to say he would not be home for dinner.

Night off for you, he said. *Enjoy.*

I decided to keep working and eat a quick salad at my desk. There was of course, a mountain of paperwork—accounts and receipts and other details. Online documents need to be printed out so the hard copies can be double-checked and filed. These were not things I could I couldn't delegate to Bethany.

By the time I snapped the lights off and locked the doors, there was still nothing from Robbie. Or Walt. Or Geraldine. They had all left me alone to manage as best I could.

But when, really, had it ever been any different? Maybe when we were younger. Maybe before Aunt Trish...but not since then. Not really.

I have to pass the old house on my way home. I pull into the parking lot. There's another car there, and for a moment, I think Geraldine must be home. But the house is dark and silent. The car isn't Geraldine's yellow Outback. It's a battered old Toyota I don't recognize.

My hands curl around the steering wheel. My cut stings and then burns beneath the bandage.

What is she doing? Where is she? Why is she...why is she...?

No. I stop myself firmly. I will not lose control again. It does not matter what Geraldine does today or where she is now. The plan can still be moved forward. I will not neglect my responsibilities.

I pull the Escalade around the back of the house, where it cannot be seen from the road. I have a little work to do yet, and I see just where I can begin.

Calmly, quietly, I climb out and extract the baseball bat I keep under the passenger seat.

2.

There is satisfaction in a job fully completed. I am glad I have this to cushion me, because as I pull up the smooth, winding drive of the Rose House, I see Grandma Millicent's Town Car parked out front of the garage.

I park and sit for a moment in the dark gathering my thoughts. This is not unprecedented, but it is unexpected. My grandmother generally does not come up to the house except for the large family gatherings, like last Sunday's barbecue.

I check my phone. I have not missed any messages.

I need to think. She must be in there with Dad. I cannot walk in on them with no idea what is happening. Not now. I need to know…something. Anything. I have to know which face to show them.

Contemplating sneaking in to my own home might seem a little childish, I suppose. But enough has happened that I feel a little extra caution is warranted.

I circle behind the garage and skirt the tree line up the slope, and then slip around through the manicured flower beds in the back. It takes a minute, but I finally get to the door in the old children's wing. We keep that locked, but of course I have my keys.

I quietly move down the long hallway to the front room. No light shines under the pocket door, so I assume I am safe. I open the door slowly, so its rumble is lessened, because it is after all, next to Dad's study and I don't want to disturb him if he is in there.

I slip inside and close the door.

And turn to see a woman's shadow on the sofa.

I slap my hand across my mouth to stifle the scream. The shadow raises a wineglass to me, and drinks.

Aunt June.

She's sitting alone in the dark. There's a bottle of wine on the table beside her. In the deep summer twilight, it looks like ink. The only light is leaking from around the edges of the closed study door.

"You sure you don't want anything?" Dad is saying from the other side. "I don't know what's keeping Marie, but I think I still remember how to make a cup of tea, or if you want something stronger…"

"No, thank you, Martin," answers Grandma. "I'm fine."

I look at Aunt June. Aunt June looks at me. She tips her wineglass up and drinks down the night-black liquid like water.

"So what brings you all the way up here?" Dad asks.

I do not have a lot of choices, so I cross the flagstone floor and sit down beside Aunt June. She holds up the bottle. I wave it away. She shrugs and pours herself a fresh glass.

"Martin, it's time to finish," I hear Grandma Millicent say from the other room.

"I don't understand, Mother."

"I mean you've done enough."

Aunt June stares out the picture window and makes little circles with her ankle as she listens to the voices from the study. The sunset's brilliant colors have darkened to purple and gray.

When Dad speaks again, I have to strain to hear him. "Do you really think that's possible?"

"I am not interested in a philosophical debate. I am saying we have enough. You have done it. You have succeeded."

Dad's little chuckle sends goosebumps crawling across the back of my neck. "I really don't understand what you're talking about."

"I'm talking about the moment that should come to any man who has worked hard all his life. It's the time to say 'I have enough. There is no need to keep trying so hard.'"

The corner of June's mouth curls up. It occurs to me that if my mother had lived, she would be about June's age. I do not think about that much. To me, Mom's always been unchanging, eternal. It is a jolt to suddenly imagine her in front of me instead of behind me, where I could watch her age and die, where I could talk with her and everyone else could admit that they do see her, rather than constantly pretending they don't.

I wonder if I would like that. I wonder if it would have been better.

Dad is talking again. "So, you're saying I should, what? Sit back and enjoy the fruits of my labors?"

"If you like. Or start something new. Something for yourself. You're free, Martin. You have more than adequately provided for the family, and we are grateful. And I am proud of you."

"You are?"

"Yes. Very proud. I hope you know that I always have been."

Silence falls again. Aunt June drinks and circles her ankle. She's impressively silent. I find myself wondering how often she's sat like this, just drinking and listening, with nobody to see, or to care.

"What do you want, Mother?"

"Nothing. That is what I have been attempting to explain. You have taken care of—"

"Yes, yes, and you're telling me I've been such a good boy. Something you never bothered to do when I actually was a boy, by the way. So, I guess I could be forgiven for asking, why now? Why's it so important that I give up everything right now?"

"That's not what I'm saying at all."

"I mean, it's a little hurtful to hear you talking like this, Mother, when I've got so many plans for us."

"I'm sure you do, Martin, but that's not—"

He isn't listening, or at least, he's pretending not to. "I was going to save this for after the graduation party, but since you're here…what is it the kids say? Spoiler alert? As soon as Robbie heads off for college, you and June are moving in here. Think about it! All my girls, together in the family seat."

Aunt June arches her brows at me. She gestures at me and then at herself, and then raises her glass to heaven. *Salut!* Her smirk is sharp.

My cut hand twitches.

"I suppose you've consulted Marie about this."

"Marie will be thrilled. You know her whole life is taking care of people."

"Well, it's a very generous offer, Martin—"

"It's what you've always wanted." Dad says this calmly, patiently. It's the same voice he used to correct us when we were children. "To live here, in this house, with the whole world at your feet."

"Martin, I never wanted anything to do with this house, or anyone in it."

That can't be right. I lean toward the door, frowning. Grandma has always wanted this house. I've heard her talk about the Rose House, about how it really belongs to the Monroes. She's said that. I'm sure of it.

The darkness presses against my skin. It's slimy. And cold. I try to shake it off, but it won't go.

Aunt June watches me, and she's still smirking.

"Martin, this house was always your obsession."

I can picture the exact way my father shakes his head at this. "I understand you don't want to inconvenience Marie. Or maybe you think she and June'll butt heads. Well, you'll sort them out, Mother. That's what you live for."

"Martin, I am very well settled right where I am." There is a tinge of fear beneath my grandmother's irritation. "I do not choose to go through the trouble and upset of moving house at my age."

"Oh, we'll do all the work, I promise. All you'll have to do is sit back and watch it all happen."

"Martin, stop this."

The snap of command makes my breath catch in my throat.

"But I don't want to stop," says Dad. His voice is buoyant, cheerful. He is enjoying himself. "This is my life, Mother. Working for my family. Making sure the Monroes have the lives they deserve."

"I told you, I do not want—"

"No, actually, you didn't." His interruption is so very gentle. "You told me something is wrong, and that you're frightened of something." There is a pause. I can picture him crossing to her, putting down his drink, taking her hand. "What is it, Mother? What's worrying you?"

"You worry me, Martin, and you refuse to listen to what I'm saying."

"But you're not making sense. I wonder if you're a little tired."

"I'm fine. I came up here to…"

"As soon as Marie gets home, I'll have her drive you back. Probably not the best idea for June to take you at this point. I think we're going to need to talk to her about her drinking. It's not good for a woman her age."

There's a pause. Aunt June raises her glass to me and slugs more wine back.

"Or, I'll drive you myself, just to make sure you're both all right."

"Martin, I'm only asking you this one more time. What are you doing?"

"Do you remember when Dad died, Mother? How you sat me down and told me I was responsible for the family name now? No? I remember. I've never forgotten. It was just me. Not Pete, or June. You knew even back then that they didn't have it in them. I'm really surprised you don't remember. You kept telling me and telling me, with every look, every word. Every time we didn't have enough and had to keep pretending that we did, every time you saw Lisa Burnovich and her kids in tow and had to remember they had this house and everything that went with it. You never said a word out loud, but you told me anyway, and I understood."

Grandma Millicent says nothing. What, I wonder, could she even want to say?

"I know you had to put on a show when I married Stacey. That was a hard time, wasn't it? But we got through it, and just look how everything's turned out. We've got the house and all the money and the Burnoviches...*Pfft!* All gone. We wiped them right off the map."

"It was never about the money, Martin. And it wasn't—"

"Don't lie to me, Mother." Dad's voice is soft as snow and just as cold. Even Aunt June pauses with her glass halfway to her lips. "It was entirely about the money, and the family name, of course. But then, they're one and the same, aren't they? Money, name. Name, money. Makes the world go 'round, right? Only now, you're saying you don't care, and I've got to admit, I'm kind of confused. Either you're starting to go a little senile, Mother dear, or something's changed, after all these long, long, long years. Now, what could that be? Maybe you've been gossiping with Geraldine?" He chuckles again. "No shame in that. She's your granddaughter, after all. I'll bet you two have had some lovely, cozy little chats since she got back."

"I haven't said two words to Geraldine."

"Well, I hope that's true. I've been meaning to warn you and June. Geraldine's come back to make trouble—no surprise, there!—and she's spouting some really twisted lies. Awful stuff. Now, I know you know better than to believe any of it, unless, you know, you'd been getting tired, or, well...We're not any of us as young as we used to be are we?"

Cold silence. Hard silence. It pours across the shadows, oil on troubled waters.

"You know, the more I think about it, the more I think there's no reason to wait for you to move in. We can start right after the graduation party on Sunday. Robbie can even help. It'll be good for him to have something useful to do. What do you think?"

Silence.

There's the distinct *thwap!* of Dad slapping his thigh. "Well, I'm going to go get June. We need to get you home. I wonder what's keeping Marie."

Aunt June gets to her feet quicker than I can. It's as if she were waiting for her cue this whole time.

"Oh, Marie," she says as she flips on the light. "You startled me! For a second, I thought you were old Addison's ghost!" She holds out the wine bottle. "Drink?"

There are a lot of princes who never get to go home. They go out and make a new place for themselves. Which means they are as trapped as the princesses. Because if they fail, there's nothing left for them to do.
—*Out of the Woods: Musings on Fairy Tales in the Real World*, Dr. Geraldine Monroe

GERALDINE, PRESENT DAY
THE COLOR MILE, M-131

1.

Well. It could be worse.

Robbie isn't actually hurt. His pupils may be the size of black basketballs, but they're the *same* size. He's wobbly on his feet, but there's nothing broken. And if he's not entirely coherent, he's very responsive.

"Don't tell Mom," he says, as we shove up his sleeves and peel back his eyelids so we can shine the flashlight into them. "Please, please, don't tell Mom."

His car isn't actually wrecked. One headlight is out, and a chunk of the bumper is missing, but otherwise it seems to be fine. It takes a bit of swearing and heaving, and the strategic application of flattened cardboard boxes to get some traction under the wheels, but Tyler and I both have some experience with this. Together we manage to get the Mustang convertible, which has to be another gift from Granddad, back onto the shoulder. Tyler gives the engine and the undercarriage a quick once-over, before offering to drive it back to the house while Robbie rides with me.

"I'm assuming you two need to talk," he says.

We do. I am so angry I could spit nails. I could rear back and smack this stupid, screwed-up, scared, spoiled baby boy. Does he know what his mother goes through every single day for him? What we've all done? All the secrets and the waiting and the pain, just to keep him safe?

"You going to tell Mom?" he asks.

"No. I'm going to shove you into the goddamned lake!" I keep my eyes fixed on the road. "What the hell did you think you were you *doing*?"

His silence lasts long enough that I think either he's not going to answer or he's drifted off. But, finally, he mutters, "I was running away from home."

"You've got, what, three months until college? And *now* you decide to run away?" The road curls sharply between the hills and the lakeshore. The striping is bad here and I have to focus very hard to keep us in our lane. "What kind of dumbass move is that?"

"I'm not going to college."

"What?"

"I am not going to U of M. I am not going anywhere near it!" he squawks.

I sigh and try to keep my eyes on the road. I'm going fast enough that if we meet a deer out here we are going to be back in trouble. Back in the ditch if we're lucky. I shouldn't even be having this conversation until he straightens out. I know that. But I can't stop myself.

"Look, Robbie, I know what it's like to want to just throw it all in their faces. But you can't really want to hurt your mom. It's just until August. Then you're down in Ann Arbor and your granddad can go fuck himself."

"I am not letting that old man keep my balls in one of his fucking slings!"

I glance at him. A passing car's headlights hit us. For a second, Robbie's floodlit, and I can see all the anger and the misery written across his young face.

"But he won't…"

"It was me," he says, and his voice is flat and dead.

"What was?"

"The 'trouble.'" He makes the air quotes. "At the old house, with the pills and shit. It was me."

We come to a four-way stop. I'm distantly proud of the fact that I don't slam the brakes. "You were dealing."

He shrugs one shoulder. "I had to get money from somewhere."

I'm going to kill you.

"And you got caught."

I'm going to drive us both into the lake. Save your mother the trouble.

"Dad did a drive-by checkup, and the fucker who was with him told Granddad what they saw."

You goddamned little idiot!

"So, he comes to me all sad and disappointed and says there's no need to tell Mom. As long as I'm a good boy and do what I'm told, she never has to find out her darling son is selling other people's pills for five bucks a pop."

I remember we're in the car, and I'm supposed to be driving. I ease us through the intersection.

"Where were you going?" I ask. "I take it you had some kind of plan."

"The plan *was* to come and stay with you," he mutters. "I thought you'd come up for graduation and then leave. Like…"

"Like always," I finish for him.

"I told Shelly, Aunt G will let us stay with her 'til we figure things out. No problem. Maybe she can even help you get into Lillywell. Shelly wants a degree in design," he adds.

"Is Shelly your girlfriend?"

"Yeah, kinda. Mostly." I take us around another curve. "Are you going to tell Mom?"

"I don't know."

"Aunt G…"

"I said I don't know!" He winces like I hit him. He has no idea. We ride on in silence for a little while longer. The country around us flattens out as the road turns away from the lake. We pass the fields and the houses, all dark for the night.

"What did you do?" Robbie asks me. "After you left. You never talk about it."

"That's because it was pretty much a disaster."

"How come?"

We are actually going to have this conversation. Well, maybe it's time. Actually, it's past time.

"I kind of did the opposite of what you did. I'd gotten into college. State University of New York at Buffalo. But I hadn't told anybody, because I didn't want anybody to know where I'd be, for a while, anyway. I hitched a ride with a friend out to Buffalo as soon as I could, and kind of bummed around for the summer. Used most of my cash to buy the car off my friend and so I was living in that 'til school started and I could get some financial aid. Made some money the old-fashioned way."

"What were you selling?"

"A little weed. Fake IDs. Stuff that didn't belong to me."

"And then?"

"And then school started, and things got better, and worse."

"How?"

"I met this girl. Jeannine. She was really smart. Really good at working the system without anybody seeing her do it." I pause. "She was a lot like your mom, actually. Anyway, she was the one who got me to expand away from just IDs."

"Into what?"

I should not be telling him this. That's how we protect the children, isn't it? We lie to them about what we've done, so they won't decide to follow our examples. That's what we tell ourselves anyway. Really, it's so we'll never have to live through that moment when they look at us and say, "Well, *you* did it."

"Term papers, bluebook tests, even journal articles. All very white collar." I still remember that strange feeling of having moved up in the world because I was selling paper instead of pills. Mostly. Jeannine would sell anything she could move. "You would not believe what college kids will pay for if they think it'll get them an easy A." *Or a quick thrill.*

"Bet I would."

Yeah, he probably would. "Anyway. Jeannine was the face of the operation. She brought in the customers. I found what was needed and packaged it to sell. We split the cash. I won a prize for writing, got into grad school, and we called it quits."

"What happened to her? Jeannine?"

The trees have closed over us, and the road is rising again. "She's chair of the anthropology department at Lillywell. At least she was."

Robbie lets that settle in, and I can feel the way his sobering brain matches it up with my being here. "What happened?"

"The board found out she padded her resume and plagiarized some of her papers." I say this looking straight ahead. "That's bad news in academic circles. She had to agree to quietly resign."

"Was this after you got fired?"

"Amazingly enough, yeah." I brake, and turn us into the old parking lot. My house sits white and squat in the headlights. Something's wrong. I feel it, but I can't see it. My mind is too divided between my past and Robbie's present.

I shut off the engine and the lights. Robbie and I sit in the dark, listening to each other's breathing.

"I won't tell your mom," I say.

"Thank you."

"But only if you do."

He stares at me, his eyes starting out of his head. "What? Why the—"

I cut him off. "Because."

Because of the water and the cold. Because of the current and the darkness. Because of the hospital room and the tubes and my raw throat and the look in Marie's eyes.

Because of what I'm doing here. Because I am *not* going to be responsible for Marie losing her son.

So, I do the worst thing I can think of.

"Either you tell your mother, or I'll tell your grandfather."

That does it. Just like I knew it would.

"Okay, okay. I'll tell her, I'll just...it's going to take a while, okay? I've got to figure out how."

Because I love him, I say okay. Because I don't want to hurt him. Because I can't stand seeing that scared, furious look in his eyes. Because I want so very badly to believe I am not the villain in this piece.

I can't blame him for what he is and what he's done. He's just another victim, and we've failed him. Marie, me, David, all of us. I know that. But I can't leave him alone to just do what he wants either. That leads right back here to the Monroe trust fund and the blank white walls that are all that's left of the Rose House.

I sigh and fumble with the door latch.

"Look, let's get you inside, and you can sleep off...whatever, and then in the morning...we'll figure it out."

I climb out of the car, keys in my hand. That's when Tyler pulls in behind us, and the white headlights of Robbie's car light up our little section of the world.

That's when I see all the broken windows.

2.

"Oh, Jesus H. *Christ*!"

Tyler's quicker, or at least less distracted, than I am. He jumps out of the Mustang and runs across to his old Toyota. The passenger-side windows have been shattered. Glass shards glint in between the weeds and gravel.

His car. The store. The front windows on the house. They've all been smashed in. Just a few jagged teeth still glint in the frames.

Robbie looks blearily at the damage. He's swaying on his feet. Whatever sobriety came from putting his car in that ditch is gone now.

"We need to find out if anything's missing," says Tyler. "Have you called the cops yet?"

"Just got here," I mumble and head for the front door. My hands shake as I struggle with the key.

I already know what I'm going to find. What I don't know is how I'm going to lie about it.

Inside, nothing's been touched. My gear, my computer, my files, all are exactly as I left them. If I looked, I know the money would still be in its hiding place.

I don't look. I head back outside.

Robbie's leaning against the hood of his car, both hands in his hair like he's trying to keep his head from coming off. I see the flashlight beam bobbing alongside the old store.

"They got all the windows in the store, too," Tyler says as he circles back around to us. "Did you call the cops?"

I didn't even touch my phone. "I'm not calling the cops."

The flashlight throws weird shadows across his face, but they are not enough to mask the utter disbelief of his expression. "Why the hell not?"

I can't look at him. "Because it'll only make things worse."

"What? Why?"

Old, familiar thoughts race through my brain. *I can still get out of this. I can still do this. I can. This is just a bad moment. I just have to get through it.* I know it's all a lie, but I grab hold of it anyway, because it's better than sinking into what waits underneath.

"I know who did this."

Robbie is staring at me, terrified of the accusation he thinks is poised on the tip of my tongue. Tyler is staring at me, waiting for me to name names.

I'm going to do it, too. I'm going to stand here and open my mouth and say it, to my nephew and lover. The two men I always intended to protect from what I'm really doing here, even when, deep down, I knew it was hopeless.

Just get through it. Whatever it takes. Figure out what to do about it later, when everything calms back down.

"It was my father," I say.

3.

Tyler looks at me, stunned, blank. Robbie isn't much better. Tyler can't believe that someone would really do this. Robbie can't believe I'd say it out loud.

"Your father?" Tyler repeats.

"He doesn't want me here. He doesn't want me messing up his money scams. He..."

"He smashed out your windows to convince you to leave?"

I nod. I can't look at him.

"And that thing you said to me, about how your face got busted up?"

I let silence do the work for me.

"Jesus, Gerie!" He grabs my shoulders. He doesn't shake me, but he swings me to face him. "Why didn't you *tell* me!"

"What were you gonna do?"

"Get you the hell out of here!"

"No." I pull myself away and reach into the car, where I tossed my purse. I yank out my phone and find David's number on the list of recent calls. He answers on the second ring.

"Geraldine? What's going on?"

Robbie has good ears. He's shaking his head violently. Tyler has fallen back, his hands hanging limp at his sides. Helpless, for the moment.

"There's been some trouble at the old house," I tell David. "Again."

"Shit. Bad?"

"Only kinda." This is a lie, because I still can't get myself to look at Tyler, and nothing can be worse than that. "But I've got Robbie here, too. He needs somebody to come get him."

"Right. On my way."

I hang up without bothering to say good-bye and drop my phone back in my purse.

David shows up twenty minutes later. It's a very long twenty minutes. Robbie spends it sitting in my car, his thumbs busy with his phone.

I try to make a flashlight tour of the damage. The two house windows that face the road were taken out, and only the passenger-side windows on Tyler's car. There was a single dent in the hood, but nothing that would make it undriveable.

All the store windows, though, had been at least cracked. Most of them were entirely shattered. *Look,* the vandal said, *I could have done this while you were inside the house. I could have done so much worse. But I didn't.*

David's wearing his security uniform jacket. His gun and radio are visible on his belt. He sees all the broken glass, his son in one piece sitting in the car, and me and Tyler without any new injuries, and he sags.

"Tyler, this is David, my ex-brother-in-law." I perform the introductions because I don't know what else to do.

The men exchange the little nod that passes for a greeting. David measures Tyler up, trying to use the space between us to gauge our relationship. Not that it's hard. But David is in security mode, and he's being thorough.

"I take it you didn't see anything?" he asks us.

"No, we were up at the fish fry," I tell him. Tyler doesn't say anything. He's looking at me, waiting to see what I'll say. I feel the pressure of his impatience against my throat.

David's gaze strays to Robbie in the car. I see what he's thinking and I shake my head.

"It wasn't him."

I wait to see that slump of relief again, but it doesn't come. David's not sure whether he believes me. I can't blame him.

I open my mouth to say I'll report it first thing in the morning, but he won't believe that either. Because David is not stupid.

"You better get Robbie home," I say. "He's still kind of messed up."

"Yeah," answers David flatly. "Thanks."

"David?"

"Yeah?" he says again.

"He's eighteen, right?"

We're looking at each other. He's understanding everything I am not saying. We're standing in the broken glass, in front of the old house, in the middle of our history, our insanity, in a present and a future that have a cracked and crazed foundation. We have power, and are powerless. We are miles apart and tied together so tightly that neither one of us can escape.

"In two weeks," he tells me.

"Try to keep him indoors 'til then, maybe. He'll miss his graduation, but that's the least of anybody's problems right now."

"Yeah. Right. Okay."

David goes to the Outback and opens the door. Robbie gets out and slouches silently at his father's side like he's in handcuffs. He's trying for belligerence, but he's too tired and too freaked out by the damage around him. He gives me one backward glance before he climbs into David's truck.

Does Robbie believe what I've said about who did this? I can't tell. Maybe he's just grateful I at least tried to tell David he had nothing to do with it. I don't know. I don't even know if I'll ever talk to him again. I picture David loading them into the car and heading out of town. Prince Charming, gone away to the woods, to find the princess and slay the wicked sister and whatever other monsters he finds. The problem is, once he leaves, Prince Charming rarely gets to go to his own family. It's not like it is for the girls.

They drive away, and I am left alone in the dark with Tyler.

"You can't stay here," he says.

"I know."

But I go inside anyway, all the way to the bedroom.

Tyler does not follow me.

I sometimes wonder what would have happened between that ugly daughter and her evil mother if the good sister hadn't come back in the nick of time.

Somehow, I suspect it would not have been a happy ending.
—Out of the Woods: Musings on Fairy Tales in the Real World,
Dr. Geraldine Monroe

MARIE, PRESENT DAY
THE ROSE HOUSE

1.

It's six in the morning when the phone finally rings.

I never went to sleep. I put on my pajamas and I tried lying down, but I knew actual sleep was entirely out of the question.

When I couldn't stand it anymore, I dressed in the dark and sat on the edge of my bed. I needed to be ready to go at a moment's notice. Someone would call. Someone had to. It was not possible that no one was coming for me.

Slowly, the world brightens from black to gray. Slowly, sporadically, the birds begin to sing. The walls lean closer, wondering what has disrupted my routine.

I have the phone up to my ear before the first ring finishes.

"David? What's the matter...?"

"It's fine, Marie. It's all fine," he says. "Robbie's right here with me."

"Oh, thank goodness." The relief is real, but strictly limited. "What's happened?"

He hesitates and I clench the phone, and my free fist. My scab pulls and threatens to break. "David, please."

His breath rasps as he sucks it in. "You need to get down to Geraldine's."

"What? Why?"

"Something happened down there last night."

"A little more information would be helpful, David."

"Yeah, yeah, I know. But…listen, it would be better if you talked to her. And then you can come talk to me, okay?"

"Let me talk to Robbie."

"He's still asleep. I'll get him up if you want me to, but I don't think you'll get anything coherent out of him. He is fine, I promise. I'll bring him home this afternoon, all right?"

"That's not all right. How could that be all right?" My voice is high and tense. I am breaking. I know it. I need to hold appearances together, but I need to see my son even more. I need to have him right here beside me, where I know that he's all right, that he hasn't vanished into the cold and the dark, or fallen down and gotten lost or…or…

Anything could happen if he's not with me. Anything at all.

"Marie," David says. "I'm asking you to trust me this once. I swear, Robbie's not going anywhere without me. I'll bring him straight home. Please, just please go talk to Geraldine. I want to know what she tells you."

I have so many other things I want to say, but they all wither and die. There's a sound outside, a rustle that does not belong to the normal breathing of the house.

My father. Dad is outside my door, listening.

"Thank you for calling, David," I say. "I do appreciate it."

David hears the shift in my tone, and he understands. "I'm sorry about all this, Marie."

I believe him, but it doesn't make any difference. "We'll talk this afternoon." I cut off the call.

"Marie?" Dad pushes the door to my bedroom open.

He's still in his navy-blue pajamas, and his hair is rumpled. I have to work not to shrink away from him. Only his eyes are as normal as he takes me in, sitting on the edge of my bed with my phone in my hand.

"Who was that?" he asks.

"David." I don't even think about shading the situation. "He says…" *What? What did he say?* "He says something's happened with Geraldine. I need to go down there. I'm sorry."

My father shakes his head. "I tried to warn you, Marie."

"Yes. I know. You were right. Excuse me, please."

I brush past him and head for the stairs before he can call me to stop. I can't risk the possibility that I might obey.

2.

The old house is silent and still when I get down there. The shards of broken glass glitter fitfully as the clear morning sun touches them between the trees' shifting shadows. There are three cars in the parking area. One of them is Robbie's.

I stare. Understanding will not come. David said Robbie was with him. Why is his car here? Why is anyone here, with all the windows broken?

The house door opens, and a man comes out. He's wearing jeans and a ragged T-shirt for some band I've never heard of. He's knuckling his eyes and scratching his chin.

It's him. The one I heard her with the other night. It must be.

"Can I help you?" he asks warily.

"I…I…Where's Geraldine?"

He squints at me and considers the question. "Are you Marie?"

"I…yes. I…"

The stranger holds out his hand. "Tyler Prescott."

I stare like I expect him to hit me. "Where's Geraldine?"

Tyler Prescott withdraws his hand, trying to cover the awkwardness by pointing over his shoulder. "Asleep. She can sleep through anything." He smiles and waits for me to smile back.

"Yes."

"Your son's okay," he tries. "His dad took him home."

"I...yes, he let me know. Thank you."

We stand there. The morning is already warm. Sweat prickles under my arms only to be turned to a chill by the breeze. I wait for the world to shift and the ground to sag. I want to see what this man will do when it happens. How good he is at pretending.

But the world stays steady, and he and I are left to stare at each other.

"Do you want me to get Geraldine?" he asks finally.

"No. Thank you. No. She..." I swallow, and I look at the broken glass. "Did she say what happened?"

"Yeah, she did."

My fear is instant. She didn't. She wouldn't. Not even at her worst. She would never lay our secrets out to a stranger.

"She said your father did it to chase her off. She said there's some kind of money..." He hesitates, editing Geraldine's words in his mind. "Problem...?"

"Oh." It's not the worst thing, but it's bad enough.

He thinks my silence is for the broken glass. "Hell of a thing. They got my car, too."

"Yes."

"Look, Ms. Monroe, we don't know each other, but I've been with Geraldine for over a year now. I love her. I swear, I didn't come up here to make waves. I just...she's hurting, and I want to help. That's all, I promise. She came up here to make things right so we could...Well, look, what I'm saying is, if there's anything...any way I can help smooth things over...just say the word."

Over a year. The words settle into me. This man, this boy, looks to be barely older than Robbie. He's been with her over a year. And she didn't say one word while we talked and planned and promised.

I look at his bright, distressed eyes and see his expression of gentle regret. He doesn't want to be saying these things. He knows it's painful. But he loves her. He just wants everything to be right.

He doesn't realize how very, very familiar I am with this expression, not to mention the arguments and behavior that go with it. I live with them every single second of every single day. I am an expert in all their shades and hidden meanings. I am not taken in, not even for a moment.

"I'm sorry," I say. "Really I am, but the only way you can help is to leave us alone."

His bearded jaw juts out. "Right. Okay. Guess I'd better go get Gerie then."

He goes back inside. The ancient screen door slams shut behind him.

She lied to me. *She lied to me.*

I can't breathe. I'm falling, from the tree, from the stairs, from the cliff over the lake. The air crawls up my arms and into my ears, whispering obscenities and accusations in my mother's voice as it spirals into my brain.

She said she was coming home to help.

She said she was sorry. She wanted to make it right.

She made me believe we were finally going to be together.

And she lied about all of it.

The house door opens and Geraldine steps out. She looks so young in her cargo shorts and a misbuttoned shirt. She's shoving her dark hair out of her eyes, showing her scabs and her bruises, all that damage she has done to herself. She stares at me, bleary-eyed, belligerent, so familiar. The person I have loved longer and more than anyone else.

I should go to her, talk to her, try again to understand her. Convince her, console her, remind her. She is my sister.

But she lied.

I turn on my heel, shut myself into the car my father picked out for me, and drive away.

The most famous of the traditional story about two full-blood sisters is, of course Bluebeard. As usual, in the original story it's very different from the version that got famous. But the moral is the same. It's more of a horror story than a fairy tale. But then again, the line between the two is very fine. "Beware of the charming stranger," the story says. "He's going to take you away from home, and you are never coming back."
—*Out of the Woods: Musings on Fairy Tales in the Real World,*
Dr. Geraldine Monroe

GERALDINE, PRESENT DAY
STACEY B'S SANDWICHES AND STUFF

1.

Marie's gigantic black car rounds the curve and is gone, leaving behind the rush of the wind in the trees and the shouts of the crows.

Tyler's moving closer to me, angling to press his body against mine, but I've already pulled away. I head for the bathroom and lean across the little sink. I brace both my hands on the porcelain, staring into the basin for a long minute. When it becomes clear I'm not actually going to be sick, I turn on the cold water and fill my hands. I smack the cold against my bruised face like I'm hoping the shock will jolt something loose. It doesn't work. So I do it again, and again.

When I'm gasping for air, I shut the water off and look up into the mirror. I want to see what my sister saw that lit her face with so much hatred. But the truth is, I don't need to look. I know exactly what I've done, and that only makes it worse. I've made and broken promises to both sides with equal speed.

I just wish I knew what I was going to do next.

Tyler moves into the mirror frame. He looks haggard and hungry. Guilt clenches my stomach. He's looking at my reflection, my bruises, scabs, and scar, studying them all for the truth he hasn't been able to find in my real face.

Mirror, mirror, on the wall, who's the fairest one of all?

"What are you going to do?" Tyler asks my reflection.

"Get some breakfast," I say. "Get your car into the shop. They should open around nine. Get some sheeting and maybe some plywood for the windows…"

Tyler's finally recovered his voice. "Geraldine, this is crazy. You cannot stay here."

He keeps saying *you*. Not *we*. My heart shrivels. I should take it out and put it in a box, in a duck, in a well, in the woods…

I close my eyes and swallow and try to stamp down on the tangle of my thoughts.

"It'll be fine," I say. "We've both stayed worse places."

But Tyler's not buying it. I knew he wouldn't. I know what is happening, I can see the ending clearly. I've read this story. I've written it.

I can still stop.

"It will *not* be fine! You said your—"

"Never mind what I said, okay? It doesn't matter." I push past him, heading for the bedroom. I'm half dressed, and feeling fully naked. Battered. Burned.

Tyler, of course, follows. "How the hell does your father smashing your house windows not matter!"

The tangle inside me snaps and, in a flash, I see red.

"See, this is why I told you to keep your nose the fuck out of my business!"

"Do you have any idea how insane you sound right now?"

"Yes, actually, I do," I say, because I have nothing left in me but honesty and anger. "That's the other reason I told you to stay away!"

"So, I was just supposed to leave you out here?"

I can still stop this.

"Yes! How many times to I have to say it? Yes! When I walked out on you, you were supposed to take the goddamn hint!"

"I love you, Gerie!"

"It doesn't *matter*!"

My scream rings off the walls. It fades and slowly dies. Tyler steps back. His expression goes blank. I can imagine him standing in front of his father, the man who tried to beat holiness into his children, wearing that same solid, stoic expression.

"You really mean that."

"Finally!" I throw my arms out wide and shout to the ceiling. "He gets it!"

"This isn't you. I don't know who the hell…"

Stop this.

"You're wrong, Tyler. This *is* me. I really am the crazy lady in the ruined house in the woods."

He's out of words. He's out of breath. He takes two steps forward. Anger seethes behind his eyes. For a minute, I think he might actually hit me. I'm ready for it. I want it.

Hit me, break me, kill me, stop this. Stop me. You can do it, Ty. You're the only one who can.

He takes my face in both hands and kisses me, hard. I freeze. My mouth stays shut, my body stays stock still. I don't even lift my hands. His tongue stabs at my lips, blunt and insistent, and I just clench tighter.

He pulls back.

"Well. I guess that's that."

Tyler turns and walks away. Tyler slams the door and heads for his damaged car without looking back.

My mouth moves, shaping words. There's no sound because there's no breath left in my body.

Let him go.

I'm moving. Toward the door. Down the hall. Out into the living room. Out into the morning air and the shifting light and shadows and birdsong. I'm still talking, still making no sound.

I promised. I have to. It's all my fault.

It always had to end this way. Because of the fire that didn't start and the accident that didn't happen and the fact that I couldn't ever convince Marie to come out with me, so I've come back to her.

Tyler slams his car door. He shoves the key in the ignition.

It's family, Tyler. I can't get away. I can't. I've tried.

He cranks the engine, and cranks it again.

This is my world. I was stupid to think there was anywhere else. This is all there is. Everything else . . . I just break everything else.

He slams the heel of his hand against the steering wheel and cranks the ignition once more. This time, it catches.

Yes, get out of here. This is better. This is the right thing.

He throws the car into reverse. I hear the gears grind. The Toyota lurches around—back, *grind*, forward, *grind*, back—making a clumsy circle like a wounded dog.

Good-bye. Good-bye. Good . . .

"Tyler!"

But he doesn't hear me.

No wicked stepfather tales. Why didn't anyone ever tell them that story?

—Dr. Geraldine Monroe (margin notes)

MARIE, PRESENT DAY
THE ROSE HOUSE

1.

Dad is in the formal dining room when I get home. He must have made his own coffee. I hope he got it right. He is very particular.

"Marie," he says mildly as I walk in. "I was worried."

"Yes, I'm sorry."

"Did you find Robbie?"

"Yes."

"Good. With the party Sunday, it would be a bad time for him to get up to some adolescent shenanigans."

The party. Oh. "Yes."

Dad puts his mug down on the coaster. He is always careful of the things we use. A little less so of the people, perhaps, but that's what it is to be human, isn't it?

"There was a phone call for you while you were out," he tells me. "Larry Kappernick."

"Oh."

"I didn't know Larry knew what eight o'clock looked like." Dad chuckles. I think I smile. I am not sure. "We chatted a bit. He said he'd been looking into a few things for you."

"Yes."

"He said you were concerned Geraldine had been shading the truth and asked him to call some friends at Lillywell."

He waits for my explanation. "I didn't want to upset you."

Dad considers this, washing it down with another sip of coffee. "He said you were right," he tells me finally. "Geraldine was fired."

"I wanted everything to be as normal as possible, so we could all enjoy graduation." No. That's not the right thing to say. Why can't I think of the right thing to say?

"Seems there was some scandal with her and the dean, and she was sleeping with a student…?"

A student. Tyler Prescott. Sloppy, sleepy, standing right behind her and trying to tell me everything he had done he had done from love. "Yes."

"I tried to warn you, Marie. I told you I don't know how many times…"

"Yes."

"I thought you were the one who would listen. I could always count on you, no matter what. We were a team, you and I. Not like the others."

"Yes."

"I'm disappointed, Marie."

"I'm sorry."

"You're going to have some work to fix this."

"Yes."

Yes, I am.

Fairy tales are not big on second chances. The wicked sister never gets to turn around and say, you know, that thing where I tried to kill you and marry your husband? That was a mistake. I have reconsidered my life choices. In the stories, redemption can only come from the hand of God, and God is a tight-fisted old bastard.
—Out of the Woods: Musings on Fairy Tales in the Real World,
Dr. Geraldine Monroe

GERALDINE, PRESENT DAY
STACEY B'S SANDWICHES AND STUFF

1.

I can't do this.

I thought I could stand him hating me because I deserve it, but I am melting down. Dissolving into anger and confusion. I hate myself, my family (like that's hard), and everything around me. I'm lost in electric, ecstatic confusion with no way to reclaim the certainty I thought had hardened inside me.

I know—I *know*—I have to let him leave.

Atonement costs. A piece of your foot. Your beloved horse. Your hands. I have to pay—and pay heavily—to stop being the wicked sister and finally prove to someone somehow that I deserve a life of my own.

But this price is too steep.

Tyler isn't answering his phone. Until he does, I can't say I'm sorry. I can't explain. The fight was a mistake. Sending him away was a mistake. Staying alone, here in the empty house with the broken windows while all the craziness closes in on me, it's all part of the same huge mistake.

I knock glass shards out of the windows, shattering them on the ground and the floor. I prowl the empty rooms, I guzzle the Diet Coke and shots of rum until I'm sick and dizzy. I try to find a way out of the endless loop of thoughts spinning through me.

I shouldn't have sent him away.

He shouldn't have come here.

I shouldn't have sent him away.

He shouldn't have come.

I shouldn't have come.

Somewhere in the back of my head, I know this rage will eventually evaporate. That only makes it worse.

I try to clean up, but it's hopeless. I don't have the tools. I catch myself standing outside with one glass shard in my hand, wondering where it would hurt the most to cut. The pain will break the cycle. Let me focus. I can pay the price with blood that I can't pay with honesty.

I drop the shard and run back into the house.

Inside, I strip all those photographs off the wall. My first impulse is to tear them up, but instead I stuff them into my purse. I'll throw them all in Marie's face. They're all going straight into her face. All of them. This is her fault.

This is my fault.

It doesn't matter. Not anymore. I'm going to blow the whole thing sky high. Just as soon as I explain it to Tyler. Just as soon as I can see past how much I hate everything I am and everything I've done and everything I plan on doing next.

Just as soon as I talk to Tyler and explain.

Tyler has left me alone. Just like I said I wanted. I said it because I could not let the outside world in and still keep my promise to help destroy my father. I could not adequately explain why Marie and I had to take matters into our own hands.

I climb into the car and fumble for my phone. I call David, but he's not answering. In desperation, I call Marie. I remember the hate in her eyes as I listen to her voice mail message.

"Marie, please, pick up. I need to talk to you. I need..."

I need a reminder that there is something real happening here. That my heartbreak has a point and a purpose.

I need my sister.

There's a click and a shuffle and my heart swells.

"Marie. Thank God. Listen, I know you're angry and I'm sorry. I am. I wanted to tell you. We were coming up last night, but we found Robbie instead and he…"

"Marie's not ready to talk to you just yet, Geraldine," says my father's voice.

The phone slips from my fingers and thuds onto the floor mat.

"Geraldine?" says Dad from down by my feet. "Your sister told me what happened at Lillywell. She's very upset that you lied."

My lungs are heaving. He probably hears, but I can't stop it.

"I've been talking to her," he says. "I told her we should hear your side of the story."

Slowly, the flood of emotion I've been drowning in since sunrise drains away. Listening to my father reminds me exactly who I am. I welcome it, even though it makes my skin crawl.

"Geraldine?"

I have to duck awkwardly around the steering wheel to pick my phone up.

"When did you ever want to hear from me?" I ask him.

"Things change, Geraldine. Even for an old man. I don't see why we can't sit down and talk this through."

Something's wrong. Something's happened, something that matters to him. He wants something. From me.

"Where's Marie?"

"You sound like you think I've buried her in the back garden."

Because that's what I do think. Because I remember the car ride out to the county asylum when I was thirteen, the endless threats to lock Mom away. And Aunt Trish, barricaded in Rose House.

As soon as I think it, cold fills me to my scalp. I'm shaking and I can't go another step. Aunt Trish pulls us in. She keeps us alive. She bangs and she rages, toothless and crazier than any of the rest of us. But she keeps us alive. She makes us hold on to each other, and does what no one else will. She tries to give us strength. She failed, we all failed, but at least she tried.

"Where's Marie?" I ask Dad again. "Put her on."

"She's not here. She forgot her phone. I know," he says into my silence. "I thought the world would end before she did something like that. She's so detail oriented."

Every bruise I have, every cut, down to my oldest scar, burns. I remember the rest of it.

I remember that they found Uncle Pete's truck on the dunes outside Whitestone. But not Pete. Never Pete.

Dad didn't come after us at Trish's for a week. That was a very long, risky time. It must have been very important to him to keep us all out of the way.

"Well, tell her I called," I say, and I hang up before he can drop one more poisoned word.

I'm sorry, Tyler. I am. But you're better off gone.

I am not a child, I am not a coward. I am not free, either, and it breaks my heart. I will rage and I will storm and be afraid. But I will not betray my sister, or myself, or our dead.

Not this time. I swear. No more missing Monroes. No more bodies in the gully, in the lake, in the house.

Well. Maybe just one more.

"Father," she said, "do with me what you will." She stretched forth her hands and let him chop them off.
— "The Girl without Hands" from *Kinder und Hausmärchen*
Vol. 1, Jacob and Wilhelm Grimm, 1812

MARIE, PRESENT DAY
WHITESTONE HARBOR

1.

I can count the number of times I have deliberately left my phone somewhere on one hand. There are so many people who depend on me, it's important they can reach me at a moment's notice. Especially Dad, of course.

But I need to think. I have to decide what to do. I cannot trust Geraldine.

But I cannot give up on her. I have worked too long and too hard to let her worst instincts take her away again.

I said I could not do this on my own, but now I will have to. For Geraldine's sake, and Robbie's, and David's. I will not let us down. When I have finished, they will understand what I have done, and why. We will be able to talk, and listen. We will at long last begin to heal.

I drive downtown. Because so much has gone wrong, I park in the public lot and walk the three blocks to the office. I see Walt's car along the way, but not Bethany's.

Good.

Forewarned is forearmed, and I have the right cheerful expression on my face when I trot up the stairs and push the glass door open. I am able to ignore the memory of glass just like this shattering under my blows.

In my office, I drop my keys and briefcase on the desk. Rattle. Thump. I leave the door open behind me while I start opening file cabinets and yanking out files.

"Marie? What's going on?"

I whip around, pressing a folder against my chest. Caught in the act. So very obviously guilty. Walt sags in my doorway, a tired anger simmering in his drooping brown eyes.

"I could ask you that. Putting in some extra time?" I add the folder I'm holding to the crooked stack on my desk.

"Just a few last-minute things," he says, but the lie is easy to read. "I would have figured you'd be busy with the party Sunday."

"That's next. You and Carla will be there, of course."

"Carla's not feeling really well," he says. "She might have to skip."

I gather up all the files and tuck them into my briefcase. I don't look at him. "Oh. I'm sorry to hear that."

"Marie. We have got to talk."

I close my briefcase and rest both hands on it. I let him see how hard it is for me to smooth away the worry on my face.

"I'm sorry…" I say. "I really need to get going…"

"This won't take long." He straightens up, trying to summon enough anger to be strong. And he is so angry. "You're screwing with the accounts, Marie, and I'm going to tell Martin. There. Done." He makes a great show of dusting his hands. "You have a nice day."

"Walt, please," I whisper. "I can explain."

Walt lets his head drop back so he can stare at the ceiling. "And suddenly, she's got all the time in the world to talk."

"Yes. Because you're making a mistake." *I'm sorry. I would not put you through this if it wasn't absolutely necessary.*

"And what mistake is that?"

I take a deep breath. What I say next must be exactly right.

"Walt, four years ago, Dad…did something indiscreet. He borrowed some money from the trust."

Walt says nothing.

"He meant to pay it back. But it was for the AbsuHomes deal, and you know how that went."

Still nothing. That's all right. I can keep going.

"When he couldn't recoup the loss, he..." I stop. "Walt, he started fiddling with the accounts. Robbing Peter to pay Paul. And...I found out." I keep my voice steady, but soft and bereft. "He was desperate, Walt. He was frightened. It was so much money, and he has so many people depending on him. I was so afraid. I thought...I thought he'd kill himself, like his father did. I thought..." I pause. I sway a little on my feet even though the floor is perfectly steady. Distantly I think that this story would work on no one but Walt. Because no one else loves my father like Walt does. The rest of us just need him.

"So, I've been trying to...make it right. That's why I've been...well, you saw..."

I look up, mute, afraid. My eyes are wide, my chin is trembling.

The skin around my cousin's eyes crinkles. He's listening. And even though he doesn't want to, he's beginning to believe.

"And then Geraldine..." he prompts.

"I still don't know how she found out. Amber might have dropped the hint, I suppose. I'm trying to convince her it's not worth making a huge ruckus over, but...She's in trouble, Walt. She...I found out from Larry Kappernick she was fired. I haven't got all the details yet. But..." I let the sentence trail away. "She might be looking to get some money out of him."

"Because Martin's bought her off before," says Walt flatly.

"Yes." She didn't take the money, but Walt doesn't need that detail right now.

I see his exhaustion and his anger. He cannot hide what is happening inside him. He has never understood that he might need to. He trusts us. Well, he trusts my father. Dad has worked hard to make sure. Walt always has to feel important and needed, but submissive and beholden all at the same time. It's a very fine line, but my father is always up to a challenge. And it would never, ever do to have Pete's son question the status quo, or how it came to be.

"Why didn't he tell me?" Walt whispers. "If there was real trouble...why didn't he say *something*?"

"Pride, Walt," I remind him gently. "He couldn't let anyone see he'd let the family down."

"He told you."

"No. I found out on my own." I smile sadly. "I've been looking after him a long time. I know...I know where the bodies are buried."

"Lousy analogy, Marie," he mutters.

"I know. I'm sorry. I...just..." I press my bandaged hand against my mouth and look away.

"So what is that you're trying to smuggle out of here?"

And just like that, I am caught. My shoulders sag. My hands shake as I pull the folders out of my briefcase and lay them on the desk.

Our eyes meet. For a split second, my certainty falters. He has lived with us and watched us and survived us and I don't know how. Walt is not stupid. He's loyal and he's weak. He loves his family. He wants them safe and together. Just like I do. But he is good at what he does, just like I am.

That is where the danger lies. He might find the fact that I have just the files he needs a tiny bit too convenient.

But Walt looks away first. He gathers up my folders and tucks them under his arm. "Okay. All right. Look. Let's just...let's just get through the weekend. We can sort this out on Monday. All right?"

"Thank you. You'll...what will you tell Carla?"

"The truth," he said. "I can't keep secrets from her, Marie. She always figures it out."

This is my cue for a tiny smile, because I care about his wife, too. "She does, doesn't she?"

"Do you think you can keep Geraldine from screwing the pooch for two days?"

"I'm going to do my best."

He nods and heads back to his office.

I emerge into the fresh evening twilight, just as the streetlights switch on. I remember when there were only two working lights on this whole street. Back then, I could stand right here and see a sky full of stars and my father's building was the only one without a NOW LEASING sign for two blocks.

Now, just look what we've done. The streets are full of cars cruising for a parking spot and the sidewalks are crowded with tourist families with their ice creams and the lifestylers on their way to their friends' pubs. The world is brimming with warmth and voices. I'm nothing but a ghost from the past, watching the living and smiling at their innocence. I am relaxed in my invisibility. I'm also starving. Perhaps I'll stop for something to eat. Stray from the path for just one tiny, irresponsible moment before I go on to finish what I have to do tonight.

I barely have time to finish the thought before a Whitestone Security cruiser pulls up to the curb and the driver lets the window glide down.

"Ms. Monroe?"

It's Kyle Shamanski. We went to high school together. He's gone paunchy over the years and shaved his head to avoid the indignity of a comb-over.

"Kyle, what is it?" My heart is sinking. My throat is tight.

"It's your sister's boyfriend," he tells me. "I think somebody better go get him."

There's a misconception that the woods are the destination in a fairy tale. The woods are just something to get through. Scary, yes. Necessary, of course. But it's when you finally get to the castle that the real trouble starts.

—*Out of the Woods: Musings on Fairy Tales in the Real World*,
Dr. Geraldine Monroe

GERALDINE, PRESENT DAY
WHITESTONE HARBOR

1.

I drive to the edges of Whitestone, hit the McDonald's, and park at the public beach. I wolf my burger and fries fast, so I won't have to taste them. I feel steadier when I'm done. The mega-grande-whatthehellever from Starbucks also helps.

It's full dark and Whitestone's clear lights glimmer on the rippling lake. My tantrum lasted a whole day. *Impressive, Geraldine.* I drink my coffee and I grimace, and try to think.

I need to get back to playing my part in Marie's plan. I'm supposed to be the big noise. The wicked sister, out to spoil the party.

I can start by talking to Amber. Amber said she wanted to help. I should let her. I'll find a way to talk with Marie as soon as I can. Send up a smoke signal or just show up on the doorstep, crash the graduation party maybe. That'd be in character. Might give Robbie a lift, too, since he's staying with his dad.

Jesus, Robbie. I hope he's doing okay.

The problem is, I don't have Amber's number, or her address.

Which is probably really sad, considering. It is also just par for the course. But I do have Aunt June's number from when she called the other day.

"Aunt June?" I say when she answers. "It's Geraldine. Sorry to interrupt, but I was hoping…"

There's shuffling in the background, and I hear Grandma Millicent's sharp voice. I can't make out the words, but Aunt June answers her instead of me.

"It's Geraldine, Mother." Grandma says something else, and I can picture Aunt June nodding before she turns to me. "We're glad you called, Geraldine. Mother was hoping to talk with you."

Shit. "Okay, sure. Put her on."

Again, that voice, sharp and clear, but I still can't hear the words.

"Can you come over here? It's important."

Because everything with Grandma is important. I swallow my anger. Because she is important, to the family, to me and Marie. I can't blow her off entirely. We might need her.

My phone beeps, letting me know a text has come through. *The hell?*

"Okay," I say to Aunt June. "I'm downtown anyway. I'll be there in five, maybe ten."

"Thank you, Geraldine," says Aunt June. There's an undertone in her voice I can't quite read. My scar itches and I rub it hard.

We say our good-byes and I hang up and check the text. All at once my ears are ringing and my breath is short, and I'm pretty sure I'm going to pass out.

It says:

Still here u love me love u not going away can't make me nope nope nope

The devil, who was still trying to harm her, came to him and exchanged the letter with one that stated that the queen had given birth to a changeling.
—"The Girl without Hands" from *Kinder und Hausmärchen* Vol. 1, Jacob and Wilhelm Grimm, 1812

MARIE, PRESENT DAY
CHARLIE'S ROADHOUSE, M-131

1.

Charlie's is a holdover from the bad old days. It's really little more than a windowless aluminum-sided shed with some neon Miller Beer signs hung on the sides. It's not even that big, so a lot of the drinking goes on in the parking lot, whether it's supposed to or not.

Everyone stares at my Escalade when I pull in, and of course at me. There is no chance of invisibility here. I have to settle for the armor that is my solid, respectable matron's appearance.

I march through the door. The patrons—mostly men in T-shirts, jeans, and gimme caps—don't exactly fall back, but they don't crowd me, either.

I am utterly out of my depth in this place. I don't see Tyler anywhere.

"Help you?" asks the bartender, plainly confused. He's old, gray haired, and paunchy, and his beard hasn't been trimmed in far too long. He has a MAKE AMERICA GREAT AGAIN cap on his head.

"I'm looking for my sister's boyfriend," I tell him, because I've got nothing else I can tell him. "I heard…he was getting a little out of control and might need a ride home."

He considers this. "Skinny guy? Short beard?" He tugs at his own flourishing growth.

"Yes."

"Yeah, he left maybe twenty minutes, maybe a half hour ago. Said he was going home to wait for her."

"Did he say anything—"

He cuts me off with a snicker. "All kinds of things. Whatever that fight was about, it was a good one."

A fight? My heart lurches. *Geraldine and her...that boy had a fight?* "Thank you."

"No problem," he answers amiably. "But, you know, he was pretty out of it. You might want to watch the ditches."

"I'll do that. Thank you."

I leave, trying not to look like I'm walking too quickly. No one needs to see that I can scarcely breathe. Because Tyler has gone back to the house. To Geraldine.

This is a gift. A gift. It can still come out all right. As long as she's not there. If I can get to him before she does, I can get him away. Let her believe he has left her. Geraldine will not forgive that.

I can make sure of it.

2.

When I open the old house's door, the beer and tobacco smell hits like a pair of fists. I am looking wildly around for my mother. She's not here. The front room is still and dark, but the lights are on in our old bedroom.

My feet still remember which boards creak, and my shoes are soft enough they make no sound as I hurry down the hall.

I take a deep breath. I push the door open.

Tyler is sitting on a rollaway bed, with an open six pack beside him and a cigarette bobbing in his mouth. He plucks it free and blows smoke at the ceiling.

The photos Geraldine taped to the wall are gone. All of them.

What did you do with the pictures?

Anger races past rationality. This is what my sister dragged home. This filthy, drunken boy who smokes like a chimney and throws away our past. This is what she cares about. Not us. Not me.

He blows another cloud of smoke, filling the air with the heat and bitterness like our mother used to. I want him dead. He doesn't belong here. He will never, ever belong here.

I know I don't make any noise, but Tyler turns his head anyway and squints at me.

"Oh," he says, around the cigarette. He wrestles another beer can out of the pack rings. "It's you."

"Yes," I agree. "And you're drunk."

He salutes me with the beer can and pulls the cigarette out of his mouth so he can take a healthy chug.

"I understand you and Geraldine had a fight?"

"What's it to you?"

Everything. It's everything to me. "Tyler, you can't stay here. You need to go someplace and sleep this off."

"Nope."

I force myself past the pain to remember how to deal with this kind of drunk. I cannot win a direct fight against beer and bleeding pride. "Come on, Tyler. I'll take you to a motel. You can sleep in a real bed and it will all look better in the morning."

"Nope." He blows his smoke straight toward me. "I'm here and I'm stayin' right here." He squints at the cigarette butt and looks for somewhere to put it out. There's no place, so he grinds it against the wall.

You *thing*. You stinking *thing*! Do you have any idea how hard I've worked to keep this place up! I saved this for her! Not for you to make into your goddamned ashtray!

"If you go with me now, I'll talk to Geraldine. I promise. Whatever it is…"

"I said *nope*!" He hurls the beer can at the wall. Amber liquid splashes everywhere, running like cold piss down the old plaster. "She's coming back and I'm going to be here. Right here. Right where she can see me. She doesn't get to kick me out like some fucking boy toy!"

Stark understanding washes through me. Geraldine did try to do the right thing. She tried to send him away, but he won't go. But she did try. She did.

He picks up his phone off the pillow and starts texting madly with both thumbs, probably telling Geraldine what he's just told me.

"Please, Tyler," I say. "Come with me. I know where Geraldine is. I'll take you to her."

"Nope." He hunches closer over his phone. "Nope, nope, nope, nope!"

He pushes a final button and falls back, spent.

Anger provides the inspiration I need. I swoop down and snatch his phone from his limp fingers.

"Hey!" He struggles to get up to follow me as I run out the door, but his feet get tangled in the trailing sleeping bag and he sprawls full length on the floor instead.

I run out the front door, punching at the phone's keys with my thumb until I call up his text messages. I was right. He did text Geraldine. She'll be on her way back here. She'll find him. I can't let her. I can't.

I bite my lip and type:

Charlie's has the best beer, HA HA HA!

I send it. Then, I drop the phone onto the gravel and stomp on it, hard. The case shatters and I leave the bits there.

That's done. Geraldine, wherever she is, will be further delayed with a detour to the roadhouse. Now, I just have to decide what to do about Tyler. If she sees him, even as he is, she might weaken and try to take him back.

I cannot let that happen.

273

A happy ending must include punishment for the bad guys. Otherwise how could it be really happy?

—Dr. Geraldine Monroe (margin notes)

GERALDINE, PRESENT DAY
CHARLIE'S ROADHOUSE, M-131

1.

"Hey, Geraldine!" Randy calls over the noise from the ancient jukebox and the would-be punks talking smack at each other by the pool table. "Your boyfriend was in here earlier. He was about eight over the limit when he left."

Shit. Too late. "Yeah, I heard." I stop in front of the bar, ignoring the men hunched over their long necks and shot glasses. "I don't suppose he said where he went?" In my head, I'm already running down the checklist. *House first, then the lake, keep an eye on the ditches…*

"Said he was headed back to your place, but I don't know. You should call your sister. Maybe she found him by now."

"My sister?"

"Yeah, she was here too, looking for him…" Randy scratches under his beard. "About, what, an hour ago, I guess?"

How in the hell…? Never mind, never mind. "Thanks." I rap twice on the bar and try not to run back outside.

I shut myself into my car, shove the keys into the ignition, and throw it into gear. Something is wrong. Marie was in Charlie's an hour ago.

That text from Tyler came through maybe a half hour ago, if that long. That doesn't make sense. But I can't call Marie, because Dad got hold of her phone, and I don't know if she's got it back yet, and Tyler's still not answering his. I've texted three times now and there's still nothing.

Something is really wrong.

I drive too fast. I'm going to hit a deer, or a late bicycler, or another car if I don't slow down. I don't slow down. I accelerate around the curves, under the tree branches, down the hills, into the dark.

Something's wrong. Right here. Right now. I can't put my finger on it. My window is open and the rush of air brings the smell of the green woods and the distant lake, and rain.

And a hint of smoke. And I know.

What's wrong is the light. There's a glow up ahead that does not belong there, not at this time of night.

I round another curve and I see it clearly—a flickering, rotten orange gleam between the trees where there shouldn't be anything at all.

I'm up on the shoulder and in the weeds before I can brake. I'm cursing and yanking on the door and the seat belt at the same time.

Heat slams against my back as I fall out of the car. Smoke flows into me as I gasp.

There are moments in your life when you cease to think. Your planning and plotting is all gone and there's nothing left but terror—for your life, for the lives of those you love. That's how you finally know you really do love them. When you become a passenger in your own body, and you're racing across the road, heading toward the fire.

Until the heat hits like a brick wall.

Until you hear the roar and crash as the house's bones break, and that sound grabs your plotting, planning, thinking self and drags it back out of the corner where it collapsed. Because that part of you is needed now.

Because somebody has to scream.

Human nature, in the Household Tales, is inborn. One sister is good, one sister is bad. There's not even the possibility of change. No one has to stop and reconsider. There's only continuous motion toward an ending where all things turn out as they are expected to. And that's happiness.
—Out of the Woods: Musings on Fairy Tales in the Real World,
Dr. Geraldine Monroe

MARIE, SEVENTEEN YEARS OLD
GERALDINE, FIFTEEN YEARS OLD
THE ROSE HOUSE

1.

Maybe if the snow had been a little less deep or the cold snap a little shorter, they could have gotten out.

Maybe if there'd been a neighbor to check in, they could have found a way to get down to Petoskey and the Greyhound station.

Maybe if Uncle Pete had been able to keep the promise he made, the one Aunt Trish decided not to tell her nieces about, they still could have made it.

But none of these things happened. What did happen was the girls lived with Aunt Trish for a week. They learned to light the cast-iron stove, and how to make sourdough pancakes and fried potatoes and onions. They learned to fill the Coleman lanterns and that the delivery boy knocked three times and that the money was in an ancient cigar box on the top shelf of the kitchen cupboard.

They learned that Aunt Trish was going blind.

"Cataracts," she said. "Maybe. Who knows? I don't know. Scurvy, rickets, misspent years, drink, sin. Doesn't matter. Goddamn."

And at the end of the week, the door opened and their father walked in, slapping his gloved hands together and smiling at Trish.

Marie saw him and froze where she stood.

Geraldine did a little better. She drove one bony shoulder into his stomach and ran past him, tearing down the stairs.

Until she slipped and fell. And he came, and he wrapped his strong arms around her and held her, not minding the blood on his jacket.

"I said to myself, I can get a new jacket," he said later when he told the story. "I can never get a new daughter."

Marie watched. Marie followed. And Marie said nothing at all. Not for three weeks solid, until the stitches were taken out of Geraldine's lip, and Geraldine herself was allowed out of their room to go back to the store and school and taking care of Mom.

"You're glad to be home where you belong, aren't you Marie?" he asked, staring deeply into her eyes, alert for any flicker of doubt.

"Yes, Dad," answered Marie. "I'm so glad to be home where I belong."

The heroine's journey is different from the hero's. The hero has left home, voluntarily or not. His quest is to find a place in the world. The heroine, on the other hand, is fixed in place—in the woods, in the castle, on top of the glass hill. Sometimes inside her own home. Her quest is to find a way to escape.
　　　　—Out of the Woods: Musings on Fairy Tales in the Real World,
　　　　　　　　　　　　　　　　　　Dr. Geraldine Monroe

GERALDINE, PRESENT DAY
THE ROSE HOUSE

1.

I wake up to craving.

It crawls up through my veins and pounds in my head so hard my vision blurs. The pillow is damp under my cheek. I'm surrounded by white walls. I'm on a soft bed. There's sunlight. I've got no idea where this is, and I don't care. I'm falling apart. I'm hollowed out.

Tyler. I was looking for Tyler. My throat raw from screaming. I remember the smoke. The heat. Running away.

No. I squeeze my eyes shut, and the craving gets worse.

I did not run away. That was the other time, the other fire. The night Mom died. This time I ran toward the burning house. I know I did. This time it was not my fire, and there was no rain to save me, or anybody else.

"Oh good." Words drift between the beats of pain. "You're awake."

My eyes fly open.

Dad is standing in the doorway, all calm and quiet concern. Absolutely unruffled. Marie stands at his shoulder.

"What's the matter with me?" My ragged throat and dry mouth break the words to bits.

"The doctor gave you something."

Oh no. Oh shit. "You let...you didn't tell..."

You didn't tell them I'm a fucking junkie?

"You were such a mess, Geraldine," says Dad, softly, tenderly. "We were terrified you were going to hurt yourself."

Dad strolls into the room and sits on my bed. Marie drifts in behind him and stations herself in the corner. Her eyes are wide and she keeps touching the walls, as if trying to reassure herself they're real.

She sees things, David said.

Get it together, I tell myself. *Remember what's important.* "Where's Tyler?"

Dad glances at Marie. A current passes between them that I can feel but not comprehend. I smell fire. Not just smoke, but the foul, complicated, chemical reek of a burning house. It coils out of the past and the present. I hear echoes of my own screaming, and I know. I tell myself I don't, but I do.

"Where the fuck is Tyler!" I croak.

"Geraldine," Marie begins, but it's Dad who finishes. The sight of his patient face and his sad eyes burns right through me.

"He's in the old house, Geraldine. Right where you left him."

2.

I have a lot of blanks after that—empty places in my mind where new memories simply failed to form. In their place, acrid smoke mixes inextricably with the feeling of Tyler's hands on my skin and his voice purring in my ear. But memory of his unique scent is gone. There's nothing left but the smell of the fire.

I stare at the ceiling, afraid to move or do anything that might distract me as I try to take detailed inventory of my own mind, and everything still in it that pertains to Tyler Prescott.

Can I see Tyler's calm efficiency as he sits Robbie up to check his eyes and his pulse? Yes. That's there.

Can I see him dancing in the shifting fairy lights of that stupid Vegas disco, and on his hands and knees in the sunlight, searching for wild strawberries in that meadow in the Allegheny Mountains? Yes. Good.

Do I remember his face as he rose over me, lost in the joy of our bodies?

Yes. Oh, yes. All of that is still with me, and it will be until the day I die.

And how he stared at me in disbelief as I shouted at him to go the fuck away?

Oh, yes. That, too.

3.

At some point, I surface from that acidic combination of darkness and memory to find there are strangers gathered around my bed.

No. That's wrong. There're four people, but only one stranger. Dad's there, at the bed's foot, so if I want to avoid seeing him, I have to turn my face away. He runs his hand through his hair, his attitude all decorous concern.

Marie is in the corner, again, in front of the armchair. She's freshly brushed and lightly made up, dressed in a plain pink T-shirt and white capris, a costume that assures the world she's still Daddy's baby girl.

The third person is David, a fact I register with dull surprise. He's in a rumpled red polo shirt and dirty jeans, and looks like he hasn't slept in a week. When Dad's gaze shifts toward him, I can feel the smug disapproval.

The fourth one, he's the stranger. He's standing beside David wearing the brown uniform of the Whitestone County sheriff's department. He lays the Smokey-the-Bear-style hat on the nightstand.

"Geraldine," says Marie gently. "This is Gary Scrope."

"She knows me." Gary smiles and actually manages to look cheerful when he does.

Now I manage to place him. He's Corinne Scrope's younger brother, so he's some kind of cousin, somewhere over in that dim blur that is Mom's side. He used to be skinny and spotty, and I think he hung around with David in high school.

"They need a statement, Geraldine," Dad informs me. "About what happened that night…about…" Dad lets his words falter and break off.

"You feel up to talking?" Gary fills in.

No. But I nod anyway and shove myself upright on the pile of pillows. Gary pulls out one of those little flip notebooks you see the cops carry on TV. His face remains absolutely neutral. I would have thought a burned-up corpse would unsettle a local boy more. But then I remember where I really am. Our idyllic rural town has plenty of ways to kill its people. This probably isn't even Gary's first fire.

Behind Gary, David watches Marie. He's all but vibrating as he wills her to look at him. But Marie's attention is pinned on me, just like Dad's. That's understandable. After all, Dad is here because he doesn't know what I'll say, and neither does Marie.

The difference is, Marie knows what I could say.

"What was your relationship with Tyler Prescott?" asks Gary.

Marie knows I could look our Jesus-knows-how-many-times-removed cousin right in the eye and tell him everything.

"He's…he was my boyfriend." *When I was with him, I could dance. I could sing. I laughed out loud for no reason at all. He pulled me fully into my life for the first time.*

Marie rubs her fingertips together, her only external sign of nervousness. Dad sees. His empty eyes dart to her face. But she's still watching me.

"How long had you been seeing Mr. Prescott?"

"A little over a year."

I could tell Gary, and David, and Dad. Oh, yes, most especially Dad, about Marie's first phone call six months ago. *My sister said she was ready to kill him.*

"Mr. Prescott was a student at the university where you taught?"

"Yes." *No, I mean really kill him.*

"Did your relationship with a student cause any problems?"

"Not really. I mean, it wasn't exactly kosher, but he was twenty-three when our relationship started." *My pink and white sister, Daddy's baby girl, was finally ready to kill our father all good and dead and bury him in his grave, right next to Mom.*

"How had things been lately, between you and Mr. Prescott?"

"It was…we'd had a fight. Before he came up. He followed me, to try to patch things up."

I could tell these men about the second call. *Okay, Marie. I'm in.* That might be a little anticlimactic though. Everybody already knows what a bad girl I am.

"How was that going?"

"It was…it started off all right."

Marie, though. Marie's kept everything hidden so well. Revelations about Marie would surprise them all.

"Can you tell me where you were around ten o'clock?"

"I was trying to find Tyler. We'd had another fight. I…he…I thought he'd left town, but he didn't. He texted me he was at Charlie's."

"I already told you about that, Gary," David says. "He took his car into Ed's to get the windows fixed and asked Ed where he could get a drink. Ed sent him to Charlie's."

Who is David's explanation for? Is it for Sheriff Cousin Gary, because it's the truth? Or for Marie, so she knows he tried to help? Or is it for Dad, so Dad knows David is still on Team Monroe and doesn't try to cut him off from Robbie and Marie?

"Randy told me Tyler had been drinking pretty heavily," I tell them. "He said…"

Marie's thumb is worrying at the scab on her palm. She's going to break it open. *I feel your feels, sis, really I do. But Dad is watching. He sees you're nervous, Marie. He's gonna know something's up.*

"Randy said Tyler told him he was going back to the house."

My throat is sore. My head is killing me. I need something. Just a little something. Just enough to get me through this. I stomp on that. Instead, I imagine myself speaking the whole truth and nothing but the truth, one crystal-clear word at a time, so Gary Scrope can get it all down in his little black book.

About how we detailed the plan: how Marie would fudge the accounts to create a story of embezzlement and fraud; how I would come home and make all kinds of noise and slowly escalate the appearance of violence and threats down at the old house by staging a series of misdeeds.

I'd start by making it look like I'd been beaten. And then the house would get damaged.

And then it'd be burnt down altogether. To make it look like Geraldine and her pesky inquiries were really not welcome here.

"By the time I got there..." My fingers knot into the quilted coverlet, and I meet my sister's eyes. "The fire had already started."

I could tell them how, when the time was right, Marie would lead Walt—gently, lovingly, with nothing but concern for the good name of all Monroes—to the evidence that Dad was embezzling from the family trust.

And I could tell them all how Dad would finally be found dead. A tragic event that by then could easily be explained away as a suicide. His car would be perched on the dunes in the same spot where his brother's truck was found all those years ago.

"I think that's enough," says Dad. "You've got what you need, don't you, Gary?"

"Last thing," says Gary. "Do you know who we should call?"

I could throw Marie to the wolves. Because right now, she's the only one who has actually broken the law.

My problem is, the wolves Sheriff Gary has the power to summon are nowhere near savage enough for what Marie has done.

"He's...was...there were some family problems, but he was still in touch with one of his sisters. Angela Jimenez. She lives in Los Angeles. I've got her number. I think, I..."

"Don't worry about it." Gary tucks the notebook back in his shirt pocket. "We'll find her. You get your rest."

Gary leaves, and then, more slowly and reluctantly, David follows. Dad comes up right behind them, setting a friendly hand on each man's back. Marie trails the masculine group, but only as far as the threshold. She closes the door and turns to face me.

Because, of course, we need to talk.

4.

Marie sits on the edge of my bed, right where Dad was. It's probably still warm. She takes a quiet moment to make sure she's wearing the correct expression of sisterly sorrow.

"Geraldine, I'm so sorry. But you're strong. We will get through this. You can stay right here. You take as much time as you need."

Marie takes my clenched fist. I feel the rough line of her healing cut. My scar burns. My skin crawls. I need something. Just to get me through this. Because there is so very much to get through right now.

"Right. Sure. Just like we planned it," I say.

"Yes. No. I don't mean…"

"Of course you don't. But we had a plan, right? You had to stick to the plan."

"You cannot talk about this now," she breathes. "We agreed. We wouldn't say anything out loud that might be misunderstood."

Because once Dad was dead and Gary Scrope, or somebody like him, came to ask us about our father, we had to be able to say what we had said and done, and we had to tell the truth. We had to live the setup, just like Marie has been doing for years. And I agreed. I'd say God help me, but there is no help.

"I tried, Geraldine," Marie whispers.

I want to go away and be sick. Because all I can see are Marie's dead eyes that night in front of Aunt Trish's when she turned from me to our father and smiled.

I press my fingers against my bruised cheek. It hurts, but not nearly enough.

"Tried what?"

"To keep you out of it. To do this on my own. But I made a mistake the first time. Eventually, I realized hadn't paid attention to the signs. I'd closed myself off, do you understand? I needed time, to learn to be open. I needed to plan more carefully, to make sure all the details were correct.

"And I needed you. We *had* to do this together. It couldn't happen any other way."

I remember the note. The note that has now gone up in smoke along with the rest of the house. Its ashes mix with Tyler's now. *I did it. I'm sorry.*

"You...what did you do?"

"I took Mom's pills. I meant to use them...The night she...the night you and she...and you..."

My mouth has gone dry. I'm staring at her. "Which pills? From her table drawer?" *The ones in the shoebox, down in the cellar?*

Marie frowns at the question, then nods.

All at once, my stomach cramps up, hard. I have to roll over. For a split second, I think I'm going to be sick, but I'm wrong. I just start laughing. It's a hard, hysterical, jagged waterfall of noise, but I can't stop myself. I can't believe it has come to this. I can't. I won't. Oh, shit, oh, shit. I hurt. I hurt so bad.

"Please, Geraldine," Marie begs. "We have to pull together. We—"

And that's when Dad walks back in, with his smallest smile turning up the corners of his mouth and lighting his eyes.

That small smile that says, *Gotcha*.

5.

How much did he hear? What does he know?

"Didn't mean to interrupt the girl talk," he says cheerfully. "But I wanted you to know, Geraldine, the doctor left you these." He fishes in the pocket of his khakis, like he's not sure what's there. Then, he holds up a bottle of pills and rattles them just a little. "In case you need something later to help you sleep."

In case I need something. Staring at that amber bottle, I am nothing but need. I want to lunge for it. I'll crawl across the floor and beg, if that's what it takes. The thing that stops me—and it is the only thing— is that little tiny, gleam in my father's bottomless eyes.

"You got a doctor to hand you a bottle of pills for your junkie daughter?"

Dad sighs at Marie. Her cheeks have gone pink.

And I have my answer. Dad didn't tell the doctor about my addiction, and he didn't give Marie any chance to. Not because he's ashamed, and not because he wants to protect my reputation in Whitestone. That kind of thinking is for other fathers. My father didn't give the doctor a full history, because my father wanted those pills.

"Dad." Marie's voice is almost as hoarse as mine. "I thought we'd agreed…"

"Look at her, Marie," Dad pleads. "She's hurting."

Oh yes. Yes, I am. "You son of a bitch."

My father returns a beatific smile.

"All right. All right. I see I'm not welcome here. You two know best." He sighs, and he considers. "Tell you what? I'll leave just one," he says. He twists open the lid and shakes one little white circle into the palm of his hand. "You're both right, of course. We do need to go easy on these. They're pretty powerful and, well, there's family history, isn't there?"

"She doesn't need that," snaps Marie.

The pill clicks against the table. Dad does not bother to turn around. "It's just one, Marie."

I don't look at it, but I feel it, like sunlight against my cheek.

"She just needs rest."

"Then we should let her rest." He straightens up to face her. "Let's go."

Marie draws herself up to her full height. It's not something I've ever seen her do in front of him. I'm kind of surprised. Or, I would be, if so much of my mind wasn't occupied in wishing they'd both go away. I want to be alone. Just me and the pill and the smell of smoke.

Marie turns her back on Dad. She bends down and kisses my forehead. Her mouth is cool and soft. "I'll be back to check on you in a bit."

Dad stands in the threshold, with his arm out, motioning for her to pass. I fall onto the pillows. The door closes. My hand gropes across the nightstand.

And finds nothing. My whole body jerks upright without my telling it to.

The pill's gone.

6.

I want to throw myself after her. Shame crawls through every nerve, but it's nothing compared to the need to be filled. The need to not care.

To not feel the hatred roaring through me.

I curl up under the sweat-dampened sheet, too exhausted to do anything but play back the conversation with Marie in my head. The memory of it spills out of my skull to fill the blank, white room.

I think about the boxes in the shop's old storeroom. I think about Robbie and all the secrets he's keeping. I think about my reasons for coming here, and my reasons for staying.

I think about how very much I have lost, and all that I owe. I have not yet begun to pay the bill that's coming due.

But I know who lit the blaze that killed Tyler Prescott. I am sure I know.

Because Tyler isn't all that's dead and dust and ash. My files went with him—my computer, all my work and all my research, the papers that were going to help me cobble together some kind of future when I'd finished here. The two thousand dollars that might have been an emergency stash, that's gone, too.

Ashes to ashes. Dust to death. I came here because I thought I could finally break the ties that bind. Instead...

Instead.

The light fades around me. The room is stuffy and smells like nothing at all.

Carefully, one limb at a time, I sit up and set my feet onto the floor. For the first time I realize I'm not wearing my own clothes. I'm in a pair of black yoga pants and a plain white T-shirt.

I want my clothes. The last things I own. What did Marie do with them? Washed them, probably. Folded them neatly and put them into one of the dresser drawers to wait until they were needed.

My stomach cramps again and I push myself to my feet.

The house is quiet as I pad down the stairs. The kitchen is empty. So is the dining room. I drift into the great room and stare out between the roses and the trees for a long time.

I'm still staring when I see my father's reflection slide into place beside me.

Mirror, mirror, on the wall...

"You're up," he says.

"Couldn't sleep." I smile at his scarlet and amber reflection. My scar pulls and twists. "What did you do with Marie?"

"I told her she should go with Robbie and David. Get out of the house a little," he says. "We had to cancel the party, of course."

"Of course." All those calls. All those apologies. Marie must have been frantic.

He moves closer. "I was hoping we'd get a chance to talk."

I steel myself to face him. The last rays of the evening sun slide through the stained glass. My father stands in the center of a glowing scarlet patch. It tints his skin. Lips as red as blood. But it doesn't change his eyes. Nothing will ever change those eyes.

Both his hands are in his pockets. I know what he's got in there. I know it like I know the feel of my heart hammering in my chest.

I think how my whole life has been shaped and controlled by the contents of little plastic bottles with their big white caps and wraparound labels. And by all the people who held on to them. My mother. My friends. And even Robbie.

"Is this about Marie?" I ask.

Dad nods without breaking eye contact. And now I understand. Dad heard. Maybe not everything, but enough. He knows why I came back, and who set the fire that murdered Tyler and finally destroyed the old house. Just like he knows what really happened to Uncle Pete, and Mom.

And, like always, Dad knows just what to do to make it all better.

"I was talking to David," I tell him. "He thinks Marie's got...problems."

Dad sighs. "Well, you know how it is. Marie spends too much time in her own head. She needs a lot of understanding."

"About who people are and what they're doing?" I suggest.

"She gets a little confused."

"And sometimes she's confused enough to do some damage, if she doesn't get that understanding?"

"What are you saying, Geraldine?"

But he knows. He's the one leading me on. Just like in the story. *Come stand in the yard, daughter, because the devil is coming to take you away.*

All right, Dad. I'll stand here, nice and clean and quiet. Let's see which of us the devil can get his claws into.

"I'm saying, Dad, that I wonder where Marie was when the old house caught fire and what she was doing."

"I'm not sure I know. I'm not sure anybody knows."

"That's not good."

"No." He pauses and looks at me from under his pale eyelashes. "But Marie's fragile, Geraldine. She needs to be handled carefully. For everyone's sake. Especially Robbie's."

Ah. Robbie. Of course. Robbie. We all want to take care of Robbie.

"She told you, I suppose, that I've been playing games with the family money?" he says calmly.

"Even Marie knows I don't care about the family money."

"You didn't used to. But now, things have changed. You're going to need something to get by on. Until your book sells, of course. Marie knew I'd set aside an account for you. Just in case. So, she would assume you had a stake in all this, and with you two being so close...I know she confides in you. Despite everything."

"Yes, she does," I agree. "And I'd say she's been under a lot of strain lately." The cliché slips smoothly off my tongue. "It's starting to show."

"I'm afraid so, yes. That's why I was so glad you came back." He reaches out and puts a hand on my shoulder. His palm is cool and soft, his blunt fingers strong despite his age.

I'm trying to remember the last time my father touched me. Oh, yes. Right. In the gully, where they found Mom. That was it.

"This can all be handled quietly, Geraldine," he tells me. "Things that look complicated in the beginning are usually pretty easy to resolve. As long as we're careful, everyone can get exactly what they need. But we don't want anybody putting two and two together and getting five, do we?"

"Especially not Marie, right?"

"Poor Marie."

"Poor Marie." My mouth twitches and I put up a hand to cover my scar. "Sorry. I'm just on edge."

"Well, this'll help." He pulls the bottle of out his pocket, twists the cap, and shakes out one white pill into the hollow of his palm. "Just the one, now."

I pluck the pill out of his hand with my cold, numb fingers. And just at the moment I open my mouth to place it carefully, reverently, on my tongue I look through the rose glass again, and this time, I think I see Marie.

But when I turn, of course, there's nobody there.

In the original stories, the happy ending is not the wedding. The happy ending does not come until the bad guys are all dead. Sometimes this takes a while.
—Out of the Woods: Musings on Fairy Tales in the Real World,
Dr. Geraldine Monroe

MARIE, PRESENT DAY
THE ROSE HOUSE

1.

I don't know what to do.

I planned, every day. I acted with care. I made myself perfect. I laid each stone and I tested each step, even as I was tested. I passed. I perfected the image of myself until no one bothered to look for anything else beneath.

I trusted one person. One.

But she did not trust me. Not enough. Now, that single stone has shifted, and the whole world is falling.

I don't know what to do.

2.

Robbie is down by the garage when I get there. He leans against the Mustang in the driveway, flicking his thumb against his phone. The light shines into his face and shows me my son—grim, distant, seeking his escape in that private world he carries with him.

I was appalled when I saw Robbie walk in behind David and Gary. But David told me Robbie wanted to make sure I was okay. He stayed, even though his father left hours ago. Here at the end of the world, he came back for me.

That must mean I've done something right. Maybe. I don't know. I don't know anything.

Robbie sees me, or at least my shadow, and shoves his phone in his back pocket.

"Mom?" he says. "You okay?"

I do not answer that. It wouldn't do either of us any good. "I need you to drive me to Uncle Walt's." As I speak, I feel my maternal tones and expressions all fitting themselves into place. It is automatic. I need to be sure Robbie is out of the way. This is the only way I can think to do that. "And pick me up again afterward. I'll text you. You can go get a pizza…"

"I don't want a pizza, Mom. And you don't want to see Uncle Walt."

"You think you don't, but you must be hungry…"

"Mom! Cut it out!"

I close my mouth.

"Just…just stop it!" he shouts. "A guy is dead, Mom! You can't just pretend it didn't happen this time!"

Oh, my dear son, you have no idea. "I know, Robbie, and we're all very upset, but you need…"

Horror rises in Robbie's eyes. Not the pained embarrassment of adolescence, but the genuine terror that comes with understanding a truth too huge and too awful to encompass. "You're letting him get away with it," he whispers.

Why doesn't the ground shift? Why doesn't the air move? Where are the familiar secrets crawling out in answer to my pain? There's nothing to help me remember how to act. Not even my mother's cold, angry presence behind me. This time, I have gone too far for them to reach.

"Robbie," I make myself say. "I promise…"

"He killed that guy and you know it!" Robbie stabs his finger up toward the house. "You know and I know and *Dad*, he knows…"

"Robbie!" I grab his shoulders and shake him, hard. He's so startled, he lets it happen. "Did your father say anything to you about this?"

"No," he admits, but there's no time for relief to set in. "But I saw the look on his face. I'm not a goddamned little kid, Mom! Grandad was pissed off about Aunt Geraldine's boyfriend and now he'd dead! It doesn't take a genius to figure out somebody ought to be asking questions!"

Somebody is asking questions. He's asking questions and he's laying plans, and he's watching us. He's staring out from under the night-black roses and watching us right now.

"Robbie, you cannot say this, not to your father, not to anyone. Do you hear me?"

"Why the hell not? Why should I protect him? I'm not like you!"

He regrets the words as soon as he speaks them. I see that. He shoves that regret beneath his anger, but it's hard and it hurts.

"Robbie, listen to me. I know you're angry. But you cannot go around saying things like this."

"Why? 'Cause he'll hear me? You think I care what he hears anymore?"

No. No. Stop it. Stop it. Robbie. You have to stop. He'll hurt you. He'll kill you, Robbie. He will kill you and he'll make me cover it up.

My hands hurt. The pain runs up my arms into my mind. Bright lines in the void.

"You say you're not a little boy anymore. All right. You're not. That means you need to think about what you're saying, and who you're saying it to." I meet his eyes. "You know what words can do, Robbie."

Look at me. See me. Please. Just this once. Really see me.

He says nothing. He just steps back out of my grip. There is a smear of blood on his arm. My scab has broken open again and marked him.

"Dad said I could come stay with him," Robbie tells me. "Any-time."

"Yes," I agree. I do not ask when David said this. It does not matter. "If you need to go, you should go," I tell him. Robin James

Pendarves. My only child. His life flashes in front of my eyes and is gone. "I'd appreciate it if you'd give me a ride to Walt and Carla's on your way."

I speak like I would to a stranger, or one of my older relations. I can't do anything else. I do not have a foundation for this. There are no habits or manners or masks to retreat behind. There isn't even darkness left to me. Darkness requires that there be light somewhere.

"Okay," says Robbie finally. "Come on."

I climb into the Mustang's passenger seat and buckle in. Robbie turns over the ignition and the radio, or streaming service, or whatever it is, blasts out…something. Very loud with a thudding bass that shakes the floorboards.

He shuts it off instantly.

"Sorry." He mutters, and he puts the car in reverse.

We make the drive in silence. Robbie puts the top up without my having to ask. He punches a few buttons and gets a classical music station to fill the silence. He drives with a caution I am sure is exaggerated, coming to a full stop at every sign, and slowing down for each yellow light.

I am grateful. I am silent. I am so very sad.

Finally, we come to town, and he turns down Third Street, and into Walt and Carla's drive. Robbie punches the button that unlocks the door. I climb out and face him. He's leaving me now. He has nothing with him. I've given him nothing, haven't packed or prepared anything. I have nothing that will help him. I never did.

"Mom," he says. "There's something you need to know. Something Aunt Geraldine told me."

I am silent and I am still. Robbie speaks softly, steadily. His voice is hesitant, almost boyish. But there is nothing boyish in what he says, or what he is doing.

My son tells me about Geraldine's past. A whole world of things she never told me. He is making a gift of it to me, even after all that I have done to him.

With these words, my son is choosing sides. He is giving me permission for what I have to do next.

I close the car door. Robbie drives away and I turn away. Neither one of us looks back.

3.

Walt and Carla live in a lovely old Victorian home complete with a wraparound porch and gingerbreading, the details highlighted in three different colors. It's a lovingly preserved remnant from Whitestone's glory days when the quarries and the timbering brought endless supplies of money. The curtains are drawn, but the light streams through onto the tidy lawn edged by yew bushes and roses. It could be a stage stetting for an old black-and-white movie. Something wholesome and hometown with plenty of happy endings to go around.

I don't want to move. If I just stand here, maybe the happy ending will still happen. Maybe I'll get to see it.

I imagine myself walking up those steps and ringing that bell. Carla will answer the door, and she will let me in, all quiet concern.

I'm sorry, I'll say. *I'm so sorry.*

I'll sit on their sofa and she'll call Walt down from the upstairs.

I'm sorry. Walt. There's something I have to tell you. Something I should have told you years ago.

You see, your father didn't just disappear, into the lake, or thin air or anywhere else. My father killed him. Another one of his tidy domestic murders. It happened the night I ran away and almost died. That was why he left me and Geraldine with Aunt Trish for so long. He had to make sure that the body would stay gone, and that no one would look to blame him. He had to make sure he had our mother under control.

But if I tell them the truth, then I am trapped. Cornered by secrets exposed both too late and too soon.

I have to go on. I have to protect my son. He is not going to be able to keep quiet much longer. He is too angry. He thinks he understands his grandfather's power. He does not, not really.

But I do.

I know that my father is friends with the sheriff, as well as the mayor, the town council, the bankers, and the owners of the remaining quarry. Many of them owe him money for one thing and another. He's made sure of that. I know that sometime very soon, he will go into his friend's office and close the door. He'll have something to say. He'll be very reluctant. It will pain him deeply, but he has to do this.

Which of us will it be?

I would have thought Geraldine. He might just be trying to put her at her ease, with his little confidences in the dark and his careful doling out of fresh pills. After all, it worked with our mother. Among the things I have learned over the years is that Dad is confident, but not terribly creative. Unless he's pushed, he goes with what's worked before. If he can lull Geraldine into a false sense of confidence, she'll be right where she needs to be when they come for her.

It would serve her right.

The problem is, of course, it could be me he's setting up. He could decide that Geraldine will be easier to keep hold of going forward. That I failed him one too many times. He could have found out why I brought her home. Walt, sitting in his bright living room with his wife, might already have told him.

And I know Dad has been preparing for the day I become a liability. He's been telling people about me. He's made sure they all know Marie is not just weak and obedient; Marie is crazy. Marie sees things. Marie hears things.

And I have to admit, it's a very good story. It fits with who we are. Because my mother was crazy, my aunt was crazy, my sister, too. A whole houseful of crazy women. And one sane, sad man doomed to love us all. It has been so hard for Dad. All these years, all the work to keep us all together. All those cold nights making sure we didn't ever stray or get ourselves into real trouble.

You need to let me take care of this, Marie, he said to me back then. *We don't want anybody putting two and two together and getting five, do we?*

I feel my mother behind me, and I know exactly what I will do.

I just don't have much time.

The idea of a kiss solving the princess's problems is actually not that present in most of the original Household Tales. The Frog Prince, for example, does not receive even a reluctant kiss from his princess. Instead, she throws him against the wall.

Snow White is not kissed, either. She's dropped out of the coffin by a careless servant, which jars that bit of apple out of her throat.

Sleeping Beauty is apparently somewhat more than kissed by her prince. In one of the earliest versions, she gives birth while she's still asleep, and the baby sucks the poisoned spindle tip out of her finger.

Is there a moral of the story? Yes. It's that real salvation is an inherently messy business.

—Out of the Woods: Musings on Fairy Tales in the Real World,
Dr. Geraldine Monroe

MARIE, NINETEEN YEARS OLD
STACEY B'S SANDWICHES AND STUFF

1.

"Please, Geraldine," said Marie. "Just this once?"

They were in the living room. Marie sat on the edge of her chair. Geraldine sprawled on her back on the sofa, glowering. Marie held her breath. Geraldine had to agree. Everything depended on it. But she might say no, just because Marie needed it so much.

Geraldine, to everybody's surprise, had scraped through high school. Marie was home from her second year of college and working for Dad in his new real estate office, just exactly like he had always planned she would. Geraldine was spending her summer…what was Geraldine doing? There were rumors, and Marie didn't like any of them.

Dad clearly didn't, either. Most days began with a cold, tense enumeration of Geraldine's faults. Most of them ended that way as well.

Mom slept through most of it.

"Fine," Geraldine sighed toward the ceiling. "I'll take her up to see Aunt Trish. That's always good for two or three hours of screaming fights and make-up drinking afterward."

"Oh, Geraldine, that's not a good idea. You know how angry Dad gets when he finds out you and Mom have been talking to Aunt Trish."

This was pure reflex. By now, it was next to impossible for Marie not to consider what their father might say and do. Marie herself had not been back to the ruined Rose House since... before. Since that time. But Geraldine knew going to the Rose House was the easiest way to upset Dad, so she did it every chance she got.

How can she stand it? But Geraldine had always been stronger. Marie couldn't even let herself think about that time anymore, or what had taken them there. It was all mixed up in her head and she got sick every time she tried to sort it out for herself. The confusion was so frightening because it was so inexplicable. She *knew* what happened. Dad told everyone, he told her, and told her, and told her.

Aunt Trish had kidnapped them. She'd held them up there overnight. It only felt like a week. Marie had been sick most of the time, so she couldn't remember properly, and then there was the fact that poor Pete went missing at the same time. She'd gotten upset and mixed up, that was all. But Dad knew what really happened.

In fact, Dad had spent a whole month afterward persuading all the people who mattered that it hadn't been as bad as it looked. The girls were safe, he said. They were home. That was all he wanted. There was no need to press charges. Patricia Burnovich wasn't actually dangerous. She was just confused. She needed understanding, that was all. It was up to the family to look out for her better.

He said that a lot.

At the same time, whenever Mom suggested she should go up to the house, Dad frowned. "It's a bad idea. She gets so agitated. You might set her off, Stacey, and we don't want that. I'll handle it, all right?"

And Mom, bleary-eyed and pale-skinned, would look at him and leave the room. But she didn't stop sneaking up there, with and without Geraldine. What did they think they were doing? Marie never knew. It wasn't like it helped anything. It just made Dad angry. And then Geraldine would stay out all night, and Mom would lock herself in her bedroom, and Dad would shake his head and talk about all the work he had to do.

"I can't manage them alone, Marie," he whispered to her. "Things are about to break wide open for us, baby girl. I need you here to help. Everything's about to change."

That was something else he said a lot, but only to Marie. She and her father had grown closer than ever. Even now that she was in college, he was always driving up to see her. She never knew when he might drop in. When she was home on break, he hardly ever let her out of his sight. She was in the office with him, or in the house helping, or driving back and forth with him. That was wonderful, really. The other girls in the dorm teased her about it, but that, of course, was just because they envied her for having a father who loved her so much and protected her so lovingly. Even from her sister. He was very gentle with her about Geraldine, but he was firm, too. He had to be. Because Geraldine was a liar, just like Mom. Just like Aunt Trish.

And of course she believed him. Sometimes, when things got bad, Marie would lie awake, staring at the ceiling and repeating what he told her. Just to keep things straight. She still got confused sometimes, about what did and did not happen. Sometimes Dad had to set her straight about the little details. But that was all right. He understood her confusion and the reasons for it, and he was always there to help her.

That was why they had to do this now. Dad would be home any second.

Geraldine peered at Marie from underneath her fringe of dyed black hair. "You want me to do the job, Marie, you have to let me do it my way."

"All right, all right," Marie said quickly. "Just as long as you promise to keep her away until at least midnight."

"What's the big deal?"

"Nothing." But the word rang hollow in Marie's ears. "Dad has a business dinner tonight. He wants me there and I just, well, I thought he might want to bring the client back here afterward."

"You think Dad's gonna bring a client back here?" Geraldine made a rude noise. "You're delusional."

"I just want everything to be nice, in case. You know how Mom's been lately."

Mom had been getting more and more agitated. There were days when she stood in the yard and screamed at the sky. The one time she'd lurched into the road like she was begging the cars to come hit her. The time they'd caught her trying to batter down the door to the store, which was only opened during the summer and on weekends now.

"Delirium tremens," said Dad quietly. "Well, Marie, it can't be long now."

Something sparked deep in Geraldine's eyes. Marie felt like the air curdled around her.

"Yeah," said Geraldine slowly. "I know exactly how Mom's been. I'll take care of her."

"Thank you," Marie said. Geraldine was up to something. It was all there, in her scarred face. Marie knew she should ask questions. In fact, Geraldine wanted Marie to ask. She was itching for it. But there wasn't any time. Dad was going to be home any second, and then she would have to head to the office with him, and there was still so much to do.

Let Geraldine keep her secret, Marie told herself. After tonight, it wouldn't matter. Dad was right. After tonight, everything was going to change for good.

"Alas, young queen, how ill you fare. If this thy mother only knew, it's sure her heart would break in two."
—"The Goose Girl" from *Kinder und Hausmärchen* Vol. 1, Jacob and Wilhelm Grimm, 1812

GERALDINE, PRESENT DAY THE ROSE HOUSE

1.

It's surprisingly easy to get out of bed in the morning. The only bad moment comes when I peel open my eyes, and the first thing I see is the little white pill sitting on the bedside table.

Just one, I hear Dad's voice in my head as I pick it up. *Just for now.*

But that moment passes. I dress in the clothes left for me: stretch pants that I think are meant to be cropped, but go down over my ankles anyway, and a pale blue T-shirt. It's probably oversized on Marie but just barely manages to fit me. I brush my hair and bundle it into a pony-tail. I smell like smoke. I don't think I'll ever stop smelling like smoke. I hope I don't. The smoke keeps the pain alive, and while the pain is alive, I'll remember Tyler and I won't lose my nerve.

Downstairs, Marie's set up the full formal dining room for us, or at least the dining area. The dividing walls and swinging door were ripped out years ago. The china and the silver and the cloth napkins are all laid out on a glass table. The scents of bacon and coffee, sugar and butter fill the room. There's a bowl of fresh strawberries next to what I assume is meant to be my place.

In the kitchen, my sister is busy beside the stove, a little frantic, like she always is when she's in motion. She's only cool when things are finished. She's rebandaged her hand, but I can see the bloodstain on it as she reaches for the ladle to drizzle more batter into the waffle iron.

That's never going to heal, Marie. But maybe it doesn't matter.

"Oh! You're up! Good morning!" she chirps, but her glance toward me is fleeting.

"Yeah," I agree. "Can I help with anything?"

"No, no, I've got it. You just go relax. Oh, can you take in the coffee?"

"Sure."

She flashes me a happy, vacant smile, and turns back to her waffle iron.

I take in the coffee, just in time to see Dad crossing the great room.

"Well!" he says as he surveys the breakfast spread, and me, in my Marie clothes. "What's all this?"

"Breakfast, of course," says Marie, bringing in the white platter heaped with fresh waffles. "I thought we could all use a good meal. I know you might not have time, Dad…"

He looks at the two of us. Tension thrums across the lines of our triangle. He meets my eyes and I put my hand up to cover my scar. It's an old gesture, but it comes back so easily, it's a little scary. From the corner of my eye I can see Marie, standing like some statue of June Cleaver, holding that plate of the steaming waffles as she watches us.

Dad notices, and I can only describe the look that crosses his face as wolfish. "Oh, no. For this, I'll make the time."

Dad slips easily into the chair at the head of the table. Marie takes her place at our father's right hand. I'm at his left. I don't remember the last time I sat with Dad when he was so visibly happy. He's absolutely in control and absolutely certain of himself and everyone around him.

Including me. Well, why shouldn't he be? I'll bet he even checked my room on the way down to make sure the pill was gone. Idly I wonder if he ever kept count of the pills Mom was taking. I bet he did. Dad's always been a detail kind of guy.

We keep busy passing fruit and bacon around on the good dishes.

Dad still drowns his waffles in syrup, while Marie spoons a few discreet berries onto hers. I heap the remainder onto my pastry. Marie watches. She's smiling. Just a little, but it reaches her eyes. Seeing us all gathered here, Marie is filled with sentiment as sweet as maple syrup. Her little family. I swear I even see a touch of pride.

Well, why shouldn't she be proud? This is everything she's worked for. I wonder what she's going to look like, later, when it's all over. I fork another strawberry into my mouth and let the juice spread across my tongue. I am eating without tasting anything. I am aware it's all rich and that I'm too full, but I don't stop. I feel like if I stop cramming something down, everything is just going to come bubbling out.

Finally, Dad pushes his plate away and reaches for the carafe to refill his cup. "I had a call from Gary Scrope this morning. About the fire," he adds, as if either of us needed telling. He leans back in his chair, crossing his ankle over his knee.

I swallow my mouthful of waffle and fork in another. Marie is watching me, carefully. Like she's not sure if I'll burst out screaming or just break down sobbing.

You have no idea, sis. Except there's a glitter in her eyes that says maybe she does.

"He says there's not a lot to go on." Dad takes an appreciative slurp of coffee. "They found that rum bottle in the ruins. Looks like that might have acted as an accelerant. He maybe got careless with a cigarette and..." He shrugs.

I notice Dad doesn't mention how that rum got into the house in the first place. Neither does Marie, of course. It wouldn't be polite.

"Anyway, Gary says the way things look right now, they're going to be putting it down as an accident. Unless something new turns up."

"Will something new turn up?" I ask him. Out of the corner of my eye, I see Marie's hand pause as she reaches for her juice glass.

"Well, I wouldn't know, would I?" Dad smiles. He saw it, too.

I wonder if the sheriff's office has gotten hold of Angela yet. I consider asking, but only for a minute. The fact that Tyler was a person, that he might have meant something to me, has been dismissed from the conversation. And anyway, I'm not sure what I'd do if I had to face Dad and Marie's mild, pitying looks in response to his name. I might not be able to hang on.

"Another waffle, Geraldine?" Marie pushes the platter toward me.

I help myself and reach for the butter.

"Where's Robbie?" I ask as I spoon yet more strawberries onto my plate.

"He's staying with his father. We decided it would be best until things settle down."

"Lots of shakeups coming," adds Dad. "Did Marie tell you, Geraldine? We're moving your grandmother and Aunt June into the house."

I glance at Marie. She's chasing soggy waffle crumbs around her plate. This tells me everything I need to know about who "we" actually is. I wonder if Dad bothered to tell her about his little plan before now.

"Of course, you can still stay as long as you want," Dad is saying. "There's plenty of room. But, well, there's bound to be some shuffling around. Still, Marie will manage everything just fine."

"It's what she's good at," I say. "I wonder if this is what Grandma wanted to talk to me about?"

"What?" says Dad, and this time, there's a frown on his face. "When?"

"Before." Despite my determination to meet and match the level of denial surging around this table, I cannot make myself say before what. "She asked me to come over. She had something to tell me. I should probably find out what."

"You can call after breakfast," Dad says.

"She's always up by nine," Marie adds.

Uncertainty churns inside me, thick and nauseating. I see the two of them, poised and perfectly comfortable in this blank modern space they've created out of Aunt Trish's ruin. Together, they've covered over so much. Everything that didn't fit the picture has been disappeared. I don't forget the pockets and piles of things Marie has squirreled away. I don't forget how I came to be here. But at the same time, when I see my father so calm and relaxed with her, I have to wonder. What if I'm wrong again? What if I was wrong from the beginning? Or not from the beginning. Just from last night.

There are so many points where I could have been mistaken, so many wrong turnings I could have made. And each one of them means there's something different waiting behind the masks we all wear.

Jesus.

I swallow and set my fork down on the side of my plate. My tongue is thick. "I think I'd rather go down there. I...need to get out. Clear my head a little."

"I've got some errands," says Marie. Although, what the hell those could be at this point is anybody's guess. "I'll take you."

"If it's all the same, I'd rather go on my own. If it's okay with you, Dad?" I add. Because that's the one move Marie cannot possibly protest.

Dad considers. He takes his time with the idea and enjoys every second. We sit here, Marie and I, awaiting his pronouncement. My scar twitches and my head pounds.

"I think it's a great idea," says Dad finally. "You should talk with your grandmother, Geraldine. Especially if...you're going to be here awhile."

"Great," agrees Marie instantly. What else is she going to do? "Maybe we can go shopping after you get back? You're going to need some things."

"Yeah, I can't keep wearing your clothes, can I?"

Dad watches us from over the rim of his coffee cup. I can tell the idea of me and Marie having a girls' day out tickles his particular fancy.

Jesus Christ. What am I doing?

Marie just beams at me. She can do that. Because Marie knows.

I let her smile and I let her look, and I let them enjoy this moment. Because whether I've been wrong, or whether I've been right, this is going to be the last little moment either of them gets.

Here's a piece of trivia almost nobody knows beyond a few specialists. All those evil stepmother stories—the ones where she abandons her children, or murders them outright, or exposes them to cold and starvation, or steals their voice, or their name, or their food to give to her other children—those wicked women weren't stepmothers in the stories told to the brothers and their associates. They were the birth mothers. The real *mothers.*

Jacob and Wilhelm had to make decisions about transcription and translation when they sat in their studies sorting through their material. They had no problem with self-mutilation, or birds pecking out eyes, or people being rolled down hills in barrels full of nails. But they thought depictions of mothers plotting elaborate infanticide was a step too far. Especially Wilhelm. Wilhelm thought the traditional tales could, and should, be improved. In modern-day language, he wanted them made more "accessible." So he softened the blow by killing off the real mothers and replacing them with more acceptable monsters.

But the mothers are still there, underneath. It's just that nobody talks about them, or if they do, nobody believes they mattered.

Somehow, that makes it worse.

—Out of the Woods: Musings on Fairy Tales in the Real World,
Dr. Geraldine Monroe

GERALDINE, SEVENTEEN YEARS OLD
STACEY B'S SANDWICHES AND STUFF

1.

Geraldine slammed the trunk shut. *Good. Done.*

She looked at her watch. Marie should be out at the restaurant now, doing what the hell ever she and Daddy had planned.

Time to go.

"Mom?" Geraldine called as she headed back into the house. No answer. The light was on in this living room, but no one was there. A whole lot of banging, rattling, and swearing was coming out of her parents' bedroom though. *Shit.*

Geraldine sucked in a breath and knocked on her parents' door. "Mom?"

There was a muffled grunt. She took it for a yes, and walked in.

Mom was there, rooting through her dresser drawer, head down, trying to see into the back corners.

Shit. Again.

"You okay, Mom?"

"No, I'm not okay." Mom slammed the drawer shut. "Haven't been okay for fucking well ever. Did you take my pills, Geraldine?"

Geraldine's heart banged once. *Okay, okay. Play it cool, G.* "You ran out," she lied. "Don't you remember? I called up this morning to refill your prescription."

"Oh. Oh." Mom sat on the edge of the bed and rubbed her arms. "Did they say when...?"

"This afternoon." Geraldine sat beside her.

"I need...something, G," she whispered in that weak, pleading voice that always left Geraldine feeling sick. "There's got to be something left, right?"

Geraldine squeezed her hand, carefully. Mom had been eating more lately, but she was still thin as a rail, and way too weak. She'd been smoking more, too. A real four-pack-a-day habit.

They'd worry about that later.

"What you need, Mom," she said, "is a vacation."

"What are you talking about?"

Geraldine grinned. "I'm talking about an absolutely awesome, girls-only summer road trip. We'll go up to Copper Harbor, and stay for a few days, and then down to the Wisconsin Dells, and then it's Milwaukee. You and me and Dad's credit card and the beer capital of America!" Okay, so it wasn't Dad's card. At least, it wasn't only Dad's card.

"How did you get your father to give you his credit card?"

"Who says he gave it to me?"

Mom blinked at her and she wavered.

"I don't know, G…" She was looking her bedside table, at the spot her pills weren't.

Where the hell did the pills even go? That bottle had been more than half full this morning. Probably rolled under the bed or something and she just forgot about it.

"Come on, Mom," Geraldine said. "We deserve it. I'll leave the card if it'll make you feel better. I've been saving up from the store." Which was even mostly true. "The car's gassed up, I even packed for you. It's all planned. We can pick up your prescription on the way," she added.

Mom swallowed and wiped at her mouth. "What about your sister?"

"I asked her, but she wants to stay here. She says Dad needs her or something." The truth was Geraldine hadn't bothered to ask. Marie would never leave Dad, not even for a couple of weeks. Marie was going to stay his baby girl until she died. But as of now, that was her problem.

"I can't leave Trish. You know she's in bad shape."

"You're not going to. We'll stop and get her on the way, too."

Mom's mouth moved, like she had to repeat Geraldine's words to get them to make sense. She ran her hand over her forehead. She was sweating. Jesus. All these weeks and she still hadn't stopped sweating.

"What's gotten into you, G? You think Trish is going to want a road trip? She won't even leave the house."

"You're going to convince her. This is it, Mom." Geraldine wrapped her hands around both her mother's. "This is our chance."

Come on, Mom. Come on. You can do it. All you have to do is believe the story. You don't have to poke holes. Just believe what I'm telling you long enough to get in the car. That's it. Please.

Mom sucked in a deep breath. She looked at the nightstand

again, and Geraldine thought something inside her was going to explode.

Then, slowly, almost like she had to try to remember how all the muscles worked, a grin spread across her mother's tired, sallow face.

"Okay, G," she said. "Let's go."

No one ever asks where the power comes from in these families. Like the hatred, it's simply taken for granted. But would anyone be that surprised to find out these two things grow from the same root?
—*Out of the Woods: Musings on Fairy Tales in the Real World,*
Dr. Geraldine Monroe

GERALDINE, PRESENT DAY
MILLICENT MONROE'S RESIDENCE

1.

I have never understood Grandma Millicent's house. Or maybe I should say, I've never understood why she lives there. Dad has always talked about how much Grandma loved the Rose House, and how happy she was that it was in Monroe hands, where it belonged. And it's not like he and Marie don't have the room for one more. Or two, if she brought Aunt June. Or even three, because Amber would come, too, at least some of the time.

But this was where she stayed—a little ranch house on the lakeshore, tucked behind a painted cinderblock wall. She could have made a small fortune renting the place out to the tourists, especially after Dad engineered Whitestone's miraculous turnaround, but she never did.

I ring the bell, grip my purse strap, and wait.

I don't want to be here. I do not want to sit in front of my grandmother and listen penitently to whatever the latest lecture is. But I've got no choice. First of all, Dad only let me go so easily because he knew I was coming here. And there's every chance he'll call and check. No matter what he says out loud, he does not trust me. That's fine, though. I don't need him to trust me.

What I do need is some cover for what I'm doing next. Not much. Just a couple hours. I suppose I could ask Carla, but I'd rather not do that to her.

I'm about to ring the bell again when I hear footsteps, and the snap of a turned deadbolt. Amber pulls the door open. Our eyes meet and I watch her swallow her immediate, sarcastic surprise.

"Jesus, Geraldine, come in!" She grabs my wrist and draws me inside. "I...I'm so sorry about what happened."

I pull back awkwardly and we stand together, too close, in the tiny front hall. What do you do in this situation? Hug? Not us. Never us.

"I was expecting your mom," I tell her.

"She's still asleep. She was kind of upset about...things." Amber meets my gaze and we both silently agree to let it go at that. Mentioning the fact that there's some chemical help in Aunt June's veins is not called for, or even really worth mentioning. Not right now, anyway.

"I wanted..." I have to stop and start again. "I had some stuff to talk to Grandma about. Is she here?"

"Yeah. She's on the sunporch." Amber jerks her chin toward the inside of the house. "You want me to come with you?"

"Yeah," I say, and I surprise myself by meaning it. "But I don't think Grandma does."

Her mouth tightens in a familiar, cynical smile. "Probably not. Well. Good luck. I'll be out on the dock if you want...anything." She grabs her sun hat off the hook and heads out the door.

I square my shoulders, grab hold of my purse like it's a lifeline, and head in.

Grandma Millicent sits in a basket chair in a puddle of sunlight streaming through the clear glass windows. There's a book lying open, and a sweating glass of iced tea on the matching table beside her. Her slippered feet rest on a cushioned stool.

She looks up, startled when I walk in.

"Geraldine. You should have called." This is my grandmother's idea of a pleasant greeting. "Sit down. Tell me how you are doing."

I sit. I rest my purse on my knees. I try to find something benign to say, but nothing comes. Instead, I look out the windows. Outside, the tiny sloping yard ends in a strip of sand. There's an aluminum dock with a motorboat moored to the end, a twenty-footer with a wooden deck.

While I watch, Amber comes around the house with a toolbox in one hand and the sleeves on her white shirt rolled up. No surprise. She's always liked boats better than cars. She drives like a maniac and can turn that thing on a dime. We used to go out together when we were younger. Usually after we were both drunk enough we could finally stand each other.

Now, Amber steps easily over the gunwale and makes her way to the engine hatch. It's strange to see her moving with so much purpose.

"Geraldine?"

I yank my attention back to my grandmother. "Yeah. You, uh, you had something you wanted to talk about. Before."

I wonder, distantly, if I'll ever be able to finish that sentence. It probably doesn't matter.

"Yes," says Grandma. But I have to wait while she slots her marker into place and closes her book. She rests her hand on it for a moment, like it's a Bible and she's just been asked to take an oath.

What's going on?

Whatever it is, Grandma has clearly made up her mind. She faces me fully and folds her hands in her lap.

"I never thought I'd say these words again, Geraldine," she tells me. "But I will give you one hundred thousand dollars to leave Whitestone."

2.

I choke on nothing but air. Being offered an enormous bribe by your got-to-be-ninety-by-now grandmother will do that to you.

"What?"

"I believe I spoke clearly enough."

"You want to pay me to leave?" I say, just in case. I'm having some trouble jump-starting my thoughts.

"Yes," she answers, a little testily, and I can't blame her. Grandma never did suffer fools. "It's for your own good as well as ours."

I rub my scar and my bruise. My eyes dart around the room, looking for clues as to what's really going on. Grandma *tsk-tsks* at my fidgets. Anger hits immediately. It also shows me a tiny detail I almost missed.

"Wait. You said 'again.' What do you mean, again?"

Grandma sighs, impatient with the fact I've caught her. But she doesn't dodge the question. Which is really surprising.

"The last time I said anything like this," she says, "was to Lisa Burnovich."

"*Lisa* Burnovich?" I echo. "Lisa was…"

"Your other grandmother. Your mother's mother."

My mouth is hanging open. I close it and try to pull myself together. The truth was, I'd never thought about my two grandmothers in the same space. Lisa and her husband died before Mom and Dad even got married. Car accident or something. Mom barely ever talked about it. And by the time I tried to get some kind of answer out of Aunt Trish, it was hard to tell whether she was talking about her own parents or a whole different set of Burnoviches from a hundred years ago.

I never stopped to consider the fact that not only had Lisa Burnovich and Grandma Millicent probably known each other, they might have been about the same age.

How very careless, Geraldine.

"What were you paying her for?"

Grandma's eyebrows arch sharply. "You honestly don't know? You hated me enough when you were growing up, I just assumed your father had told you."

"I hated you because you were a raging bitch, Grandma. You treated Mom like…"

"A tramp?" she suggests without any rancor at all. "I suppose I did.

I couldn't separate her from her mother. I suppose I should have tried a bit harder, but at the time I simply didn't have the strength."

"I don't understand. You had us all by the—"

Grandma Millicent, though, is not in the mood to listen to another of my pointed accusations. "Dear Lord, you girls. You blunder around blind to anything except what's happened to you."

That's the second time that somebody's said that to me. I glance toward Amber. She's fishing around in her tool kit now. I wonder how much of this she knows. I wonder how much of this anybody knows.

"My own fault, I suppose. Again." Grandma's sigh is short and sharp. "I should have sat you down and told you the full story. But you were so young, it seemed needlessly cruel, especially after Stacey died. And the truth was... the truth was there was so much I couldn't admit. I was willing to take any excuse, just so long as it allowed me to keep silent."

"Grandma..."

"Lisa Burnovich," she says, "was having an affair with my husband."

3.

I stare at my grandmother. My eyes must be popping out of my head like in an old Warner Brothers cartoon. This cannot be happening. I cannot possibly be hearing this.

"Mom's mom was..."

"Screwing Martin," she says, and my cheeks burn. I swear she smiles a little at having successfully made me blush. Payback's a bitch on so many levels. "Martin Senior, I mean, of course. My Martin. Your grandfather. He was infatuated with her. She made him feel like a boy again, he said. They were, according to him, going to run away together." Her gaze is turning inward. Grandma's never been one for sharing family stories with me and Marie. She's always left that to Dad. And now I'm getting some idea why.

"My husband explained it all very carefully. How he felt, how she felt, all the plans they'd made while I was out at my bridge nights and committee meetings. He wanted to be sure I understood the legal procedure for asking for a divorce on the grounds of abandonment. He was confident I could handle it all, once I had the details in hand. He was a great one for plans. He always had so many, and he would spend hours explaining them. Usually over dinner. Sometimes Martin Junior and Pete would almost forget to eat their dessert listening to them." She is seeing her past, and it is leaving her pale. "Unfortunately, he was less successful at carrying them out."

I can't even begin to think what I should say.

"Regardless, after our little heart-to-heart, I went up to the Rose House to see Lisa. I was prepared to plead with her. Even tolerate her, if it proved necessary."

"You loved him that much?"

Her mouth tightens, so do her hands. "I did not love him at all. Not by that point. I'd stood by him because I had no choice. You girls have no idea what it was like for divorcées back then, especially in a small town. What he really told me that night was that I was about to become an abandoned woman with three children to support and no income beyond whatever alimony the court assigned. I would put up with anything to avoid that. Even my husband's floozy."

I try to imagine her then, a wife and mother in a prosperous rural town. As someone who could have married for love, and then spent her life trying to keep up appearances and remember what her sacrifice had been for. And then...and then...

I can't do it. I've spent too long thinking I know her. It's going to take more than these few moments to tear down all those old images and start fresh.

Guilt wells up inside me, cold and unfamiliar.

"Lisa listened," she tells me. "I will never forget the look on her face. Then, she just burst out laughing.

"I thought at first she was laughing at me and my pathetic pleading. But that wasn't it. She was laughing at the idea that Martin thought she'd run away with him. You see, she was perfectly happy with her life. The Rose House was a social hub then. She and Forrester had plenty of money. She liked her men on the side, and he liked his women, and they were furiously jealous of each other. They kept on cheating, kept on blaming, kept on…" She struggles to control herself. "I didn't understand it. I'm not sure she understood it, but it didn't matter. She wasn't going to change it.

"She promised to set Martin straight for me. She offered me a drink. I don't know why that was the final indignity, but it was. I left her there." Grandma's trying to control herself and speak calmly of her wrongs, but it is not easy. "I promised myself I'd never set foot in that house or have anything to do with its occupants again."

She waits for me to make some little remark about the patently spectacular failure of this promise, but I've got nothing.

"Did Lisa do it?" I ask instead. "Did she break it off?"

"Oh yes. I know she did, and she told him about our talk."

"He told you that, too? Jesus, Grandma…"

"I know because two days later, my husband climbed up on our roof and jumped."

Her words are heavy, and sharp-edged from disappointment. I wonder if she's ever told anyone this story before. I mean, she must have, at least once. But not often. That tone is too raw.

"I've never known how your father found out that Lisa was involved with his father," she says, talking right over my thoughts. "I think Pete may have known, and perhaps he let it slip. But I don't know."

"You mean…you didn't tell him?"

"What on earth makes you think I'd tell my son something like that?" She's genuinely shocked, and I'm genuinely surprised.

"Because he's always said you were the one who wanted the Rose House. He's always tried to impress you and—"

"Impress me? He's spent his whole life humiliating me," she snaps. "He blamed Lisa for his father's death, but he also blamed me. I'd failed him, you see. I lied to him. And he decided he was going to get his revenge on me as well as her. He's spent years parading his victories in front of me—destroying his brother for not hating well enough or long enough. Bringing my family under his thumb. Making me watch while he tore any shred of independence out of any of them. And, of course, marrying Lisa's daughter. That was a brilliant move. He flowered early, my..." She chokes and she stops.

My son. She tried to say it and she failed. My ruined heart finds a way to break just a little for her.

"And now comes the grand finale," she says. "I am to be locked up in Lisa's house to die."

Her eyes are glittering. That's the biggest shock yet. In my world, Grandma Millicent is hard as nails. Grandma Millicent is my father's co-conspirator, his support and confidant.

But she's right. I have been blind. And now, she's about to cry.

"What do you want me to do?" I ask.

"I am hoping against hope I can save at least some of my children," she says. "If you are...established somewhere, perhaps Amber will have someplace to go when it all falls down. Perhaps Walter, or Carla. All I'd ask is that you do not leave them in the lurch if they come to you for help."

She doesn't mention Marie, and that's what gives her away. Grandma knows who started the fire. Grandma is trying to get me out of town before I can spill any beans I might have. It's the same kind of desperation that took her up the hill to plead with her husband's mistress. Because her family, her second son, might be deeply, desperately, fatally flawed, but they are all she has.

I don't understand that choice. I will not understand it. Because I don't want to.

I watch Amber instead, kneeling on her boat deck, elbow deep in the hatch. She sits back on her heels, takes off her hat, and wipes her forehead. She looks at the sky, and then toward the house. She must see me here, because she waves.

I wave back.

"Will you do it?" asks Grandma impatiently.

I lower my hand. It curls into a fist. No surprise.

I consider what she's said. I really do. She's offering me a chance to get away. A chance to establish—I don't know—some kind of sanctuary against what's coming. I wonder who she's been talking to. Besides Dad and Marie. Grandma's not stupid, and she's got her own friends. The club ladies. Those old women in their hats who get drunk on Bloody Marys and mimosas, decrying the rest of us who are simply lazy and unmannered. They still know everybody who counts around here. They can find answers when they need them.

"I'm sorry, Grandma," I tell her as I get to my feet. "Maybe before. But not now."

"I think I understand."

I think she does, too. Something else I never expected.

4.

There's a side door out to the yard and the lake. Amber watches me walk out onto the grass and down to the edge of the sand. She wipes her hands on a shop towel and comes to meet me at the foot of the dock.

"She's tired," I say. "I'm heading out."

"Sure," Amber says, but I can tell there's more to come. I'm not sure I can take it. I'm completely wrung out. I want to go hide myself from...everything.

"Geraldine, I don't know whether you'll believe this or not, but I really am sorry about what happened. He seemed...I would have liked to get to know him."

I do believe her. I'm just taking everybody at their word today. "Thanks."

"Do they...did they find out what happened?"

"Not yet. But they will." Because Dad wants them to. He's made that pretty clear.

Unless, of course, Dad is playing another game. Which is never, ever out of the question.

"Amber? I need a favor."

"What?"

I suck in a long breath and try to push past the exhaustion that fills my shattered self. "If anybody asks, and I mean *anybody*...after I got done with Grandma, you and I hung out for a while, okay? I didn't want to go h...back to the house."

She watches me for a long minute. "Maybe we took the boat out?" she suggests. "You love it on the water, and I wanted to help you take your mind off things."

"Yeah. I appreciated that."

"We didn't talk much," she adds. "Small stuff. I don't even really remember what."

"Me either," I agree. "We just kind of hung out. Drank some wine."

"There was definitely wine. Kind of a lot."

I say thanks and she says you're welcome and I walk back to the driveway and out the opening in the cinderblock wall.

I leave my car right out front where I parked it, and instead I head up the road. When the traffic clears, I cross both lanes, and make my way across the ditch and up the hill on the other side.

I catch myself hoping I remember the way. So much has changed. Not that it matters. Because I'm not going to stop.

Where do they come from, all these powerful women? The birth mothers strong enough to make children from wishes, but so weak they can't save themselves afterward?

—Dr. Geraldine Monroe (margin notes)

GERALDINE, SEVENTEEN YEARS OLD
THE ROSE HOUSE

1.

Something's wrong.

Geraldine felt it the second she and her mother walked into Aunt Trish's clammy kitchen. The trash stank and the flies buzzed, and even though it was getting dark, the kitchen lantern hadn't been lit yet.

Is that it?

"Trish?" Mom called into the empty kitchen. "Trish! Come on out, Trish! We got a surprise for you!"

"Maybe she's in the great room?"

Aunt Trish had cleared some space between the ruined books. Sometimes they'd all sit there, looking out the rose window, and pretending to make plans. They were going to fix up the house, finally. They were going to go shopping. They were going to leave town, going to move down to Florida or out to Montana.

Going To games, Geraldine always thought. *Is that what everybody does?*

Mom picked up the flashlight they kept by the door and pushed the switch. Somewhat to Geraldine's surprise, the beam flickered on.

"Trish!" Mom plunged into the dark. "Trish!"

Later, when she could stand to think about it, Geraldine would re- member that she wasn't surprised. At least, not by how they found her.

She was lying at the foot of the staircase, on her face, with her ragged hair spread out around her shoulders. There was a paint can beside her, spilling a dark, tacky puddle across the tiles that mixed with...other things. The smell made Geraldine stagger.

But she wasn't surprised. The surprise was how calm her mother re- mained. Stacey didn't scream. She didn't cry. Maybe she'd already felt it, like Geraldine had. Either way, Stacey just knelt down beside her sister. Geraldine couldn't move. Geraldine wanted to hurl. Stacey put her hands underneath Trish and turned her. She tried to be gentle, but Aunt Trish flopped and thudded. Geraldine clapped her hands over her mouth, holding back the screams and the sick.

Mom laid her hand on Aunt Trish's forehead. She drew her palm across her sister's eyes so they closed. She touched one hand, and then the other. And folded them neatly across her sagging breasts.

"Go find a blanket, or something," Mom said. "She needs to be covered up."

Geraldine wanted to argue, but how could she? She thought fran- ticly and then ran up the stairs into the twilight of the second floor. She blundered her way to the old children's wing. Bits of paint and plas- ter crunched underfoot as she opened the old cupboard. Inside was still a mostly anonymous pile of junk, but there was an old bedspread in there. She'd seen it at some point. Maybe Aunt Trish had told her a story once about who made it and how and when.

I should have listened more. I should have...done something.

Dirt and who-knew-what showered down when Geraldine shook the thing out, but it was better than nothing. Barely. She carried her find back downstairs.

Mom was still on her knees. She took the bedspread and draped it neatly across her sister's body. It was covered in rings and roses, Geraldine noticed. That probably meant something.

"I'm sorry, Trish," Mom whispered. "I am. I was...I'll do better now. I promise."

Geraldine was amazed. Geraldine was appalled. She wiped her palms on her jeans, like she was the one who'd been handling the dead. But in her mind all she could think was they couldn't let their chance go. They might not ever have another shot. Mom might not be strong enough. Dad and Marie might not be distracted enough. It was sad. She felt terrible. But she'd tried her best, really she had. If only Aunt Trish had been able to hang on just another couple of days…

But it didn't matter. Not anymore. They had to move.

"Mom?" Geraldine forced the word out. "Mom? We should go. We need to…tell somebody," she finished lamely.

Just got to get her back in the car. She can't stop me once we're in the car.

"You go," Mom said. "I'll stay with her."

"No, Mom. You shouldn't be here alone. It's…it's…a bad idea. We'll come right back, okay? With help," she added.

But Mom looked up, and when Geraldine saw the look on her face, she took a step back.

"I'm not going anywhere," said Mom and her voice burned in the dark.

"What are you *talking* about? You can't…"

Mom heaved herself to her feet. Her face was wrong. She was *happy*. Intensely, dangerously happy. "She's dead. The house. It's mine."

"What?"

"It's mine!" she shouted. "And I'm going to hold it over his fucking head!"

"Mom! Are you crazy? What are you talking about?" But she knew. Of course she knew. After all these years, how could she not?

"He's tortured us for fucking *years* to get hold of this place. And now it's mine! Trish had her will written, and I'm the heir. He's never going to get it! I can't wait to see the look on his face!"

"Mom! Stop it!"

But Mom wasn't listening. "He never got it from Trish, and he won't get it from me. He's gonna die of a fucking heart attack when he realizes I'm not going to give it to him!"

"Mom! It'll never work! Please! Just…just let him have it. If this is what he wants, then he can keep it, and we can go. We don't have to be his slaves anymore! We can do whatever we want, have real lives, *our* lives!"

"Fine. You go. I'm not stopping you. But I've waited twenty god-damned years for this and I am *not* going to miss it!"

"No! I am not leaving you with him, you stupid, crazy bitch!"

Mom slapped her. A good, hard backhand right across the face. Geraldine didn't even think about what to do next. She just balled up her fist and swung. Randomly, blindly. She felt the connection and heard the thump.

Mom fell onto the floor and lay there, almost as still as her sister beneath her rotten shroud.

2.

Geraldine stared at her mother's limp frame. She lifted her gaze to the ruined house and breathed in the dark and desolation.

After that, she kind of lost her mind. Probably she screamed. Maybe she grabbed up the hammer Aunt Trish had left behind during one of her attempts to fix things and attacked the walls. Maybe the ancient world so carefully created by poor, crazy Addison tore like paper, raining dust and faded paint into her blinded eyes.

But she didn't remember. She only retained the anger, and the despair.

When the storm passed and Geraldine came to, she was in the great room. Her arm ached. She looked around her. Paint cans were scattered around. More paint was splashed against the wall. There were gaping holes in the plaster. She was staring at the rose window, vaguely aware she'd been about to smash it. She looked at the hammer again, and then tossed it away. It clattered against the hearth and fell still.

Geraldine stood still for a minute, staring at the hammer and the black and empty hearth. Then, she turned and walked calmly into the kitchen.

The Coleman lantern was in its usual spot beside the cast-iron stove. She shook it. It was empty. But the rusted can of fuel beside it wasn't.

"G?" She heard her mother's voice, thin and wobbly. "Geraldine?"

Geraldine wiped her mouth with the back of her gritty hand. Her scar hurt. She picked up the fuel can and wrenched open the cap. The smell of white gas was a shock to the system and her head cleared in a single, painful burst.

"G?"

She poured a puddle out onto the cracked tiles and kicked the empty lantern over on top.

She was breathing like she'd run a marathon. She felt curiously calm. It was like she'd closed a door on the normal part of herself. It might be screaming and clawing to get back in, but it couldn't. Not yet.

"Goddamn it, G! I need…I need…"

Geraldine yanked open drawer after drawer. In one, she found a moldering envelope that turned out to have a whole pile of cash in it. There were words scrawled on it. BACK LATER TONIGHT. HANG ON TO THIS. She thought she should recognize the handwriting, but she couldn't make her brain move that far.

She counted five thousand dollars before she crammed the whole thing into her pocket. They'd need it later.

She found what she was really looking for on the next try. Kitchen matches. The box was damp and torn but the matches themselves seemed pretty dry.

Six tries. On the seventh, the match lit. She dropped it, and the rest of the box, into the puddle.

Whomp!

Flame went up and Geraldine ran. Back in the front hall, Mom was sitting up, awake, but woozy.

"What the fuck…?" she demanded.

Shaking, wordless, Geraldine dug her hands into her mother's armpits and heaved.

"No," Mom groaned as she staggered to her feet.

Geraldine didn't answer. After all these years, she was an expert at moving her mother when her mother didn't want to go. Mom stumbled and sagged and struggled, but Geraldine hauled her out the front door and around the terrace to the remains of the carriage house, where they'd parked the car. The rain was coming down harder now and Geraldine swore.

"I said no!" Mom tried to wrench herself away.

"I told you, I am *not* leaving you with him!" Geraldine planted Mom against the side of the car and struggled to get the door open.

"I don't care what you say!" screamed Mom.

"You think I don't know that!" Geraldine screamed back. She shoved her mother into the car and slammed the door. She ran around to the driver's side, splashing in the puddles, praying that outrage and concussion would confuse Mom just enough. Praying the rain was still too light to make any difference to what was happening inside the house.

She threw herself into the driver's seat and jammed her keys in the ignition.

But by then her mother's vision had cleared enough that she saw the flickering light shining between the rotted boards. Or maybe it was the smell of the smoke that got to her.

"What the fuck did you do?!"

Geraldine revved the engine. Mom struggled with the latch. The rutted lane that passed for a driveway was tight and the rain was coming down harder, and she couldn't see. She banged the car's back end into something but managed to wrench it around, just as Mom wrestled the door open.

She half-jumped, half-fell onto the buckling asphalt.

"Mom!"

But if her mother heard, she didn't let it stop her. She hoisted herself to her feet and staggered through the rain, toward the house. Toward the fire.

"No!" screamed Geraldine.

Mom spun around.

"What are you going to do? Kill me? Go ahead! Kill me!" She

dropped her head back and threw her arms out and stood there, cruci-fied on the dark. "For fuck's sake *somebody* just kill me!"

Something snapped. Geraldine felt it go.

That was when she screamed.

That was when she gunned the engine and felt the thud and saw her mother fall.

That was when she drove away, roaring down the hill, the passenger door flapping open and the rain blowing in. That was when she drove to the lakeshore, to wait out the rain, to drink and screw David, and to try to swim away from life itself.

That was when she did not do the one thing she should have done. That was when Geraldine Monroe did not look back.

"And what should be the punishment, for someone who has done all these things?"
—"The Goose Girl" from *Kinder und Hausmärchen* Vol. 1,
Jacob and Wilhelm Grimm, 1812

GERALDINE, PRESENT DAY
STACEY B'S SANDWICHES AND STUFF

1.

Houses never burn completely. No matter how hot the fire, there's always something left: a jumble of blackened sticks, the scattered remnants of ruined possessions, some cracked brick, some scorched steel.

And the stench, of course. Ash and grease and chemicals.

The old store didn't escape unscathed. One wall is entirely black and the vinyl siding is blistered and cracked. I wonder if Marie watched the blaze. I picture her sucking in a worried breath as the wind shifted. After all, she wouldn't want her stash damaged while she was killing Tyler.

There's no one to see me duck under the police tape strung between trees and sawhorses. The store's front entrance is still locked, and I still don't have a key, but that's okay. The screen is on the ground where we left it. The window's even still open.

I toss my purse through and I climb in after. I crouch on the scuffed tile for a long minute, listening to the eternal sound of the wind in the trees. Nothing comes to disturb it. Well, nothing but me.

I hug my purse to my chest and scuttle toward the basement door. I stay crouched down, just in case. I don't have a high opinion of the Whitestone County sheriff's department, but David might have his own ideas about what constitutes proper procedure right now. His family is involved after all, and he's going to protect them, because that's what he does.

Sorry, David.

I hurry down the stairs. It's dark, but I don't try to switch on the light. Instead, I take my phone out of my purse and use it as a flashlight. This shouldn't take long. I know exactly what I'm looking for.

I need the shoebox Marie saved. I have something to add to her stash. A gift from her wicked sister. Belated payment for all that she has given me.

I didn't manage to save anything from the fire. Not my computer, my writing, my money. Not Tyler. But I had the photos. The ones I'd kept for my sister. The ones I'd planned to throw in her face before I left for good. Again. They're still there, in my bucket of a purse. Marie's past, all jumbled up with mine. Deeply personal. Absolutely irreplaceable.

And I'm going to find them.

They're going to be hidden in that old shoebox. I'm going to show them to David. I'm going to express my great shock and consternation.

She gave them to me, years ago, I'm going to tell him. *I'd put them up in the house when I moved in. I…they should have burned down with everything else. How in the hell did they end up in here? David…* Well, no, maybe not David. David knows me too well. Gary. *Gary, you don't think that Marie…*

Gary. You can't think that Marie…!

The box was on the set of shelves on the far wall. Third one up. Right at my eye level. I shine the phone light there. I'm imagining Cousin Gary's blank face as I tell him the tale. I hear him sigh and say *we'd better take a look.*

There's one problem. My hand freezes, and the light shakes.

There's no box. There's a hole—a dark gap where the old shoebox used to be.

I stand there for a long time staring at it. I will myself to move my phone, shining its bluish light so I can search the nearby shelves. Maybe I moved it. Accidentally put it back in the wrong spot. Maybe Tyler did. I was a little distracted at the time. I could have. He could have.

But we didn't. It's gone.

So that's that. That is fucking well that. My sister was one move ahead the whole time. Stupid Geraldine. Slow Geraldine. Can't even get her revenge right. Can't even...can't even...

I'm sorry, Tyler. I'm so sorry.

But it's pointless, because it can't change anything. It never could.

I consider trashing the place. I could. Smash everything to bits. It is, after all, what I do. I know it would feel good. But eventually I'd run out of things to break and nothing would be changed. Like always.

I climb the stairs because I don't know what else to do, with my bag full of useless evidence and my ruined plans. I've lost. I've been outsmarted by my sister, used by my father. I'm nothing but the wicked sister at the end of the story. Come, give me my punishment. Put me in a barrel full of nails and roll me downhill. Send your birds to peck out my eyes. Put on the red-hot iron shoes. I'm ready. I'm done.

Somebody just fucking kill me. I lean against the wall. *Please.*

My phone buzzes. I have it out and in my hand, and hope is clawing at my insides before I remember it can't possibly be Tyler, because Tyler is dead.

I blink back the tears I didn't even feel form and stare at the screen. It tells me I have one missed call. I thumb the buttons so I can see who it was.

It's not Tyler. But it is Angela. His sister called while I was in the basement. I hesitate. How can I talk to her? What can I tell her? There's nothing.

But while I'm staring, the phone rings. I jump and almost drop it.

Angela. The screen lights up to display her name. She's calling again. Right now.

My fingers move to turn it off, but I stop, because I've got that much sympathy left. I deserve my pain, but she doesn't. I can do this much for her before...

Before.

I hold the phone to my ear with one shaking hand. "Hello?"

"Geraldine?"

"Yeah, Angie. It's me." We've met a couple of times. Talked some on the phone when she called Tyler, for his birthday, for Christmas. I liked her. I wanted to be friends.

"Oh my God, Geraldine. I've been trying to…I just…"

"I'm so sorry, Angie. I…I'm so sorry."

"What happened? I…this guy, a cop, whatever, he wouldn't tell me anything. He just? Shit. Hang on." She's saying something rapidly, maybe in Spanish, to somebody else. "I'm at LAX now. I'm trying to get a flight. Please. Talk to me."

She means about Tyler. I have to talk to her about Tyler. What can I possibly say? "We haven't got all the details—"

She cuts me off. "Did you guys have a fight?"

"Yeah. We had a fight. And I thought he'd left. I thought…" Those tears are falling now, trickling down the sides of my face. They run down the groove that is my scar and sting my dry lips.

Angie doesn't make me struggle any further. "He called me," she says.

"Wh…what?"

"He called me. It must have been right before…before it happened. He was really wasted. He told me you'd broken up again. He told me he wasn't done. He understood everything."

Tyler you stupid, sloppy drunk.

"He said you didn't mean it. He'd met your dad and he knew—"

"Wait. Wait." I press my hand against my eyes. "Stop. Tyler said he met my dad?"

"That's what he told me. He said your dad was just like a high-class version of ours." She pauses. "He…told you about Pop, right?"

"A little."

"Yeah. Well, he said it wasn't your fault. He…anyway, I thought you should know that."

"Yeah."

331

She hesitates. She's registering that something's wrong, but she's not sure what to ask. "Shit," she says. "They're calling my flight. I'm on my way. We'll…figure out what to do when I get in, okay? Can somebody pick me up? I'll text you all the info."

I say yeah. I hang up. I stare at the ruin where my old house used to be. I clutch my purse strap and breathe in the smoke and ash.

I remember.

I realize.

There's only one possible way Tyler could have met my father. Only one moment unaccounted for. That's if Dad came to the old house and found Tyler there, waiting for me to come home.

A loose end. A picture that did not fit the frame.

Dad found Tyler. Not Marie.

I turn toward the road and the hill and I run.

"King, what art thou doing now? Sleepest thou or wakest thou?"
—"The Three Little Men in the Wood" from *Kinder und Hausmärchen* Vol. 1, Jacob and Wilhelm Grimm, 1812

MARIE, NINETEEN YEARS OLD
STACEY B'S SANDWICHES AND STUFF

1.

This was, quite literally, the night they had both been waiting for.

For Dad, it was a business dinner with his first major client.

For Marie, it was something quite different, but her own quiet plans very neatly intersected with her father's.

The client was Teddy Ford, of the car-company Fords, not the political Fords. Marie had arranged for a private dining room at the yacht club. She'd coordinated with the chef to make sure all Mr. Ford's favorites would be available. She'd even explained to the manager how vital the evening was and he assured her they'd have a team of experienced, and pretty, servers. The two hundred dollars she gave him to help ensure that everything went smoothly came out of her own savings.

She made sure that Geraldine and Mom would both be out of the house.

Once they left, she spent hours on her hair and makeup, so she'd be just exactly what Dad needed.

Men appreciate a graceful figure at the table, he told her. *It's not politically correct to say so, but it's true. It helps set the stage. I can count on you, right, Marie?*

Of course, Dad, she answered. What else was she going to say?

During dinner, Marie sat at the foot of the table and made her best small talk. Mrs. Ford had not been invited. Mr. Ford was very appreciative, just like Dad predicted, but thankfully kept his hands mostly to himself. *One less thing to deal with*, Marie thought, but she carefully kept that thought from dimming her smile or making her questions lag.

She left the table after one cup of post-dinner coffee. "I'm taking some summer courses and I need to study," she said, and Dad gave a tiny nod, approving the little social excuse. It was time for him to get down to business. She was not needed anymore.

Besides, she had other things to do.

Despite what she had told Geraldine, Marie did not really expect Dad to bring Mr. Ford back to their house. Dad cultivated a certain image for his clients, and this little old house didn't fit with it. He needed to be seen on a grander stage. But that didn't mean she couldn't make things comfortable for when Dad did come home. It was all in the details. Like putting Duke Ellington on the stereo and fixing a glass of good Scotch.

She took her time making sure his drink was just right. But even when she was certain she had everything perfectly arranged, Marie couldn't make herself sit still. She circled the room, straightening and adjusting and inspecting. *Be patient,* she told herself. *You've waited two years. You can wait another half hour.*

Two years ago, Dad had come up to the Rose House to save her from Aunt Trish, and Geraldine, in a way. She had stood at the top of the steps, watching her sister fall, watching her blood spill onto the snow. Dad had gathered her up, so tenderly, and held her so tightly, not caring that the blood got all over his jacket and his hands. He had his daughters close again, and he would never let them go.

It was in that moment that Marie understood what she would have to do. The understanding had never once wavered, and tonight those two years of planning and waiting would come to their conclusion.

But despite her certainties, she still couldn't calm down. The sound of every passing car made her cringe. The rain had started up again. She could hear it patter on the roof, and it felt like each drop was tapping on her skull.

Where is he?

It was eleven now. She'd only asked Geraldine to keep Mom away until midnight. She sank into the creaking armchair and gripped her hands together in front of her. What if they came back before Dad did?

When she heard the door slam outside, Marie literally jumped to her feet.

What if it's them? She faced the door, heart hammering. *What do I do?*

The door opened. Marie felt like she was going to scream. But it was Dad who walked in, and he was beaming.

"Well?" she asked, too loud and too high. She could only hope he'd mistake that for enthusiasm. "How'd it go?"

Dad didn't answer right way. Instead, he settled onto the sofa and stretched his arms out across the back. "We got it."

"I knew you would!" Marie turned away, biting her lips to try to get herself under control. "Drink to celebrate?"

She handed him the glass of Scotch she had all ready. Dad took it easily and leaned back.

"Aren't you going to have one?"

Marie felt herself hesitate. That was a mistake. She should have been pouring the second drink right as he walked in. That would have looked better, more relaxed. She couldn't neglect those details. It looked strange to only have the one ready.

Dad laughed at her. "Oh, come on, Marie. I know you're only nineteen, but it's okay. Your father says so." He hoisted his own glass toward her and took a swallow. "You should learn to drink, you know. The right way. Not like your mother. Don't worry," he added patiently. "I'll help you. Just a little to start with, okay?"

"Okay," she agreed, because what else could she do. Dad leaned forward so his elbows were on his knees and watched while she poured Scotch into a second tumbler. When she had about two fingers, he lifted his hand.

"That's plenty to start."

She sat in the armchair with her drink. Dad smiled and lifted his own glass in another toast. He drank and watched her over the rim. Marie looked at the liquor and sipped.

He wants me to learn to drink the right way. He said so, she told herself. *That's the only reason he's watching so close.*

But that didn't stop her from running down the mental tally of her appearance. Hair. Face. Clothes. It was all still perfect. There was nothing strange or out of place. She sat back in the chair, not on the edge. She held the glass in only one hand instead of clutching it in both. After all, she was relaxed. Everything was exactly as it should be. She was sharing a sophisticated drink with her father, to help him celebrate.

He took an appreciative swallow.

"So, Mr. Ford has decided to take the house?" she asked brightly.

"Lock, stock, and barrel." Dad nodded, and sipped and watched her. Marie took another sip and tried not to gag or cough. "Wants it dressed and staffed, and for us to handle security and grounds. The works. This is the big one, baby girl. The one we've been waiting for." He drained his glass. She had to work not to stare. "You're going to have a busy summer."

"That'll be terrific!" Marie smiled and she sipped. There was a wrinkle in her skirt that she couldn't smooth down, because she didn't want to look nervous, but she felt it pressing against her thigh.

"And we're going to have to decide what to do about Geraldine."

Marie started. Her Scotch sloshed. Dad frowned just a little and Marie blushed. Dad hated twitchy women.

"Things are happening, baby girl. We can't let Geraldine's shenanigans slow us down."

Marie sipped her drink. The gesture could take the place of an answer. For now. She felt the seconds sliding across her skin.

"It's only a matter of time before she gets into real trouble or winds up like Stacey. She needs help. You know that. We've talked about it."

Yes. We've talked about it and talked about it. Like we've talked about Mom, and Aunt Trish, and you and me.

"It's for Geraldine's own good, Marie. I know we don't want to air our problems in front of strangers, but you will be asked questions. I've found a good treatment center for her. They'll..."

"Why are you talking about sending Geraldine away but not Mom?" The words slid out, and Marie pressed her fingers across her mouth. What was she saying? It must be the Scotch. It must be.

Dad's mouth twitched. "Stacey's problems are far enough gone that they'll resolve themselves soon," he said. "But Geraldine..."

That was when the phone rang.

Marie jumped. Dad frowned.

Not at me, not at me, it's still all right, she thought frantically as he got up to answer. *We just need a little time now. That's all. Just a little more time.*

But how much time?

"Martin Monroe," Dad said into the receiver. He waited, listening. Someone was babbling on the other end of the line.

Dad swayed. He mopped at his forehead. Marie's heart tried to jam itself into her throat.

"Calm down. Calm down!" he ordered whoever he was talking to. "I can't...I...Just say it again. Slowly." He pressed his hand against the table.

Marie gripped her knees with both hands to force herself to stillness.

"All right," said Dad, heavily. "All right."

He hung up. He looked at her, a little dazed. Then, he sat back down on the sofa, and looked around for what was missing. Marie poured some more Scotch into his empty glass.

"Who was that?" she asked.

"David Pendarves." He picked the fresh drink up and stared at it.

"David?" His name leapt out of her before she could remember that she wasn't supposed to know David, not really. He was just one of the Whitestone boys they had grown up with. No one special. She had no one special. "Why? I mean..."

"Geraldine's had an accident." Dad slumped backward. "She's in the hospital."

"What?" Marie was on her feet without realizing she'd moved.

"The emergency room. Sit down, Marie," Dad said heavily. "You know I can't stand it when you're looming."

"Yes, but, I..." *Oh, God. Oh, Geraldine. Why* now? "I...Shouldn't somebody go out there?"

"I suppose. If you think it's important." He picked up his glass again and stared into the Scotch. "Remember last time we had to take her in? When she messed up her face so badly? Jesus, I hope she hasn't done anything like that again."

Marie ran to the door. She grabbed her purse and the car keys off the rack on the wall and bolted out into the dark and the rain. Puddles splashed underfoot, and she skidded in the mud, tumbling against Dad's Taurus.

"Oh, Jesus *fuck*!"

Marie's head jerked around. *Mom?*

She was a wavering white ghost on the road's sandy shoulder, staggering from tree to tree. Soaking wet from rain, mud streaking her white hair and pale skin. Drunk. Stoned. Something. Again.

How could she even be here? Geraldine promised to stay with her. Geraldine was in the emergency room. Mom should be there, too.

Mom lurched forward, but this time she missed her step and dropped to her knees. That was when she looked up and saw Marie.

"Well, don't just stand there, you stupid little shit!" There was something wrong with her face. "Help me!"

Geraldine was in the emergency room. Her mother was right here in front of her, so messed up she couldn't stand. Dad was in the house with the drink she'd fixed. She couldn't be in all three places at once.

Marie climbed into the car.

I'm sorry. I'm sorry. I have to choose. This is better, she told herself as she started the engine and peeled away, down the hill, toward the town and the hospital. *She'll pass out and that'll be that. No explanations needed. It's better this way. Much, much, much better.*

The words rang through her mind, blotting out all other thoughts. She was barely able to focus the road in the headlights, on not hitting the ambulance as she turned into the hospital drive, on making sure she had her purse when she ran through the hospital's doors into the sterile white waiting room.

On the fact of the square-faced young man who jumped off the bench and ran to intercept her.

"David?"

He smelled like beer and weed and fresh water. His hair was plastered to his head, his chin was a mess of pimples and five o'clock shadow. His shirt was half-tucked into soaking wet jeans.

"Marie!" David put his hands out, like he didn't know whether he'd need to catch her or fend her off. "Christ! I am so, so sorry!"

"What's happened? Where's Geraldine?"

"She...oh, Jesus Christ, Marie. I don't even..."

I don't have time for this.

Marie pushed past him to the nurses' station. Mrs. Mayor—Becca and Lucy Mayor's mother—was on duty. "Mrs. Mayor! What's going on? Where's Geraldine?"

"Oh, Marie." She was on her feet and coming around the desk. Marie couldn't tell whether it was surprise in her voice or exasperation. Naturally, Mrs. Mayor had been expecting Dad. But she recovered quickly. She was an experienced small-town nurse. She knew how tangled things could get. "Come on, honey, I'll take you to her."

"Marie...Marie...wait..." stammered David.

"I'm sorry, David, family only," Mrs. Mayor answered for her.

Whitestone Harbor's emergency room was three hospital beds separated by curtains. Geraldine lay in the middle one.

The first thing Marie saw was that Geraldine's ankles had both been bandaged. Then, she saw the red and pink stains on them. Then, she saw how white her sister's legs and arms and throat were against her blue hospital gown. She had a tube in one arm, and another up her nose.

Then Marie saw Geraldine's face—eyes closed, lips a sick gray-blue, her scar a stark scarlet thread cutting across her white, white skin. She saw Geraldine's dyed hair spread in black snarls on the thin pillow.

"David saved her," Mrs. Mayor said. Slowly, Marie became aware she had been speaking for some time.

"Wh…what?"

"David saved her, honey," she repeated, more slowly this time. "Now, we don't know for sure what happened, but it looks like she went for a swim, and couldn't make it all the way back. David pulled her out of the lake and called the ambulance."

"What was he…how was he…"

"You can't worry about that now, honey," Mrs. Mayor said firmly. "Just be glad he was there. Here. Come on. Sit down."

I don't want to sit down. I want to know what happened. She was supposed to be with Mom, not David Pendarves. She promised. She was going to see Aunt Trish.

"Marie," said Mrs. Mayor. "Are your parents on the way? Geraldine's still underage. We need them to sign her paperwork as her legal guardians."

My parents. My mother is staggering drunk. My father… Marie closed her eyes and swallowed. But that was enough for Mrs. Mayor.

"All right. I'll just get everything ready and they can sign when they arrive. You just…be here in case she wakes up."

Marie nodded. Mrs. Mayor drew the curtain in a rush of metal on metal, and she was alone with Geraldine in the little white cave.

Time passed. Marie didn't have a watch on, so she couldn't tell how much. Geraldine didn't move. There were voices outside, and the rattle of metal carts, and the squeak of rubber shoes on tiles. None of it penetrated far enough to make any sense to her. The glowing green lines on the monitors bobbled. The machines beeped randomly.

Geraldine didn't move.

Eventually, Marie got up. *She can't be comfortable like that.*

The sheet felt stiff as cardboard as Marie pulled it over her. She pressed her hand against her sister's forehead. *Like I think she's got a fever.* But she felt only ice and bone. Her hair was all snarled.

Marie took one damp knot between her fingers and started picking at it.

"You didn't have to do this," she said. "But it's okay. I've taken care of everything. I'm sorry it took so long. We had to wait until I was a legal adult, otherwise they wouldn't let me keep you, or the house, or anything. Especially with…what he's been saying about you. But he can't make you go away now. He's dead, Geraldine. I'm sorry I didn't tell you before. But, it's over now, so, you can wake up, okay?"

The curtains rattled and rushed back. Marie jerked her hands away from her sister's tangled hair. Mrs. Mayor walked calmly up to Marie, but her face was almost as white as Geraldine's.

"Marie…" Her confidence was gone and she licked her chapped lips. "Oh, God. I am so sorry. Marie, they've just…honey, it's…"

"Dad?" she croaked before she caught herself. Before she remembered she wasn't supposed to know.

Mrs. Mayor looked confused. "Oh, no, hon. Your father's fine. It's your mother."

Your father's fine.

Your father's fine.

It's your mother.

Your father's fine.

That was when she passed out.

MARIE, PRESENT DAY
THE ROSE HOUSE

1.

I can still change my mind.

The old shoebox is heavy in my hands. It rattles and clinks as I carry it into my father's study.

This is what it is like to walk into a room you will never leave: it is cool and slow and silent. I am fully open. Fully present. Every whisper of sound and each physical sensation is critically important—the release of setting the box down, this taste of dusty cardboard in the back of my throat.

The house breathes its approval. I feel it slick against my skin. I know this feeling. Just not from this source.

I don't have to do this again. I can stop.

I dig my fingers under the ancient pink rubber band. It snaps in two, twanging against the cardboard and the back of my hand.

It's a sign. Things breaking. A bad sign. I should stop.

I lift off the crumpled lid. The faint scents of dust and stale alcohol waft out. Inside waits a heavy-bottomed tumbler and the amber plastic bottle of pills. I saved them. What was left of them anyway. I always knew I'd need them. If not for somebody else, then for me.

I bring a new tumbler out of the sideboard. My fingers relish the smooth curve of the clean glass as I set it next to the old one. They match perfectly. I made sure they would when I bought the new set. I contemplate the bottles that decorate my father's sideboard. But there's really no question as to which I should choose. I reach for the Scotch.

There are no windows in here. But because I want my father to be able to find me easily, I've left the door open. Burnished gold sunbeams stream in from the front room. The sky at my back is salmon pink and lavender. It's all utterly exquisite, and I'm glad. Tonight should be beautiful.

I can still stop.

I can't think why that idea won't go away. What part of me thinks there ever was any choice for us?

The childproof cap bites against my palm as I struggle to open the bottle. The anonymous white, pink, and red pills click and slosh as they drop into the glass. I use the ancient wooden muddler to crush the pills into the seven-year-old Scotch, and then a long, swizzle-handled spoon to stir them into a slurry.

Around me the house holds its breath. I feel its textures and anticipation against my skin. It's not disapproving anymore. It embraces me like a lover. This is what the house has been waiting for. What we've all been waiting for.

Finally, it says. *Finally.*

The only worry is that the pills might have broken down. Lost their potency. But the devil is always in the details, isn't it? And I've prepared for the possibility. As I passed through the kitchen, I put the paring knife in my pocket. Now I understand why I cut my hand. It was so I would think to bring the knife. I hope I don't have to use it. I don't want to leave a mess. A thread of panic runs through me at the thought and makes my hand shake as I carefully pour three fingers into both glasses. I will not repeat the mistakes I made before. This time I will have both drinks ready.

I put the lid back on the pill bottle and crank it down tight.

People do not act like this. I know that. These are things that people do not do out in the normal world. But out there, they haven't spent their lives trying to save the things that should have been allowed to rot decades ago. Out there, they know there's a point where you just have to say, I failed and it's sad, but I just give up. Out there, they walk away.

I could do that. Right now. Nothing has happened yet. I could spill the glasses. I can. If I stop now, then I can...

If I stop now...

If...

"Marie?"

I lift my head but do not turn around. "Oh, Dad. You're home."

2.

Dad snaps on the light and I have to blink. The light has faded while I've been working. I didn't even notice.

"I've been looking for you," he says.

"I've been right here." Through the open door, I glimpse the glowing bands of red that stretch over the iron-blue horizon. I don't look at my father. I can't, not yet.

The thick carpet pile crunches under his shoes as he comes toward me. I feel warmth. Polo aftershave. Mild curiosity. My father is all these things.

"Scotch?"

"There's been so much going on, I thought we could both use a drink," I tell him.

But he's ignoring me. Dad has seen the pill bottle. He picks it up, shakes it, looking inside at the random mix of ancient tablets, caplets, and lozenges. So pretty, really.

"What are these, Marie?"

I set the glasses back down. "You already know."

He does know. His face crumbles under the weight of that knowledge, and of the associated memories. He's remembering being down *there*, down into the bottom of the gully, where Mom stares up at the sky, waiting for one of us to care enough to try to find out what happened to her. But Geraldine is in the hospital and I'm sitting next to her and there's only Dad to see. Only Dad to know what happened between the time I saw her staggering across the road, and when he came to the hospital to take my hands and sit me down to tell me one more hard truth.

At the time, he thought my confusion came from hearing that my mother was dead, while my sister was only hurt. He has never realized that he was the one who was supposed to die.

I've never known what went wrong. Perhaps I should have asked Geraldine about dosages. She was, after all, the expert when it came to dealing with Mom's pills. I was supposed to be shielded from all that.

"Oh, God, Marie…" Standing beside me now, my father chokes on the rest of that sentence. It's an undignified noise and I don't like to hear it coming from him.

"Don't, Dad. Just…don't. Here." I pick up both glasses. I hold them out, equal distance from me, a move I have practiced any number of times. "We both need a little something."

Dad doesn't take either glass. He's staring at me, wide-eyed, white-faced. At first I think he might be scared, but that's not it at all. He's angry.

"What did Geraldine tell you?" His whisper is low and rough and it grates against my bones.

"What makes you think she told me anything?"

"You got these from her, didn't you?" His hand shakes the bottle, rattling the ancient pills. "She stood there. Right in front of me. She looks like butter wouldn't melt in her mouth and all the while, she kept *these*!"

"No," I say, because it is the truth. I do not lie to my father. Not ever. "Geraldine had nothing to do with it."

"Don't keep covering up for her! What's it going to take for you to realize she's not *worth* it!"

I'm not expecting the shout and I stagger away from him. The sideboard bumps into my back and the drinks slosh, splashing dirty liquid against my palms and fingertips.

For a second, I think he's going to throw the bottle across the room, but no. Even as angry as he is, that kind of crude and open display is beyond him.

"What was she planning to do?" he demands. "Try to get my finger-prints on the bottle? Did she actually think she could frame me like that?"

He's heading for the door, half-stumbling, half-running.

"Where are you going?" I ask, stupidly standing here with both glasses in my hands. Splashed liquor and condensation are making my fingers slippery.

"I'm going to flush the whole goddamn bottle down the toilet, what do you think I'm going to do?"

He's leaving with the pills. He might not come back. I can't let him.

"It won't do any good," I say.

That stops him, right on the threshold. Dad swivels around, his brows knitted tight together. "What are you talking about?"

I have to set the glasses down or I'm going to drop them. I wipe my damp hands on my slacks. I shouldn't do that. There'll be a smell, maybe a stain. "I told you, Dad. I didn't get the pills from Geraldine."

Because this isn't about her. Geraldine is a distraction. Like Mom and Aunt Trish and Robbie, and everyone else.

This is about you and me.

"Marie, don't say that."

This is about everything you made me into. Everything I had to be. All my life. Your good daughter, your baby girl. Your perfect, obedient, loving Marie.

Because the price of being anything else was too high.

I shrug and slip my hand into my pocket. My fingers curl around the knife. "All right. I won't say it."

But it's too late. And after all these long years of being exactly what my father needed, I have the highly dubious satisfaction of watching new reality forming inside him. All the things he has denied spread out from the back of his mind in long, slow ripples.

He doesn't want to see, of course. Who would? He's already trying to turn away. He scrubs at his face like he can wipe the truth off along with the sweat and condensation on his palms. "Marie, you know it hasn't been easy for me, either, but I had to be strong. There was no one else to take care of you."

Memory rises to the surface of my skin, the walls, the world around us. I remember his hands holding mine. I feel us together, sitting in my stuffy little bedroom.

We have to be strong, says Dad in my memory. Which time is this? Maybe none of them. Maybe all of them. *I know it's hard. I wish things were different. But they're not. I'm counting on you, Marie. We don't want anybody looking at this the wrong way. We don't want anyone thinking that what happened to your mother was anything but an accident.*

"Yes, Dad, I know," I say, and I don't recognize my own voice pressed flat under the weight of bitter memory. "You were always very clear about how things were."

She was sick, Marie, says my memory of us together. *Sick and weak. But that's over. Now, it's our job to hold things together. I need you, baby girl. Geraldine . . . we love her, but we can't count on her. It's up to you and me.*

"Drink your drink." I use my free hand to push the glass toward him. "Tell me how much you need me. How perfect I am. How much you depend on me."

"You know all of it is true. But Marie, I never, *ever . . .*"

We have to be strong. We can't let this tear us apart. I wish there was something we could do, but . . .

"It doesn't matter," I say, and I can't tell whether I'm talking to the father who's in front of me now or the one who was holding my hands when I was still nineteen. "What matters is that we've kept the family together." I measure the distance between us. I feel the knife handle against my palm. I took my bandage off. I didn't want it there tonight. The handle digs against the cut, seeking the blood.

Dad picks the glass up and looks into it. He raises it to his mouth.

He sets it down and, instead, takes my hand. Just like all those other times across the years. Those endless years of stage setting and secret smiles and silent approval and patience with my little flaws and my reasonless love of my scarred, unstable sister.

"Oh, my baby girl," he whispers. "What's she done to you?"

She, the syllable repeats heavily in my mind. He means Geraldine. The new reality has been revealed and he has examined it carefully.

And discarded it absolutely.

"She didn't do anything, Dad." I'm exhausted. I don't want to fight anymore. But I will make sure he knows who is responsible for us being here now. "Nothing new anyway."

"I know that's what you want to believe, but I also know Geraldine. Here, I think you need this more than I do." He picks up the glass and hands it to me.

I have never refused anything from my father's hands. There was no time to form the thought before my body acted. I smell the acrid tang of the Scotch and I feel the cold curve of the tumbler.

Its twin is still sitting on the sideboard. I don't know which one I'm holding. The realization catches me all wrong. I start badly, and Dad sees.

And Dad gives me that special little smile.

Gotcha.

The rules of a Household Tale are simple: If you are polite, if you share and keep your promises, you will be rewarded beyond your wildest dreams.

But if you are selfish, if you are cruel and careless, if you break that promise you made to the stranger in the woods, you are doomed.
—*Out of the Woods: Musings on Fairy Tales in the Real World,*
Dr. Geraldine Monroe

MARIE, SEVENTEEN YEARS OLD
STACEY B'S SANDWICHES AND STUFF

1.

Marie wouldn't have been there at all, except she needed her purse. Not the plain, square one that she used for every day. The cute little beaded one she kept for special occasions. Occasions she didn't want Dad to know about.

She really should tell him. She knew that. She was a good girl and she loved her father. Only bad girls lied to their fathers.

She knew both these things were true. She just couldn't make them hold together. Somewhere along the line, she just stopped trying.

Mom was back in the store, maybe closing up, maybe getting a new case of beer. It was six o'clock and dark outside already. The snow was just starting to come down. At least she didn't have to worry about Geraldine. Geraldine had gone to Becca Mayor's party, which meant she'd be out until at least midnight.

Which meant Marie had to get out of here before Mom finished whatever she was doing in the store. Because without Geraldine here,

Mom would make her stay and help make dinner and take care of anything else around the house.

Marie sprawled belly down on the lower bunk where Geraldine slept. The sheets smelled like her sister's mix of Enjoli perfume and weed. She fished a quarter out of her pocket and loosened the screws on the vent. The angle was awkward, but she'd had practice. She'd grab the bag and be back outside before anyone even knew she'd come home.

After all, why should it just be Geraldine who got away with things? Why'd Marie always have to be the perfect one?

Well, as of tonight, everything was going to change.

She reached into the vent and wrapped her fingers around the beaded bag. There was two hundred dollars in there. She needed to get it out of the house and somewhere safe. Two hundred dollars was a bus ticket. Another two hundred was a cheap motel room. But only as long as no one found out she had it or could wonder what she did with it.

David would hang on to it for her. She could trust him.

Marie heard the front door open and she froze.

"…*boots were made for walkin'*…" Mom bellowed off-key and Marie cringed. She was trapped now. Unless…She eyed the window. Well, why not? Geraldine did it all the time.

Mom was banging around the kitchen, singing loud and off-key. Marie yanked the purse out of the vent and stuffed it under her shirt. Her heart hammered and for a moment she felt dizzy with excitement. Was this how Geraldine felt all the time?

She leaned the vent cover back in place. She'd put the screws back later. Marie shimmied off the bed and tiptoed to the window.

A car's headlights flashed on the other side of the blind. Marie froze again. Nothing to worry about. Just traffic. Dad wasn't here. He was working late. He'd said so.

But then she heard the gravel crunch, and the sudden silence of an engine shutting off.

Mom was still singing about boots and walking and just what she'd do. Marie stood with her hands on the ice-cold aluminum frame and tried to make up her mind.

She heard the door open again.

"I'm glad you're in such a good mood, Stacey," said Dad. "I've got some news for you."

2.

Oh, no. Oh, darn, oh shoot, oh shit. Marie cursed and prayed. But it was too late.

"News?" Mom was saying. "Oh, joy. More earth-shattering developments from the world of the Mighty Monroes."

Dad laughed, and Marie felt her stomach churn.

"I think you're going to be interested in this. I was out at Ed's."

"Ed's? What…?"

"Pete's gone, Stacey. Packed up and skee-daddled." Dad drew out the word.

What? Uncle Pete left? Marie drifted toward the door. *Why? Have he and Aunt Florence made up? Did he go to get them?* She had a fleeting vision of the rusted red pickup pulling back up the drive, with Walt and Ruby hanging out the sides and waving.

But the silence on the other side of the door stretched out until Marie thought something was going to break. "Where'd he go?" Mom asked.

"What's the matter, Stacey? You don't look very well. Do you need your pills?"

"Go to hell, Martin. I asked where Pete went."

"Why do you care?"

"Fine. Never mind. I'm calling Ed."

"No need. I've got all the information you could want right here." There was a noise. A rustling. A click. "You know I'm always looking out for you, Stacey."

Marie eased the door open. From here, she could see a slice of the front room and her mother's back. Mom stood beside the dinner table, staring at something box shaped. Marie couldn't see Dad. But she could hear him.

"He's left you, Stacey," said Dad, satisfaction dripped from each word.

Mom grabbed the table edge. "What…are you talking about?"

"I'm so sorry. But it's better this way."

"You're lying."

"No. He sold you out for five thousand dollars, and he left."

Dad's hand came into view. His index finger touched the thing on the table. Marie realized that box was Dad's recorder, the one he used for taking notes and leaving himself reminders. There was a click, and then Uncle Pete's voice crackled through the room.

"Look, Martin, I know this is rough. But let's face it, you and Stace don't exactly get along anymore. Why not just…" There was a pause and more static, and then Dad's voice.

"I'll give you five thousand dollars."

"What?" said Uncle Pete.

"Five thousand dollars," repeated Dad. "I've got it right here." There're some clicks and rustlings. Marie pictured a briefcase being opened, and an envelope being extracted, like in a spy movie. "It's all yours, if you leave us alone instead of taking her with you."

Mom's breath was harsh and ragged. Her hands gripped the table and leaned over the box. Marie couldn't move, couldn't register any fact except that Mom was going to leave. Mom was going to run away with Pete and leave her behind, with Dad and Geraldine, and no way out.

"It's not for me, Pete," Dad's voice said. "It's the girls. She's their mother." More crackling paper. "Please. I'll get more, if you'll just leave us alone."

"Martin, that's not what this is about," Uncle Pete answered. "I love her."

"I know. You always did."

Mom had gone completely rigid. *Don't take it,* Marie could practically hear her thinking. *Don't take it.*

But there was only the rustle of more paper and the whisper of fabric. The envelope was being stashed.

"She's hurting, Martin. They all are. You...you expect too much."

"I know. I don't blame any of them. I've been neglecting her and the girls."

Another pause. "And now a change of heart?"

"You opened my eyes, big brother," answered Dad, and Marie could hear the smile in that recorded voice. "I'm turning over a new leaf."

He meant it, too. He always meant everything he said. Pete had to believe him. Everybody always believed him.

Tears streamed down Marie's cheeks. She didn't wipe them away. If she moved, she might catch someone's eye.

Another pause stretched out on the recorder. Maybe Pete nodded, maybe not, but there was a crunch, like gravel under boot soles.

"Good luck," called Dad's voice.

Uncle Pete said something back, but Marie couldn't understand it.

Dad in the here and now reached out and snapped the recorder button off.

"He didn't take it," Mom whispered. "You're lying. He wouldn't."

"Is he here?" asked Dad. "Did he tell you what happened? Call him, Stacey. Go ahead. I'll wait. He won't answer. He's already gone." He came around the table. Marie saw his silhouette, tall and strong, coming to stand so close to Mom.

"Liar!" Mom spat. Marie slapped her hand over her mouth. Her knees buckled and she sank down.

"You love me, Stacey." Dad's voice didn't change at all. It stayed absolutely even and certain. "I know that. Pete is a distraction. I understand. I've had a few myself, but I always come back, don't I? Because I love you and you love me."

"You hate me, you son of a bitch. You don't love anybody but yourself!"

"You're not going to get me mad, Stacey." His hands flashed out and gripped both her wrists. At the same time, his voice remained impossibly gentle. Why didn't he get angry? What would it take? "Test me all you want, but I promise you. I'll never break. I'll always love you. No matter what you say. No matter what you do."

Something was going to happen. Marie could feel it. Something new. Something bad.

I have to stop it.

"I'm leaving!" Mom shouted. "You can take your house and your family and your endless goddamn Monroe pride and shove it…"

Geraldine would stop them. She'd scream at them, get them looking at her.

"You think you know why he took that money, don't you?" Dad was turning her around now, slowly, like he was dancing with her. "You think he's going to use it for a bribe for poor Florence, so she'll allow his whore mistress and bastard daughter into her house."

What's he mean? Move, Marie! You have to! There's nobody else.

"You think Pete's coming back for you, Stacey. But he's not. He's not ever coming back for you, or your sister, or your bastard."

Marie threw the door open. She hadn't turned the lamp on in the bedroom, so there was no flash of light. At the other end of the hall, Dad bent Mom backward, until she was flat on the table. Marie tried to gather the breath to scream. She meant to run toward them, like she knew Geraldine would, but she couldn't. It was like a nightmare. Her body would not obey her. She couldn't get the signals right.

She could see, though. She could see how her father was holding her mother pressed down with his hands, and how he had his body shoved between her legs.

"I called Florence, you know. She wasn't that hard to find. We had it out, she and I. She was almost ready to do it, do you know? Pete had just about talked her round. I'm sure that money would have sealed the deal, if he'd ever intended to come back for you. But he won't, Stacey. He won't ever hurt any of us ever again."

"Let me go!"

"Not until you say it, Stacey."

Marie finally convinced her feet and legs to inch her forward along the wall. *He'll see me. I won't have to scream. I can just stand here. That'll be enough. He'll stop just as soon he sees me.*

"I just want to hear you say you know how much I love you, and how important you and the girls are to me. We are each other's every-thing, Stacey. Just like it's been from the beginning." He yanked her hands together, pinning her down. She struggled, trying to kick, but she couldn't.

Mom screamed. She screamed again, but nothing happened. There was no one to hear, except Dad and Dad didn't care.

And Marie…Marie couldn't move any further.

Dad got his hand up under her denim skirt. There's the sound of ripping fabric. Mom screamed again, longer and louder this time. She screamed like it was the end of the world.

"Get off me! Get off me! Get off me!"

"I'm your husband, Stacey." Dad's fingers were at his fly now. He yanked open the button and the zipper. "You chose me. Forever. You said so, the very first time."

Marie saw his penis, swollen and red. She saw his hand grab it and she saw him shove.

"Stop it! Stop it! Stop it, you son of a bitch!"

"There's only me, Stacey. You know that. I'm the only one who loves you."

Marie whimpered. And Dad heard, and he turned his head. And he saw his daughter.

"No one else will ever love you. You're mine. Those girls are mine. I will never let you go. Never let you go. Love you. Love you."

And he smiled at Marie and he didn't stop even once. Not even when he watched her turn and run back into her room, with his voice a hot, sick smear of sound behind her.

"Loveyouloveyouloveyouloveyoualwaysloveyou. And. You. Don't. Ever. Leave."

The miller was frightened and did what he was told. The next day the devil returned.
        —"The Girl without Hands" from *Kinder und Hausmärchen*
                    Vol. 1, Jacob and Wilhelm Grimm, 1812

MARIE, PRESENT DAY
THE ROSE HOUSE

1.

My father is watching me.

It's always the same, whether he's miles away or right in front of me, like he is now. The touch of his gaze wraps me up and pins me down. Especially when it's that sad, patient expression he uses every time I disappoint him. Like now. Like then. Like always.

Life isn't flashing in front of my eyes. I'm wading through it, like I'm in mud up to my knees, and my life is composed of all my father's sorrow.

I need you, Marie. I need you to keep it together. I need you to be strong. We all do, Marie. Please. I know it's hard, I do, but we have to stay strong. Otherwise they're going to think Geraldine had something to do with your mother's accident. And you don't want that, do you?

"I know what really happened to your mother, Marie," he says. "That night."

"Which night?" I hear myself asking. There have been so many.

He smiles like I've made a terrible pun. "The night she died, Marie. I know you did it for us. You knew she was trying to leave us, again."

No. Stop.

My mind clears of memory, and I'm not plowing through mud anymore. I'm filled with a knife-edged clarity.

He's telling the story over again. He's changing the story.

He's putting it on me.

"What kind of woman abandons her kids?" he says to me. "I've never blamed you for being angry at her. I just, I've always been sorry I couldn't protect you better. I did try. I swear to God I did."

Leaving. That was true. That was real. She was going to leave. Like a normal person. She was going to cut her losses and get out.

I didn't know. I swear I didn't. I'm trying to shape the words, but I can't. There's no air in my lungs, no strength to draw breath. My hand's trembling so bad, I almost drop my glass.

I almost forget the knife in my other hand. Almost, but not quite.

I raise the glass, so he's watching me. I ease my hand from my pocket. The knife is small and my hands are careful.

I swirl the amber liquid in the glass he's handed me. The ice clinks. It's a very different shade from the amber of the pill bottle. More dark gold, far less orange. My father's sad, patient eyes are watching me, waiting to see if I really understand. This is the only way I will be allowed out of this house, this town, this family, this life.

And he's showing me why I have to take it. Because if I don't, he's going to start telling people a new story. He's never actually laid the blame for my mother's death at any particular doorstep. Not really. Not outside the family, anyway. He's held that back.

Just in case.

"You know how hard this has been, baby girl. It's killed me to see what this has done to you, how hard you've worked and tried. I wish…"

"What do you wish?" The ice clinks. The cold of the glass is burning my fingertips.

"I wish I'd tried harder to keep her away. I should have done something the second she showed up. I knew she would ruin what we had.

357

But you wanted your sister back so badly, I just didn't have the heart. I should have been stronger, for your sake."

I look into my father's eyes. He is so sorry that this is the way it has to be. He wants me to understand him and forgive him. He has tried so hard to make his family what it is supposed to be.

"It's all right," I tell him.

I raise my glass. I down the drink—the whole bitter, foul mess—all in one gulp. I cough, I retch, and I blink hard. I lift my eyes to him again. I thought I'd see shock. I thought I'd at least surprise him this once. But no. It's still that eternally sad, eternally patient, nightmare look of his. That's all he has to give me. That's all he's ever had.

"I'll take care of Robbie," he tells me. "You don't have to worry."

I set the glass down.

And I lunge forward, right for his guts. He's inches away, he's old and he's worn and he trusts me.

And he's still faster than I am. He grabs my hand and he twists hard and the knife is gone from my fingers and I can't even see where it went.

"Oh, Marie," he says. "What has she done to you?"

He shoves me backward onto the couch, and I let him. The knife is in his other hand, but neither one of us needs it anymore, do we?

I let my head fall back on the couch, and I wait for what's coming. Heat drags itself up the sides of my throat until it gets to my head and leaves me dizzy. I am never leaving this room.

I just thought he'd die first. I thought I had finally done something right.

I feel my father's cool, steady fingers, feather-light as he brushes back my hair and kisses my forehead.

"Goodnight, baby girl. Sleep tight," he whispers.

My drink churns my stomach. Its vapors swirl through my veins and my lungs. I feel the walls peel gently open, like wings. I feel my mother at my shoulders.

"I don't think so," says someone.

My father lifts his gaze from me. "Geraldine."

2.

Geraldine strolls through the doorway, as comfortable here as my father ever was.

She is dark and solid against the white walls.

"Quick, call the ambulance," says Dad. "I think your sister might have—"

"Taken mom's old pills?" Her voice is as flat, as dead as his. They are playing their scene out together. Saying what has to be said so they will remember it correctly for later.

And I have to watch. Because I'm dizzy and I can't move. The whole room is spinning. *This is new.*

"You okay, Marie?" asks Geraldine.

My tongue is thick and uncomfortable. And there's something else. "No. I think. I'm going to be…sick."

She's ready for it. Geraldine is always ready for the unpleasant. She grabs the wastepaper basket and shoves it under my face. I vomit. It's painful and it's ugly and it stinks and it doesn't stop. I feel her hand on my back.

Dad doesn't move.

"It's okay," Geraldine says. "It's okay. Just let it come out. It'll be okay."

I lift my head. I am hot and hollow. Geraldine looks at me, and I wait to see the triumph, the awareness of betrayal. My last sight before Mom takes me into the walls and under the floors with her and Aunt Trish.

That's not what I see in my sister's face. I see anger. I see hate. But it's not for me.

Geraldine eases me back on the sofa. She stands up. She turns around.

"Fun fact, Dad," she says. "Marie tried to poison you, once upon a time."

"What are you talking about?" Is there a lilt in his voice? I can't tell. My ears are ringing.

"Marie tried to poison you," repeats Geraldine slowly. "The night Mom died. She used the pills from the bedside table." She holds the bottle up and rattles it at him. Why is she doing that?

"You're lying." He reaches for the bottle, but she snatches it back.

"Not this time. And you should be grateful, Dad. Because of me, you got twenty-five extra years."

"Geraldine, this isn't funny. Marie is—"

"See, I'd been trying to sober Mom up. I figured if I could get her off the junk at least a little, she'd get stronger and I could get her to run away with me. So, I'd been swapping her pain pills for aspirin and stuff."

She pauses to let that settle in. It takes a long time.

"That's what Marie gave you when she tried to kill you. An overdose of aspirin. And that's what you've given her. Twenty-five-year-old stale goddamn aspirin."

"Of course, you didn't know that," Geraldine continues. "You thought you were killing your daughter. Just like you thought you were hooking me."

She reaches into her pocket and brings out a fist. And opens it. Little white pills rain down like hail.

"Those were plan B," she tells him. "And you handed them to me. A half dozen over forty-eight hours, because you wanted to be sure you had me hard on the line before you made your move." I can't see her face from this angle, but I hear the wild grin in her voice.

Dad sighs. "I know you like to think people believe your stories, Geraldine…"

"Yeah, well, they will this time," she says. "Because I've got backup. Right, Marie?"

I lift my face. There's vomit on my chin. I don't know what's in my eyes. It's hard and hot and completely unfamiliar. I have no name for it.

"Yes, Geraldine," I say. Because what else am I going to say?

Snow White said, "We will never desert each other."
  Rose Red answered, "No, not as long as we live."
  And the mother added, "Whatever one gets she shall share with the other."
  —"Snow-White and Rose-Red" from *Kinder und Hausmärchen*
                    Vol. 2, Jacob and Wilhelm Grimm, 1812

GERALDINE, PRESENT DAY
THE ROSE HOUSE

1.

It is a sight to behold. My father is staring at Marie and Marie is staring right back. She's a more complete disaster than I've ever seen her. Except the once, when I dragged her through the cold. But then she looked dead, and now she looks alive. Really, truly, fully alive.

"No, Marie," says Dad. Calmly, of course. No need to get excited. Not yet. He's got one hand in his pocket. Very casual. "You agreed. You promised me you would be strong."

"Cops are already on their way, Dad," I tell him. Marie's going to live, but she can't be in good shape. I need to keep his attention on me. People are coming, but I don't know when. There's still time for all this to go very, very wrong.

Dad turns toward me, one motion at a time.

"You bitch," he says, calmly, of course. "You goddamned useless junkie bitch."

He brings his hand out and my breath seizes up in my throat.

He's got a knife. A paring knife. Where the hell did that come from?

Dad lunges. That tiny blade is out and down, and I feel it graze my skin as I dodge. Dad isn't expecting to miss. He stumbles against the threshold. I shove him forward, letting his momentum help him down.

Where's the knife? I think. *Where's the knife!*

But that's a mistake. I'm looking for the weapon, and I take my eyes off Dad. He gets his hands around my ankle and he yanks. The world spins and I fall. My head cracks hard against the floorboards.

"You're just like her." His voice grates as he looms over me. "None of you will ever learn!"

He lunges, but, somehow, impossibly, Marie is there.

"Don't you touch her!"

She dives. She's trying, but my sister doesn't know how to fight. Not like this. He twists and shakes and throws her off. By then, I'm on my feet.

"Tag," I whisper, wiping at my mouth. "I'm it."

My heart is hammering. My mind is full. I'm alive, too. I'm filthy, angry, brazen, and burning, but I'm alive and all the restraints, all the terrible, tyrannical reality is gone. I can do anything here and now. And I will.

Dad's gaze slides off me, to Marie. I feel her beside me, but I don't dare look. I have to keep my eye on Dad. Whatever he sees, that'll remain between the two of them.

Whatever he sees, Dad turns. And Dad runs.

I'm laughing as I take off after him. The front room flashes past. I barrel through the pocket door and cut left, getting between him and the front door. I think I hear Marie, but I don't stop. Dad wavers and dodges and pivots toward the great room and the French doors. I swing around, right at his heels.

He misjudges, stumbles against a chair. I see the knife flash in his hand. I'm right on top of him. Grab and swing and shove and scream. Hard. He topples forward, into the pines, into the roses.

The crash shatters the whole night.

"My child, if I do not chop off both of your hands, then the devil will take me away...Help me in my need, and forgive me the evil that I am going to do to you."
—"The Girl without Hands" from *Kinder und Hausmärchen* Vol. 1, Jacob and Wilhelm Grimm, 1812

MARIE, PRESENT DAY
THE ROSE HOUSE

1.

I see Geraldine shove my father forward with all her might. The window, the crowning glory of the Rose House, explodes into a thousand pieces around him. It is beautiful. It is terrible.

My father falls onto the terrace and is still.

I walk across the carpet, slowly, softly. Geraldine is there. Perhaps she touches me. I am not sure. I do not have the attention to spare her now. I have to see to our father.

He groans, and rolls onto his back, and he screams. I've never heard him scream before. It is a high-pitched, terrible sound.

I don't blame him, though. He is hurt, very badly. He's bleeding from...well...everywhere. His scalp is very bad. His arms. His legs. There's a large shard embedded in his thigh. Black blood surrounds the shattered glass spreading out beneath the moonlight.

He's done screaming, for now at least. He sees me coming toward him.

"Help me," my father whispers. "Marie."

I would, but unfortunately, I don't have a free hand. Both my hands hold the pillow I picked up off the couch as I passed. I thought I might need it. It is good to be prepared. My father has taught me I need to be prepared for anything.

"Marie. Marie. We agreed. You wanted this."

"Marie, stop."

Who said that? Geraldine? No. It can't be. Geraldine would not talk like that.

"I protected you, from them, from all of them," Dad whispers. His words are slurring. "I saved you. Baby girl. You know I did. You told me you understood."

I kneel down. The glass is everywhere. It cuts me deep like the knife cut me, but I don't mind.

"But I lied to you, Dad," I tell him. "Every day since I was seventeen. Since you killed your brother and raped my mother and pulled me out of Aunt Trish's house, I lied to you and you *believed* me."

I lean over my father and the mask that is Marie in the mirror falls away, like the stained glass fell. I look into those bottomless eyes, and my father sees me. Finally. Truly.

And I see him. He is an old man, my father, and he has finally worked out exactly which of his girls he should fear.

Finally.

I bring the pillow down, hard, fast, silent. Just like I've practiced. Blood is warm on my hands, glass from the shattered roses bites into my knees. His hands grab my wrists.

"Stop. Marie. It's enough! It's enough!"

I'm bleeding. I'm screaming. The house is screaming. Mom, Aunt Trish, Uncle Pete. All of us. All my living. All my dead. All his dead. Screaming together.

Geraldine, too. *"He does not get to do this to you!"*

Hands grab my shoulders and drag me back. I'm thrown sideways, so I roll and crash against the hearth. My skull cracks against the stone. My empty hands come down on more glass. The pain blinds me. When I can see again, I see my sister standing between me and my father, an avenging angel, a mad witch, like our mother, like her sister.

"It's over, Marie," she says. "You don't have to do any more."

I am trying to understand. I push myself up onto my knees. I reach my hand out, looking for support. And Geraldine is there. Her hand is strong in mine, and she pulls me to my feet.

Geraldine would never let me fall. I remember that. Not really.

"Marie?"

Dad's still here. That's a surprise. He's calling for me. I've never refused him. I don't know how.

"Marie, please."

We look at each other, my sister and I. She sees me, too, but then she always did. Geraldine steps aside.

I reach my father's side and settle onto the carpet again, more carefully this time. Behind us, there's a thump and a whooshing noise. A smell of burning cloth and foam. I know what's happened to the pillow, which, of course would have my father's blood all over it and might have been somewhat difficult to explain, if it comes to that.

"Marie, help me," Dad whispers. "Marie. You love me. You're my girl. You've always been my girl."

"I was never yours, Dad," I say, and he hears, and he sees my face and my hands, covered in the blood. Mine. His. Ours.

I press my ruined hands against his heart, and his face. He struggles feebly under my attentive touch. I want this memory under my palms to blot out all the others.

There's noises coming from somewhere. Voices. Footfalls. None of it is important. What is important is this moment, here between my father and me. What is important is my hands on his heart, feeling the beat spasm and slow. My gaze holding his. The memories raging between us.

"It's okay, Dad," I tell him. "You can let go now."

"Marie…"

"I'm here, Dad. Let go now. You're done. It's all over now."

All over but the shouting, isn't that what they say? And there is shouting. I can recognize the voices.

"Hurry. Please," Geraldine is saying. "David, thank God it's you. He tried to kill her, David. He tried to kill Marie."

"Mom!"

It's Robbie. Oh, my son. Of course you came, too. And it's David. My hero. Always where he's needed. He's almost too soon this time.

But not quite.

Beginnings are unavoidable. But endings need trust. We made it
through. We got this. The wicked have fallen. We can look away now.
—Dr. Geraldine Monroe (margin notes)

GERALDINE, PRESENT DAY
WHITESTONE HARBOR MEDICAL CENTER

1.

"Tell me what happened," David says. "All of it."

We're back in the emergency room, David and me. At least, we're in the waiting room. It's comfortable, in that carefully designed impersonal style of modern hospitals. Marie has been admitted and the doctors are with her. They're removing the shards, stitching the wounds, searching out the extent of the damage.

They're never going to find it all.

"Geraldine?" David prompts grimly.

My cuts were less extensive than Marie's. I'm already cleaned up and stapled shut. I refused the painkillers. I need to stay alert. Because I knew this was coming. Cousin Gary and his team are back at the house, but they'll be here very soon. Somewhere, Tyler's sister Angela is trying to rent herself a car and find directions from the Traverse City airport.

I am not looking forward to her arrival. But I can't think about that yet.

I feel like this is the moment that everything else has led up to. All those stories. All those years coming to understand why people tell fairy tales, and how they are important. And all the time with Dad, of course. I should be grateful, and I am, in a perverse sort of way. It was

Dad who taught me and Marie how to lay down tracks and wear the masks until we couldn't tell them from our own skin. It was all so we could tell the stories that need to be told and make people believe.

With all this behind me, I tell David the tale.

I tell him how Dad abused us. I tell him how he stole, from Mom, and from Aunt Trish, the other sister, the crazy, rebellious, bad sister in the castle.

I tell him we weren't ever kidnapped by Aunt Trish. We ran away. I told him why Marie did her about-face and became the perfect, loving, obedient daughter when Dad showed up on her doorstep to take us home.

Marie knew if she didn't give Dad exactly what he needed, he'd peel us off one by one, looking for it. She was trying to save me, and our mother, and herself in the only way she could. It wasn't her fault it didn't work.

I tell David that Dad killed Mom. Pushed her down into the gully while Marie stood beside my hospital bed. This is true enough.

I tell him Dad burned down the old house. He used the remains of the rum he'd brought me as accelerant. I say he knew I'd been fighting with Tyler (oh, Ty) and wanted to frame me for my lover's death.

I wonder out loud when he decided killing Tyler would be a better idea than killing me.

I do not tell him about the pillow, or Marie's long-ago attempt at poisoning Dad on the night Mom died. None of that is important to anybody but me.

"The house," he says. "The fire. You're sure about that?"

"Yes. I'm sure. Dad even bought the rum. I'll bet Marie kept the receipt."

He doesn't even question the likelihood of this.

"Jesus Christ, Geraldine," he says.

I am silent, and that is agreement enough.

David pushes himself to his feet. We are the only ones in the family waiting area tonight. He paces to the door, and back again.

"You're lying," he says. "Again."

I don't bother to argue. "What are you going to do about it?"

We stare at each other, measuring, judging. We each know how far the other will go now, and it is not an easy feeling.

We are still standing like this when the orderly knocks softly on the threshold. "Dr. Monroe?" He looks at David first, but has the grace to look embarrassed when I get to my feet. "You can see her now."

"Thanks." I'm still a little wobbly as I stride past him. David follows me.

"Sorry," says the orderly. "Just family for right now."

2.

The room is dim and quiet. My sister is propped up on a pile of pillows. There're tubes in her arm and a monitor that's mercifully way quieter than the old-style ones. Her right hand has a fresh bandage. So does her left.

She doesn't stir as I walk into the room. Not until I lay my hand over hers.

Her eyes flutter open slowly.

"Hi," I say. "How are you?"

Her tongue pushes against her teeth. I fill a cup with water from the in-room sink and help her swallow. She settles back on the pillow.

"Better?"

She nods.

I glance at the door. The orderly hurries past. No one is paying attention to us.

"I've told David what he needs to know. Everything's going to be okay."

Marie doesn't care. Yet. That's the drugs. Blunting memory as well as pain. "Home now?" she whispers.

"Soon."

Her wounded hand spasms in mine. "You? Like we said?"

I am silent for a long time as I look into my sister's bleary eyes.

Slowly, I feel doors open in the back of my mind. I see it then, the way she does. The long years ahead of us. Me and Marie in the Rose House. Remaking. Rebuilding. Restoring the walls that have been torn down. Carefully building up our broken lives, with David watching, instead of Dad. I see us making a place where we can stay. We will be safe this time. No one will ask too many questions or expect difficult answers. We can finally be real sisters. We're going to build our tree house, our rope bridge, our castle. Snowy White and Rosy Red, looking out for each other, for better or for worse. And if David or anyone else decides they don't like it…

No. I don't have to think like that. Not ever again. That's over. This is it. Happily ever after. The end.

Except maybe not quite.

Because something else has happened. I don't know yet, but I think. I believe.

I think maybe I'm pregnant.

ACKNOWLEDGMENTS

No book is created by the author alone. I'd like to acknowledge the hard work and tremendous help I had from my editors and agents, the honest feedback of all the members of the Untitled Writers Group, the unflinching support of the SFNovelists and Michigan Sisters in Crime who saw me through the rough spots. And first, last, and always, the constant support of my husband and son. Thank you all.

ABOUT THE AUTHOR

Sarah Zettel is an award-winning author. She has written more than thirty novels and multiple short stories over the past twenty-five years, in addition to hiking, cooking, stitching all the things, marrying a rocket scientist, and raising a rapidly growing son.